SCRATCHGRAVEL ROAD

ALSO BY TRICIA FIELDS

The Territory

SCRATCHGRAVEL ROAD

TRICIA FIELDS

MINOTAUR BOOKS

A Thomas Dunne Book
New York

A THOMAS DUNNE BOOK FOR MINOTAUR BOOKS.
An imprint of St. Martin's Publishing Group.

SCRATCHGRAVEL ROAD. Copyright © 2013 by Tricia Fields. All rights reserved. Printed in the United States of America. For information, address St. Martin's Press, 175 Fifth Avenue, New York, N.Y. 10010.

www.thomasdunnebooks.com
www.minotaurbooks.com

ISBN 978-1-250-02136-6 (hardcover)
ISBN 978-1-250-02278-3 (e-book)

Minotaur books may be purchased for educational, business, or promotional use. For information on bulk purchases, please contact Macmillan Corporate and Premium Sales Department at 1-800-221-7945 extension 5442 or write specialmarkets@macmillan.com.

First Edition: March 2013

10 9 8 7 6 5 4 3 2 1

*Dedicated with love to Molly Fields—may your fascination
with science provide you a lifetime of discovery. Hail Purdue!*

ACKNOWLEDGMENTS

Many people were involved in the research and revision of this book. A teacher, doctor, chemist, quality assurance specialist (ammunition surveillance), state trooper, and firearms expert all took the time to offer commentary and support. I am truly grateful for their time and expertise. Special thanks to Linnet Harlan, Mella Mincberg, Merry Caston, Dr. James Preston, Kelly O'Sullivan, Ken Harwell (wishing you safe travels), and especially, Frank Disbrow, for offering great insight and hooking me up with the right people. Thank you to Todd Fields—you are the best! Finally, a special sigh of thanks to my agent, Dominick Abel, for seeing and communicating the big picture, and to my editor, Peter Joseph, a first-rate problem solver of all things great and small.

SCRATCHGRAVEL ROAD

ONE

Teresa Cruz knew that people watched her. *There's nothing more satisfying than catching a cop's kid,* her mom had told her. Yet here she was, standing in front of a pickup truck an hour past town curfew, with Enrico Gomez, the twenty-year-old guy her mother had forbidden her from seeing.

"No cars past here," he said, pointing down into the Hollow.

Teresa looked out into the black desert but could see nothing. She had cotton mouth and her eyes stung from the hot night wind. She felt Enrico fumble in the dark for her hand, then wrap her fingers inside his.

"You scared?" he asked, his voice barely above a whisper.

She shrugged, not trusting her voice.

"Stay with me, you'll be fine. Everybody's cool. We walk down a slope into the Hollow. Can't see it from the road. Cops don't even know it's here."

Teresa's throat constricted.

"Even if she drove by here she couldn't see the cars from Scratch-gravel."

She turned away from him. He had misjudged her silence.

He dropped her hand and dug into his front pocket. "I got a surprise. Hold your hand out flat."

She held her palm out and watched him twist open the top of a small container. He laid a round mirror in her hand and she forced herself not to pull back.

She felt suddenly self-conscious, too young in her shorts and flip-flops and tank top. She wore her black hair straight, falling just below her shoulder blades, and worried Enrico's friends would look down on her—just some sixteen-year-old girl. She had no idea who would be there but was too proud to ask.

"Hold still," he said.

She held her hand motionless, torn between the fear of getting caught and the thrill of watching.

In his other hand he flipped open his cell phone and shone the dim light onto the mirror, where he tapped out a line from the container. He handed her his cell phone and she held the light over his hand as he tightened the lid on the small vial, stuffed it back in his pocket, then bent over her hand and used a thin straw to snort the powder into his nose.

Teresa felt nauseous. She had crossed a line her mother would never forgive, certainly never understand.

In the pale light Teresa watched him shove his hand back into his front pocket. "Want a hit?"

She shook her head.

"You ever done a line?" he asked.

She said nothing.

"Come on, girl. You'll feel like Superman. Feel like you can do anything. Just a small one."

He unscrewed the lid and her skin prickled.

"Let's just go," she said.

He hesitated and then replaced the lid and shoved it back in his pocket. She should have told him the truth—she didn't want it. She liked Enrico, but she didn't like the person she became when she was with him.

He walked back to the truck's driver-side door and she listened as he turned the key and rolled the windows up, then locked the doors.

It was a warm July night and the air felt hot on her skin. The sky was wide open with a three-quarter moon that cast a deep purple light, revealing the jagged shadows of desert cactus and low-lying mountain ranges in the distance.

He came back and stood in front of her. "You know anyone who's been out here?"

Like most high school kids, she had heard of the Hollow but never been. It was a desert hideout accessible by invitation only. A kid didn't wander into the Hollow without being asked first by a regular. By someone who had already been accepted. Rumors ran through school about what went on: drugs, sex, alcohol, but it was the allure of the unknown that made kids talk.

She shook her head no.

"That's cool. Just relax. Street etiquette, right?"

"I know." She did not know. She had no idea what she would say. She felt entirely out of place and wanted him to promise not to leave her side.

Taking her hand again, he laced his fingers between her own and began walking.

Enrico pointed toward the land in front of them. "Look. You don't need lights now."

Teresa made out the silhouettes of two small mountain ranges to the north. Creosote bushes, agave, Spanish daggers, and mesquite clumps blended with large boulders that disguised vehicles from view. Enrico was right; her eyes had adjusted and the land spread out before her like a movie screen. It was the same desert she'd grown up in, but everything looked different. The boulders and bushes she wouldn't have given a second thought to in the daylight now appeared to hide things inside their shadows.

"How will you find the truck with no lights?" she asked.

Enrico laughed. "You stick by me. Ain't nothing to worry about."

His hair was cut military style, short on the sides, longer on top, and he wore the loose jeans and tight shirt of guys who claimed gang status. She could feel the energy buzzing through his body, his grip on her hand so tight it hurt.

As he pulled her along she struggled to keep her bearings, beginning to feel anxious that she couldn't find her way out on her own. Enrico had pulled off of Scratchgravel Road onto an arroyo that she hadn't even known existed. He had put the truck into four-wheel drive and followed the arroyo heading east for close to a mile before stopping. There were a half-dozen trucks and Jeeps parked behind the tail end of a small mountain range that appeared to have been chopped into pieces. It made good cover for the vehicles and the Hollow that lay somewhere on the other side.

Enrico laid his arm over her shoulder and it felt heavy. He was built thick and worked out obsessively. She struggled to keep up with him, worrying she would trip over a cactus, leaving cuts that she would struggle to explain to her mother the next day.

She smelled the sweet musky smoke before she saw the faint light from the bonfire in the distance. Enrico put a finger to his lips and they listened to hushed laughter, maybe fifty feet in front of them. She couldn't tell if the voices' owners were walking or were inside a vehicle. After a few seconds the sounds faded into the distance.

With no city lights the stars and moon lit the desert floor a soft gray. The ground appeared to be reflecting back the absorbed light from the sun's afternoon glare. The light from the fire, still partially hidden behind a large boulder, appeared bright suddenly.

"It's a half-mile walk from here. You cool?" he asked.

"I'm fine."

"Watch for the long skinny cactus. They rip into your skin like a fishing hook. Hurts like hell to pull them out."

Enrico stopped suddenly and Teresa ran into his side. He pointed to his left, toward the road, in the direction of an approaching vehicle. "Hold up. Truck's coming."

They stood and watched the yellow parking lights of a dark-colored, full-size pickup as it drove slowly forward, just to the north of them. Without a word, they both crouched in the sand and watched the truck slow to a crawl, then circle behind a large thick grove of bushes roughly thirty feet in front of them.

"Don't you know all these people?" she whispered.

"Nobody comes to the Hollow off Scratchgravel like that," he said, pointing in the direction of the truck. "Got to be safe."

She wondered what he meant. Safe from the cops?

The truck stopped. The driver exited, slammed the door, and walked to the back end.

"What the hell's this guy doing?" Enrico said.

Teresa could feel his arm tense against hers like he was ready to take off after the guy in the truck. Enrico had an intensity that she respected, like he could handle anything.

The man laid the tailgate down and dragged something forward. They heard him grunt, obviously struggling with the load. Teresa wondered if they were watching a drug exchange. The Rio Grande, the border to Mexico, was less than a mile away, and crossing it in the middle of nowhere was no big deal. The Border Patrol rarely made it to Artemis. With two thousand miles of international border their little town barely got noticed, and drug mules and coyotes transporting illegals were part of life.

The man at the back of the truck continued to struggle for another minute, and then they heard a heavy thud as the load hit the ground. The man bent and worked for several seconds arranging something, then stood abruptly, shut the tailgate, and walked back to the driver's side. They listened as he shoved the truck into gear and drove slowly away, around the bushes and back the same way he came, straight back out to the road.

Enrico stood and Teresa grabbed ahold of the back of his shirt. "Maybe we should turn back. If that's a load of weed we should get out of here."

Instead, he walked forward, toward the dark mass lying on the ground. Teresa followed a few feet behind him.

Enrico stopped suddenly and threw his arm out to stop her. "Son of a bitch."

Looking over his shoulder, she gasped and stifled a scream into her fist.

TWO

At noon on Monday, Chief Josie Gray followed her bloodhound outside, then locked the front door of her small adobe house in the foothills of the Chinati Mountains. She watched Chester lope up the long lane behind her house to the cabin owned by her closest friend, Dell Seapus. His place was the dog's second home while Josie went to work. She unlocked the driver's-side door of her dusty blue and white jeep and leaned in to start the car. The blast of hot air sent her back to the shade of the front porch while the car cooled. Her police uniform was standard garb: thick gray pants, navy blue short-sleeved shirt, and heavy black work boots that made little sense in the West Texas desert, but the mayor and commissioners were convinced they conveyed the proper image. Josie wore her uniform carefully pressed and the brass polished. She recognized that her public image as chief of police had to remain impeccable on every level. Not everyone thought a thirty-three-year-old woman fit that role.

She pulled her cell phone out of her uniform shirt pocket and called dispatcher Louise Hagerty, to log on for second shift.

"Anything going on?" she asked.

"Otto's taking a report at the Gun Club. Tiny called and said somebody stole all the trash cans from behind his store."

Josie sighed.

Lou told her she was cleaning out the refrigerator and wanted Josie to tell Otto to quit leaving open Coke cans on the shelves. Lou was a forty-seven-year-old chain smoker with a voice like sandpaper who complained about having to work as secretary, detective, intake officer, custodian, and psychologist on top of her real job as dispatcher. But Josie knew Lou was first rate at all her various tasks, and probably would have complained bitterly if someone tried to take one away from her.

"I'll talk to him," Josie said. "I'm going to drive by the watchtower before I come into town. Call me if you need anything."

With the steering wheel cool enough to touch, Josie backed out of her driveway onto Schenck Road, the gravel lane that led to her and Dell's property. The Chihuahuan Desert spread out before her, sparsely marked with cactus, scrub bushes, and pinyon pine, with not another house in sight for miles. Josie drove slowly down the lane, appreciating the quiet and the solitude.

She glanced down at the gold medallion that lay in the tray on her console; her father's ten-year award for his service as a police officer. It was the only memento she had of her father's work as an officer and she kept it with her, a talisman to protect her on the job. Her father had been killed in a line-of-duty accident when she was eight, and in her own mind, it had always been a given that she would become a cop as well. Looking out at the lonely desert before her she knew the job was a good fit. She preferred watching people to talking with them, asking questions rather than answering them.

———

Cassidy Harper wiped the sweat out of her eyes with the sleeve of her T-shirt and turned to face the road, a quarter mile back through scorched desert sand, to where her water bottle sat in the front seat of her car. With thirty minutes before Leo returned home, there was no time to turn around.

She pulled a folded piece of paper out of the front pocket of her shorts and stared at the words she had heard two days ago. At one thirty in the morning she had awoken to the sound of Leo's voice in the other room. She got out of bed and crept down the hallway to see him sitting in the dark on the living room floor, hunched over the phone. She had only caught pieces of his conversation before the fear of being caught eavesdropping forced her back into bed. But she'd grabbed a pen, and a paperback book from her nightstand, and in the light from the digital clock she scribbled down fragments of the conversation she had heard on a blank page: *I'll take . . . to Scratchgravel Road. Half mile before River Road, on the right. A quarter mile downhill. Can't see . . . from the road.*

Then he'd disappeared for three hours. Gotten in his car and driven away without waking her up or leaving her a note about where he was going. Cassidy had remained rigid when Leo crawled back into bed near dawn the next morning. He had curled away from her and said nothing. A mix of fear and anger kept her from saying anything that morning, but she couldn't let it go.

Over dinner that evening, she had asked where he had gone in the middle of the night. He'd given her a startled look and then concocted some ridiculous answer about not being able to sleep. "I just took a ride, got some fresh air. I didn't want to wake you." *Bullshit,* she'd thought.

Cassidy had allowed the words she had written down to chew at her for two days, but the not knowing was driving her crazy. She'd heard rumors about a dirt road somewhere off of Scratchgravel that led to a place where kids partied on the weekends. The druggies called it the Hollow. But she had never known Leo to take drugs or even show any interest; he rarely even drank alcohol. None of it made any sense.

With fewer than 2,500 people, Artemis was a remote desert town situated on a dead-end road between two ghost towns. For an outsider, it was not an easy place to meet people, especially if you didn't fit the mold. Cassidy wasn't sure what the mold was, but it obviously wasn't an out-of-work physics teacher. Leo had no friends and only a part-time research job he worked at from home. She was basically his only friend in Artemis, or so she had thought, and she couldn't imagine who he would be meeting at one in the morning. So she had decided to investigate. She wanted proof before he had the opportunity to spin the lies she was sure would follow.

She looked back toward her car, but it was behind a low hill, just out of view. She was not good at judging distances, but she was fairly certain she had walked at least a quarter of a mile. In the heat, it felt like five miles. Twenty-two years old, and she was stalking her lousy boyfriend in the desert.

Cassidy turned away from the road and began walking toward a patch of mesquite bushes and several large boulders about fifty feet in the distance. If there was nothing there she would turn back. Her head hurt, and the sun, now directly overhead, was making her dizzy and nauseous. She could see a depression in the sand directly in front of her, maybe another quarter of a mile from Scratchgravel, and she assumed it was the crater-shaped area the kids called the Hollow. Curious, she wanted to check out the spot, but she would need to come back with water if she intended to hike any farther.

Fifteen feet from the small grove of bushes she caught wind of a horrible smell. She stopped and wrinkled her nose. It smelled putrid, like a rotting animal—not a familiar smell in the desert. She realized suddenly how hot she was. Her sweat evaporated instantly and it was difficult to measure how much water she had already lost.

Growing up in the swamps of the Everglades she had hated the dank decay that permeated everything she owned. When she left home at sixteen she hitchhiked west and stopped in Texas for the smell alone, the clean baked smell of desert dirt. She wrinkled her nose in disgust. Whatever it was now, a dead jackrabbit or coyote, it definitely did not smell clean.

There were six mesquite bushes, approximately five feet tall and just as wide, with only a sparse covering of small green leaves that allowed her to see through to the other side. Before she walked behind the first mesquite she noticed a lump. She held a hand over her eyes to block the sun's glare and after several seconds she made out the shape of a body, a man, flat on his back.

"What the hell?" she said, her voice surprising her in the silence.

She walked quickly around the grove to the back side, then advanced several steps before her windpipe swelled with fear. She struggled to pull air down into her lungs. She put a hand to her mouth and dropped to her knees. The sand burned her skin as she crawled forward, a sickening curiosity pushing her on. Had Leo known about this man? Did he have something to do with this man's death?

Cassidy's long red hair hung in ringlets around her face. Sweat stung her eyes. Riding a wave of nausea she had a clear vision of her blistered body passed out beside the decaying corpse in front of her. Stray flies buzzed from the corpse toward her face in search of new prey. She watched the sand in front of her begin to move like ocean waves.

Josie pushed her sunglasses on to avoid increasing the spray of wrinkles around her eyes. At her age, the desert sun was just beginning to take a toll on her skin. She wore her brown shoulder-length hair straight, usually pulled back into a ponytail, which did nothing to soften her angular cheekbones and jawline. While on duty, Josie wore nothing that would draw attention to her physical appearance or gender.

She turned south onto Scratchgravel Road, toward River Road, which ran a parallel course with the Rio Grande. The river served as the fragile border between West Texas and Mexico. Across the river was Piedra Labrada, Artemis's sister city. The fifty-mile strip of land on either side of the river was known locally as *the territory*, a once-quiet area where two cultures had shared their differences peacefully for several hundred years. The cartels had recently chosen Artemis as their route into the United States, a disaster that taxed local law enforcement beyond all available resources. Since the Medrano and La Bestia cartels had begun negotiating over territory and drug routes in the area rather than killing each other over it, her small town of Artemis, Texas, had settled back into an uncomfortable peace. People wanted to believe the brutality was over, but the memories were fresh; the fear still dominated conversations at the diner and gas stations. She knew the peace was nothing more than temporary.

Josie made a habit of climbing the fifty-foot-tall watchtower built alongside the river at least once a week at various times of day and night to keep an eye on several hot spots for illegal crossings. She looked for signs on the ground: trash bags, discarded clothing, empty water bottles—all trash left behind by illegals lightening their load as they made their way across the desert. A shallow bend in the Rio Grande had been a recent crossing point for the Medrano cartel's gun and drug running, but Josie hoped the entrance point had been shut down with the arrests of several high-ranking leaders.

About a half mile before reaching the watchtower she spotted a light blue economy-sized car parked on the east side of the road. As she approached, she made out Texas plates. The car looked as if it had lost at a game of bumper cars; there were multiple dents, faded paint, a smashed left taillight, and a loose right fender. Josie thought the car looked like Cassidy Harper's, a girl who had worked as a fill-in janitor at the Artemis Police Department for a few months last year. Josie had liked the girl and had offered her some advice that Cassidy seemed to want but never followed. Josie met Cassidy's type frequently; many of the people she arrested weren't bad, they just made horrible choices.

Josie parked behind the vehicle and surveyed the area, scanning for movement. She saw no one. She walked around the car and found all of the windows up and the car doors locked. A woman's yellow tote bag lay on the backseat and about a dozen music CDs were scattered over the passenger seat in the front. Nothing looked tampered with. It looked as if she had parked and taken off hiking on a day forecast to hit 104 degrees.

Josie called the plate in to Lou and climbed onto the hood of her jeep, and then the roof, to view the area. A quarter mile east of her jeep she saw two shapes that she was certain were not native. The shapes were in the midst of a group of bushes so she was not able to distinguish what they were, but the coloring was off. She could make out bright yellow, and a patch of navy blue, neither of which were colors found in the desert in late July.

Worried the shapes could be people suffering from heat exhaustion, Josie climbed down from her vehicle to grab a small pair of binoculars from her glove box. Lou radioed back confirmation that the car belonged to Cassidy Harper: twenty-two years old, red hair, brown eyes, five foot four, 119 pounds, a resident at 110 River Road in Artemis. Josie told her to send Otto her way for assistance, and then got back up on the roof of her car.

She yelled Cassidy's name twice, but saw no movement through her binoculars.

With her heart pounding now, Josie climbed back down, slid inside her jeep, and threw it into four-wheel drive. She could think of no rational reason for Cassidy to be outside. She'd lived in Artemis long enough to know this kind of heat killed in a hurry.

Resisting the urge to floor it, she drove slowly into the desert, feeling her way, sensing the movement of the tires in the sand beneath her. There were areas she wouldn't take the jeep, even in four-wheel drive, because the sand was so soft the tires would get buried. Having never driven off-road in this area, she advanced carefully.

Josie rarely became emotionally tangled with other people's lives but occasionally her guard slipped. Cassidy had remained in Josie's thoughts since leaving the department. The girl lived her life by being at the wrong place at the wrong time and Josie often wondered about the situation with her boyfriend. She hoped it hadn't just ended in tragedy.

About fifty feet from what she was now certain were bodies, Josie felt the sand give way under her tires. Rather than chance getting the jeep buried, she grabbed her water bottle from the center console and opened the door, leaving the jeep and its air conditioner running. She pulled her gun and ran toward the bodies.

As she approached it was obvious she was facing the possibility of two dead. She found Cassidy, lying on her side, her face in the sand. Josie glanced at the body lying ten feet to the left of Cassidy but didn't bother checking vital signs. The man was already dead: swollen, deteriorating, and smelling rank. He had been there a few days. Even with the decomposition she could tell he was not Cassidy's boyfriend.

Josie kneeled close to Cassidy's head to block the sun from her face and placed two fingers on her neck. The girl's face was bright red and her pulse racing. Her skin was dry to the touch and Josie feared heatstroke, which could turn fatal fast.

She pulled her portable radio out of her belt and signaled Lou.

"Call the clinic. Tell them we have a probable heatstroke. I need a medic fast. She needs IV fluids. Then call Otto. We have a dead male. Possible illegal. Body is due east of the blue Ford Focus on Scratchgravel Road. Call the coroner."

During her time as a custodian at the police department, Cassidy had been good-natured and friendly. She had been a hard worker and Josie had hated to see her leave when their regular custodian came back from his medical leave. Jimmy was a sixty-something-year-old who was slow and quiet and rarely interacted with anyone in the department. Cassidy had been a welcome addition.

She lived with a man quite a few years older than she was, an odd guy, close to forty years old with a long scruffy beard and dark eyes that bothered Josie. During a traffic stop several years ago, he had avoided Josie's eyes, never once meeting her gaze. She could not imagine what the attraction was for this pretty young girl.

Waiting for Lou to respond, Josie opened the water bottle and took Cassidy's head in her hand, tilting it up, trying to wake her and get her to drink something. There was no response. She poured water over Cassidy's face and her wrists, attempting to lower her body temperature. Cassidy's hand moved but nothing more. Josie stood and put the water bottle in her gun belt. She bent at the knees and lifted Cassidy's torso over her shoulder, then used her leg muscles to slowly stand and balance herself. She took careful steps through the fine sand back to her jeep. In the intensity of the afternoon heat, each breath felt like fire, but she had to get Cassidy into air-conditioning until the medic arrived.

Josie stood at a trim five feet seven inches, but the walk to the car was slow. The heat magnified every movement, slowing every bodily function. Just as she started to worry the girl would not make it in time she saw the dust of an approaching car, then the unmistakable flash of Otto's patrol lights.

Officer Otto Podowski was sixty years old, a large man with little tolerance for the desert heat. He drove his own jeep to where Josie had parked, then ran to her and took the young woman over his own shoulder, carrying her the last forty feet to Josie's car. She ran ahead and opened the backseat door, then helped Otto position Cassidy inside.

"Paramedic's been called. I'll try and get some water into her," Josie said, climbing in beside Cassidy and slamming the back door.

Otto got into the driver's seat of Josie's jeep and aimed the air vents toward the backseat. Josie slowly poured water over the girl's face. Her body was limp and leaning against Josie's side. Otto turned the jeep around and headed out to the road to meet up with the paramedic.

"Is that the Harper girl?" he asked.

"Yes. She's not doing well. Her face is red. Her pulse is rapid, and she's not opened her eyes since I arrived."

As Otto maneuvered carefully through the sand, Josie filled him in on the position of Cassidy and the dead body when she arrived.

"Think she found the body and passed out?" he asked.

Josie glanced up and saw Otto looking at her in the rearview mirror. She shook her head in doubt. "What are the odds Cassidy would pick this spot to take a hike on a day like this? She couldn't have seen anything from the road. I had to climb on the roof of my jeep before I realized something was out there. It's not like she saw someone and ran to help."

"Since when did you quit believing in coincidence?"

"My first year on the job." She looked away from him and tried to pour a trickle of water into Cassidy's mouth again.

Otto pulled the jeep onto the side of the road as the ambulance made the turn onto Scratchgravel so fast Josie thought it might tip.

"That guy drives like a maniac. I'm gonna cite him for reckless driving after this is all over," Otto said.

"Cut him a break. He's just a kid."

"You were hired on as a kid too, but you didn't drive like a jackass."

Thirteen years prior, while he was still chief, Otto had hired Josie as an officer. He had retired as the chief three years ago after a hip replacement surgery and aching knees kept him from doing the job he expected of himself. Josie had applied for the job as chief with Otto's encouragement and he had been quick to accept her as his boss when she received the promotion.

Marvin Levin hopped out of the ambulance already sweating heavily in his EMS uniform. He had a paunch, and walked as if his belly slowed him down and annoyed him. He left the engine running and went directly to the back of the unit and opened the double doors.

Otto and Josie climbed out of the jeep and opened both back doors. Josie helped Marvin roll the stretcher over to the jeep.

"Fill me in," Marvin said, already looking into the backseat.

"A female, twenty-two years old. Possible heatstroke," Josie said.

Josie helped Marvin pull the girl out of the backseat and lay her on the stretcher. Marvin strapped her body down, and they rolled her back to the ambulance and slid her inside. He climbed into the back and started preparing IV fluids as Josie explained what she knew.

"I found her a quarter mile east of here. Passed out. She's unresponsive. Won't take any water." Josie watched Marvin slide the needle smoothly into Cassidy's arm and get the fluid dripping into her body. "She hasn't opened her eyes since I got here."

"Any idea how long she's been outside?" Marvin asked. He pulled packs of ice out of a small freezer and laid them in between her inner arms and her body, her armpits, and her groin.

"No idea."

He stood up quickly and headed toward the front of the ambulance. "Anybody taking the ride with me?"

Otto motioned Josie into the back of the ambulance. "Go on. See if you can get something out of her when she wakes up. I'll get measurements."

She nodded and stepped in beside the stretcher. Marvin turned the ambulance around and Josie shouted toward the front, "Hey! Drive like you got sense. I don't want to end up in a ditch on the way there."

"No worries," he yelled, laughing at what he thought was a joke.

Sitting on a small bench beside Cassidy's head, Josie pulled her cell phone out of her pocket. She dialed Officer Marta Cruz's number. Marta was the third member of their three-person police department. Artemis needed at least five officers to handle the recent spate of violence, brought on by the cartels in northern Mexico, but resources were scarce. Marta wasn't due in to work for several hours. Josie hated calling her off duty, but it was an accepted drawback of police work in a small town.

When Marta answered, Josie told her about finding Cassidy in the desert beside the dead body.

"Why am I not surprised to hear this?" Marta asked. "How can such a sweet girl attract so much stink?"

"The body is a male. I'm guessing he's been outside two to four days. Looks like he might have been an illegal making a break for it. Check with Border Patrol and ICE for any recent missing persons reports."

She felt the ambulance lurch through the lone stoplight in Artemis and continue forward. She could see the courthouse tower out of the front window and knew they were just a block from the Trauma Center.

Josie hung up with Marta, called the sheriff's department, and asked for Sheriff Roy Martínez. He was a burly retired marine who took his job seriously, was fair-minded, and operated on the same shoestring budget she did. The sheriff also ran the Arroyo County Jail. The majority of his staff was needed just to keep the jail running smoothly, which left Josie's police department in charge of both city crimes and often the county calls that the sheriff's department should have taken.

The sheriff answered with a gruff, "Martínez."

"Hey, Roy. It's Josie. I'm headed to the hospital with a probable heatstroke victim. And we've got a body in the desert."

"I heard from dispatch. I'm headed to Marfa in about ten minutes. I've got a prisoner transport. The body in the desert a Mexican?"

"That's what I'm calling for. We're not sure. It's your case to take at this point, but I talked to Lou this morning and she says you've got problems."

She listened as he blew air out in frustration. "I got one officer in Guadalajara for his wedding and two on sick leave. Peterson called in this morning. He's got a broken leg and won't be back for weeks. Fell off a ladder painting his damn kitchen." He paused. "You okay to take this one?"

"Otto's getting measurements now. I'm hoping with some fluids Cassidy will come around and tell us something about the body.

I'll keep you posted." She watched as the girl tried to move her arm, which was still strapped down to the stretcher. She moaned quietly and Josie took it for a positive sign.

"I appreciate it. I owe you one or two," Martínez said.

Marvin pulled the ambulance up to the side entrance of the Arroyo County Trauma Center and killed the sirens. The building was split into two discrete halves, each with a green awning covering a separate entrance: one for the county health department, another for the Trauma Center. Mayor Moss had won a homeland security grant after 9/11, and the money was used to build and outfit a Trauma Center to deal with the increased border violence. Josie was amazed they had survived so long without the center when the closest hospital was two hours away in Alpine. It was the one credit Josie could give to the mayor.

Vie Blessings, the nurse on call, pushed through the Trauma Center's double doors and rushed outside wearing a set of purple scrubs. Her expression was all business, but her spiked red hair and brightly colored makeup and eyeglasses indicated her real personality. Marvin met Vie at the back of the ambulance where the doors swung out as Josie stood from the bench.

"How is she?" Vie asked.

"She's trying to move her arms some. She's moaning too but hasn't opened her eyes," Josie said.

They pulled the stretcher out and the legs folded down and locked into place with a kick of Vie's foot.

Vie nodded at Josie. "Got it from here. Give me a call in a couple hours."

She and Marvin pushed the stretcher through the open doors, leaving Josie standing beside the ambulance in the hot afternoon sun.

Marvin called over his shoulder, "I'll give you a ride back. Give me five minutes!"

THREE

After Josie left for the hospital, Otto returned to her jeep and sat in the driver's seat with the air-conditioning vents pointed directly at him. He was certain Artemis would beat the record books that day. His shirt was already soaked. He pulled his ball cap off and wiped the sweat from his head with the handkerchief he kept in his back pocket. He hated wearing the Artemis PD ball cap, but he had burnt his balding head enough times that he finally started taking the extra precaution.

He opened Josie's metal evidence kit that lay on the passenger seat, certain she wouldn't mind him using her equipment. They worked well together. He respected her as an officer, and liked her as a person. It was his opinion that Josie needed to spend less time worrying about her job and more time worrying about her love life. She had not had much luck in that arena, and Otto worried her current romance with the local accountant was doomed for failure if she did not move things along. He had told her this, and was told to mind his own business in return.

Otto found the plastic accident template that was used to draw accurate pictures of the scene, as well as a graphite pencil and a sketchpad in the back of the kit. He opened the notebook and used the template to draw straight lines representing Scratchgravel Road, a rectangle showing Cassidy's car pointed south, the bodies roughly a quarter mile east of the car, and *X*s to signify the larger mesquite and creosote bushes and boulders in relation to the body. Once he had a rough sketch of the area he looked at his watch and sighed. The hottest part of the day. He knew it would be instant nausea when he stepped back out into the desert furnace, but he had to take the measurements, which meant leaving the air-conditioning to walk from the road to the corpse.

Otto pulled the measuring wheel from the back of Josie's jeep and pushed the button to reset the distance to zero. He took off walking, counting steps to ensure he was getting an accurate measure with the rolling wheel in the thick sand. He recorded 825 feet from the road to where he and Josie had stopped their vehicles in the sand, and another 47 feet to the body. It was almost a quarter of a mile from the road to the crime scene.

As Otto finished making his second sketch to scale and labeled the distances, the ambulance returned and Josie exited from the passenger-side door. Several minutes later she had driven her jeep to where Otto's was parked. She grabbed her evidence kit and camera and walked the remaining distance to the body.

"How's the girl?" Otto asked.

"I think she's coming around. Vie said to call back in a couple of hours." Josie placed her kit under a mesquite bush for a small amount of shade and pulled her camera strap around her neck. She held the 35-millimeter camera up to her eye to check the settings. "The coroner is on his way," she said.

"Mr. Personality?"

Josie smiled. "Have you ever once heard that guy laugh?"

"I suspect he doesn't know how."

Josie pointed to the ground around the boulder, about ten feet from where Cassidy's body had lain. "These are fresh prints. Make sure you get them noted on your sketch, and I'll get pictures." She focused her camera and snapped several pictures from different angles, trying in vain to keep her mind off the putrid smell. "I'd like to get a cast of one of the prints but that sand is just too fine."

"There aren't any prints around the body. It's blown clear," Otto said. "Makes it pretty obvious whatever happened to him took place first, then Cassidy came into the picture."

"Or she came *back* into the picture."

Otto swore and swiped at the flies swarming them.

After twenty minutes, they were satisfied they had thoroughly photographed and logged the area.

"Let's get this over," Josie said.

They approached the body and Josie handed Otto her camera.

"You snap pictures. I'll record."

"You're a good person. I'll be smelling that tonight in my nightmares."

Josie shuddered. She had volunteered for the task that would require getting personal with a dead body that had been out for several days in blistering heat. The bugs and small animals had already started on the exposed flesh. She was surprised the coyotes had not finished him off.

Otto pointed toward the man's ankle, where blackened flesh had been torn away from the bone. "Looks like the vultures have already started on him."

Josie looked up into the sky expecting to see the circling birds, angry at the human intrusion, but there was nothing but blue. She pulled her plastic gloves from her back pocket and said, "I heard once that the reason vultures are bald is so they can stick their head into decomposing roadkill and not get their feathers all nasty. You ever heard that?"

"You have to quit hanging out with cops. You need a life."

Josie smiled and pulled a mask out of the evidence kit lying under the bush. The kit was already so hot the metal clasp burned her fingers when she touched it. She slipped the mask over her nose and mouth, then pulled the gloves on. She turned on the handheld recorder she pulled from her shirt pocket, tested it once, then started her recording.

"Today is July twenty-third. It is 1:34 P.M. This is Chief of Police Josie Gray, in Artemis, Texas. Location is a quarter mile east of Scratchgravel Road, about a half mile from River Road. I am examining a deceased male, age undetermined due to breakdown of the body. Decomposition is visible on face, hands, neck, and on the right ankle." Josie paused and leaned closer to the man's face, forcing her gag reflex down at the smell. "There are larvae around the eye sockets and mouth. The neck and face area also appear to have been eaten by small animals."

Josie paused the recorder and stood suddenly, walked several steps away, and removed her mask, taking in fresh air. Otto handed her a water bottle and after several minutes she returned.

She kneeled again in the sand, and held the recorder to her mouth. "The man is bald. Dressed in a button-down Western-style shirt with a thin black bolo tie. He is wearing blue jeans and black work boots." She paused and lifted the man's untucked shirt slightly above his waist. "He is wearing a black belt with an expensive silver buckle. Clothes are in good condition. No other bags or luggage in the area."

Josie grimaced and pushed two fingers gently into the front pocket of the man's jeans. She fished out a wood-grained Case pocketknife and several coins.

Otto opened a plastic bag and she dropped the items inside. He held it closer for inspection. "That's a fifty-dollar pocketknife. This guy's not some down-on-his-luck Mexican trying to cross the border."

She checked the other pocket while Otto labeled the bag with an evidence marker. "Want to roll him over?" Otto asked.

Josie was kneeling beside the corpse in the shade provided by Otto's shadow. She turned back and narrowed her eyes at him. "I'm afraid the body will fall apart. I'll let Cowan deal with that one."

She turned back to the man, and noticed a black-and-purple-colored lesion stretching from under the dead man's shirt sleeve onto the back of his hand.

Josie said, "Hand me another set of gloves, will you?"

Otto pulled another pair of plastic gloves from the evidence kit and handed them to Josie. She wiped the sweat out of her eyes on her shirt sleeve and strained to get the gloves over her first pair in order to double up. She knew it was paranoia, but she was more afraid of unseen parasites than a gun or a knife. At least she stood a chance if she could see what she was fighting.

She struggled to unbutton the cuff on the man's sleeve and then slowly slid it above his elbow, grimacing at what she saw. Large black and red sores, some open wounds, covered his arm. "Think this came before or after his death?" she asked.

Otto leaned over her back and snapped several pictures. "Nothing I've ever seen."

Josie leaned across the man's torso, unbuttoned the other sleeve, and pulled it slowly up. A half-dozen lesions were revealed on the top of his forearm. Josie used the fabric on his cuff to lift his arm and look at the underside. One sore, with pus oozing from the center, stretched several inches from his wrist up his arm. She unbuttoned his shirt and found no wounds on his chest or abdomen.

Josie pulled his shirt closed and stood. "I don't like this." She walked to his feet and pulled up the bottom of his jeans, struggling to raise the jeans a few inches above his black work boots. She stood and shook her head. "Nothing. Only appears to be on his arms."

Otto took a step backwards. "I think we'd better leave this for Cowan. We don't know what this might be, or how contagious it could be."

They both turned toward the sound of a car in the distance.

"Speak of the devil," Josie said.

They watched the 1978 Dodge station wagon that had been

painted white and converted into the county hearse approach Cassidy Harper's little blue car.

"That has to be the ugliest car in all of Texas," Josie said.

"You don't think he'll try and drive that thing back here, do you?" Otto asked. County Coroner Mitchell Cowan was known for a supreme intelligence that translated into negligible common sense.

"Better get him on your cell phone before he tries it," she said. "I would trust that man with my dead body in a heartbeat. I sure wouldn't want to rely on him with my life though."

Otto dialed his cell phone. Josie turned back to the body and listened to him tell Cowan to wait by the road to be picked up.

"Hang on, and I'll go with you. I have to get out of this heat for a minute," she said.

"I'll drive. You take a break."

Josie pulled off her gloves and mask and dropped them on the ground by the body. She would put them in a hazardous waste bag when they got ready to leave. She found hand sanitizer in the evidence kit and rubbed a liberal dose onto her hands before climbing into Otto's jeep.

When temperatures hit above ninety they always left one of the cars running to have a cool place to escape the heat. They both sighed at the cool air blowing from the vents. Otto pulled a gallon jug out of a cooler in the backseat and they traded drinks of water before Otto took off to meet Cowan.

Josie and Otto got out of the car as Cowan was assembling his materials from the back of the station wagon. He was built like an ostrich, with a small head and thin neck that ballooned into a large midsection and ended in stick legs. Josie had always liked Cowan. He appeared to have no joy or humor in his life, but he showed up and did the job to the best of his ability with no complaints. She respected that.

"Nice day for a murder in the desert." Cowan looked up from

the black medical bag he was packing and glanced briefly at Josie and Otto before returning to his bag.

"You have a hazmat suit with you?" Josie asked.

"That I do. And, if I wear it, I will certainly stroke out from heat exhaustion before the examination has even begun. Plastic suits are not very practical on a day like today."

"The arms of the dead man are covered with oozing lesions. Doesn't look good," she said.

"Any idea on time of death?" he asked, ignoring Josie's comment.

"I'm guessing two days."

"Because?"

"Because there are flies and fly larvae in the eyes and nose," she said.

Cowan nodded. "Blowflies, yes. Have they hatched?"

"No."

"Good work, then. You're probably right. Sounds like about forty-eight hours."

"You taught me well," she said.

He grunted an acknowledgement and slammed the tailgate shut. He walked past the two of them and got into the backseat of Otto's jeep. Josie smiled at Otto, who rolled his eyes and got into the driver's seat.

"Blowflies don't typically deposit eggs at night," Cowan said.

Josie nodded, still smiling. "So, what are you saying? The time could be off by eight hours?"

"Blowflies are the best watch a dead man has."

"Cowan, you have a unique way with words," Otto said. He drove cautiously and pulled to a stop beside Josie's jeep.

Cowan stepped out of the car without speaking and, wearing his brown dress loafers, trudged awkwardly through the sand. Once he reached the body, he set up a plastic tarp and his equipment. He then performed a cursory examination that included his own set of 35-millimeter photographs. He was able to turn the body over and Josie asked him to check the man's pockets for iden-tification. When he found none, she stepped back over to wait with Otto. After another twenty minutes Cowan turned to face Otto and Josie, who were standing in the narrow shade of a mesquite bush, waiting impatiently to get out of the heat.

Under the rolls of deep-set wrinkles running across his fore-head, Cowan's customary sad expression had turned grave. "Two things. First, cause of death was most likely blunt force trauma to the head. Bruising on the back of his skull indicates he was hit with a heavy object, and with considerable force. The injury wasn't caused accidentally or by a fall."

"But the injury could have caused death?" Josie asked.

"Certainly. I'm not ready to rule it as his cause of death, but I wouldn't rule it out either," Cowan said. "Second, I've never seen necrotizing fasciitis in person, but the lesions certainly fit the de-scription."

"What is it?" Otto asked.

"It's a bacterial infection. Rare. It destroys skin, tissue, fat, and muscle. Regardless, the flesh is certainly dead, apparently eaten away by something."

"Could the wounds have happened after the man died?" Josie asked.

"I'm guessing not, but we need to get him into the lab. This heat is doing a number on the body."

"Wouldn't the flesh be dying because the man laid out here for two days?" Otto asked.

Cowan frowned. "Not the same kind of dead. I'm fairly certain this man's flesh was dead before his body was."

Otto looked at Josie, then back at Cowan. "Could it be conta-gious?"

"Too early to speculate. I would recommend a hot shower and copious amounts of soap after we're done here." He gestured to-ward the hearse parked along the side of the road. "Now. How do you suggest we transport this body out of here?"

"We could fold down the seats in the back of my jeep. Would it be safe to bag him and drive him out to the hearse?" Josie asked.

Cowan pulled his glasses down his nose and looked wide-eyed at Josie. "You understand why we installed the plastic mats in the back of the hearse? There's a fair chance that this body will leak fluids. This won't be pretty. And the smell will most likely permeate your vehicle for some time to come." He pulled his glasses off and stuffed them in his shirt pocket. "Have you ridden in the county hearse lately? Lysol can't touch that smell."

Josie glanced back at the body and grimaced. Not a good start to the work week, she thought.

Otto opened his phone. "Let me call Danny. We'll get him to bring the county truck over. He can transport in the back of the pickup."

Josie didn't argue. Thirty minutes later, Danny Delgado, sanitation supervisor, also known as the Dump Man, drove the Arroyo County four-wheel-drive pickup truck through the desert like a pro. Weighed down with large rocks in the bed of the truck, he could maneuver through sand, mud, and water like a stunt driver. He backed up to the body without a question. Josie figured he'd transported worse, but she couldn't imagine what that might be.

Otto had driven Cowan back out to the road where he retrieved disposable plastic jumpsuits, thick plastic gloves, and face masks from the hearse. He insisted each of them put the outfit on, including Danny, before they touched the body. Even with the heat, no one complained.

With considerable effort, and a fair amount of stomach distress, Josie, Otto, and Cowan bagged the corpse and loaded it onto the bed of the truck. As soon as the body was deposited, they stripped off the jumpsuits and stuffed them into a hazmat bag that Cowan said he would dispose of at the morgue. They were all sweat-soaked and Cowan passed around cold bottles of water, which they drained. Danny hopped into the pickup truck and hollered that he would meet Cowan at the morgue.

Cowan headed to the hearse. "I'll call as soon as I know anything." He pulled away with a parting toot of the horn.

Standing by the side of the road, Josie examined Otto, whose face was bright red. His uniform shirt was sweat-stained and his flyaway gray hair was a mess.

"I would just like to go home and sit on my front porch with the dog and drink a beer," Josie said.

"I got a close second. A cool shower and clean clothes. Then we meet up again for an ice-cold Coke and a bologna sandwich from the Hot Tamale. My treat," he said.

———

The phone on the bedside table rang and startled Cassidy out of a half-sleep. She looked around the hospital room, not sure what she should do. Hers was the only bed in the room and she'd seen only two people since she woke, both of them nurses. On the fourth ring Cassidy propped herself up on her elbow and closed her eyes at the flaming sunburn on her arm. Tears ran down her cheeks as she picked up the receiver and placed it gingerly against her ear.

"Hello?" she asked. Her voice barely registered.

"Hey, it's me. What's going on?"

She closed her eyes, relieved to hear Leo's voice, but dreading the inevitable questions.

"I passed out from heat exhaustion. I spent too long outside."

"Are you okay?"

"I'm fine. Got a bad sunburn, that's all."

"What were you doing outside?"

"I was just out for a walk."

There was silence for a moment. "What do you mean you were out for a walk? It's like an incinerator out there."

She forced the words out, clenching her eyes shut. "I found a dead man."

The line was silent for a beat too long. "What are you talking about?" he asked.

"I was over by the river, just hiking, and I came across a body. I passed out and Chief Gray found me."

"Where were you?" he asked.

"I don't know, over by the river."

"What do you mean over by the river? Where?"

"I don't know. Just out in the desert."

He blew air out in frustration. "Why can't you just give a straight answer?"

She closed her eyes against the anger in Leo's voice.

"What was wrong with the guy?"

Cassidy opened her eyes and stared at the computer monitor attached to an arm that connected to the wall. She stared at the blank screen as Leo's question replayed in her mind.

"What was wrong with him?" Leo repeated.

She wanted to hurl her own questions back at him. *Why were you talking about Scratchgravel Road to someone at one in the morning? Why did you leave in the middle of the night without a word to me?*

"I don't know," she said. "Maybe he was an illegal, crossing over, and the heat got to him."

"Can you come home tonight?"

"You can come get me. I'll pick up my car tomorrow."

"I'll be there as soon as I can," he said, and hung up.

She stared at the white sheets on the bed wondering how her life had collapsed in such a miserable heap in just one day. She leaned back into the pillow to get the weight of her body off the burnt arm, closed her eyes, and began to cry.

The door to the room opened and the nurse bustled inside wearing her white starched uniform and carrying a tray full of medical supplies. Cassidy willed the nurse to turn around and leave the room, but she didn't. She approached the bed and reached out for Cassidy's wrist. The nurse placed her fingertips on the inside of her arm and pressed into her flesh. After a moment she wrote numbers on her clipboard and laid it on the bedside table.

She grabbed a tissue from the box next to her clipboard and handed it to Cassidy, who sniffed and wiped her eyes. The nurse found a tube of ointment in the cabinet and unscrewed the cap as she walked back to the bed. Her expression was kind but worried.

"How's your pain?" Vie asked.

"It's okay."

"You want me to call your mother? A friend maybe? Someone who can come sit with you?"

Cassidy shut her eyes and tried to stop the flow of tears as the nurse began to gently rub the cream into her arms.

FOUR

After Cassidy Harper's car was towed to the county garage, Otto and Josie both drove home to shower and change into fresh uniforms. Josie was struggling to keep the images of the lesions on the dead man's arms out of her mind, and hoped that whatever killed him wasn't now invading her own bloodstream. It would be a frustrating waiting game until the coroner came back with his results.

Driving back to the Artemis Police Department, she turned her jeep onto River Road, hugging a curve that followed the natural path of the Rio Grande on her right. From the high point in the road she could see downtown Artemis, a couple dozen businesses surrounding the courthouse in an orderly grid, and a spray of middle-income housing and shabby apartments on all four sides. She thought about the considerable risk that Macon Drench had taken when he developed Artemis, for a second time, back in the early seventies. Fed up with the excesses of the city, he had used a good portion of his oil fortune to purchase the West Texas ghost town and remake it into a place where hard work and an independent spirit could pull a family through even the roughest of times. Josie had asked him several months ago if he considered his desert experiment a success. In reply, he had said that his vision was a town where crime was nonexistent.

"Considering the nightmare across the border, and the tough economic times, I'd say you've succeeded," she said.

Drench had frowned. "Napoleon Bonaparte said, 'The infectiousness of crime is like that of the plague.'" He had rubbed a finger along the brim of his cowboy hat and studied Josie for a moment. "You keep that in mind. Once those bastards infect our town with their drugs and violence we'll never get them out. They'll infiltrate every corner, just like they've done all over Mexico."

Driving down the straight stretch of River Road into Artemis, Josie thought about Drench's words. She stared out at the rugged low-lying mountains of the Chihuahuan Desert running haphazardly on either side of the Rio, and thought it was a small miracle that anyone could settle a land that could be so unforgiving. She agreed with Drench completely, and had to force herself not to obsess over the problems when she was away from work. She would give everything she had to keep the cartels across the river, and that obsession sometimes took precedence over everything else in her life.

The cell phone in her breast pocket vibrated and startled her.

"Where are you?" Otto asked.

"Just outside of town," she said.

"I'm pulling up to the Tamale. I'll order your usual."

The Artemis Police Department sat between the Gun Club and the Artemis City Office across the street from the courthouse. Catty-cornered to the PD was the Hot Tamale, Josie and Otto's favorite spot to eat. Josie pulled her jeep beside Otto's and parked in front of the restaurant. On the front of the building a newly painted sign read *The Hot Tamale: Quick Service, Authentic Recipes, and the Most Accurate Gossip in Texas*. Josie smiled at the sign. She wasn't sure if the gossip was accurate, but it was abundant.

She walked inside and found the waitresses wiping down tables and preparing for the supper crowd. The tables and chairs were up for grabs and were moved to fit whatever configuration the current group of customers cared to arrange. The waitresses wove their way through the jumble and typically knew every customer by their first name, as well as their daily order. Josie found Otto at their customary spot in the front corner of the diner, at a table with a clear view out the large window facing the courthouse.

She sat down and discovered a Coke already waiting for her.

"You look refreshed," she said to Otto.

"Lucy special-ordered dill kraut to go with my bologna. The woman is a saint." He smiled and shook his head, obviously touched by her effort. "Do you know how hard it is to get quality bologna in West Texas? Let alone dill kraut!"

Lucy Ramone, owner and head cook of the Tamale, doted over Otto shamelessly. Josie wondered if Otto's wife, Delores, realized Otto had an admirer.

"How long has it been since you and Delores went back to Poland?" Josie asked.

"Ten years. Since our parents both passed we haven't made the effort. We need to, though." He leaned forward in his chair and propped his arms on the table, his expression pensive. "Sometimes I physically ache for the food from my childhood. The pierogi and gnocchi, the kraut and sausage. My mother would cook for hours for Sunday dinners."

"Delores is a great cook," Josie said.

He sighed as if talking to an amateur. "She is, of course. But a pierogi constructed in a Polish kitchen is comfort food like no other."

Lucy ambled out from the kitchen and pulled up a chair. She ran the back of her hand across her forehead and sighed dramatically. "You missed it. Every table filled. A madhouse in here for lunch today."

Josie smiled and leaned back in her chair.

Lucy was not from Mexico, but she spoke a fair amount of Spanish, and she had developed an authentic-sounding accent over her twenty years of running the Hot Tamale. She was a squat woman with black hair and dark eyes that fit the Mexican persona she affected.

Lucy leaned in to the table conspiratorially. "So? Everyone talked dead bodies today at lunch."

Otto looked at Lucy in disbelief. "Who spreads this stuff?"

"I never reveal my sources," Lucy said. She smoothed her white apron across her thighs. "Now, fess up."

"Lou stopped in, didn't she?" Otto asked.

Lucy smiled, her lips pressed tightly together.

Sarah, who did double duty as short-order cook and waitress, yelled from the kitchen, "Bologna sandwich and a cold tamale?"

Josie looked up and saw her standing behind the pass-through window in the kitchen and gave her a thumbs-up.

"Five minutes!" Sarah yelled, and turned back to the kitchen.

"One body," Josie said. "Singular."

"I heard multiple," Lucy said.

Josie held up a finger. "One dead body."

Lucy considered the answer. "Okay. How many live bodies?"

Josie looked at Otto and smiled, then looked back to Lucy. "We found one dead body, and a local woman who passed out, probably from heat exhaustion. Know anything about it?"

"An illegal?" she asked, ignoring Josie's question.

"We don't know yet."

"Who was the local?"

"Cassidy Harper. You know her?" Josie asked.

"Vaguely. Doesn't come in here much. Her boyfriend does, though."

"What do you know about him?" Otto asked.

"I know he's a lousy tipper. A loner. Always sits by himself. Looks ready to slash his wrists most of the time."

Sarah brought their plates out and set them down, along with a bottle of Tabasco sauce. She was in her late twenties, and wore the unofficial Hot Tamale uniform: shorts, T-shirt, and tennis shoes. She wore her blond hair in a short bob and was covered in freckles from head to toe. Josie pointed at a button pinned to the pocket of her apron that showed her son holding a T-ball bat, a proud smile revealing two missing front teeth.

"Cute kid," Josie said.

Sarah grinned. "You should see him hit that ball and run like the wind. He's amazing." She sat their drink refills on the table and hustled back to the kitchen.

Lucy stood to leave. "The monsoons are supposed to start tonight. Forecaster says it's the hundred-year flood. Calling for a foot of rain over the next couple days." She pointed a finger at Otto, then Josie. "Mark my words. Things are about to get bad."

After they finished eating Josie offered to start her car while Otto paid. She tried to hand him a ten-dollar bill but he refused to take it.

"You pay tomorrow," he said.

Josie went outside to start her jeep and waited for Otto to join her, but the car was still blazing hot during the three-minute trip across town to the Trauma Center. She left her jeep running outside the emergency room entrance while they both went inside to check on Cassidy.

The Trauma Center's wing included a nurse's station and patient waiting area, two small examination rooms that also served as patient rooms, and a surprisingly well-equipped surgery unit. Vie Blessing was bent over a computer at the nurse's station talking into a phone and staring intently at something on the monitor below her. She glanced up and waved, then went back to her conversation. Otto and Josie wandered over to the TV mounted on the wall in the waiting room. A woman from the Weather Channel was discussing the forecast for heavy rain across northern Mexico and into Texas and Arizona.

Vie hung the phone up and called out, "Sorry. We're so understaffed it's ridiculous. There are two of us on duty in the center today. Not because someone called off. Because we're it!" She walked over to them, crossed her arms over her chest, and huffed in frustration. "Someday this town will face a lawsuit because they have a registered nurse serving in the capacity of a doctor about fifty percent of the time."

Otto said, "Want the truth? If I was in bad shape, I'd take you over most doctors any day of the week."

Vie winked at Otto and patted his arm. "You big suck-up. Are you here about the Harper girl?"

"How's she doing?" Josie asked.

"She'll be fine. Her temperature was down below one hundred when I checked about ten minutes ago. She's a lucky girl, though. If you hadn't picked her up when you did, she'd be dead by now. She knows it too. She's pretty shook up."

"Anyone been to see her?" Josie asked.

"No. She told me about finding the body. I told her she needs to talk to you. Tell you what she knows, but I don't expect you'll get much from her."

"Did she give you any details?" Josie asked.

"No, nothing like that. She looks scared to death, though."

"Any idea where the boyfriend is?" Otto asked.

"Nope."

Vie pointed and they all walked down the hallway. She stopped in front of Cassidy's room with her hand on the door. "I told her we need to keep her under observation until supper time."

Josie nodded and looked at Otto. "Good. That'll give us a chance to check her car out before she leaves."

Vie pushed the door open into a dimly lit room with two patient beds in the middle of various monitors and pieces of medical apparatus. In the first bed, Cassidy lay flat on her back staring up at the ceiling. Her face and arms were sunburnt, and her pretty red ringlets were matted around her head. She looked far older than her twenty-two years. She turned her head slowly in their direction.

Josie approached her first. "Vie tells us you're going to be okay. You had us pretty scared for a while."

Cassidy lifted the corner of her lip in a weak attempt at a smile.

"Do you remember us carrying you out?" Josie asked, trying to get her to relax.

Cassidy shook her head no, and then her attention shifted to Otto, who folded the flap back on his notebook and clicked a pen open.

Otto noticed her watching him. "It's okay, kid. We just need to ask you a few questions about this afternoon."

"What were you doing out in the desert in this kind of heat?" Josie asked. She kept her tone kind rather than accusatory.

Another shoulder shrug.

"Were you hiking?"

Cassidy looked at Josie as if deciding how to answer. "Not really. I just wanted to be outside." Her tone was soft and timid.

"How did you end up off Scratchgravel?" Josie asked.

She shrugged again, and when Josie continued to wait for an answer she finally said, "It just looked like an okay spot."

"For what?"

Cassidy looked confused for a moment. "For being outside."

"Couldn't you have gone outside at your own home?"

"Not really. We live in town. We don't really have a yard. It's—" She hesitated. "The grass is all dead. It isn't very pretty."

"How did you find the body?" Josie asked.

A shrug. "I just saw it. I was walking and I smelled something. It was awful, then I saw something behind a bush. When I saw the body, I got dizzy. Then I don't remember anything. I guess I blacked out."

Josie glanced back at Otto, who nodded to let her know he was getting everything. "You're saying you were just out walking in the desert on a day supposed to hit 104 degrees?"

She nodded.

"Why?"

She shrugged.

Josie tried to keep the frustration out of her voice. "Do you know who the man was?"

Cassidy opened her mouth slightly as if she couldn't believe the question. "You couldn't even tell who he was. He was—" She stopped and shuddered, then closed her eyes and turned her head away.

Josie adjusted her gunbelt and stepped forward to sit on the edge of the bed. "Cassidy, I'm trying to understand why I found you lying beside a dead body. Can you help me out here?"

She opened her eyes again but kept her head turned. "I told you. I just went for a walk and I found him there. It's not like I wanted to find him."

"Did you touch the body?"

Cassidy's jaw dropped and she turned to Josie. "Are you kidding? He was disgusting! Why would I touch him?" She shuddered.

Josie turned to look at Otto, who jerked his thumb toward the door.

"If you remember anything, or come across any information about the man or why he might have been out there, promise me you'll call?"

Cassidy nodded and Josie placed a business card on the hospital table.

"We had your car towed to the county garage to get it off the side of the road. We'd like to take a look inside it. Get some fingerprints around your doors. Are you okay with that?" Josie asked.

"I don't care."

Otto had a consent form and pen ready and approached the bed. "We just need you to sign a consent form. Make it all official."

Cassidy pressed the remote on her bedside table to raise the bed and used the table to sign the paper. Josie noted that she didn't give much thought to the paper or the idea of having her car searched. She seemed more concerned with the pain of bending her arms and the sunburn.

Cassidy pointed to a folded pile of clothes atop a bureau across the room. "Keys ought to be in my front shorts pocket."

Josie felt a piece of paper in the first pocket she looked in and resisted the urge to unfold it and read it. She found the car keys in the second pocket and took them instead. She and Otto thanked Vie and left for the garage.

The county garage was located on the east side of town, beside the Arroyo County Jail. The dark green metal garage was eighty feet long by thirty feet wide and had a poured concrete floor. Inside were several bays where the county four-wheel-drive pickup and two ancient plow trucks were parked and maintained. The plows were used to clean the roads after the monsoon hit each summer. They had been purchased by Macon Drench at a Houston auction several years ago. Before the plows were bought, the town had to rely on locals with pickup trucks and push-blades to clean up the roads. Drench had also paid for the construction of the garage himself rather than raising taxes. Josie wondered what would happen to the town if Drench ever tired of his desert experiment and headed back to the city.

Josie and Otto rode together in Josie's car and parked just inside the open garage door. Industrial-sized fans pulled air in one side of the garage and out the other. The air movement and shade from the brutal afternoon sun made the job they were facing still miserable, but tolerable.

Danny was in charge of the garage and maintenance on the trucks. The garage typically closed at five, but Danny had offered to keep it open as late as necessary so they could examine Cassidy's car. When Josie shut her jeep off, Danny appeared from behind the engine of one of the plows, wiping his hands on a rag. He smiled widely and flipped his rag to hang over his shoulder like a dish towel. His coworker, Mitch Wilson, walked behind Danny and waved hello. He was a lanky, heavily tattooed Harley rider who had served several tours in the second Iraq war as an explosives expert with the army. With his laid-back disposition it was hard for Josie to imagine him using explosives in a war zone.

"How's tricks?" Otto called.

"Trying to get these old rust buckets ready for the epic rains," Danny said.

"We appreciate your help today," Josie said.

"No problem."

"Cassidy doing okay?" Mitch asked.

"She'll be fine. She got lucky, though." Josie looked back at Danny. "You and Cowan get the body unloaded at the morgue?"

He shook his head slowly. "That was some nasty business."

He pointed to Cassidy Harper's car, parked directly behind them in an open area on the concrete pad. "Mitch and I unhooked her from the tow truck. Car's ready for you. We didn't touch any of the door handles. Didn't get inside the car."

Josie thanked them and they wandered back to the plow truck and turned the music back up. Over the hum of the fans Josie heard George Jones singing to Tammy Wynette about the "Crying Time."

"That's some classic music," Josie said. "Makes me want to find a lonely spot in the desert."

Otto turned up his lip. "That stuff'll put you in an early grave. You ever listen to a good polka?"

Josie got inside her jeep and turned it around so the back end faced Cassidy's car. She opened the hatch and Otto spread a plastic tarp over the carpet inside. She opened up her evidence kit, then backed away to face Otto, hands on her hips.

"Did you forget something?" she asked.

"You have issues," he said. "I borrowed your sketchpad and pencil. And I stuck them right back in there when I was done."

"*Right back in there* isn't where you found them. The pad and pencil don't belong with the evidence collection. That should be obvious to you by now. There is a section in the back for files. There's even a nice clip to hold the pencil."

"You need to lighten up, Josie."

"How many years have we been having this same conversation?"

"Learn to enjoy your life a little." He grabbed the black powder and brushes and walked over to the car to take latent prints off the silver door handles.

"I would if I didn't have to suffer a slob as a partner."

He smiled and winked at her.

She laughed. "Delores deserves a medal. I wouldn't put up with this at home."

Josie got Cassidy's keys from the cup holder in the front of her jeep and unlocked Cassidy's trunk. She snapped pictures of the contents: a bowling ball bag with a bowling ball zipped inside, a messy collection of college math and science textbooks ranging from calculus to nuclear physics with pages and covers ripped, an oily bath towel, and torn newspapers. With the closest bowling lane thirty miles away in Marfa, she wondered about the bowling ball. She didn't picture Cassidy or the boyfriend as the bowling league types. Josie picked up one of the newspapers and saw the date was from two years ago. She thought she ought to do the girl a favor and throw everything from the trunk in the trash.

Josie jotted down a list of the items and slammed the trunk closed. Otto was peeling the tape off the passenger-side door handle. "That's a pretty print. That'll run for sure."

"You done with the back yet?" Josie asked.

"Yep. This is my last door. I got two decent prints on the front driver side. This was the best one, though."

Josie opened the back passenger door and leaned down to examine the items on the floor.

Otto stood and stretched his back. "How about a drink break?"

"Give me a minute," Josie said, and got down on her knees beside the open car door. She used a pair of tweezers to lift a man's wallet off the floor and drop it into a one-quart plastic evidence bag. She also found several coins that she dropped into the bag. There was nothing else on the floor of the car except for a straw wrapper and small pieces of trash.

Otto leaned over her. "There's a Coke machine in the corner where you can buy me a drink."

Josie stood and wiped the sweat away from her eyes. "I might have something."

She walked over to the trunk of her car and Otto followed. She dumped out the evidence onto the tarp and Otto hummed beside her.

"Is that Leo's wallet?"

Josie used a pair of large tweezers to open the wallet. "No driver's license. But there's cash in it." She bent over the wallet to examine the clear windowed space for the ID more carefully. "At some point there was definitely something in this space. There's a square ridge all the way around where the license was."

"Looks like Ms. Harper might know more than she says," Otto said.

"Why would she take the ID and pitch the wallet in her backseat?" she asked.

Josie used the tweezers and a gloved hand to open the bi-fold brown leather wallet. A twenty and four one-dollar bills were in the bill section. She backed up to let Otto look.

"Odd amount of money for an illegal trying to cross the border," Josie said.

"Who would steal a guy's driver's license and leave the twenty-dollar bill?"

"That's assuming the license was still in there when she took it." Josie wiped the sweat off her forehead with her arm and sighed. She dropped the wallet into another plastic evidence bag, then put her hand in her front pocket and pulled out several dollar bills. "Come on. I'll buy you a drink."

They walked over to an enclosed office area with a humming Coke machine. They got their drinks and each drained half a can at once.

Josie nodded absently. "You figure Cassidy found the body and took his wallet back to her car out of some kind of morbid curiosity?"

"You hear about killers keeping items as souvenirs after they kill someone."

"Come on. You don't see her as the killer," she said.

Otto nudged her arm with his own. "You being sexist? She's a cute young girl, so she couldn't possibly kill this guy?"

"Tell me how many cute young girls you've arrested for murder."

"Not my point."

"Besides, you know Cassidy. She's clueless. Not a killer."

"What's that saying about desperate times?" he asked.

Josie ignored the question. "We're assuming the wallet is the dead man's. Maybe it's her boyfriend's. Maybe he bought a new one and switched wallets out while sitting in the car," she said. "Just pitched the old one in the backseat."

Otto gave her a skeptical look. "He has so much extra money that when he switched his wallet out he just left the twenty-four dollars."

She tilted her head, conceding his point.

Josie stopped at her trunk and slipped on a fresh pair of rubber gloves. "I just can't figure why she'd take the wallet. Think about the timing. She'd have found the body, taken the wallet, walked it all the way back to the car, dumped it in the backseat, then walked back to the body in this deadly heat, and passed out from exhaustion."

"Maybe she took the stuff and got a guilty conscience. Decided to go back," he said.

"Still doesn't work. If she felt guilty she would have called the police. Why walk back to a body that was obviously dead? There's no point in that."

"Maybe someone else put the stuff in the car," Otto said.

"Nope. The doors were locked. All the windows were rolled up.

Her car keys were on her." Josie opened the backseat of her jeep and pulled out her camera case. "We'll need to check if she has another set of keys."

Josie passed Otto the 35-millimeter camera and he nodded slowly. "Here's another one. How'd she get the wallet? The guy is lying on his back. His body is decomposing. She had to work hard to get that wallet out of his back pocket. Fight the flies and the smell. I can't imagine the wallet being worth that kind of grief."

"Maybe he carried it in his front pocket, along with his pocket-knife," she said.

"I thought she looked pretty disgusted with the whole idea of the dead body. Remember her face when you asked if she could identify him? She looked ill even thinking about it. I can't see her putting her hands into that dead man's pants pocket." Otto looked doubtful. "Front or back."

"And why would she dump it in her backseat? Would you work that hard to get something and then throw it on the floor?" Josie shook her head no to her own question.

"You'd put it on the front seat, or you'd hide it," he said.

"Let's go back to the keys. If there's a second set, it makes sense that Cassidy's boyfriend would have them. What if Leo planted the evidence?"

"And why would he do that?" Otto asked.

"Maybe he's planting evidence on her to keep the focus off him," she said.

"Doesn't make sense. All it does is draw more attention to both of them. If he had the evidence he'd want to hide it. Ditch it."

"The body has been there several days. Maybe Leo drove Cassidy's car out there and took the wallet himself. Killed the guy and took his identification. Left the wallet in the backseat," she said.

"Although it still doesn't make sense why he'd dump it in the backseat for Cassidy to find."

Otto handed Josie a pair of latex gloves and grabbed himself a pair as well.

Josie absently slipped a glove over her hand, trying to make sense of the details they were collecting. "Meanwhile, we have a man with a curious mess of sores on his body, who was banged on the back of the head, then most likely left for dead in the middle of the desert."

They spent the next twenty minutes inventorying everything in the car. It amounted mostly to music CDs, hair ties and headbands, and the items in Cassidy's purse. The license from the man's wallet never showed up.

Josie was packing up the evidence kit and Otto was locking the car when the first raindrops pinged off the metal roof of the garage. Within ten minutes the temperature dropped twenty degrees. They walked up to the open garage door as nickel-sized drops of rain pooled on the dry ground like water on a waxed car. The sky directly above them was still relatively clear with the setting sun casting light onto the ground in patches. Across the Chihuahuan Desert the rains were coming.

The country music stopped and Danny and Mitch ambled up to join them.

"Ain't nothing better than the first rain of the season," Danny said. He smiled widely and stepped out into the rain with his arms thrown wide, his head tipped back, and his eyes closed.

"Crazy shit. He'd be running through the raindrops if you two weren't here," Mitch said.

The sky to the south was moving fast, the clouds rolling like boiling water as the sun became completely blocked out and the light faded. The rain tapped louder and faster on the roof and Danny finally came back into the garage for shelter. They listened in silence and watched the display for a long while before Otto said they'd better get back to town. West Texas had experienced no rain in over nine months and it wouldn't take long before the roads began to fill with mud. When the sand in Arroyo County mixed with rain it formed a frustrating combination of slick mud and concrete. Some areas received rain and compacted so hard the ground cracked when it finally dried. In other places sand mixed with soil and sediment and turned into a sludge that could turn instantly dangerous in the right conditions. Mudslides weren't common, but they could be deadly when they hit.

In a suburb just south of town, two dozen modest, one-story homes were located around a road shaped like a race track. The center of the track, referred to as the infield by the kids in the neighborhood, was a park; mostly just a large empty lot with brown grass for a playing field that the kids used for baseball or whatever pickup game they could arrange. Most of the homes were rental units owned by Macon Drench, including the one where Officer Marta Cruz lived. Her house was located on the far end of the block, a small two-bedroom home covered in white siding with white vertical blinds covering all of the windows. A stone shrine to the Virgin Mary, surrounded by colorful plastic flowers in terra-cotta pots, decorated the front of the house. The landscaping consisted of gravel and a few cactuses. The house was clean and unassuming.

Inside, the walls were painted white, the decorations primarily religious in nature: an ornate gold cross hung on the wall above the couch, religious poems and plaques hung from the other walls. A floral couch and love seat and oval-shaped coffee table filled the small living room to capacity. The only room in the house painted anything other than white was Teresa's. When she had turned thirteen she had insisted on a deep purple that now felt dark and overpowering, especially with the rain falling outside. She lay on her bed staring at the cracks in the ceiling. She imagined each line as a choice. She thought if she studied long enough the lines would connect and her life would make sense again.

She had never seen a dead body. She'd been to a funeral once when her grandpa died, but she'd not been allowed to walk up to the casket. But this wasn't just a body. The man was murdered. She had seen the guy who last touched the body. She knew what the truck looked like. This wasn't about sneaking out of the house with Enrico. Each minute she let go by without telling her mom increased her guilt. Now, two days had passed and she'd said nothing. She wondered if she might be arrested herself for something—for hiding information. She had lain awake for hours that night, listening to the soft tap of the minute hand on the clock, then the rain pounding on the roof and sliding down the windows outside her room, and still she had done nothing.

Her mother had walked into her bedroom early that morning, at the end of her shift, kissed her on the forehead, and whispered good night. Teresa had faked sleep, unable to admit what she had done. Then her mother had been called back into work that afternoon, and Teresa had said nothing. She had already waited too long. How could she tell her mother she had lain in bed, silent, knowing that a man had been killed?

She'd always imagined herself as tough, as someone who could take care of herself and stand up for what was right. But she had discovered she was a coward. Teresa closed her eyes and wondered what Enrico was thinking at that moment. When they had climbed back into his truck and driven away from the Hollow he had made her promise she wouldn't tell her mom. At the time, she had thought it was an empty promise. She had imagined confessing everything to her mother, but now, the thought of telling her seemed impossible.

FIVE

Officer Marta Cruz was a ten-year veteran of the force—twelve if her first two years working as a custodian were included. She left Mexico fifteen years ago after an abusive relationship with her then husband had forced the relocation. She was a compact woman with a deeply lined face; the permanent scowl lines that fanned out from her eyes and mouth belied her generally positive outlook. Marta attributed the recent deepening of those lines to constant worry over her sixteen-year-old daughter, Teresa. The girl had the curves to turn a grown man's head, and a smart mouth that would either serve her well in life, or prevent her from finding success. Either way, the girl kept her mother and the parish priest up nights with worry.

Marta was thinking about her daughter as the first raindrops slid down the windows of the police department. She was sitting at her desk, on hold, waiting for the Border Patrol agent, Jimmy Dare, to come back on the line with a report on missing illegal immigrants in the West Texas area. Marta was struggling to remain focused on her job. Teresa was draining all of her energy. She was infatuated with a boy who was too old and too experienced for her own good. Marta predicted Enrico Gomez would be in jail before the year was out, but she couldn't convince her daughter that he was anything more than misunderstood.

Jimmy finally came back on the line. "There's a group of three kids missing. They took off about a week ago and supposedly headed up north through Presidio, but they were in their early twenties. Doesn't sound like your man."

"Thanks for checking. You'll let me know if you hear anything?" she asked.

"Will do."

Marta hung up with Jimmy and called her home phone to check on Teresa. They had been fighting nonstop lately and Teresa had started threatening to run away from home with Enrico if Marta didn't allow her to see him. Marta listened to the busy signal on the phone and sighed, relieved her daughter was at least home. As a single mother she had no idea how to handle her hardheaded teenager with a rotating shift and no family in town to help.

———

By the time Josie and Otto arrived back at the Trauma Center the rain was coming down in sheets. Josie parked just outside the emergency room door and she and Otto made a run for the building. Standing inside, shaking the rain off, they watched as Cassidy walked down the hallway with Vie on her heels. Josie was relieved to see she had apparently made a full recovery, aside from the angry red burn covering her arms, legs, and face. Josie had talked with Vie about thirty minutes prior to tell her they were coming back to talk with Cassidy. She must have decided to make a quick getaway, and Vie was determined not to let it happen.

Vie threw her hands in the air when she saw Josie and Otto. "I told her you needed to talk to her!"

Cassidy was dressed in the same yellow shorts and brown T-shirt she had been wearing when they carried her out of the desert that afternoon. She looked as if she were ready to cry.

"Hold on a minute. What's the rush?" Josie asked.

"My boyfriend's on his way to get me. I have to go."

Josie turned from Cassidy and gestured back toward the entrance door. "I'm sure he'll come in. Nurse Blessings can explain we're talking."

"He called a few minutes ago. He'll be here any minute."

"You've been here all day. Surely he can wait a few minutes while we talk," Josie said.

Her lips quivered and she squinted through tears. "He doesn't want me talking to you. I told him you were coming back and he said he was coming to get me. I can come by your office tomorrow." Her voice had grown shrill.

Josie motioned to the brightly lit patient waiting room. "Let's sit down for a minute. We need to ask you some questions today. I don't think you want to come down to the police station later, do you?"

She shook her head no and sat on the edge of a plastic chair with her hands underneath her thighs. Her eyes darted around the room as if searching for an escape route, and her forehead was creased in worry. Josie wondered if it was an act to get her way, or if she was truly fearful of the boyfriend. She considered taking Cassidy in to the station just to remove her from the boyfriend's influence so she could try and talk sense into her.

Otto sat in the seat next to Cassidy and passed her a digital camera that he had turned on and queued up. "Take a look at that picture."

Cassidy looked at the camera, then back at Otto.

"Recognize it?" he asked.

She shook her head no.

"It's a wallet."

"Okay. But I've never seen it," Cassidy said.

He took the camera back and advanced to the next picture. "Recognize that?"

She leaned forward to look at the picture and looked confused. "Is that the backseat in my car?"

Otto nodded, his expression grave. "You recognize it now?"

Her eyebrows furrowed in confusion. "That's not my wallet," she said, pointing at the camera screen.

"What do you see in the picture?"

Cassidy frowned. "A wallet, in the backseat of my car." She looked up at Otto.

"Whose is it?" he asked.

"I don't know. I've never seen it."

"Does it belong to the dead man?"

Her eyes widened. "I told you, I don't know. I've never seen that wallet."

"Is it your boyfriend's?" he asked.

"No. He doesn't carry a wallet. He carries a money clip."

Otto glanced at Josie, who remained impassive.

A horn honked several times outside of the emergency room doors where Josie's police car was parked. She assumed it was Leo.

Cassidy looked toward the door but didn't speak.

Josie said, "Did you see any other cars drive by while you were in the desert?"

"No."

"Would you have noticed someone driving by while you were walking?"

She shook her head. "From where the dead man was I couldn't see the road at all."

The driver of the car outside the Trauma Center lay on the horn.

"Please. I have to go," she said.

Josie handed her another business card. "Put this in your pocket. You call me first thing tomorrow. We'll find a time to get your car back to you."

She stood and Josie put a hand out to stop her. "Hold on. You have some homework to do tonight. I want you to make me a calendar that details your day, from the time you got up, through your sleeping hours, for the last four days. Start with last Friday, end with today."

"I will. I promise."

Josie blew air out in frustration. She didn't know how to get through to her. "One piece of advice and you can go. Tell the truth. Whatever has happened, you need to tell me what's going on so I can help you figure out a plan." Josie gestured toward the honking horn outside. "He may not have your best interest in mind."

Cassidy turned from Josie and ran from the building.

Josie pulled her keys out of her front pocket and smiled grimly at Otto to keep her anger in check. "I'll be visiting Leo tomorrow."

She and Otto thanked Vie for her help, but as they turned to leave Vie asked if she could talk with Josie for a minute. Josie pitched Otto the keys and he went outside into the rain. She followed Vie over to the waiting area and sat down beside her.

Vie crossed her hands in her lap and pursed her lips. "I need to talk to you in confidence." She paused and Josie nodded for her to continue. "I'm worried about someone you work with. About their child."

Josie considered Vie for a moment. The only one of her coworkers with a child who lived in the area was Marta.

"Okay," Josie said, her tone cautious.

"Obviously I can't tell you specifics, and I can't go to the parent, but I'm worried about the direction this young person is headed."

Josie nodded. She knew discussing patient care violated federal laws and would be cause for dismissal. The only thing that came to Josie's mind was a rumor she'd heard recently that involved Teresa dating Enrico Gomez. Josie had dismissed it as nasty small-town gossip.

"Should I be concerned about Enrico?"

Vie nodded once, her lips forming a thin line as if forcing her to not say more, but her eyes were filled with worry.

Josie had heard enough. It meant the rumors were true. Teresa was seeing Enrico behind Marta's back. Marta worked third shift and Teresa was often alone at home in the evenings. Enrico was a known meth user, a twenty-year-old who had done time in juvenile hall for drug possession and dealing several years ago. Josie felt sick.

Vie patted Josie's knee and walked away, back to the ringing phone at the nurse's station.

Josie leaned back in her seat, and stared blankly at the TV hanging from the wall, its volume muted. The weather forecaster, standing with rain dripping off the hood of her yellow rain slicker, was no doubt delivering more bad news. Josie sighed heavily and watched Vie talking on the phone. For such a smart kid, Teresa was one of the worst judges of character Josie had ever met. Her mom, who would do anything for her, got nothing but grief. Teresa made excuses for her alcoholic dad and cut her mom zero slack. And now she was running with a convicted meth user.

———•—

Cassidy pulled the car door shut and Leo slammed the accelerator, spinning the tires on the wet pavement. He didn't speak until they were out of town on River Road. "What the hell is going on?"

She looked out the passenger window and said nothing as she tried to force down the knot in her throat. She focused on the raindrops pelting the ground, all falling at precisely the same angle. Before she had met Leo he had been an assistant physics professor. But then he had lost his job due to cutbacks. When they first started dating he would impress her with his ability to use wind speed and velocity to figure out the precise angle of raindrops, or he'd tell her exactly how long it would take to drive somewhere at a certain speed. She didn't care, but she liked that he tried to impress her. Most guys wanted nothing more than an easy date. Now, here it was six months later, and she wondered if he was capable of murder.

He took a deep breath and blew it out in frustration. "What

were you doing on Scratchgravel Road, in the middle of nowhere, passed out by some dead guy? That deserves an answer."

Her attention remained on the rain. Numbness ran through her entire body. She felt it all the way to the middle of her brain. He had to know that she knew about his conversation the other night. Or, maybe he suspected she knew much more than she did. She wondered if her own life was in danger. She forced words out of her mouth. "I felt like getting out and walking. I just took a walk."

"And ended up by a dead man."

She didn't respond.

Leo slammed on the brakes. Cassidy's body jerked forward and she threw her hands out to keep from hitting the dash. The car fish-tailed on the wet pavement and stopped in the middle of the road. She looked forward and backward and saw no other cars, but she knew it wouldn't have bothered Leo if there were.

He turned his body toward her and squeezed her sunburned arm. She cried out in pain.

"What the hell is wrong with you! I won't put up with this shit. I don't like it when I can't trust you."

Tears stung her eyes. They were a defense she used with him that often worked. Now she cried openly, swearing to him that she just went outside to walk.

A car slowed to ask if they needed assistance, and Leo waved them on. He let go of her arm and started toward home again, leaving his questions unanswered. Cassidy's head throbbed, and she wondered how she could force herself to climb into the same bed with him that night.

A glass entrance door opened between two large windows in the front of the Artemis Police Department. Inside, the brown-paneled office was narrow and deep. The receptionist/dispatcher area snugged in behind a waist-high counter that kept the general public just out of reach. Behind the dispatcher and her computer and radios were two metal desks used for officer intakes and interviews. Beyond the desks were a dozen filing cabinets against the wall on either side of the room, and the flags of the United States, Texas, and Artemis in the rear corner. A set of stairs in the back led upstairs to one small unused room and a large classroom-sized room that held desks for the two officers and the chief of police. A wooden conference table was located in front of the entrance to the office. When Josie became chief she declined the use of the small private office in favor of working in the same room as Otto and Marta.

Josie and Otto arrived back at the police department at eight o'clock that night. Otto stayed downstairs to discuss information Lou had for him on an ongoing burglary investigation. Josie found Marta at her desk upstairs. She was on the phone, but turned and waved hello at Josie when she entered.

Josie hung her dripping rain slicker on a hook in the back of the office and poured a cup of burnt coffee. A small table with a coffeemaker and condiments sat under one of the large plate-glass windows. The view from upstairs was one of her favorite lookouts in Artemis. Even on a gloomy rainy night she could picture the neighborhood behind the police department, lined with colorful small adobe homes with postage-stamp lawns filled with tricycles and toys and plastic swimming pools. On most spring and summer days kids bicycled endless laps around the block while men worked under the hoods of cars and women tended to small backyard gardens, fussing at the kids and gossiping with friends over the fence. As a girl, growing up without a father, Josie had imagined herself in a home just like the ones she stared at; she had imagined herself married with two kids by this point in her life, but the happily-ever-after had proven elusive.

Josie sat at her desk and watched Marta finish her phone conversation. She looked bad; her eyes were tired and her cheeks sagged. Marta wiped perspiration from her forehead as she hung up the phone even though the room was cool and damp from the rain.

She opened the notepad in front of her and flipped through a few pages of notes. "I called Border Patrol. Talked to Jimmy Dare. He doesn't know anyone using that area as a crossing point right now. And no missing persons fit the victim's description."

Josie nodded. "I don't think he was crossing the border."

Otto entered the office and said hello to Marta, then sat down at his computer and hit the power button.

Josie continued, "It's an odd one. The body was already decomposing, but we should still get a decent autopsy. Cowan's guessing he was in his sixties. Hispanic. Nicely dressed. Western shirt and nice belt, jeans, and work boots. Expensive knife in his pocket. No luggage or extra bags. He had some money in his wallet, but his wallet was gone."

"How do you know there was money if the wallet was gone?" Marta asked.

"Guess where we found the wallet?" Otto asked.

"No clue."

"In the backseat of Cassidy Harper's car," he said.

Marta groaned.

Josie nodded and sat down at her desk. "Doesn't know how the wallet got into her car."

"And the boyfriend doesn't want her talking to the police," Otto said.

"She claims she went hiking because she wanted to be outside. She just happened to find a dead man. Then we search her locked car and find a man's wallet lying on the floor of her backseat," Josie said.

"She says she's never seen it," Otto said.

Marta rolled her eyes. "Of course not."

Josie pitched her pen on her desk, frustrated with Cassidy's unwillingness to help herself.

Otto pointed to the sketchpad in front of him. "From the angle of the bodies, it appears she crawled toward the body, then passed out about five feet from him. Her story works, we just can't figure out why she was there."

"Any idea how the man died?" Marta asked.

"He'd been there a few days, so cause of death is anyone's guess," Josie said. "The scary part was, he had sores on his arms. Multiple open lesions. Cowan's talking about some kind of flesh-eating disease."

Marta looked horrified. "The stuff where entire villages are killed?"

"Cowan was pretty evasive," Josie said.

"He wasn't his usual chipper self, if that tells you anything," Otto said.

Josie smiled. "Leave Cowan alone. You know how lucky we are to have a coroner in a town this size who actually knows something about dead bodies?"

Otto glanced at his watch and Josie noticed it was after nine o'clock. After working second shift this evening, she and Otto had to turn around and work first shift in the morning. They drew up a quick list of priorities for Tuesday morning and she and Otto left Marta to finish out the night on her own—one of the many hazards of an understaffed, underfunded border police department.

Charcoal gray light hovered over the horizon as Josie drove home from work. The rain had momentarily slowed to a drizzle but a downpour loomed in the thick layers of clouds. Josie rolled her windows down to smell the wet earth, a smell she associated with a sense of longing and dread. She loved the sound of raindrops on her roof, listening to the deep endless roll of thunder across the desert, and watching the sheets of rain travel across the land like a curtain being drawn across a stage. But the aftermath would be ugly. Mud and sand would be on the roads for days, making travel on the back roads time-consuming, and in some areas impossible. She would start tomorrow helping the crews assess the damage to determine if roads needed to be temporarily closed until the county trucks could plow. She had a meeting scheduled with Sheriff Martínez and Smokey Blessings, the county maintenance director, at 7 A.M. to discuss plans. Smokey was married to Vie, and was her laidback opposite. He was built like a grizzly bear with a full beard and thick head of hair, but his demeanor was kind and always polite.

Josie turned right onto River Road, the best paved road in Artemis, and saw that it was already covered with debris. Most of the town's roads were gravel, some just worn paths through the desert, or arroyos that were used only during the dry seasons. They were even harder to clean after a major storm.

Josie drove slowly and enjoyed the balmy temperature and moist air on her face. She turned onto Schenck Road and caught a glimpse of Dell Seapus's ranch, tucked into the foothills of the Chinati Mountain range, just beyond her own home. Dell had deeded her ten acres to build a house on after she brought back his prized Appaloosa horses that a band of horse thieves had taken to New Mexico. Dell was a seventy-year-old bachelor, short and wiry, stooped and bowlegged from too many years on horseback. He was also Josie's closest friend.

Josie looked at her house with pride as she approached. It was a small, rectangular adobe with a deep front porch. She and Dell had framed the house with brick over a two-month period, and she had hired an old Navajo Indian to plaster the faded pink exterior. Pecan timbers were used for the front porch and lintels. Josie had oiled and hand-rubbed the wood to a deep brown patina. The house looked as if it had been there for a hundred years.

As she pulled into the driveway her headlights caught Chester trotting down the lane from Dell's house to her own. He held his head high, probably searching for a scent, but it gave him a serious look that Josie loved. Most days, Chester had already made the quarter-mile walk back down the lane to Josie's and was lying on the front porch when she got home. She knew the dog would give his own life for hers, but at heart, he was a chicken. He didn't like the dark.

She slammed the jeep's door and laughed as the dog made his way up to her, his tongue hanging, back end swaying in the opposite direction of his wagging tail. He moaned and barked, his entire being happy to see her. She rubbed his long velvet ears and finally followed him up to the house where he forced his way through the door ahead of her and made a straight path to the kitchen. She heard the plastic rattle as he pushed his nose down into an open bag full of rawhide bones. Before she made it to the pantry to hang her gun belt on the hook, he had lain down on his rug in the living room for an evening snack and nap.

After she hung her uniform and bulletproof vest in her closet and changed into cotton shorts and a Texas A&M T-shirt, she wandered back to the kitchen to search the pantry shelves for dinner. She opened the cabinet to scavenge and found a can of roast beef and a can of baked beans, which she thought matched surprisingly well. She pulled them down and found the can opener in the silverware drawer. She dumped the contents into two plastic bowls with lids and stuck them in the microwave for two minutes.

As her dinner cooked, Josie pressed the button on the answering machine that sat at the end of her kitchen counter. One message.

"Hey, it's me."

Josie smiled. It was Dillon Reese, her longtime, semi-serious love interest. He sounded tired and lonely.

"I'm still in Kansas. The conference is predictable. The feds want more than is humanly possible to give. I'm going out tonight for dinner and drinks. Nothing like twenty accountants to liven up the streets of Topeka. Call me later. I'll keep my phone with me." He paused. "Miss you."

Josie stood at the counter, staring at the answering machine, imagining Dillon in his Dockers and pressed white shirt and striped tie, sitting in a hotel eating conference chicken for lunch, chatting amiably with the other accountants at his table. He was the most stable, the most predictable man she had ever met. She could count on him like the earth's rotation. She knew what his reaction would be before she knew her own. And she could not fathom why he seemed to love her when she could not offer him the same level of commitment in return.

The microwave buzzed and startled her. She dumped the contents of both containers onto a plate and sat on the couch with Chester gnawing on his rawhide at her feet. She clicked on the local news to watch the grim weather forecast, then clicked it off again. She was tired of bad news.

Her thoughts drifted to Marta, and her daughter Teresa. She wondered what dinner must be like at their house: an angry teenage girl and her frightened mother, trying to look brave and in control across a plate of food that Marta scraped together from a paycheck that never went far enough. Josie wondered if the hole in her own heart would be filled by a child, or if the emptiness she felt so often was just part of her nature. She envied Dillon, lanky and easygoing, able to say what he felt with no forethought or anxiety.

She walked into the kitchen and dug back in the cabinet beside the refrigerator to find her bottle of bourbon. She'd hid it one night after Dillon commented on how quickly the alcohol was disappearing. He had hurt her feelings and she was irritated with herself for hiding something that she knew was not a problem. She poured a juice glass full and went back to the couch, hoping to fill the hole, at least temporarily.

SIX

Tuesday morning Otto awoke at six, but before he made the ritual beeline to the kitchen coffeepot, he walked outside through a light rain to check on his small herd of milk goats that roamed freely on his sixty-five acres of pasture. He found them huddled under the stable, but as soon as they caught sight of him they stumbled up off the ground, their skinny legs propelling them forward as one group, their brown eyes concerned, bleating like scared children. Their routine had been interrupted and they were not pleased with the chaotic weather. Otto had raised goats for twenty years and never tired of their quirky personalities and social nature. He stopped to check the rain gauge on the fence post. Six inches in one night, most likely a record breaker. The desert was a place of extremes, but that year they'd experienced drought, record-high temperatures, and now possibly record-high rainfall. Otto tended to blame the weather patterns on nature's fickle whims, but at times like these he wondered.

After feeding and watering the goats, he sat down with Delores for a breakfast of waffles and milk, and then showered, dressed, and left for work by seven thirty. On the drive to work the rain turned heavy again: from ground to sky was a gray wash. The West Texas monsoon season, when the area received most of its rainfall, typically lasted from July through September, with an average annual rainfall totaling just sixteen inches. Artemis had received eight inches in two days and it was still July. The old-timers at the Hot Tamale were predicting the hundred-year flood this season, and in his experience, the old-timers had a sense for all things weather. The lack of vegetation across the flat land made perfect conditions for flash flooding, and all officers were on alert for emergency calls.

Sitting at his desk in the office he made a few phone calls and answered e-mails while he polished off two cups of coffee. Then he called Mark Harper, Cassidy's dad, and asked if he could stop by and see him at the shop. Mark owned a bulk food store that he operated out of a small warehouse located by the Arroyo County Jail, several miles east of town. It was a successful business, used by the jail and several restaurants in town to purchase dry goods at a reasonable price. Otto knew Mark from his membership in the Kiwanis Club. He and his wife had moved to Artemis several years ago after Cassidy had landed here. Otto wasn't sure if they had seized a good business opportunity, or just moved to Texas to support their wayward daughter.

The wooden sign standing in front of the large warehouse read HARPER'S BULK DRY GOODS. The building was a green metal pole barn surrounded by tasteful desert landscaping that curved to the front door.

A buzzer sounded when Otto entered the empty front lobby, and a minute later Mark appeared from a door that led to the storage area beyond. He wore blue jeans and a green polo shirt with the company name embroidered across the breast pocket. He was medium height with a hefty build and thick brown hair. He wore wire-rimmed glasses and gave the impression of a confident, successful small-business man.

They said their hellos and commented on the rains and the

flooding that was sure to come before Mark motioned for Otto to have a seat in a small lobby. It was furnished with two leather couches, a coffee table covered with magazines, and a dusty TV that looked as if it had never been turned on.

"What can I do for you?"

"I have some questions about Cassidy." Otto noticed the change in his expression, from friendly to one of dread. As a police officer, Otto was used to that look when he appeared unannounced, but he thought Mark might have had conversations about his daughter frequently and had learned to anticipate the worst.

"She okay?" he asked.

Otto nodded. "Yes."

"Is she in trouble?"

Otto put a hand up. "Don't worry. She's fine. I just hope you can help shed some light on her situation."

The tension in his shoulders relaxed slightly and he nodded as if he understood and needed to sit back and listen.

"Did she talk with you about what happened yesterday?" Otto asked.

"No."

Otto pulled his notebook and pen out of his chest pocket. "Here's the situation. You know Chief Gray?"

Mark nodded. "Sure. Cassidy worked at the police department for a while."

"Chief Gray saw Cassidy's car along the side of the road yesterday and stopped to check. She located her about a quarter mile from the road. Found her passed out in the sand, suffering from heat exhaustion."

Mark's eyes widened and his face reddened in anger. "What was she doing in the desert? It was over a hundred degrees yesterday!"

"That's not so much the issue. We found her lying beside a dead body."

"What?" His expression was incredulous.

Otto put a hand up again. "We don't think she had anything to do with the man's death. Apparently she took a walk at a random location on the side of the road. She smelled something, looked around, and saw a body. She passed out. That's when Josie found her. We carried her out and got her into an ambulance and to the Trauma Center. She's fine now."

He paused, allowing Mark a second to consider what he'd heard.

Mark rested both hands loosely in his lap, and stared at Otto, his eyes not blinking. "This is my punishment. This is God making me pay for the grief I gave my own parents."

He stared for a moment more and Otto sat quietly waiting for the story he was sure would come.

Mark finally leaned forward and rested his forearms on his knees, avoiding eye contact with Otto. "Pam and I were young when we met. We had Cassidy right away. We experimented with various things—some drugs, alternative lifestyle. Nothing too bad, just trying to figure out life. My family got this crazy idea we were worshiping the devil. We got tired of the BS so we moved to Florida to start over. We finally grew up and decided we were tired of raising Cassidy in poverty. We wanted a better life. She was eight by then, and she'd lived all over the place." He looked up, his expression pained. "She didn't exactly have a stable upbringing. Pam and I blame ourselves. It's like she floats through life with no grounding."

"Cassidy's a good kid. Some just take longer to grow up than others."

"Point taken." Mark smiled weakly. "But who hikes in the desert on a hundred-degree day and finds a dead body? It's like—" He gave up, at a loss for words.

"We had the same thought. What bothered us was that she couldn't answer that question either. It's the reason I came here today," Otto said. "I've got some concerns about her boyfriend. Nothing I can put my finger on, but I wanted to get your thoughts."

Otto did not need an answer. Mark had sat up suddenly, and

the look on his face was answer enough. "I hate that kid. I wasn't going to bring him up. I've never blamed Cassidy's bad behavior on her friends. She's got her own mind. She needs to use it. But, that kid, that *man*, is not right."

"Give me an example of *not right*."

"In his own mind, he's brilliant. I guess he was a science professor at Texas A&M before he got fired for sleeping with his students. "

Otto looked surprised. "Cassidy told Josie he got laid off."

Mark cocked an eyebrow. "Cassidy can believe what she wants, but I know the truth."

"What's he do for money meantime?"

Mark's face reddened again. "My daughter is supporting him. She works as a cashier at the Family Value Store so he can sit on his lazy butt and watch cartoons."

"You think he might be involved in something illegal? Organized crime, drug running?"

"Hell no, Otto. He's too lazy to organize anything. Besides, he's got a girlfriend paying his bills now. What more does he need?"

Josie's morning meeting with Smokey and Sheriff Martínez was canceled. Smokey and the sheriff were helping a tow truck driver pull a stranded pickup truck out of a ditch that was flowing like a river. Martínez told her they had it under control so Josie took the opportunity to stop by the Arroyo County Jail, where Mitchell Cowan's office was located.

As Josie pulled into the paved parking lot she could barely make out the shape of the brown cinderblock-and-brick building due to the rain pelting her windshield. She parked as close to the entrance as she could and pushed the car door open. She popped her umbrella up, but by the time she reached the awning and pressed the button to be buzzed inside, her uniform pants were soaked.

She walked into a small lobby area furnished with two chairs and a framed picture of the Pledge of Allegiance. A buzzer sounded and a second set of doors opened into a central hub where Maria Santiago, intake officer, smiled warmly and waved hello. The room was octagonal, with Maria in the center surrounded by a bank of desks filled with baskets of paperwork, several phones, and computers—cluttered but organized and neat. The large room was well lit and painted a deep blue with white trim. Several doors led to different areas of the jail such as the booking room, interrogation room, and the prisoner pods. Josie chatted with Maria about the weather for a few minutes before Maria buzzed her through another set of doors to the coroner's office. Josie walked down a hallway toward the back end of the jail by the basketball court, past several offices and storage rooms to her right.

She knocked on a closed steel door with the words COUNTY CORONER painted in black block letters. She heard Cowan yell, "Enter," and found him leaning over a body laid out on a stainless steel gurney. Josie stared at the opened head cavity a moment too long and turned her head, forcing herself to keep a passive expression over the revulsion she felt.

The room was constructed similarly to the jail's kitchen. Both were outfitted with stainless steel cabinets and countertops with the equipment stored neatly away.

Cowan wore a white lab coat, plastic gloves, white mask, and blue surgical cap. He looked up at Josie over his reading glasses. "Stop!"

She stopped and raised her hands.

"No farther until you suit up."

"What's this all about?"

"I don't like what I see."

"The sores?" she asked.

"I have no idea what this is. It isn't necrotizing fasciitis. Beyond that, I'm not sure. I've never seen sores like this."

"Are they all over his body?"

"Both arms, and two spots on his head, which would indicate the sores were caused by exposure to something external."

"Was the blow to the head what killed him?" she asked.

"I'm not ready to say, but it was obviously a brutal blow."

"Intended to either kill him, or knock him unconscious to die of exposure?"

Cowan shrugged.

"It's enough to officially rule this a murder investigation?"

"I would agree with that," he said.

Josie thought about the information while staying twenty feet away from the body. "I came for fingerprints and to get the evidence. It is safe?"

"Suit up."

Not looking forward to the task ahead of her, and now wishing she had not come, she walked over to a wall of stainless steel cabinets. Cowan asked her to wash up in the sink across the room, then directed her to the correct cabinet where she found gloves, a mask, and a cap and lab coat like the ones Cowan wore. She used her fingers to pull her hair out of her ponytail, then pulled it back up again into a messy bun that would fit under the surgical cap. If he had offered her a full-body hazmat outfit she would have gladly taken it.

As she approached, Cowan was bent over, examining a section of the man's brain. "The cerebellum and hippocampus. They can clue us in to possible asphyxiation."

Josie murmured a response and studied the open head cavity, slowly getting accustomed to the sight and antiseptic smell while willing her stomach to settle.

"I've cleaned the hands and prepared them for you. Feel free to jump in." Cowan continued working as he talked. "Preliminary findings are, male, about sixty years old, five feet eleven inches, one hundred sixty-five pounds. No identification present on the body. Identifying marks are a dark brown birthmark on his left calf, approximately two inches long and a half inch wide. He has no hair on his head or his arms. It appears he may have received chemotherapy, although I've seen no evidence of any surgeries or cancer. It's still early."

"When do you expect to finish?"

"It may be tomorrow. The lesions are a continuing mystery. I'll have fluid, specimen, and tissue samples ready for toxicology today, but you're looking at seven to ten days for results."

Josie had brought a small fingerprint kit with her and opened it on top of the counter next to the body. Cowan could have taken prints for her, but she typically took her own for a homicide. It was a good chance to talk with him about the body.

Trying to warm him up, Josie asked him, "How did you end up here? Weren't you a family doctor in Presidio?"

Cowan pulled away from the body and rested his hands on the gurney, giving his full attention to the question. "In case you have not noticed, people skills are not my forte. I did not have the bedside manner people wanted. So, I found a way to practice without having to chitchat."

"Smart move."

"I am the primary care physician for the dead," he said, and bent back over his microscope. "It is gratifying work."

Josie nodded in admiration. Outwardly Cowan didn't appear to be a happy man, but Josie suspected he led a very content life as a loner.

The body lay prostrate, covered by a blue disposable sheet. The head was uncovered, as were the arms, which were lying on top of the sheet. The open wounds were grotesque and Josie forced herself to focus on the hands, which fortunately were not affected. She held the hand, still cold from the cooler, and rolled each finger on an ink pad, then printed it on a card attached to a small clipboard. The process for both hands took about ten minutes. Cowan talked quietly to himself throughout the process, measuring areas of the brain with calipers, photographing and making notes in a tablet that lay beside him on a rolling table.

"Have his clothing and personal effects been cleared? I want to take them back with me to the evidence locker."

He looked up and frowned. "Not until I get toxicology back.

You're welcome to pull everything out." He pointed to a row of six lockers at the end of the wall cabinets. "His effects are in the top locker. Everything is stored in a plastic bag. Just keep your mask and gloves on as a precaution."

Josie pulled the plastic bag out and laid it on a steel examination table to the right of the table Cowan was using. She pulled out a pair of black work boots, blue jeans, and a blue and white plaid Western-style cotton shirt. She also pulled out several other small plastic bags with evidence inside, and recognized Otto's angular handwriting. He had written a brief description, the time, and the date on a white rectangular area on the outside of each bag with a black permanent marker.

Josie opened her notebook and wrote down the size of the man's jeans, noted the brand was Wranglers, and checked them for tear marks or any sign of damage. Finding none, she went through the same process with the shirt. The clothing appeared to be fairly new and in excellent condition. It did not appear that he had experienced any kind of fight, or that he had been dragged through the sand to the spot where Cassidy found him.

Josie looked at his work boots. They were black, made of smooth high-grade leather. They appeared to be the kind of boot purchased for military or law enforcement use, although Josie did not recognize the brand. She jotted down the name, Secure-Wear, size 11 wide. She examined the bottom of the boots and noted that the wear looked typical on the soles, although the red stitching appeared fairly new. It looked as if the shoes had been re-soled.

She took photographs of the clothing before returning it back to the bag. She turned her attention to the items in the small resealable bags, hoping they might lead to some piece of information to help identify him. The Case knife was most interesting. She pulled it out of the bag and snapped a picture of it. The wood grain was stained a deep forest green with silver inlay and caps on the ends. She opened each blade and noticed the heft. The sheen had been worn off the wood, so the knife had been used for some years, but the blades were oiled and had been well cared for. She took a few additional pictures so she could run the knife by Tiny at the Gun Club.

The objects from the man's left pocket consisted of eighty-seven cents in American currency and a packet of Dentyne cinnamon gum. His right pocket held the knife and a small glass vial that appeared to be empty.

Josie turned toward Cowan and held up the vial. "Can you test a vial like this for drug residue? It appears to be empty, and I don't see anything in it, but it might be worth a test."

He looked up from the microscope and squinted. "Yes. I can test it. Leave it out of the bag and put a note on it with instructions. I'll get to it tomorrow."

Frustrated that she hadn't found more to go on, Josie placed the evidence back into the large bag and put it back into the top locker. She threw her cap, mask, and gloves in a waste receptacle marked with a hazardous waste symbol, then took her lab coat off and placed it in a hazardous materials tub for the laundry. She washed her hands and forearms thoroughly with hot water and a medicinal-smelling soap in a large sink, anxious to leave the room and whatever pathogens were floating in the air. After a quick good-bye to Cowan she was walking down the hallway when her cell phone rang in the pocket of her uniform shirt.

She flipped it open and smiled at the number.

"Hey! You on break?" she asked.

"Yep. You busy?"

"I was holding some guy's hand."

"Should I be jealous?"

"He was dead. He's not much of a threat," she said.

"I don't think normal people have conversations like these."

Josie could hear the smile in his voice and laughed. "I never promised you normal. What's your schedule today?"

"I'm coming home early. I miss you."

"You're coming home because you miss me, or because the conference sucks?"

"You should learn to accept a compliment at face value. I'm *also* coming home because today's lectures don't apply to me. It's corporate accounting. Not exactly my thing."

She smiled, happy just to hear his voice. "No, Artemis doesn't really qualify as a corporate kind of town." Josie waved good-bye to Maria, who buzzed her out into the lobby area of the jail. "Want to meet at the Tamale for supper?" She walked outside, stood under the awning, and saw she wouldn't need her umbrella.

He groaned. "I was hoping for a home-cooked meal."

"Ramen soup?"

"Sounds delicious."

"I'll see you about six at my place," she said.

"Perfect."

"Hey," she said before they hung up. "I miss you too."

The downpour that she had walked through upon arriving at the jail had turned into a sprinkle. The sun was still buried in thick gray clouds, but a reprieve from the rain would be nice. She decided it was time to have a talk with Enrico Gomez.

SEVEN

Josie drove south of the courthouse to the San Salba Pawn Shop, located between the Family Value Store and the Pay-Day Quick Loans. San Salba was owned by Carlos Gomez, but his grandson, Enrico Gomez, ran the business. Josie could forget most of what she saw as a police officer, but crimes committed against old people and kids stayed with her. A year ago, after a two-day party in the living quarters behind the pawn shop got out of control and turned violent, Enrico's grandfather arrived to restore order. Enrico shoved his grandfather, an eighty-year-old man, down a short flight of steps, causing him to be sent to the hospital. Mr. Gomez had refused to press charges. Josie had worked the case and watched Enrico walk out of the police department with the same arrogance as when he entered.

The rain had ended by the time Josie pulled her jeep in front of the pawn shop. The street was slick with streams of thin mud running across the road. Puddles of water covered the ground around the storefronts, but she knew that with the next deluge the puddles would turn into wide swaths of running water flowing over the already saturated ground. The depth of the running water in the arroyos was deceptive and could carry a car away in a matter of seconds. She made a mental note to check in with the sheriff on the current conditions of the county roads after she was finished with Enrico.

Josie saw the old man standing beside a burro in front of the pawn shop. Several men still rode burros through town rather than walking or driving. Josie liked the nod to the past, although some of the townspeople found the animals annoying and the occasional mess they deposited usually led to a rant in a letter to the editor in the local weekly newspaper.

Mr. Gomez was feeding slices of apple to the burro, his hands holding the animal's reins loosely, his head turned to the store. Despair settled around the old Mexican like a wool blanket. Josie had talked with him at length about his safety, about the need to lock the boy up before he spun completely out of control, but Mr. Gomez refused to listen. It wasn't fear that kept him from pressing charges; the fear had been worn out of him long ago. It appeared to be misguided loyalty to his grandson that kept the man silent. And Marta's daughter thought she was in love with this kid. Josie wondered again at the wisdom of having kids of her own.

Still sitting in her jeep, she looked up the unpaved street, at the burro and the wrinkled old man beside him, at the overcast sky and ratty storefronts, and the picture appeared like a gray smudge from sky to earth with no visible horizon line. She wondered how the same characteristics that gave the desert its beauty could also tear your heart apart.

She radioed her location to dispatch, slipped the portable into her gun belt, and laid a hand on the grip of the Smith & Wesson at her side, a heavy reassurance. As she approached the San Salba, the old man turned, his suspicious eyes never changing expression, the skin around them wrinkled like cross-hatching.

"How's it going, Mr. Gomez?"

"It's going okay. How's it going with you?" he asked. His words were slow and deliberate, as if the act of speaking took a great deal of effort.

"Is Enrico inside?"

He nodded yes and patted the burro on the right side of his neck to turn him toward Josie. The burro shifted, slowly lifting one foot, then the next, a perfect companion for the old man.

Josie noticed movement at the San Salba door. Enrico stepped outside wearing black jeans, a white V-neck T-shirt, and several gold chains around his neck.

"Hey, it's Josey Wales come to visit. What's up, man?" Enrico slurred his words and drew them out like a rapper. He was a nice-looking kid if you could get past the gangster arrogance. He wore his black hair buzzed short on the sides, longer on top. He tilted his head and gave her a heavy-lidded, intentionally bored stare.

Josie didn't answer and chose to ignore the movie reference. With her hand resting on the butt of her gun, she squinted in Enrico's direction. She knew he liked meth and didn't trust his actions straight, let alone jacked up on a two-day buzz. A second man stepped out of the store behind Enrico. He had the slow, measured moves of someone attempting to impress his power upon others. Even at a distance of twenty feet, Josie could see the three tattooed teardrops falling down the left side of his cheek: a prison symbol in which each teardrop represented a murder. He looked to weigh close to three hundred pounds and wore loose-fitting black jeans and a black T-shirt. He carried his weight proudly, as though his size intimidated. His hair was long and greased straight back on his head. Josie wondered what value he added to the world.

"You looking for something?" asked Enrico. "Maybe a camera or a cell phone? I give you a good deal, cop girl."

"I don't disrespect you, Enrico. Ought to go both ways," she said.

His eyes went wide at the suggestion. "Sure, man, lighten up. I ain't disrespecting nobody."

She started walking toward the pawn shop door.

"Hey! You got business with me?" Enrico asked.

She walked toward him and up the first step. "You said you want to cut me a deal. Let's go inside and look around."

"Store's closed, man. We open at eleven o'clock."

"Do I need a warrant?"

"What the hell? What you jumping my ass for?"

The second man took several steps toward Josie, his gait slow, his eyes hooded. "You got an issue with Enrico we need to discuss?"

Josie faced the man with the tattoos. "What's your name?"

He hesitated. "Jeremy."

"Last name?"

"Smith."

She nodded once and wrote his name down in the small black notebook she kept in her breast pocket. "Hope you aren't lying to me." She replaced her notebook and pen inside her pocket and faced him directly. "This doesn't have anything to do with you. I'd suggest minding your own business."

He tilted his head and crossed his arms over his massive chest. "You wrong there. If you got a problem with Enrico you got a problem with me. Me and Enrico is partners."

Josie was still facing the man on the porch but heard the old man behind her. "We got no problems here. We're just getting the store open."

Enrico laughed. "That's it, man! We're just getting the store open. You come back later and I'll cut you a deal."

Josie turned toward Enrico and stepped within a foot of him. In a voice just loud enough for Enrico to hear she said, "The next time I get a call to your house and find your old man lying on the floor? I will find you, at whatever rat hole you're staying in, and I will drag you out and beat the life out of you. You won't live to do it again."

Satisfied the smirk Enrico wore had at least temporarily been replaced with a degree of anger, if not fear, she said, "One more thing to think about. I better not catch you messing around with little underage girls. I'd love an excuse to throw your ass in jail."

Enrico gave her a doper's heavy-lidded smile again. "She is anything but little. That girl could teach you a trick or two, Chief Josie."

Josie got back in her car in a foul mood, and decided to use it on Cassidy's boyfriend. Leo Monaco lived with Cassidy on River Road, which ran parallel to the Rio Grande. West of town, the road climbed in elevation and the water pushed through five miles of canyon below. Several switchback roads were located along the canyon and held a few houses that clutched the sides of the red rock. Their home sat atop the road, fifty feet from the canyon, next to a row of a dozen other shabby houses. The homes were one-story shacks, built when a small army post had been located nearby, before the camp had left and turned the first Artemis into a ghost town in 1969. The original town had arisen around the outpost, which was constructed to guard a now defunct weapons plant located five miles north. When Macon Drench purchased the land to resettle the town, he'd bought it for an unbelievably cheap price. When cleanup of the plant started a few years later, he feared his experiment might come to a quick end.

Josie turned into a short driveway beside a mailbox with the number 110 hand-painted in red. A patch of brown grass out front managed to look dry even under two inches of water. No wonder Cassidy went searching the desert for a place to walk.

Josie parked her jeep, picked up her notebook off the passenger seat, holstered her gun, and locked the door. She slid her keys in her front pocket and walked along a narrow gravel path, sidestepping puddles along the way. Two wood steps sagged as she walked up them onto a four-foot-deep front porch that shaded the front of the house from the normally blistering sun.

She heard a TV blaring. Behind a screen door, the front door was open. The inside of the front room was dimly lit. Blackout curtains were pulled shut against the front window, effectively keeping what little sun there was outdoors. When Josie knocked on the wooden screen door it banged against the door frame, frightening the person lying on the couch into a sitting position. When he sat up, Josie recognized Leo in the dim light of the room.

"Cassidy's at work," he said, his voice groggy and irritated.

Josie held her badge up to the door. "Mr. Monaco, my name is Josie Gray. I'm chief of police with Artemis Police Department."

He raised a hand and waved her off, indicating he'd heard enough.

"I'm here to speak with you. Mind if I come in a minute?"

He tilted his head back, obviously put out, then stood and approached the door where he unlatched a lock and pushed it open. His chest was bare and he wore baggy, faded jeans that hung low on his hips. His body was pale and hairless except for a patch of black hair below his navel. The long beard Josie had last seen him with had been shaved, but stubble grew on his chin and cheeks.

She entered a living room with a couch pushed up against the wall, and a TV on a low stand under the front window. A small brown recliner was located on the other side of the TV and Josie pointed to it. "May I?"

He gestured a hand toward it and picked up a T-shirt off the arm of the couch. As he pulled it over his head Josie did a cursory look over the house. The living room was picked up. No clutter. Green, threadbare carpet led to the left, down a short hallway, and to the right into a small combined kitchen and dining room. From what she could see, the kitchen was clean, no dishes on the counter or table. All of the rooms had lined curtains drawn against the gray rainy weather outside.

"How's Cassidy feeling today?" Josie asked.

"Fine. She's fine. No problems." He sat on the couch and pushed his hands through messy dark hair very much in need of a shampoo. The house may have been clean but Josie detected sour body odor.

"I tried to understand why Cassidy had gone into the desert on such a hot day but couldn't get a straight answer from her yesterday. Can you help me with that one?" she asked.

He rolled his eyes. "She worked for you. You know she talks in circles."

"Talking in circles wasn't the issue. She just didn't have an answer."

"If Cassidy can't explain it, I don't know how I could do any better."

"I want to know how she stumbled onto a dead body, almost a quarter mile from the road, on a day that hit 104 degrees."

Leo interrupted her with laughter. "Don't you get it? If anyone could stumble over a dead body, it's her. Nobody has luck like her. Or lack of it." He smiled and leaned back into the couch, relaxing into the conversation. He had a rich, baritone voice and Josie figured he liked to hear himself talk. "She calls me her good-luck charm. If I'd been with her she'd have never been out in that heat."

"Where were you yesterday when she found the body?"

"Out of town."

"Where?"

"I was at the library."

"What library?"

He tilted his head to the side as if considering his answer. He finally stood, walked into the kitchen where four books were stacked on top of a microwave on a rolling cart. He pulled a piece of paper out of the first book on the pile. He walked back into the living room and handed it to Josie.

"I was at the library in Presidio. There's my library receipt."

"Is that a regular visit for you? To the Presidio library?"

"I don't get the connection between my reading interests and Cassidy's ordeal."

"Humor me," she said.

"They have several periodicals related to my profession. I actually visit several area libraries frequently."

"I didn't think you had a job."

He grinned slightly, as if amused at her offensive question. "I conduct research as a part-time job. I'm post-secondary science.

How many professorships do you suppose there are in West Texas?"

"So why stay?"

His smile remained. "Must be the great weather and all the friendly people."

"How did you find out Cassidy was in the hospital?"

"She called me."

"When?" Josie asked.

He sighed, finally frustrated. "She said she'd be home when I got back into town. When I got home and she wasn't here, I called and left a message on her cell phone. She finally called from the hospital and told me what happened. She said her cell phone was in her car, which I gather you still have."

"You didn't visit her? Check on her after she left you a message?"

"Why don't you tell me where all this is going? I'm not seeing a point to your questions."

Josie shifted in the seat, turned her body more toward him. "When you asked her why she was in the desert? What did she tell you?"

He frowned and leaned forward, picked up a plastic cup from the coffee table and sipped. "Nothing. She just wanted to hike, to get outside."

"Has she ever hiked before?" Josie had worked with Cassidy long enough to know the answer. She was not a physical person, not athletic, and she complained about the heat frequently.

"Sure. She spends time outside."

"Hiking?"

He offered a humorless smile. "Got to start sometime."

Getting nowhere with the interview, Josie looked at her watch and stood abruptly. She left him her business card, and said she would be in touch. At the last minute, Josie had changed her mind and not questioned Leo about the wallet. She had a hunch that Cassidy hadn't told him about the dead man's effects that were found in her car. Josie wanted to know why Cassidy was holding back information from her boyfriend.

Josie drove to town and parked on the street in front of the Family Value store. Only two other cars were parked along the street. As she walked up to the front door she saw Cassidy leaning against the empty checkout counter in front of the lone cash register. She wore jeans and a bright green smock with the words FAMILY VALUE in large yellow block letters on her back. Her long red ringlets fell down her back and she looked as if she had recovered. When Josie entered, Cassidy turned, and in a split second, her expression changed from heavy-lidded bored to frightened.

Josie looked around the store, glad to see it appeared free of customers. "How are you feeling?"

Cassidy stretched her arms out in front of her and looked at the deep red sunburn. "The sunburn's the only thing. Even my freckles hurt."

Josie smiled. "You gave me a scare."

Cassidy leaned down, reached under her register, and pulled out a tattered canvas purse, which she placed on the counter. She unzipped a side pocket and handed Josie a folded piece of paper.

Josie unfolded it and found a chart, with lines drawn with a ruler and a green marker. The boxes had been carefully filled in with a blue pen in neat cursive writing, detailing her whereabouts for the past week.

"I know I didn't answer your questions very good yesterday. I was so freaked out by the whole day I wasn't thinking right." She gave Josie an imploring look. "I swear, I didn't have anything to do with that dead man. I don't know him, and I don't know why he's there. I really did just find him. I know it sounds crazy, but that's the truth."

Josie scanned the chart and noticed that aside from yesterday, for the past four days, Cassidy had done nothing more than leave the house to work, other than a trip to the grocery for fifteen minutes on her way home from work on Saturday evening.

An older woman dressed in a bright pink cotton sweat suit stepped up to the register and began placing dozens of cans of cat food on the counter. Cassidy turned and rang her up, then helped her count out the right number of dollar bills and change in her wallet. The woman apologized, saying she forgot her glasses.

When she left the store Cassidy turned back to Josie. "She can't read or write or count. Just hands her wallet over to whoever waits on her."

"Somebody's always got it worse than you."

Cassidy tipped her head. "I guess."

"I just left your house. I talked to Leo." Josie couldn't decide if the wide-eyed change in Cassidy's expression was fear or something else. Dread, maybe.

"What did he say?"

Josie pursed her lips, then leaned her hip against the counter. "Can I ask you a personal question?"

Cassidy sighed heavily and hopped up onto the other end of the counter. She looked down at her feet. "I know what it is."

"Yeah?"

"'What do you see in him?'" Cassidy said. "Right?"

Josie smiled. "That's what I'm wondering. You're a nice girl, you're intelligent, a hard worker, pretty. Artemis is small, not a lot of options, but—" Josie stopped, unsure how to proceed without offending her.

Cassidy stretched her legs out and stared at her feet. "He's not that bad. He just says things to people because he doesn't feel good about himself. He knows people look down at him. It makes him mad and he gets defensive." She looked up. "He doesn't do that to me. I swear it."

"He doesn't talk down to you?"

Cassidy didn't answer the question. She crossed her arms over her chest and pulled them in tight as if she were cold.

"Would you tell me if you were in trouble? If you needed help?" Josie asked.

She sniffed and lifted a shoulder but said nothing.

"No one can figure out why a girl who's shown no interest in hiking would suddenly choose to go out in the middle of a record-breaking heat wave."

"I don't know what else to say. I just did."

"Any explanation about the wallet?"

She looked up then, her face finally animated. "I swear, I didn't put it there. I never saw it before."

"Why didn't you tell Leo about the wallet in your car?"

Her face registered surprise, and then worry. "Did you tell him?" she asked.

Josie shook her head. "Why didn't you tell him?"

Cassidy's eyes remained large and confused. Josie often had the sense that Cassidy was trying to concoct a story, but she wasn't good enough at lying to keep her stories straight, so she panicked and said nothing. Josie opted to wait her out.

Cassidy finally said, "I was just afraid he wouldn't believe me."

"About what?"

"That someone put a man's wallet in my car, and I didn't know why."

Josie pulled away from the counter. "Here's the situation. You are the only connection to a dead man. You found him. His belongings were locked inside your car. I suspect you know quite a bit more than you're telling me. I would suggest you think this over, and come see me tomorrow. If you're worried that you'll get someone else in trouble, put that out of your head. Trying to protect someone usually ends up backfiring."

EIGHT

When Josie arrived back at the station she found a packet of cheese crackers in her desk drawer, and borrowed one of Otto's Cokes out of the refrigerator at the back of the office. She carried her lunch downstairs where she asked Lou for the evidence room keys and logged the time she entered the room on a clipboard that hung beside the door. She flipped a switch to the right of the door and the fifteen-foot-wide by forty-foot-long room slowly came to light under the flickering fluorescent bulbs. The floor was poured concrete, but the walls remained the rough red brick that covered the outside of the department and the Gun Club next door. At one time, evidence was kept upstairs, in a small locked room that was now used for the custodian's cleaning supplies. When the amount of evidence grew too large for the small area, the alley between the two buildings was bricked up on either end and the space finished to house the growing number of objects and boxes of paperwork. The only access to the locked room was a door cut into the police station wall.

Twenty-five feet of metal shelving units were attached to the brick on the Gun Club side. Otto had made wooden signs in his workshop at home and hung them from the top of the shelving units. The years were noted on the signs to aid in locating evidence more quickly.

Josie took a deep breath. The room smelled like rock and sand and musty paper boxes. The smell seemed old and comforting, like her grandma's cellar back in Indiana. She found a shoebox-sized cardboard box on the shelving unit labeled *2012–2014* and pulled it down and placed it on an eight-foot-long library table that sat to the right of the door. The room had no windows, so the only light was the yellow fluorescent flicker from ten feet above. She turned on two hundred-watt lamps on either end of the table and sat on a metal folding chair.

When a case was going nowhere she liked to walk through the crime, altering the variables and playing out different scenarios in her mind. With the rain, there was no chance of getting back to the crime scene, where any trace evidence that may have remained would have been washed away. All she had was a small box of objects collected from Cassidy's car, while the majority of the evidence still sat in a hazardous material bag at the jail. Her only connection to the dead body was a young woman who Josie suspected knew something but refused to talk.

Josie laid her pad and paper on the table and opened the box. She pulled out the man's wallet in the sealed, clear plastic bag. She knew Cowan would have wanted it quarantined so she left it sealed. The wallet was opened so she could see the inside. The leather was worn around the edges, as if the man had carried it in his back pocket. Due to the curve of the wallet, Josie was certain it had not been carried in the front of his pants, so how had Cassidy pulled the wallet from underneath the man? Had she taken it before the man died? Someone had placed the effects in her car, Josie was certain of it. But why? How had they gotten there? And why lock the car again—was the person attempting to mess with the investigation, or with Cassidy?

She had told Josie the only other person with a key to her car was Leo, and he had been in Presidio at the library, with a library receipt that showed his checkout time was two hours after the time that Josie found the car. Cassidy had told Josie that she was certain the wallet had not been in her car when she left for the desert that morning because she had removed a container of laundry soap from the backseat that she had left in the car after work the day before. Cassidy said she would have noticed if it was on the floor. Josie had a sense that Cassidy was telling the truth.

Josie examined the other items she and Otto had confiscated from the car and found nothing more of interest. She pulled her camera out of her shirt pocket and turned the power on. She clicked through the pictures slowly, examining the details. On the second time through the pictures she stopped at the picture of the dead man's work boots. There was a close-up of the seams on the bottom of the boot, and Josie remembered that they had been resoled. The only cobbler she knew of lived out past the mudflats, north of town. Jeremiah Joplin had fixed her gun belt last year, and sewed together a belt and pair of sandals a few years prior. Now long retired, he worked out of his home. Josie figured he had to have been approaching a hundred, but he appeared thirty years younger. She frequently ran into him in town, where they always spoke, with him remembering her name and personal details about her that he would bring up in conversation. He was the kind of person who seemed to be in a perpetual good mood.

She replaced the items in the evidence room and logged out on the clipboard, then returned the key to Lou. Josie found Joplin's number in the phone book. She called and he told her to come on over, that she would find him on the back porch.

Josie stood at the front door of the police department and unlatched her umbrella. It was late in the morning but the sky was not visible through the sheets of rain pounding the pavement.

Continuing to type at her computer, Lou said, "Not fit for man nor beast. Better wait till the rain quits."

"I don't think it's going to quit." Josie looked at her watch. Otto was due in to the office any minute to start a noon-to-eight-thirty shift. "Tell Otto I'll be back in an hour. I'm going to talk to Jeremiah Joplin."

Josie popped her umbrella open and dashed to the jeep. By the time she got the door unlocked, slid inside, and pulled her umbrella through the door, she was soaked. She pulled a napkin out of the center compartment and wiped the water off her face, then pulled her wet hair back into a ponytail again with her fingers. Her uniform felt heavy and steamy and she thought ahead to the end of the shift: shorts, a T-shirt, and Dillon. It would be a good night.

At the stoplight on the courthouse square, she turned north, and drove toward the mudflats. Josie snaked along the road where Vie and Smokey Blessings lived, crossing sections of gravel where running water ran directly across. Smokey would be working twelve-hour shifts for days. It would take the maintenance guys weeks to get the roads back into shape after the rain finally ended. They were on a shoestring budget, like all the other county and city agencies, and could not afford to dump new rock. They would have to use the county trucks to scrape the rock back into place.

A half mile from Jeremiah's trailer, the incline was steep enough that the rain had produced ruts running the length of the road where the gravel had been washed away. Josie put the jeep into four-wheel drive and kept her wheels on the high parts of the road. Each year, they lost cars that were carried away because people tried to drive on running water. Four-wheel drive accomplished nothing with water rushing under the wheels.

Josie turned off onto Jeremiah's lane: it was a mudpit. She cussed herself for making the trip, but she had so few leads that it had seemed worth the risk.

She parked in front of the trailer and grabbed a clear rain poncho and black rubber boots from the backseat. Utilitarian, she thought, but effective. She scooted the driver's seat back and struggled into the raincoat, then took her work boots off and replaced them with the knee-high rubber boots. Encased in the plastic, she felt her skin steaming in the enclosed car.

She stepped outside and trudged up to a poured concrete walkway that led around to the back of the trailer. Rain pelted her poncho and dripped off the hood in front as she walked. Jeremiah's place was decorated like a Florida retirement home with concrete statues of rabbits and deer hidden around bushes and benches. Lacy blue curtains hung in the window and a WELCOME FRIENDS sign hung on the front door.

She found Jeremiah rocking in a lawn chair on the porch, a contented smile on his face, watching the rain fall on the patches of grass and desert scrub that covered the land for miles behind his home. He wore black shorts and no shirt. His body appeared completely hairless and deeply tanned. He looked like a sleek sea otter with his round head and leathery wrinkles that stretched across his head, neck, and abdomen. He leaned forward in his seat and shook her hand.

"Good to see you again," she said.

He patted the chair next to him. Josie pulled her raincoat over her head, draped it across a small end table, and sat next to Jeremiah, facing the rain.

"Haven't seen rain like this since before Grace passed. That's going on twenty years now," he said.

"You've kept the place up nice. Even in the rain it looks cheery," she said.

"She'd be proud. Made me promise on her deathbed that I wouldn't let her roses die. They were her pride and joy." He pointed to a trellis-covered bench in the backyard. Splotches of white and red color showed through the rain from where the blooms covered the climbing plant. "Takes a lot to make them grow in this heat. Grace had the touch, though."

They small-talked about the weather and the forecast before Josie settled in on the purpose for the visit.

"I'm working on an investigation, and I'm trying to make some kind of a connection to a man we found dead with no identification."

He nodded, his eyebrows raised.

"I'm trying to find something in his personal belongings that will give me a lead to his identity."

"Makes sense."

Josie took her digital camera out of her shirt pocket and found the picture of the boots the man was wearing. She passed him the camera and said, "You're the only person I know who repairs shoes."

"Lost art," he said. He picked up a pair of glasses off the side table and slipped them on.

"This is a picture of the boots the man was wearing. They're good quality, but they're definitely broken in. I thought they looked like work boots, maybe from a factory. Then I looked at the soles and saw the bright red thread where they had been resoled."

He smiled broadly. "I know these boots."

She raised her eyebrows. "You recognize the brand?"

"I recognize the *boots*."

Josie laughed. She had expected nothing to come of the visit.

"Do you know where I worked before I retired?" he asked.

"I assumed you'd always repaired shoes. Had your own shoe store," she said.

He stood from his chair slowly, easing his joints into an upright position. "Be right back," he said. He disappeared through a sliding glass door and Josie got a whiff of what she assumed was a pot roast in the oven. She realized how hungry she was.

Through the downpour she could barely make out streams of water rushing down the tail end of the Chinati Mountain chain behind Jeremiah's property. It reminded her of the mudslides that washed down the mountain a few years ago. Several of Jeremiah's neighbors had lost their homes. She hoped he would manage to stay lucky.

A gust of wind blew a fine mist across the porch and caused goose bumps to run up her arms: a welcome relief from the heat the day before.

Jeremiah appeared carrying a pair of boots that looked identical to the pair the dead man had been wearing, and he placed them in her lap.

"Where did these come from?"

"The Feed Plant." He grinned and winked. "That's where I worked fixing boots."

"You worked at the nuclear weapons plant?"

"For over twenty years. That's what brought me to Artemis. I worked here in the fifties when the plant was in full production. When the plant shut down I moved away, but came back when I heard about Drench's project."

Josie attempted to keep her face neutral. The place, now closed up behind barbed-wire fences, had always given her an uneasy feeling. "Didn't it bother you working there, knowing the kinds of deadly material you were working with? Weren't you scared you might be exposed to radiation?"

He leaned forward to pick his chair up and turned it slightly to better see Josie. His face was animated, his bald head beaded with sweat. She had touched a nerve.

"What scared me was what happened in Japan at the end of World War Two. Those bombs we dropped stopped the war. If we hadn't dropped them, someone else would have dropped them on us. Don't you believe otherwise."

Josie gave him a skeptical look.

"The science was out there. We just figured it out first."

She squinted at him, trying to understand his logic. "So, we needed to build weapons capable of killing millions? I just never understood that."

He looked at her, wide-eyed. "One of the safest eras in American history? You don't understand that? We were top dog during the Cold War. We were proud to call ourselves American. There wasn't any flag burning back then. We went to work at the Feed Plant because that's what the country needed."

"But it turned into a race to see who could build the most bombs," she said.

He crossed his arms over his bare chest and clamped them down. His expression had turned intense. "We knew, and the Russians knew, we were stockpiling enough weapons to blow each other to kingdom come. And neither country wanted that." He reached over and grabbed Josie's arm. "We were in a stalemate. Neither of us could make a move without destroying not just their country, but everyone else on earth! Every country in the world had their safety in our hands. It was science and strategy." He frowned and leaned back in his chair. "And then it all came crumbling down. And look at us now. There's no strategy. War today is like street fighting."

Josie didn't want to get into a political debate with him so she returned back to her original questions. She needed to get back to the station before the road washed out.

"So, why would a nuclear weapons plant need a cobbler?" she asked.

"Was a time we went through a lot of boots. Back in the fifties? We had two thousand people who rode the railcars into work every morning. Got dropped off in their civvies, changed into regulation uniform and boots, then changed back before they left. That helped keep the radiation inside the plant. We took good precautions."

He picked his glasses up off the coffee table again and put a hand out for Josie to pass him the boots she held in her lap. He took them and studied the bottom. He pointed to where the leather met the sole and held them up for Josie to examine them. It looked as if the leather had been melted. "See that? That's from what they called boil-overs. There were eight or ten stations in the factory, and each one used chemicals that did something to the uranium to make it ready for the bomb." He glanced up at her from over the top of his glasses. "They were powerful chemicals. When they would boil over, workers would walk through the sludge on the floor and the soles of their boots would melt. Rather than throwing the boots away they hired me to resole them."

Josie shook her head in amazement. "The workers had to walk

through chemicals so hazardous they melted the rubber and leather on their boots?"

"Yep. I never saw anybody get burnt from the chemicals. Least-wise, not their feet. We were careful. We took precautions. Wouldn't happen like that today, but back then we had a serious job to do. We were protecting our country, and we took the job serious. We did what we had to do."

"If the plant is closed down, how would the man in the desert have a pair of the boots? Especially if the workers weren't allowed to take the uniforms home at the end of the shift," she said.

"I'm guessing they're using the old leftover boots for the cleanup. From what I hear, they're pretty lax on safety. They probably let the workers wear their uniforms home now since there's no produc-tion. No new uranium coming in."

Josie considered what he said for a moment. Jeremiah had worked at the plant in its glory days and he was obviously proud of the work he had done. She wondered at the validity of his com-ments.

"When you say 'lax on safety,' have you heard workers complain-ing about something specific?"

Jeremiah frowned and rubbed at his chin, a gesture Josie took to mean he was uncomfortable with the question.

"Just stuff I hear from people," he said. "Makes me wonder what those workers might be carrying out on the bottoms of their shoes."

She nodded and decided to let it go. "You ever see anyone who worked at the plant with sores on their arms?"

"What do you mean?"

"Open sores. Something that might have been caused by expo-sure to the chemicals or the radiation?"

He looked insulted. "No, ma'am." He paused, and then asked, "You aren't going to turn this into a witch hunt, are you? The me-dia did enough of that. We don't need the local coppers stirring things up."

Josie assured him that was not her intent. "You did an important job for the country. I respect you for that."

His face softened a bit and he nodded at her peace offering.

Josie thanked him for his time and pulled her poncho back on
to wade back out through the mud.

On the slow drive back to town she replayed her conversation
with Jeremiah in her mind. Artemis had been ready for war the
year she moved to town and took her job as a city officer. As in the
Erin Brockovich case, the town was convinced there was groundwater contamination, although instead of chemicals leaching into
the groundwater from a gas company, they were leaking from a
nonoperational nuclear weapons facility. Artemis received national
media attention when a group of local mothers staged a sit-in
around the courthouse, protesting the high rates of cancer in the
youth living in Arroyo County. A small group of citizens signed
with a law firm who specialized in environmental disasters. As a
result of the lawsuit the government hired a research company who
finally revealed two years later that the rates of certain types of
cancer were slightly elevated in and around Artemis. The court
ruled against the citizen group in the first trial, citing insufficient
evidence due to the small sampling size from the small number of
people living in Artemis and Arroyo County. The group appealed
and the case returned to court.

During the same time period, the Environmental Protection
Agency came to town to survey and evaluate the Feed Plant and
discovered abysmal conditions: hundreds of rusted barrels containing nuclear waste, cracked concrete silos filled with radioactive gas-
ses, contaminated soil and water, equipment used in the production
of uranium sitting unprotected and unmonitored. The EPA put
the plant on a fast track for cleanup and a private company, Beacon
Pathways, was hired for undisclosed millions to clean the plant up
over a period of ten years. The media coverage died down after the
citizens' case was lost on appeal, and Beacon's ten-year cleanup contract was extended an additional ten years. Other than occasional

grumblings in the local paper about the abuse of taxpayer money, it was a one-time sensational issue that most residents preferred not to think about. For others, Beacon paid well during troubling economic times and those workers hoped the cleanup would be around for decades. Josie wondered if the extensions would ever end.

Josie pulled her jeep in front of the police department, anxious to tell Otto what she had discovered. She ran through the rain and into the building, forgoing her umbrella. The bell above the door dinged and Lou, who was pulling folders out of the filing cabinet, turned around, an irritable look on her face.

"Better tread lightly," Lou said.

"What's the problem?"

"You heard about Teresa?" Lou scowled and looked behind her as if scouting for spies. She loved gossip. Josie thought the world of Lou, but she had a mean streak a mile wide and she looked ready to use it.

Josie shook her head, and Lou motioned Josie back to her desk.

"That girl did it this time. Teresa took her savings account money and posted bail for Enrico Gomez!"

Josie looked confused. "I just saw him this morning."

"Sheriff must have got him right after you left. Sheriff Martínez just got off the phone with Marta. He told her that Teresa was at the bail bondsman's before the ink dried on the paperwork."

"Damn that kid. What were the charges?"

"Possession. Couple grams of coke. Teresa paid standard bond fees and he was out within two hours."

"Who arrested him?" Josie asked.

"Sheriff's deputy. Pulled him over for speeding, driving toward Marfa. Deputy found the drugs in the glove compartment. Boy wasn't even smart enough to throw it out the window."

Josie sighed heavily. "How did Teresa find out about Enrico getting arrested?"

"Supposedly the jailer allowed him two phone calls. He placed two collect calls, one to his grandpa, who didn't answer. Then he called Teresa."

"How can a kid with so much potential be so hell-bent on destroying her life?"

"Teresa claims he was framed. He's the love of her life and all that garbage. Marta's ready to rip her kid's eyes out over it."

Josie shook her head and walked toward the stairs in the back of the office. Gossip, especially accurate gossip, was torture in a small town. Marta would be living in her own private circle of hell when word got out on the streets that her daughter had bailed out a drug dealer.

Josie saw Otto leaning against the office doorway when she reached the top of the stairs, his expression grim. "Lou filled you in, I have no doubt."

Josie nodded.

Marta was sitting at her desk talking loudly into the phone.

"Who's she talking to?" Josie asked.

"Wee Wetzel."

"You've got to be kidding," she said.

Otto poured them both a cup of coffee, placed Josie's on her desk, and carried his back to his chair. "Marta wants to know how a bail bondsman could let a minor bail out a convicted felon," he said in a loud whisper. "Wetzel said Marta's daughter paid cash, and she had picture identification. Nothing he could do about it. Marta is threatening to sue him and throw his butt in jail."

"Where's Teresa?" Josie asked.

Before Otto could answer, Marta slammed the phone down, stood from her desk, and planted her hands on her hips. "I will have his ass in jail by nightfall. I don't care if I arrest him for loitering or jaywalking or peeing on a tire, he will break a law by sundown." She was breathing heavily and her voice was low and measured.

"Hold on. Let's think this through," Josie said.

"How could Wetzel allow a sixteen-year-old girl to implicate herself with a sleazy bastard like Gomez? Why didn't he call me first? No professional courtesy?"

Josie stood and shut the door to the office and pointed to the conference table. The three sat down and allowed Marta to rant against the bail bondsman for several minutes.

Josie finally cut her off. "Wetzel is scum. He has no concept of professionalism or courtesy. Don't waste your time trying to figure someone like that out. You can't do it." She leaned forward in her seat, watching Marta closely. "You know we're behind you on this, one hundred percent, but my advice is to slow down."

"She had to sign a contract—a legally binding contract—to bail him out of jail. You can't tell me a sixteen-year-old can legally do that!"

Otto cleared his throat. "The worst thing you can do is go after him and have it backfire. You need to make sure you can wrap him up tight before you do anything."

Josie nodded agreement. "I'll call the county attorney and ask his opinion first. We need to make sure the law backs you up. Then we'll take care of Wetzel."

Marta blew air out as if a balloon deflated in her chest. "That girl is going to kill me. She will literally be my death."

"She's just being a kid," Josie said.

Marta closed her eyes. "Please. Do not make excuses for my daughter's behavior. She's gone too far this time." She ran her hands back through her hair several times, blinking her eyes, trying to keep the tears from coming. "I appreciate you both, more than you can imagine." She took a deep breath and looked away from Josie, her voice softer. "I hope this doesn't cause problems for you."

"You let me deal with that. Your conduct isn't at issue," Josie said. She imagined the notion had been weighing on Marta since the sheriff had called her with the news.

Marta's expression lightened and she nodded slowly as if forcing herself to move on. "I'm okay then. Tell me where we are with the body."

Josie smiled. "This'll take your mind off Teresa. I think I know where our dead man worked." She was pleased at their startled expressions. "The old Feed Plant."

"The dead guy was on the cleanup crew?" Otto asked.

"It's a good possibility." She watched Otto's expression turn to dread.

"Is that where the sores came from? He was exposed to radiation? And we were exposed. You better call Cowan ASAP."

She tilted her head and held a hand up. "Don't panic yet. The old cobbler—Jeremiah Joplin? He worked there for years during full production. He said he never saw anyone with sores like what we saw. If anyone in the community had seen wounds like that they would have exposed it when the big cancer scare took place."

Otto shook his head. "This is bad."

"Sauly worked at the plant when they first started cleanup. He worked there for years," Marta said. "I'm sure he'd talk to you."

"I'll go visit him tomorrow." Sauly Magson was one of Josie's favorite local characters. He was an old hippy who lived by his own set of standards and was one of the most content and happy people she had ever met.

"Have you talked with the manager at the Feed Plant yet?" Otto asked.

"No. Can you call and schedule an appointment for us to meet with him tomorrow? We could meet in the morning if you can work an earlier schedule."

"Will do."

Lou buzzed the intercom and her voice came through the speaker on Josie's desk phone.

"Chief?"

"Yes."

"National Weather Service announced a severe thunderstorm warning for West Texas. Stretches from El Paso down to Presidio.

Six inches tonight. They expect the Rio to flood Presidio before dawn. They've started evacuations down by the river. They're moving families out into a temporary shelter they set up at the elementary school in Presidio."

"All right. Thanks, Lou."

"Mayor wants everyone sandbagging tomorrow in shifts. I signed you and Otto up for a two-hour shift. Seven to nine in the morning."

"Thanks, Lou," Josie said.

They looked out of the large windows in back of the PD. Fast-moving gray clouds stretched as far as they could see in all directions.

"What an ugly sight," Marta said.

Otto looked grim. "This is supposed to keep up for the next week."

Josie looked at her watch. It was almost five o'clock. "Otto, can you call Cowan and fill him in?"

He nodded. "Will do."

"Just have him call my cell if he has any questions," she said. "Marta, we'll call the county attorney when I get done at the Feed Plant in the morning. Find out where we stand." She stood and grabbed her keys off the desk. "For now, let's pay a quick visit to Mr. Wetzel. Rattle his cage a little."

Josie left a phone message for the county attorney and then she and Marta made a dash out the front door to Josie's car. Dripping wet and cursing the rain, they drove to Wee Wetzel's bail bondsman's shop, one of three ranch-style homes located directly across the street from the Arroyo County Jail. His CERTIFIED BAIL BONDS-MAN sign hung from a chain off the TV antenna that climbed the front of his house.

"I asked Teresa how she knew about Wetzel and she said Enrico told her. He promised to pay her back after he got out and proved his innocence," Marta said. She opened her door and spoke to Josie over the top of the car. "How could she fall for such trash?"

Josie thought about Javier, Marta's ex-husband, an abusive alcoholic, but she said nothing.

They walked under umbrellas across the front yard, a twenty-foot-wide patch of sand, and Josie knocked on an aluminum screen door that hung crooked in its frame. The mesh screen had apparently been shredded by the dog that they could hear yipping and growling on the other side of the scarred wooden door.

A woman in a neon-colored velour track suit opened the door and stuck her head out. Her hair had been dyed a burnt orange and teased up around her head. Josie showed her badge and Marta stayed behind her.

"You here for Wee?" she called out, raising her voice just above the dog's.

Josie nodded and the woman put a finger up and slammed the door. Several minutes later a man opened the door just a few inches. A red veined nose and thick fleshy lips appeared in the crack of the door.

"Yeah?"

"We need to have a talk," Josie said.

"What do you want with me?"

"I'm here to ask you some questions. Mind if I come in a minute?"

Wetzel huffed and opened the door. He wore a pair of mechanic's navy work pants and a V-neck T-shirt with yellow underarm stains. The small dog had stopped barking but growled and hunkered down in a corner as Josie entered with Marta following behind her.

A noisy window air conditioner recirculated lukewarm air that smelled of cigars into a small living room space that had been converted into an office. The space included a desk, filing cabinets, and piles of file folders, loose papers, and brimming ashtrays. A neat stack of *People* magazines lay on the floor and Josie figured the woman spent at least some time in the office. She wondered at the idea that Wee could have found a woman desperate enough to live with him.

Marta stood with her legs slightly apart and her arms crossed across her chest, her expression grim. "You make it a practice to allow kids to make bail for convicted felons?"

"I ain't breaking any laws." Wetzel sniffed deeply as if he might spit onto the floor.

"That's not what I asked," she said. "She's sixteen years old. She's using her babysitting money to bail out a meth user. A person with any conscience would at least have called the minor's parent."

He smiled widely. "I think you owe me an apology, Officer Cruz." He turned and walked back to his desk. He dug around on his desk, muttering to himself. He finally held a paper up in triumph, his smile revealing teeth stained the same yellow as his underarms.

"Take a look at this. That wasn't no kid that signed those papers. That was a twenty-one-year-old woman. I got a Xerox copy of her license to prove it."

Marta took the paper from him and examined the photocopy. Josie looked over her shoulder. The license was a good forgery. It looked clean on the copy. Marta was quiet for a time, staring at the page, obviously not prepared for this new revelation.

"You knew that was my daughter. You can't tell me you thought she was twenty-one years old. She's a baby!"

Wee laughed a low and seedy chuckle. "That wasn't no baby that came in here in that tight pair of jeans and skintight T-shirt."

"You nasty son of a—"

Marta took a quick step across the room toward Wee. Josie had no doubt she aimed to punch, and no doubt about her ability to do damage, and in spite of a strong desire to watch it all unfold, she grabbed Marta by the arm and took the paper out of her hand.

"We're not wasting any more time," Josie said, and pulled Marta to the door.

"Give me that paper back! That's my document! I don't got another copy!"

"I'm seizing this as evidence," Josie said.

They walked out the door and Josie folded the sheet and put it in her shirt pocket as they approached the car.

Marta turned to face Wee as she opened the passenger-side door of Josie's jeep. "Listen to me closely, Wee. You are scum. And when scumbags start messing with kids I take a personal interest. And when it's my own kid I get vicious. I'll figure out a way to nail you for this. Next time I'll have you in cuffs."

"You and what army, sweetheart?" he yelled, and let the door bang shut.

———

Josie arrived home that evening and found Chester lying on the front porch, his head atop his crossed paws and long bloodhound ears splayed out on either side. He looked mopey.

"You're as tired of this rain as I am, aren't you?" Josie reached down and scratched the top of his head and behind his ears. Appearing thoroughly exhausted, he struggled one leg at a time to a standing position, but he still managed to push himself through the door first.

Josie hung her gun belt in the kitchen pantry and got Chester a snack before starting the shower. She turned the water on hot and laid her uniform on the bed so she could change over to a fresh one for the next day. She'd have to polish the brass and switch the badge, nameplate, and medals over before morning. She'd always thought undercover work would be preferable for the sole reason that she would not have to change a uniform over.

She laid a pair of khaki shorts and a lacy pink sleeveless blouse on her bed. After her shower she swiped concealer on to hide the dark circles under her eyes and then brushed her brown hair out and pulled it behind her head in a clip. She looked in the mirror and thought about Dillon's pretty secretary, the classy Christina Handley, and dug through the vanity drawer to find mascara and lip gloss. She applied both and flashed a smile into the mirror, feeling a bit ridiculous, but satisfied with the final effect.

Josie was generally comfortable in her role as a thirty-something-year-old tomboy. But Christina caused Josie to picture herself as Dillon might, or even as a complete stranger might, and it made her uncomfortable. Christina accessorized. She wore heels and makeup and had her hair done in a salon, not the Quick Clips across the street from the courthouse that Josie frequented. It wasn't that Josie couldn't choose appealing clothes and shoes to match; she just didn't want to. The process was tiresome and she preferred to spend her time doing other things. And until Dillon had hired Christina as his secretary, Josie hadn't given her wardrobe a second thought.

As she walked into the kitchen, considering her need to go clothes shopping, she saw a sporty white BMW approach the house, with a long, sleek hood and short tail-end. Dillon was a car snob. For such a practical man, Josie thought his obsession with luxury cars was out of character. She wanted dependable and good gas mileage in a car; Dillon wanted style and panache.

He pulled in front of her house and unfolded his long, lanky body from the sports car and smiled wide when he saw her and Chester standing at the door waiting on him. He wore navy pants and a starched blue shirt with thin yellow stripes, and a yellow tie. He walked quickly toward the house, dodging the puddles. His dark hair was cut short, neck shaved, face sleek, teeth bright. Josie smiled and felt her stomach flip. He stepped inside the door and pulled her in to him. He had sad, downturned eyes that melted her heart. He kissed her lightly, then pulled back and looked at her carefully, smiling.

She smiled back at his expression. "Why are you looking at me like that?"

He laughed and drew her in to his chest, squeezing her tightly. He pulled her back again and looked into her eyes. "Because I missed your quizzical looks." He kissed her forehead. "You're always trying to figure me out, and I have no secrets. There's no mystery to me. You know exactly how I feel about you."

Dillon leaned down and kissed her, a slow welcome-home kiss that made her body tingle and the world around her fade to black. His hands ran the length of her back and chills ran up her spine. She trailed a string of kisses down his neck and forgot all about dinner, until the dog broke the moment, nudging his nose between them.

Dillon followed Chester onto the back porch to watch him sniff around in the rain while Josie went into the kitchen to fix their dinner. She opened a can of fruit cocktail and split the contents into two bowls for their dessert. She poured water into the coffeepot to heat it up for brewing iced tea. Next, she opened two packages of Ramen and started water to boil for the soup. It was one of her favorite meals.

While standing at the stove she felt Dillon approach her from behind, felt his hands slip around her stomach and his body press into her back.

"I'm kind of busy," she said, breaking up the noodles into the boiling water, and smiling at his touch.

"It's the cooking."

"What is it with you and cooking?"

"It makes me crazy," he said.

"You're barking up the wrong tree if you think I'm a Betty Crocker girl."

"It's not what you cook. It's just seeing you there, standing over the stove, your hands occupied." He kissed her neck. "I'm going to come up with a combination apron-negligee. We could sell it and make a million."

Josie laughed. She turned the knob on the burner to zero and slipped around in his arms to face him. "Let's save the cooking for later. I think I'd like to keep my hands occupied elsewhere."

—————

Cassidy Harper parked in her driveway, turned the engine off, and then gripped the steering wheel again. She looked at her cell phone lying on top of her purse. Her dad had left her several voice messages, practically begging her to call. If she called, she would be in tears in seconds, with the whole sordid story spewing out of her like a volcano erupting. She looked up at the living room window where a slit of light came through the closed curtains. It was 9:12 P.M. and Leo was waiting for her, knowing to the minute how long it took her to drive home after her shift ended. He pulled back one of the drapes and stood staring out at her. The light from a table lamp illuminated his face and she watched his lips turn down into a frown.

She choked back a sob and picked up her phone and purse off the passenger seat. As she closed the car door, Leo walked out onto the front step, the screen door slamming behind him.

"You planning on coming inside tonight?" he asked.

"I'm coming."

"What are you doing sitting in the car?"

She tried to judge his mood by his facial expression, but it was too dark outside. "I was just looking through my purse for something." She looked at the ground, trying to dodge the pools of water covering the walkway up to the porch.

She walked by his body without touching him and went inside the house. He followed her into the kitchen where she laid her purse on the table and opened the refrigerator for a snack. She had absolutely no appetite but she needed to stall, to think of something to talk about.

"The cop stop by to see you today?" he asked.

Her heart pounded in her chest and she kept her head in the

refrigerator to avoid looking at him. "Yeah. She just stopped by to make sure I was okay."

"Really. She didn't question you?"

Cassidy grabbed the gallon of milk and found a glass in the cabinet. "Not really. Nothing really to say."

"That's funny, because she came here. Questioned me like I was a criminal."

Cassidy said nothing. She faced the sink and drank the milk. She placed the glass on the counter and he grabbed her by the shoulder and spun her around.

"I'm tired of the games. Tell me what the hell is going on!"

Tears appeared instantly. "I don't know what you mean."

"What the hell were you doing out by Scratchgravel Road? You hate it outside! Never once have I seen you go outside to take a walk."

She jerked her arm away from him, furious suddenly at everyone's accusations. It was as if she had done something wrong. She stared at him, seething with anger, and wanted to confront him about the phone call. He was the reason she went hiking on Scratchgravel Road, and she wanted to tell him that. She wanted to tell him that she was protecting him from the police, that she was ruining her relationship with her family, and that she hated everything about him. Nothing in her life made sense anymore. But she had no idea what his reaction might be. He had always taken the dominant role in everything, and she had been fine with it. It kept her from having to make decisions. But now what? She had no idea how to take control.

"How would you know what I like or don't like to do? You don't pay any attention to me. The only time you talk to me is to complain about something I did. This whole thing is pointless."

He stood motionless, staring at her.

"I'm moving back with my parents," she said, forcing herself to look at him, shocked at herself.

He hesitated then came to her as if consoling a child. "Cassidy, come on. You don't mean that." He cupped her face in his hands and searched her eyes. "Can't you see how stressed out I am? This job thing is messing with me. I don't mean to take it out on you. I love you. It would kill me if you left right now."

Leo wrapped his arms around her and she laid her cheek against his chest because it was expected. She felt nothing. Her limbs felt like lead weights, as if she had lost her sense of touch. She wanted to ask the question: How did you know the location of the dead man? But she was certain the answer would require something from her, and she didn't think she had anything to give.

———•——

When Teresa Cruz heard her mom pull into the driveway she was curled up on the couch, physically ill with shame, thinking about her mother, Enrico, and her father in Mexico. The engine stopped and the car door slammed hard. Teresa closed her eyes and gritted her teeth, praying for an answer to the mess she was in. Her mom walked into the living room wearing her uniform, one hand propped on the nightstick hanging from her belt, the other hand held out as if she was going to shake a hand, except her fingers were rigid, her hand directed at Teresa.

Teresa sat up and her mother stood in front of her, the rage in her eyes unfocused. She accused Teresa of throwing her life away on a drug-addicted convict, of bringing shame into their home, of heading down the same path her father had, of making a mockery of everything she stood for, of ruining her good reputation in the community. She yelled and paced around the living room, finally coming back to point at her again. When she noticed the blank look on Teresa's face, her mother stopped as if slapped and began to cry. She turned and left without another word. Teresa sat numbly on the couch and listened to the squeal of tires as her mother backed out of the driveway.

Teresa had no tears left. She couldn't cry, she couldn't explain any of it to her mother. She'd called Enrico countless times but he wouldn't answer his cell phone. She walked to the front window, pulled the curtains open to the gray night, and listened as the rain pelted the roof. She thought about the sound the dead body had made as it hit the ground. The man had rolled it out of the pickup truck like a sack of garbage. She looked down at the phone sitting on the end table and made the only decision that made any sense. She called her best friend, Angela, who had her own car, and asked her for a ride to the bus stop in Presidio. She walked into her bedroom and opened her dresser, pulled several outfits out of the drawer, and stuffed them into her school soccer bag.

When Enrico had called that morning and said he'd been arrested, framed by one of his friends for drug possession, he had been desperate. He said he loved her, that he would make it up to her, all of it. And it wasn't that she believed him; she knew it was a story to get him out of trouble. But he was the only person who knew what she had done, who knew the kind of person she was, and yet he still loved her.

NINE

At six forty-five Wednesday morning Josie and Otto arrived at the Rio Camp and Kayak. Josie wore a pair of Adidas running shorts, an old Indiana University T-shirt, and hiking boots, with her hair in a high ponytail to keep her neck cool. Otto was dressed in a pair of cut-off jeans that stopped just above his knees, and a pair of rubber boots and white socks that reached almost up to his shorts. When Josie picked him up that morning, Delores had stood in her housecoat at the living room door waving to them both as they pulled away. Aside from Dell, they were as close to family as Josie had, and she loved them both dearly.

Rio Camp and Kayak rented boats and camping gear for river excursions. The canoes and kayaks had already been driven by truck to higher ground. The area along the river was one of the lowest spots in Artemis. A flat bank had been excavated to resemble a beach where volleyball nets, picnic tables, and horseshoes were usually erected. The family-owned business was surprisingly lucrative thanks to Marsha Smith, the market-savvy wife who drew in tourists. Josie parked her jeep beside a half-dozen other cars and walked toward the beach area, which was now mostly flooded. All traces of recreation had been removed.

The six additional inches of rain that had been forecast for the previous night had materialized and the river was flowing faster and higher than Josie had ever seen it. The brown frothing water rushed south carrying logs and debris at an alarming rate.

By seven o'clock an efficient system had been organized to fill sandbags and stack them along a fifty-foot stretch of the Rio Grande. The goal was to stack a four-foot-high wall to keep the water confined and the highly erodible banks from giving way. They all knew the sandbags would work for only a short time. If the rain kept coming, even Artemis would feel the effects of the flooding that was now hitting Presidio to the south.

After two hours of bagging and stacking, Josie dropped Otto off at his house so he could get ready for the shift and pick up his department car. Josie showered and changed into her uniform, then met him back at the station where he filled her in on their upcoming meeting at the Feed Plant.

"Plant supervisor's name is—" Otto dug through the pile of papers on his desk and found a sticky note, which he read. "Diego Paiva. Talked with a lady, last name of Moore. She's not too happy to see us, but she set up the meeting. Said she'd meet us in the parking lot at ten."

Josie looked at her watch. "Better hit it then. I'll drive."

The plant was located eleven miles out of town on a gravel road that was well maintained by Beacon Pathways, the company hired to clean and dismantle the buildings and ultimately charged with taking the land back to so-called pristine conditions. Josie wondered how a former nuclear weapons plant could ever really return to pristine conditions.

The plant took up over 750 acres of desert ground and was

surrounded by several thousand acres of state-owned property and a large private ranch. There was only one reason to drive down Plant Road and that was to access the Feed Plant. After the media attention died down, and Beacon moved in with their toxic waste trucks and massive equipment and men in white suits, the area acquired a taboo aura. No one talked about it anymore. The community preferred to trust that the government was quietly supervising the cleanup and looking out for their safety. Josie had her doubts.

All 750 acres of the plant were encircled by an eight-foot-high chain-link fence. It signified a border, but anyone wanting inside could scale the fence and cut through the barbed-wire top. Josie just couldn't imagine anyone wanting in.

She stopped the jeep in front of the entrance, rolled her window down, and pressed a button on a red box mounted on a post next to the gate. As she waited for a response she scanned the area. To the north of the plant, the small Norton Mountain range extended its chocolate-colored ridges on either side of the plant, causing the grounds to feel fortified from the outside. Rocky hills stretched for miles alongside the mountains and the land was dotted with clumps of green grass, mesquite bushes, and jagged boulders, scattered as if someone tossed them from above. The ocotillo cactus grew above the rest of the vegetation, its spiky fingers reaching awkwardly toward the sky. Josie was glad to see that the plants appeared to be thriving, a hopeful sign that the groundwater wasn't contaminated.

The speaker on the post finally crackled. "Name please."

Josie pressed the button and said, "Chief of police, Josie Gray, and Officer Otto Podowski. Artemis Police Department."

After several seconds the woman said, "You're free to enter."

Josie grinned at Otto. "Kind of pointless, isn't it?"

He got out of the car, unlatched the gate, pushed it open, and then closed the gate behind them before getting back in beside her. They drove through, onto a paved drive.

Yesterday Otto had been told that the main office was located directly through the front gate. A parking lot at least an acre wide separated it from another fence that surrounded the actual buildings.

Josie could see six or seven buildings from her vantage point, and they were all built from steel with corrugated rooftops that appeared rusty even from a distance. She could see the neck of a crane sticking above the middle of the buildings but she saw no movement of machinery. The parking lot had approximately thirty cars, all parked near the front entrance gate.

Otto pointed at the yellow lines and arrows painted on the asphalt that directed cars straight ahead. "We're supposed to park in the visitor area. An escort will meet us at the car." He gave Josie a cynical glance. "You'd think they were still making bombs."

As Josie pulled into the space marked VISITOR, a middle-aged woman carrying a black umbrella, wearing a beige pant suit and sensible brown shoes, approached. She wore a large pocket watch as a necklace and looked as if she kept a close eye on its movement. Her hair, brown like her shoes, was in a tight bun behind her head. She smiled grimly as Josie and Otto got out of the jeep, her hands clasped tightly at her waist. *Repressed* was the word that came to Josie's mind.

"Welcome. My name is Sylvia Moore. Please follow me, and I'll take you to Mr. Paiva."

Josie raised her eyebrows at Otto and popped her own umbrella open against the light rain. They followed the woman at a quick pace down a concrete walkway that led to the one-story office building. Newer than the rest of the site, it was covered in light blue corrugated metal with a brown metal roof. Josie assumed the bosses worked out of this building. The woman slowed slightly to walk in line with them and seemed to sense Josie's thoughts.

"I'll be taking you into the staging facility. This is where all of our office staff are located. I'm sure Mr. Paiva can help you with the information you require."

"What's a staging facility?" Otto asked.

She pursed her lips and glanced quickly at Otto, as if trying to decipher his intentions. Apparently convinced he wasn't harassing her, she said, "This building is the planning area where the various job superintendents and foremen meet. Our site office is located here."

She offered a thin-lipped smile again and opened the door to the building, allowing Otto and Josie to enter before her.

A man who looked to be in his forties stood just inside the door, smiling widely, holding his hand out to greet them both. "Chief Gray? Diego Paiva. Very good to meet you."

Diego wore a charcoal gray suit jacket with a casual navy blue shirt open at the neck. He had fine gray hair with a receding hairline, and a closely trimmed goatee. He was an attractive man with dark deep-set eyes and a strong jawline who emanated confidence and ability.

Josie extended her hand and shook his. "Thank you. This is Officer Otto Podowski."

They shook hands and Diego gestured for them to walk down a short carpeted hallway and into a mid-size office decorated in conservative wood furniture with comfortable chairs. A small round table and four stackable conference chairs were located to the left of the door. One long, narrow window allowed light into the office but gave little view into the operations of the plant. To the right of the window about a dozen framed certificates, a collection of degrees and awards, covered the wall behind his desk. Josie noticed a picture of him shaking President Bush's hand, but she saw no pictures of family in the office.

After coffee and soft drinks were declined they sat down at the table. When he addressed Josie, his demeanor was warm and friendly.

"I'm always curious when meeting new people. What brings you to such a remote location? In Puerto Rico, where I grew up, we imagine everyone wants to live in the big cities enjoying the exciting nightlife."

Josie smiled. "I have no desire to spend my days in the city or my nights in a club. Artemis actually suits me well."

He tipped his head. "Excellent point. Nor do I." He turned to Otto. "And you? May I ask what brought you here?"

Otto leaned back in his seat and Josie noticed the gaping spaces around the buttons on his uniform shirt. She would work on him to cut back on the pastries and Cokes.

He said, "I worked twenty-five years with the highway patrol. It was a good career, but I was ready to slow the pace. When I left the patrol, Artemis was looking for a chief. It was a good change for my family."

"How does someone get from Puerto Rico to the Chihuahuan Desert?" Josie asked.

"Ahh. I was born in San Juan. Joined the military right out of high school and ended up stationed in California. I became involved in engineering while in the service. I've been in the States for almost twenty years now as a nuclear engineer. Beacon hired me to manage their cleanup projects."

"You travel quite a bit then?" Josie asked.

"My last post was in rural New York. When this post came along?" He put a hand in the air and wavered it back and forth. "I don't like the big city, but I do like people." He looked at Josie. "It's difficult to connect with people here. Would you agree?"

Josie felt the heat in her face and hoped it didn't show. "I would agree."

Otto redirected the conversation. "We actually came by here today to discuss one of your workers at the plant."

"Of course. What can I do for you?"

Josie glanced at Otto. He tended to judge people quickly and sometimes harshly, and she wondered if the abrupt turn in conversation meant that Otto had already made up his mind about Diego Paiva.

"We have some disturbing news and would like to ask you some questions concerning a possible employee of yours. Would you know if any of your employees have been absent for the past several days? Most likely an unexplained absence," Josie said.

He raised his eyebrows. "I'm afraid I wouldn't know that for most of our employees. All of our supervisors have been here. I'll have to consult them to ask about their crews. May I ask why?"

"A man was found dead, about twenty minutes from here. His body was found by a hiker in the desert," she said.

He gave a quizzical look. "How does that connect to us?"

"He was wearing the same black boots that the workers here used to wear. We're not aware of any other local factories or businesses that use this brand of boot. We're assuming he worked for you at some point."

He frowned, his expression concerned. "I certainly hope it isn't one of our employees. Do you have a name?"

She shook her head. "We're hoping you might be able to help us figure out his identity."

He placed a forefinger on his lips, nodding his head. "I do have a way we can narrow this down. Our attendance records are online. I don't use the program, but Sylvia monitors the information." He stood from his chair. "Excuse me a moment." He walked over to his desk and picked up his phone to ask her to join them.

Sylvia entered the room, unsmiling, notepad clutched to her chest with one hand, a pen ready to take notes in the other. Diego said, "Can you please pull up the attendance program on my computer? I need you to check unexcused absences for the past—" He paused and looked up at Josie. "How many days?"

"Can you check for the past two weeks?"

Sylvia sat down in his desk chair and began clicking and typing.

"How's the cleanup progressing?" Otto asked. "We don't read very much about it in the newspaper anymore."

Diego turned from looking over Sylvia's shoulder and gave Otto a half smile. "It has been my experience that communities prefer the cleanup progresses quietly. Negative media attention causes exponential increases in time and resources for any project. I'm sure in your position you've experienced the fickle nature of the media. One never knows when the ally may become the opponent. It is in our best interest to do the work quietly and efficiently."

Sylvia turned slightly and looked up at Diego to get his attention. She pointed to the computer screen.

"This doesn't look good," he said. He asked Sylvia to print the attendance record. He retrieved the piece of paper from his printer and read the name. "Juan Santiago. His job classification is listed as Unit Seven Shutdown Crew." He ran a finger down the printout, squinting slightly at the page. "It says he's been absent from work since last Wednesday." He looked up from the paper, his brows furrowed. "I don't know this person, but his supervisor is Skip Bradford. He's supervisor in Unit Seven." He looked at Josie and Otto. "Would you like to meet Skip in the unit? I'll give you a brief tour of the plant and you can see the cleanup firsthand."

Otto looked surprised, but pleased. He and Josie had both agreed on the ride over that they hoped for a look at the facility. There was something about off-limits areas that fed a cop's imagination.

"Sure. I'd like to see the plant," Otto said.

As they stood, Sylvia turned to leave the room. Before she reached the door Josie said, "Excuse me, Sylvia?"

The woman turned, looking startled.

"Could you provide me a home address for the employee as well?"

Something flickered across her face, but Josie couldn't read her.

"Yes, of course," she said, and left the office.

Diego pointed to a framed map hanging on the wall. "Take a look at the layout of the plant before we leave. It will give you a better sense of the scope of the cleanup."

Josie and Otto stood behind Diego and looked at a series of buildings that were situated around an oval driving track, each one notated with a number from one through ten, except for one building labeled the pilot unit. It was the first unit past the building they were in now.

Diego pointed to the building labeled with the number one. "The processing started in Unit One with the uranium ore, and moved through each of the remaining nine buildings until enriched uranium was ready for shipment. Each of these buildings contained an amazing array of chemicals that we're still working to dispose of." Diego turned and motioned toward the door. "Let's suit up and I'll take you over to Unit Seven to meet Skip."

Josie and Otto followed Diego to the back end of the building where they each grabbed a hard hat off a metal rack with a sign that read SAFETY FIRST. Before they walked outside Sylvia approached Josie and handed her a Post-it note with Santiago's name and address neatly written on it. She said nothing, and turned and left after Josie thanked her for the information. Looking at the address, Josie realized his apartment was above the Family Value store.

She excused herself for a moment and called Lou on her cell phone. "Do me a favor. Call Marta at home and ask her if she'll check an apartment in town to see if anyone's home. Ask her to check with neighbors, see if anyone has seen the tenant in the past three days." Josie read off the name and address Sylvia had provided. "Also, check BMV to see if there's a car registered to that name. If there is, make sure the address is the same as the one I just gave you, and have Marta check it out as well."

Following Otto and Diego outside, Josie looked up into what seemed to be a perpetually gray sky. The rain had diminished to a drizzle that didn't merit an umbrella, but it still made for a miserable morning. They walked down a sidewalk and through an unlocked gate.

"Inside this fenced area is what has always been referred to as 'production.' You can see each of the ten units I showed you on the poster inside my office. Each unit is marked with a sign outside the main entrance." He pointed to a building on the back side of the oval track. A sign that read UNIT 7 hung beside the entrance door. "Let's use the golf carts to keep from walking through the mud."

The scene behind the main office building was a set out of an old black-and-white horror flick. Driving up to the plant and approaching through the front gate had made the size of the plant deceiving. Most of the buildings had massive steel pipes and drums attached to the sides and tops of the structures, and two large silos, at least thirty feet tall, were located near the back of the plant. Several buildings were connected with enclosed conveyor belts that rose twenty feet off the ground.

Two golf carts were parked by the building in front of a wooden fence that looked like a hitching post. They followed behind Diego and sat in one of the golf carts. Diego started the electric engine. "The most startling fact about this plant?" he said. "In 1956, the year it reached peak production, 2,045 workers came here every day."

"That's almost the size of the entire town of Artemis," Josie said.

"The railroad brought them in and out every day. It was a long commute for some, but the pay was top-notch. Talk to the people who worked here. They were proud to serve their country. Production stopped in 1969. Transportation became too expensive."

As they drove past the empty crane Otto said, "I thought we'd see more demolition."

Diego nodded. "Taking the buildings down is the easy part. Removing what's inside the buildings is the problem."

He drove the golf cart on the track, around the center of a massive courtyard that was a muddy mess. A recent load of gravel had been spread in order to keep the machinery from getting bogged down.

Diego drove past several large structures toward a steel building surrounded on all sides by round vats and pipes. He pulled the golf cart in front of the entrance, which was gated by chain-link fence. Diego continued with what sounded like a prepared tour speech as they walked through the gate to the front door.

"Unit Seven made enriched uranium ingots during the fifties. Today we're experimenting with a waste stabilization project. The biggest issue we face at plants like this one is what to do with all the waste. For every pound of uranium that was refined, two and a half pounds of waste was created. And who wants it? With Yucca Mountain lost in political purgatory we're back to containing it here the best we can."

Josie pointed behind the production buildings to where hundreds of black metal barrels were stacked on wooden pallets. "So we have our own little Yucca Mountain here in Artemis? Except it's above ground and could leak into our groundwater."

Diego opened the building's door for Josie and stepped aside to allow her and Otto entrance. He smiled sternly at her as she walked past him. "That's why I'm here. To make sure that does not happen."

Josie looked around the room and felt her stomach seize up in a knot. At the back end of the building a group of four people dressed in white hazmat suits with helmets were working on a machine that was about the size of her kitchen. A tank was attached to each person's back and she assumed these were some type of respirators. Large fans and machinery roared throughout the building.

Diego placed a hand on Josie's back and talked close to her ear to be heard above the noise. "Don't worry," he said, pointing to the men in white. "The suits are precautionary. Better to be safe." He gestured toward the rest of the building. "Would you like a quick tour before we meet Skip?" Diego yelled.

Josie and Otto both nodded and he motioned for them to follow. They began walking over concrete where steel beams had been filed down to the ground, revealing that something had obviously been removed. "This area of the plant was where the uranium fuel core was finished. The core was then shipped to other factories where it was fed into reactors to make nuclear weapons." He walked them across the plant floor to a wall with several metal doors. "The first two rooms are storage areas. One contains chemicals waiting for disposal. The other is dismantled apparatus waiting for shipment." He approached the third door and opened it. "This room houses our security tapes. Part of our contract with the government promises the site is secure. We have an expansive security system to ensure that."

Josie noted that the room housing the security tapes wasn't locked. She wondered if the security operations at the plant were mostly for show. She imagined very few people not already associated with the plant ever visited. But then, who would want to?

Diego shut the door and walked them over to the large machine where the men in white suits were gathered over a large metal pipe they appeared to be feeding into a furnace. He stopped Josie and Otto about thirty feet away and they watched the men working in tandem. She wondered if they had radios inside their suits. After several minutes Diego moved on and finished a quick tour of the building. He had neglected to explain what the men were doing and she wondered if it was simple oversight or intentional.

Next to the building's entrance door was an enclosed office area. Diego opened the door and motioned for Josie and Otto to enter. Once he closed the door the noise from outside stopped, almost completely. It was uncomfortably cold, and Josie could feel air movement. The room was approximately twenty feet square and had three metal desks that looked like they had been scavenged from offices in the 1950s.

A man in his sixties wearing a short-sleeved button-down shirt, striped tie, and black dress slacks sat at one desk. Diego introduced him as Skip Bradford, and he stood and shook hands with Josie and Otto. He was average height and build and had the serious, introspective demeanor of a scientist, complete with a calculator and pens in his shirt pocket.

Skip excused himself to answer the ringing phone on his desk and Diego continued. "Skip supervises a crew of five men, including Juan Santiago. The men are on the floor working on a vitrification project. We take waste sludge and contaminated material that needs long-term storage to give it time to stabilize. We basically heat it, mix it with glass fragments, and resolidify it. The result is waste contained in glass that is highly resistant to water. Then it can be stored underground for several thousand years until the radioactive material is safe."

Josie shook her head in amazement. "We have waste in our backyard that is so toxic it has to be stored inside glass and buried underground for thousands of years."

Diego tipped his head at Josie. "True enough. But we've found an excellent, safe solution."

Skip hung up his phone. "Sorry about that."

"No problem. We appreciate you talking with us," Josie said. She didn't have any idea what kind of relationship Skip had with his subordinate. And she had intentionally not told Diego that they expected foul play. She wanted to gauge his reaction when she told Skip. She had found that people performed for the police when asked a question directly, and often provided more honest reactions when listening from afar. If Diego showed no sign of surprise when learning about the murder, then her suspicions would multiply fast.

"I have some disturbing news. I'd like to talk with you about someone who might be an employee of yours," she said. "We found a man's body in the desert several days ago. We suspect he may have been murdered."

Skip's mouth opened and his eyes grew wide. "What do you mean?"

"You didn't mention murder," Diego said, his expression more angry than shocked.

Skip placed his palms on his cheeks and sat back down in his chair. "Santiago's been absent since last week. Is that who you mean?" The gravity of what he had just heard showed in his face. "I called him at home on Monday and yesterday but got no answer. I just figured he went to Mexico, back to his family."

Diego walked over to a kitchenette area in the corner of the room that contained a water cooler with disposable cups beside it. He filled a cup and handed it to Skip, who looked at his boss, bewildered. "I never thought about calling the police. I never dreamed of anything sinister. I assumed he'd just left." He turned back to Josie and Otto. "People do that. Employees just don't show up for work one week. No call or notice. They just quit."

"We're still trying to identify the body," Josie said. "Can you tell me if Mr. Santiago was bald?"

His eyes widened. "Yes," he said, almost in a whisper.

"Has he been bald as long as you've known him?" she asked.

He nodded.

"Were you aware of any serious illnesses he may have had? Cancer or something that would have caused him to lose his hair?"

He frowned. "No, ma'am. He rarely missed work. I'm not aware of any illnesses."

She wondered how that played into their chemotherapy theory.

Josie sat down in an office chair beside Skip and put her notebook on her lap. "Would you have expected him to quit? That he would leave with no notice?"

The shock of the news weighed heavily on his movements. He sipped from the cup slowly, then looked again at Josie as if she had asked a strange question. "No. I wouldn't think so. He was a good worker. Not stellar, but he showed up each day. He worked while on the clock. You know?"

"Did he have another job that you were aware of? Anything else that consumed his time after work?" she asked.

"His family was the only thing I ever heard him mention. I think his paycheck was sent home. He lived by himself."

"In Artemis?" Otto asked.

He looked surprised to hear from Otto, and turned in his chair slightly to see him. "Yes, downtown. Somewhere near the Family Value. I don't know exactly."

"Do you have a photo of Mr. Santiago that would help us identify him?" she asked.

"Yes. Employees have a picture on their ID badge. I believe it should be in his personnel file," Skip said.

"Would you be willing to come to the coroner's office to identify the body?" Josie asked.

He looked shocked at the question and took a moment to answer. "Of course."

"I assume he was in the country legally?" Josie asked.

"Absolutely." Diego cut Skip off. "We follow strict protocol.
His papers are on file if you wish to see to them."

Josie put a hand up to wave off the suggestion.

"We actually have quite a few legal immigrants working at the
plant," Diego said.

"Did he socialize with anyone? Ever talk about dating anyone,
or going out for a beer with someone from work?"

Skip looked miserable. "I don't think so. He kept to himself.
You can talk to the crew, though. There's four other guys. I'll call
them all in here if you want."

"He ever fight with anyone?" Otto asked.

Skip frowned. "No. Not that I know of. He didn't get close
enough to anyone to fight. He'd worked here about three years, and
I bet the guys he worked with don't know much more about him
than me." He paused and looked from Josie to Otto. "I just can't
imagine anyone wanting to kill him."

After the interview with Skip was over, Diego asked him to assemble the other workers from Santiago's unit in the cafeteria, located back in the staging facility. Josie was glad to walk back
outside. Her hands felt like ice from the cold office.

She followed Otto outside while Diego stayed back to talk with
Skip. Josie saw Otto looking up into the moving clouds.

"I don't want to be back here when it starts pouring down rain,"
she said.

Otto nodded, his eyes focused on the sky. "Place gives me a bad
feeling. Like doomsday."

"I keep thinking about all those rusted barrels." She looked behind the fenced-in production area to what appeared to have once been a large parking lot. The space was now covered with tightly packed metal barrels. From a distance they appeared to be corroded, but she hoped it was just peeling paint. "What do you think all this rain does to the chemicals and the rusted drums?"

The wind picked up and blew the fine gray hair around the top of Otto's head. He tried to smooth the hair back as he climbed into the backseat of the golf cart, leaving the front passenger seat for Josie. "I'd like to know what these guys do on a daily basis."

"I still don't think we mention the sores on Santiago's arms. We need to talk to a few more people. Make sure we know who can be trusted," she said. "Agreed?"

"Absolutely. Weren't you going to see Sauly?"

She nodded. "I'll talk to him this afternoon if I get time."

Diego walked briskly out of the building toward the golf cart and Josie was struck by how attractive he was. He conveyed assuredness and the ability to get things done. She imagined he was a good fit for what seemed to be an overwhelming task.

He climbed in the cart and they drove off immediately. "I would have appreciated some advance warning."

He glanced at Josie but she kept her attention focused on the barrels across the lot.

"You hadn't mentioned anything about him being murdered. I assumed he'd just come up missing," he said. His tone was sharp.

"Our goal is to find a killer. Sometimes that doesn't leave room for common courtesies," she said.

He said nothing in return. She knew her comment had sounded rude, but those were the ground rules.

As they approached the main office again she pointed behind them toward the lot full of metal barrels. "What's the problem with the rusted barrels? Seems like you'd want to get those out of here before they rust through."

He took a moment to respond and Josie wondered if he was considering his response, or if he was still angry. "Sometimes it's more dangerous to move material like that than it is to leave it be. We monitor the containers carefully. It's not a pretty sight out there, but there's no leaching." He glanced over at her. "People don't realize what a task it is to move dirty material to another site. It's not like taking your trash to the city dump."

"By dirty material, you mean material with radiation in it?"

He nodded.

A light rain began to fall as Diego maneuvered the golf cart through the sludge on the ground. When they reached the staging facility, Josie turned before entering the building to scan the lot one last time. She could not imagine going to work every day in that kind of environment: the combination of corroded metal and disassembled buildings, some nothing more than steel skeletons, made for a scene of bleak desolation.

In the cafeteria, several women in hairnets and white smocks teased each other good-naturedly as they placed silver pans into a buffet line. Josie glanced at her watch. It was 10:45. The room smelled like canned green beans and boiled potatoes.

The room was set up like a high school cafeteria. It was well lit with poor acoustics and neatly lined rows of tables that would seat groups of ten. The laminate-and-chrome tables looked straight out of a fifties diner. The room looked larger than necessary and Josie wondered if the number of employees was being kept low due to need or cost overruns.

As they reached the tables Josie received a phone call from Lou.

"What's up?" Josie asked.

"Marta called back. The door to Santiago's apartment was locked, no one home. No one at Family Value or the other businesses on the block has seen him recently, but they confirmed they knew who he was. They all said he didn't make much of an impression."

"Okay. What about the car?"

"No car registered in his name," Lou said. "Marta also took prints around the door. She said to give her a call if you want her back there," Lou said.

"All right."

"One more thing. Marta talked to the postmaster. He said they left mail in front of his apartment door for several days and just took it back to the post office this morning until further notice. Nobody has picked up for five days."

"Great. Thanks, Lou. That's a start."

Josie sat at the table where Diego and Otto had just settled.

"I've heard stories about why they named this place the Feed Plant," Otto said. "Any truth to the rumors?"

"There's a little truth in every rumor." Diego smiled slightly. The intensity in his demeanor had subsided somewhat, but his face looked worn since hearing the news that one of his employees might have been murdered. "The name is actually quite accurate, although the motivation for using the name was probably twofold." Diego crossed his legs and settled into the role of tour guide again. "The Feed Plant took in uranium materials; most of it shipped to us from the African Congo. The raw material was processed using a variety of steps in several units within the plant until we had enriched uranium. It was then sent to other nuclear sites around the country. Our material became fuel for nuclear bombs. We helped feed the bombs. Thus the name."

Josie didn't hide the suspicious look on her face. "They didn't call it the Feed Plant to trick people in the community into thinking it was harmless? A place that created animal feed?"

He smiled. "Of course they did! This was back in the day when secrets were respected. When people knew the government kept secrets for their own good. And people were fine with that. They appreciated the grave responsibility the president carried. There were secrets and respect. Frankly, we could use more of both in today's world."

Four men walked through a door at the far end of the cafeteria.

Diego's expression turned serious. "Skip told the men the basics of what you shared with us. He explained that you had questions to ask about their coworker."

Josie watched as they walked across the cafeteria. All four men wore loose-fitting blue jumpsuits with their names machine embroidered on their breast pockets. As they walked across the room, Josie noticed each man wore the same style boots that the body had been found wearing.

Diego stood as they approached and thanked them for coming. An earnest-looking man in his early twenties, with an unruly mop-top haircut and square wire-rimmed glasses, led the line of men. An older man, who looked to be in his forties, remained standing as the other three sat. He had a buzz cut, protruding ears, and fleshy lips. In a loud voice reminiscent of a drill sergeant he said, "My name is Andrew Magnetty. This is Bobby Cahill." He pointed at the mop-head, who nodded once at Josie and Otto. "This is Jim Sanders and Brent Thyme." Jim was a gangly young man who looked like a high school ball player still fighting acne and awkward social manners. Josie recognized Brent from around Artemis. He was about her age, early thirties, and was married to Sarah, one of the waitresses at the Hot Tamale. He had red hair and a spray of freckles across his face and hands. He smiled politely and nodded as he was introduced.

Josie introduced herself and Otto. She explained their purpose for being there, and said, "I appreciate you all talking with us. I want you to understand that the man's identity hasn't been confirmed. The man we found may not be Juan Santiago. But his time of death corresponds with the day he showed up missing from work. We're hoping to find out information from the four of you that will help us find him or confirm his identity." She was quiet for a moment, allowing the information to settle. She often used wait-time during interviews. Rushing people in high-stress situations rarely resulted in good information.

"We'll interview each of you separately. That will give you a chance to answer based on your own observations of Santiago, rather than your answer being influenced by your coworkers."

Otto started his pocket recorder and laid it in the middle of the table. He went through the basic information of time and place and collected all of their names and their relationship to the deceased man.

Josie nodded at the drill sergeant, who took the lead in introducing the group. "Mr. Magnetty, we'll start with you. The rest of you can take a seat here in the cafeteria and we'll get you back to work as soon as possible."

The other three stood and walked to a table at the far end of the cafeteria and sat down without talking. Josie faced Magnetty. "Officer Podowski will be recording the interview unless you have an objection."

"No, ma'am, that's fine."

"Okay. The first thing we need to do is start piecing together Santiago's life, and right now, the four of you are the only links we have."

He nodded.

"Why don't you start by describing Juan, both professionally and personally."

"Juan took orders and followed through. He kept quiet and did the job. No questions." Josie noted that Diego was watching him intently. "I tried to cut up with him a few times but he didn't like it. He'd smile, but that was it." He looked over at his coworkers sitting across the room. "They probably never saw him cut up either. Pretty serious guy."

"Do all of you share the same job?" she asked.

"Yes, ma'am. We're ground crew. Our job is safe shutdown. Sometimes we all work together, sometimes we're on our own or with a partner. Just depends."

"What are you currently working on?"

"We're taking apart a machine." He narrowed his eyes, settling into his role. "It's a complicated process. Not like you can take out a machine with a wrecking ball. Every piece is evaluated, monitored. There's a written plan for everything in the plant. And the machine we're working on is part of the respiration unit."

Not wanting to get too much technical detail, she cut his explanation off. "Did you ever work as a partner with Juan?" she asked.

"Sure."

"Did he ever talk about friends or family?"

"Just that he missed Mexico. I know he was lonely. I tried to get him to go out a few times, after work, but he never would. Always said he was saving money to go home." The veins in the drill sergeant's forehead throbbed. He looked across the table at Diego. "That's why we didn't think much when he didn't show up for work. We figured he got enough money to move back home and left."

"How often did he send money home to his family?" she asked.

"I think he went home each month to visit and deliver the cash." Magnetty smirked. "He didn't trust us. Americans, I mean."

"What do you mean?"

"He didn't have a bank account. No credit cards or anything. He was always thinking someone was going to kick him out of the country."

"But he wasn't here illegally?" Otto asked.

"No, he was just paranoid."

"You don't know of any friends he had outside of work? Not even one?" she asked.

He frowned. "No. I guess not."

"Did you ever visit his apartment after work?"

"No."

Josie dismissed Magnetty and then called over Jim Sanders, the tall young kid with acne. She asked him the same questions but he offered little. He blushed at each question and shrugged, basically repeating that he never talked with Santiago about anything.

Skip Bradford, the group's immediate supervisor, entered the cafeteria and came over to the interview table. He apologized for taking so long, then listened closely as the mop-topped Bobby Ca-hill described Santiago as an old guy with no sense of humor.

"What do you mean by that?" Josie asked him.

He shrugged and ran a hand through his unruly hair. "I just never talked to him. He was too quiet. Brent talked to him more than anyone, but the guy never really smiled."

"Was he unfriendly?"

He nodded. "Yeah, I guess. I just ignored him."

Brent Thyme was the last person Josie interviewed. He had a short, slim build and a friendly demeanor.

"I always thought he looked kind of embarrassed to have a conversation with you. He was really shy, kind of backward with people." He paused and thought for a moment. "But, at the same time, he was mentally tough."

"What do you mean?" she asked.

"He went through a lot to get here. To get this job. He lived by himself. Focused all his energy on getting a better life for his family back home. I had a lot of respect for him." Brent's face burned red under the freckles at his comments. He seemed embarrassed to talk about Santiago's personal matters.

"Was his quietness caused by a language barrier?" Otto asked.

"No, he spoke English fine. He was just quiet," Brent said. "I drove him to work every day. He didn't have a car. But he still didn't talk. He'd sleep in the morning and look out the window at night. I finally gave up trying."

Josie's cell phone vibrated in her pocket and she opened it, saw it was from Marta, and allowed it to go to voice mail until she was finished with the interviews.

"Was he likeable? Did he have a good personality?" she asked.

Brent gave an apologetic smile. "I hate to repeat it, but he didn't say enough to even let you know what his personality was."

Josie asked Brent if he had ever had a conversation with him about his personal life.

"He missed his family. He was married and had kids, but they were older. He had a large family in Juarez, I think. Lots of extended family. He was homesick. Trying to scrape up enough to build a house back home."

"Do you know the last time he visited?" Josie asked.

"No idea. I never met his family. I wouldn't even know how to contact them to check."

Josie's cell phone buzzed again. She pulled it out of her pocket and saw the call was from Marta. She wouldn't call twice unless there was an issue. Josie excused herself and Otto nodded, indicating he would take over the interview.

Josie answered as she walked across the cafeteria. "What's up?"

"It's Teresa. She's gone." Josie heard the anguish in Marta's voice.

"From home?"

Marta took a long breath and exhaled, moaning in the background. "I worked third shift last night. About the time I got to bed this morning Lou called and asked me to run over to Santiago's apartment. I got back home just now and looked into her room." Her breathing hitched.

"How do you know she left home?"

"She left a note."

"What did she say?"

Marta was quiet for a moment and Josie realized she was crying.

"Marta," she said gently. "We can't talk this through until you quit crying. Put the phone down. Take a deep breath. Grab a Kleenex. Then give me details."

Josie turned back to the group of men at the cafeteria table and saw Otto taking notes. She had no doubt he would be thorough. As she watched, waiting for Marta to return, Diego turned and caught her glance, a beat longer than was necessary.

Marta returned to the phone. "I'm sorry. I never expected this. She's never done anything like this. And, no warning."

Josie turned her back on the group in order to focus on the call. "What did the note say?"

"We got into a fight. It got ugly. I said horrible things."

"Was the fight over Enrico?"

"Yes." She sniffed again, trying to slow her breathing. "I accused her of terrible things, but she wouldn't even respond. She just stared at me with this blank expression. I was so angry I left the house. I couldn't deal with her." She paused a moment. "I knew we needed to resolve things today. Then I found a note in her bedroom. She said she couldn't live with me anymore. That she's leaving home for a while."

Josie felt her shoulders slump and sighed. "Oh, Marta. I'm sorry. You wait at the department. Otto and I will be right there. We're at the Feed Plant. Start making phone calls to all her friends. Make sure you talk to the parents too. The kids may tell their parents, but they might not be willing to tell you if Teresa told them not to."

"I should have never left the house so angry. I'll never forgive myself if something happens to her."

TEN

Josie and Otto were quiet on the drive back to town. Josie's head was filled with scenarios of Teresa's departure, wondering where she would go, mixed with images of the grim scene they had just left behind. As the rain intensified, Otto turned on the local radio station, which was playing a recording from the National Weather Service, a flash flooding alert for all of West Texas along the Rio Grande. A female radio announcer came back on and said Mexican dams on the Conchos River were spilling floodwater, and with the failure of several levees on the Mexican side, flooding was already an issue in Piedra Labrada, the Mexican city across the border from Artemis. The International Bridge that linked Presidio and Ojinaga had closed due to flooding. The announcer was connected by phone to a Texas senator who explained that the wastewater treatment plant just a few miles from the bridge in Piedra Labrada had ruptured, sending sewage streaming into the Rio Grande. "This is not a natural disaster," he said. "This is manmade. There are hundreds of people who are losing their homes today because of poor management practices in Mexico."

"Disaster and politics," said Otto. "Where do you come up with the money to plan for the hundred-year flood when you can barely pay the phone bill?"

Josie and Otto found Marta standing in front of her desk talking on the telephone. Worry lines formed a V in between Marta's eyes and her face was red and splotchy. Josie thought she looked as if she had aged ten years.

Marta hung up the phone and faced them. "One of her friends' mothers called back. Her daughter finally let loose. Teresa left last night while I was at work. Got a ride from her friend Angela to the bus station in Presidio. Then took the bus across the border before they closed the bridge into Ojinaga. That's where her father lives." She paused, her face haggard. "I came home last night and glanced in her room. I thought she was in bed. She'd piled pillows up to look as if she was asleep. Any other night, I would have kissed her goodnight. Last night, I was still too angry."

Otto pulled a chair out at the conference table and stood behind it. "Come sit," he said to Marta. "Tell us everything you know."

Josie grabbed three mugs from the back of the office and carried the coffeepot to the table. She poured them each a cup and sat.

"So she took a thirty-minute bus ride to Presidio, then crossed the International Bridge to stay with her dad in Ojinaga?" Josie asked.

Marta nodded. "Now the bridge has closed and the forecast says the rain won't stop. But I have to find her."

"What about driving to El Paso? They haven't had the rain we have. You could still cross there," Otto said.

"No. It's almost four hours to El Paso. Then I have to go through customs. Then drive all the way back to Ojinaga. It's twelve thirty now. It would be ten o'clock tonight before I got to town." She closed her eyes and made fists with her hands on the table. "I can't leave her there. Her dad's a drunk. If he's off the whiskey she'll be fine. If he's on it, he could stay passed out for days. Who knows if he's even home. It's not a safe neighborhood in broad daylight. And, God forbid, if she hasn't made it to his house by nightfall I can't even begin to think what could happen to her."

"Have you called?"

"He doesn't have a phone. I took Teresa's cell away from her last week. She's grounded from it. I have no way of getting hold of her. I tried Javier's father's store but no one answered."

Josie hesitated. "With the river flooded, the only way across is out by Ellis's house. There's a footbridge over the Rio that Border Patrol hasn't shut down yet."

"Can you get me there?" Marta asked.

"If Border Patrol catches us you'll be in some serious trouble, Josie." Otto was staring at her. He knew where she was headed.

"I've already called Sergio," Marta said. "He's offered to help any way he can. If I can get across the footbridge I'm sure he'll drive me to Javier's house and get us back across the border in the morning. Hopefully the bridge will be open again and we can drive."

Sergio Pando was a Federales who lived in Piedra Labrada, just across the river. He was also a childhood friend of Marta's. Josie respected him as a person and as an honest Mexican law-enforcement contact whom they relied on frequently.

"Can't he just get Teresa and bring her to the footbridge? Or, if you trust him, take her to his home until morning?" Otto asked.

"He would never do that. Javier's a drunk, but he's a Curandero. He still commands respect. Sergio would never enter his house and take his daughter." Marta frowned and shook her head.

"I'll cross by myself. I won't take you with me." Josie stared hard at Marta, who she knew would fight the decision.

"Absolutely not. Teresa's my daughter. I hate to even drag you into this, but—"

Josie broke in. "I won't talk about it. The river's at flood level. What if something happens to you? You think Teresa has problems now? What happens to her with no mother?"

Marta was quiet, her face in anguish.

Josie said, "I'll meet you out at Ellis's trailer. I'll call and let him know what's going on. If the bridge doesn't look safe, we call it off."

Josie and Otto came up with a list of items that Otto would work on for the Santiago case in her absence. His first priority was a meeting with Skip Bradford at the coroner's office to get a positive ID on the body.

Next, she called and talked to Ellis Burns about the strength of the footbridge. He said he had used the bridge four days ago to cross on foot, and it was in good shape, but he didn't know what the rain might have done to it. He said he would walk down and check it out.

Josie had known Ellis for years and would trust his judgment on the safety of the bridge. Ellis dated a woman who lived in Mexico, about a half mile from the river. He crossed the bridge weekly and the local law enforcement, including Josie, turned a blind eye. Ellis was a Vietnam vet in his sixties who had no intention of moving to Mexico at this point in his life. His girlfriend ran a successful horse ranch in Mexico, and felt the same way: she would not leave her country for America. They used the bridge to conduct an illegal cross-country romance that suited them both just fine.

On the drive home to pack a quick change of clothes, Josie pulled her cell phone out of her pocket and held it before dialing Dillon's number. She dreaded the call. He would give her grief about the trip, she would get angry, he would say something ridiculous like "you can't go," and she would hang up wishing she hadn't told him.

When she finally called, she gave him the basics, and he stuck to her predicted script.

"You can't do that, Josie. It's suicide!"

"What happens when you tell me I can't do something?"

"This isn't a joke."

"I'm not laughing."

"I'm asking you to be reasonable. There are men in Mexico who would murder you for bragging rights."

"This isn't negotiable. Marta can't go. Otto can't go."

"It isn't your fight. You can't even carry a weapon across the border for protection!"

"Dillon. I promise you that I will take every precaution. I will be with Sergio as soon as I cross the river. He'll take me to Teresa and I'll bring her home. Simple."

The argument finally ended in an unhappy stalemate. She promised to call him at the first opportunity, and she hung up glad for his concern, but slightly annoyed all the same.

Once she had a few things stored in a light backpack she could carry across the bridge, she loaded Chester in her jeep and drove back to Dell's place. He walked out on his front porch in jeans and a plaid shirt with a cigar dangling from the corner of his lips, and a shotgun broken open over his arm.

Josie got out of her jeep grinning. "What's up?"

"Cleaning my guns." He watched Josie open the back door of her jeep, and he patted Chester on the back when he loped onto the porch. "What's up with you?"

"I'm headed to Mexico for the night. Wondered if you'd keep Chester at your place."

Chester pawed at the top of an old ammunitions box beside the front door that Dell kept filled with dog treats.

"That doesn't sound like a very good idea," he said.

She shrugged. "It'll be a quick trip."

"Work-related?"

"Sort of."

"Not going to fill me in, are you?"

She smiled. "Nope. You'd follow me with your arsenal. We'd

both end up in a Mexican prison. And who'd take care of Chester?"

By the time Josie met up with Ellis and Marta at the entrance to the foot crossing it was after three o'clock. There was a light rain, but the forecast showed a break in the activity later that afternoon through midnight.

Ellis wore rugged brown sandals, jean shorts, and a brown T-shirt that perfectly blended with his surroundings. He looked as if he had recently buzzed his own hair with a pair of clippers. He stared down at the bridge and the rushing water about six feet below it. "It's made it through worse than this," he said. But Josie couldn't remember seeing the water any higher than it currently was.

Across the bridge was the expansive Chihuahuan Desert with low-lying mountains, cactus, and scrub brush that was already turning green with the recent rain. The river cut through the east end of a canyon that traveled through Artemis. The opening of the canyon was relatively shallow, with twenty-foot-high walls. The bridge was attached to the sides, on either side of the river, about five feet down from the ledge. The canyon rim was a rocky slope down to the bridge, hiding it from the road, but making the entrance accessible. The crossing was only visible from within the canyon walls so there was no cartel traffic, just an occasional local wanting quick access, usually to family members.

The muddy brown river had reached the banks, flowing fast and dragging debris. Josie knew if she fell in, or the bridge gave out, she would almost surely drown. She hated the water and was not a good swimmer, although the current was flowing so fast that swimming would be a moot point. If the water didn't kill her, the trees and limbs floating down the river would.

The rope bridge spanned twenty feet, with three-foot-wide wooden slats, and was surprisingly taut across the water. Josie had crossed it easily with Ellis several years ago just to check out what was on the other side. Desert scrub, it turned out, and a cattle road heading south from Piedra Labrada into Ojinaga, Mexico.

Marta had called Sergio back after they had formed a plan and he had agreed to drive Josie into town. Unless the road was severely washed out from flooding, she figured the drive would take about ninety minutes.

Josie wore blue jeans, hiking boots, a long-sleeved navy T-shirt, and carried her Artemis badge and passport in a black backpack. Her hair was in a tight ponytail and she carried the backpack secured tightly to her back. She didn't carry a weapon of any kind. Federales escort or not, she was still entering the country illegally.

She stepped onto the bridge gingerly and took several steps out. The water was pushing at the metal supports and the bridge dipped under her weight, but felt secure. She walked several feet out and came back to the edge where Marta and Ellis stood, looking on in concern.

"I think it's fine. I don't feel comfortable bringing Teresa back across it, though."

Marta nodded. "Sergio said he would reserve a room at a little motel downtown. It's safe. You can stay until morning. Sergio said the closing was precautionary. He's predicting the International Bridge will open again in the morning."

Josie frowned. The idea of staying overnight in a motel room with Marta's sixteen-year-old daughter worried her worse than the water. And Josie wasn't as convinced as Sergio that the bridge would be open again that soon.

"What if we can't cross in the morning?" she asked.

Marta's expression froze at the question and Josie regretted it instantly. She reached out and squeezed her shoulder.

"You can't imagine how much I appreciate you," Marta said. Her eyes carried worry for her boss, but Josie could see the deeper fear of a mother desperate for her daughter's safe return. "I don't know how I will ever repay you for this."

"Marta, friends don't require payment. I'm helping you because I care about you and Teresa."

Marta hugged Josie tightly, tears streaming down her face. She pulled her cross from under her blouse and clutched it in her fist. "I will pray nonstop for your safe return."

Several minutes later a small dark blue car with the words POLICIA FEDERAL painted in large white letters across its side pulled to a stop across the river and a stocky gray-haired man got out. He was wearing street clothes, a white T-shirt tucked into jeans and running shoes. He waved and the three did likewise. Josie agreed to call Marta as soon as they'd found Teresa and then stepped back onto the bridge.

Two-inch-thick rope handrails ran down either side of the bridge, and Josie had to bend awkwardly to reach them. She wondered if Ellis had helped construct the bridge—if so, he had seriously miscalculated the design. Her five-foot-seven-inch frame felt off balance on the narrow boards.

About three feet in, she stopped and stood still, focusing on the slats under her feet, not the churning brown water below her. Once she steadied herself, and accustomed her eyes to the rushing water under the bridge, she gained some confidence. She took slow six-inch steps, rubbing the skin off her palms as she slid her hands down the rope rails.

By the middle of the bridge, the feeling that it was ready to flip, dropping her into the churning water below, was almost unbearable. Not daring to let go of the railing, she forced her muscles to relax slightly and took smaller steps, carefully sliding each foot across the slippery wet slats. She kept her focus on the wood so she wouldn't trip. After a five-minute walk that seemed to take hours, she made it onto the other side to the applause of Sergio, who'd just allowed her access into his country illegally, now smiling as if Josie were the prodigal daughter come home to stay.

ELEVEN

"Well done, my friend. Well done!" Sergio hugged Josie and patted her back, laughing into her ear. Josie stood about six inches taller, but Sergio was powerfully built. He had the kind eyes and smile of an old-world gentleman, and a demeanor that put everyone around him at ease.

Marta had grown up with Sergio in Mexico and had been gently pushing away his advances for many years. Josie thought the two loved each other, or at least deeply cared for one another, and couldn't understand why Marta accepted only his friendship.

The landscape was rocky, with mountainous desert sprawling south into Mexico. The hour-and-a-half-long drive back to Ojinaga took them along a canyon road high enough to avoid most of the flooding. One small detour took them around a tributary that flowed into the flooded Conchos River. Sergio said that at least twenty residents had drowned in the Conchos after they refused to evacuate their homes along the river. Sergio said the International Bridge wasn't flooded, it was the street in Ojinaga that the bridge fed into that was currently underwater. He expected the water to recede within the next several hours, and for the bridge to reopen by daybreak.

Sergio spoke fluent English, occasionally mixing the two languages, but Josie had no trouble understanding him as he filled her in on the local feuds and battles that sounded identical to stories she heard about Presidio, the city across the border from Ojinaga and just to the south of Artemis. Mostly though, Sergio talked about Marta, and their childhood growing up together.

"As small children we lived in Barrio Montoyam, along the canyon. We spent our childhood in the river, scrabbling up and down the rocks and valleys. Thirteen kids between our two families. It was a good life. Then both our fathers took jobs in Ojinaga at the new *maquiladora*. That's when Marta met Javier." Sergio looked at Josie and smiled, shrugged, giving a look that said, *What can you do?*

"Was Javier always trouble?"

Sergio hesitated. "Marta was always spiritual, even as a child. She looked to the angels and the saints in place of her mother. I used to tell her, 'Marta, your home is here. Make better use of your time here, instead of wishing away for something you can't know.' When we settled in Ojinaga we were both sixteen. I was in love with her, but too proud to risk the truth of her knowing. Then, she met the Lazoyas and I lost her to Javier. His father was a curandero, a spiritual healer. Very respected in the region. Javier has the gift as well, but he never grew comfortable with his sight."

"Why is that?"

"He was afraid of the responsibility. He was a coward, and I told Marta. It just made her angry with me. She thought she could fix him. That's always been Marta's goal in life, fixing up people. She says that's why she could never love me. Nothing to fix."

Sergio glanced at Josie and smiled sadly. "Marta was too kind to give me the truth, but I knew. Her heart was with Javier."

Josie sat quietly a moment, watching the waterlogged desert pass by them, thinking about Marta's life growing up along the river.

"Would Javier have been considered a priest?" Josie asked, not entirely certain she understood Sergio's explanation.

Sergio laughed. "No, no. The curanderos learn their art from the Indian shamans of hundreds of years ago. A gift passed down, an understanding of the spirit world. Javier's father was consulted when the *brujas,* or the witches, brought harm or mischief to families. He heals with herbs and potions. People still seek out his remedies, but he's old and tired. Javier is a great disappointment to the family."

"What kind of healing?"

Sergio lit a cigarillo as he drove and rolled his window down to the warm evening outside. "Curanderos say prayers to bring you luck in bingo, to help you find your lost husband, to get rid of warts and cancer and diarrhea. You think of it, they have a saint and a prayer to help you through the problem."

As they approached the city the sun had fallen enough to cut the harsh glare from above, and the city's edges were not so rough. It was 6 P.M. and Josie hoped there were enough daylight hours left to find Teresa and get her in a safe place for the night. However, the daylight also left Josie more exposed. As an American police officer in the country illegally, she was very cognizant of her situation.

Josie had only visited Ojinaga a few times, and was always struck by the angular shapes: the buildings were cubes with square windows and rectangular doorways stacked atop each other like kids' building blocks. The stucco and arches she associated with Mexico were not found in these neighborhoods, but the brightly painted blues, reds, and oranges turned the streets into a kaleidoscope.

Sergio pointed out a small Catholic church with rooms to rent and said a room had been prepared with two twin beds. A tall stone wall encircled the church for protection. Josie thanked him for the arrangements and hoped she and Teresa were inside their room by sundown.

Javier's house was in a tumbled row of flats with power lines draped precariously along the rooftops, dangling almost to street level in between. The street had a dusty, slapdash feel to it, but Josie noted how clean of debris the area was. Sergio pointed to a small brown apartment, no more than a box perched atop a bright blue building with a large advertisement painted in yellow and red across the storefront: AGUA CHILI!

"You're sure this is Javier's place?" she asked.

Sergio frowned. "No doubt. His father has begged him to move home, but what can you do?" He turned the engine off and removed the key. "I'll walk up with you, make sure he doesn't give you trouble. If Teresa is here you can get her, and I'll take you to your room for the night."

"And what if I can't get her to come with us?" The question had troubled Josie since she first decided to cross the border.

"After spending the day here, she'll be ready for her mama. That's my prediction."

Sergio opened a street door on the building. The door led up a dark, narrow set of stairs nailed together with no regard to conformity. A tape measure and plumb line had not been part of the building process.

"Watch your step," Sergio called. The street door slammed behind them as they started up the stairs. He turned on a pocket flashlight to illuminate the stairwell. Cockroaches scurried from the light.

At the top of the stairs Sergio shone his flashlight on a narrow wooden door. The landing wasn't large enough for Josie to stand on as well, so she remained behind him. He knocked, but after several minutes no one answered and neither heard any sound from inside.

"Teresa? It's Sergio. Come answer the door." He listened again, ear to the door. "I just want to check on you. Make sure you're okay."

A half a minute later the door opened three inches, as wide as the door chain would allow. Even in the dim light Josie could see Teresa's smile at the recognition of her mother's friend. The door closed and opened again, with Teresa stepping into Sergio's warm embrace. She stepped back, suddenly noticing Josie. Her eyes were wide and she looked down the stairs as if for her mother, or a police force come to collect her.

"Chief Gray?"

"Your mom's pretty worried. She sent me looking for you."

She looked confused. "But they closed the bridge."

Josie noticed her red eyes and could tell she had been crying.

Sergio gestured toward the apartment. "Can we come in?"

Teresa looked back into the dark space and nodded reluctantly. "He's sleeping. But he won't wake up."

She flipped a light switch on the wall and the room was bathed in the light from a bulb hanging bare from the ceiling. There were no windows in the room. Javier lay in a drunken stupor, curled on his side, passed out on a frayed dark green couch. He snored quietly and one arm dangled to the floor. Teresa looked around, as if noticing there were no seats. A twin-size mattress lay on the floor opposite the couch, and a sink and toilet against the other wall. A small refrigerator was in one corner of the room while the opposite corner was a makeshift shrine filled with statues and trinkets and candles all arranged neatly on a small table covered with a lace cloth. Josie noted several candles were lit. It was an oddly personal touch in the dirty, forsaken space. She wondered how much Teresa understood of her father's unused spiritual talents.

Sergio said, "I'll wait outside while you two talk. I'll call your mother." He gave Teresa a stern look. "You've put her through torture. She's very worried about you. And this woman risked her own life to come check on your safety." He walked over to Teresa and placed her head in his hands and kissed her forehead. Her eyes softened, but her expression remained resolute.

Sergio shut the door quietly behind him as he left.

Teresa sat on the mattress and Josie sat down beside her, her legs bent at the knees and crossed in front of her. Teresa wore a pair of shorts and a bright yellow top covered with a man's grease-stained plaid flannel shirt. She smelled of engine oil and cigarette smoke. She stretched her long brown legs before her and Josie noted she was at that awkward age, stuck somewhere between a woman and a girl, that made grown men uncomfortable. Her black, sleek hair hung down, partially covering her face. She wouldn't make eye contact.

"How did you get here?" Teresa asked.

"I crossed the river on a footbridge. Your mother tried to come with me, but I wouldn't allow it. The current is too fast. Sergio found a room for us at a church. We can stay the night there and hopefully cross the International Bridge in the morning."

She nodded slightly, her eyes toward the floor. Josie was relieved there apparently would be no fight about leaving.

"I'm sorry I did this to you. I just wanted out of my life, away from my mom. I didn't mean to drag anyone else into this."

Josie paused, feeling like she had the bruised soul of a child in her hands, with no idea how to hold it.

"You know, you have a lot of people who care about you."

Teresa let her head drop as if the topic had been discussed too many times. "Yes, I know. All of Artemis is looking out for my well-being. Everyone wants the best for poor little Teresa. You watch. I'll have a tracking bracelet on my ankle by tomorrow so you can watch me easier."

"Why do you want people tracking you down?"

She faced Josie, her eyes wide and angry. "I don't! I wish she'd leave me alone!"

"So you can live like this?" Josie regretted the words as soon as she'd said them.

Teresa's dark eyes fixed on Josie. "You're just as bad as she is. You think because Daddy drinks he's bad. She doesn't even give him a chance. You ought to hear the way she talks about him." She looked toward the couch and lowered her voice to an angry whisper. "He treats me a hundred times better than she does! At least he believes in me. He tells me how smart I am, how pretty I am, how good I am."

Josie sighed and stared at Javier, his body diminished by a life of alcohol and poverty. He lay on his side, his mouth open, his face covered with several days' worth of patchy beard. He had a thick head of hair plastered to his head and wore a dirty flannel shirt similar to the one Teresa wore. It was difficult for Josie to imagine what Marta had seen in him, or what possessed Teresa's loyalty. Was it pity, or simple love for a father?

"You don't think your mother believes in you? Thinks you're pretty and smart?" Josie asked.

"What does she say? I've embarrassed her again." She stood up from the bed and faced Josie. "No. That's not what she'll say. I've disgraced her and her good name. That's fine. I'll just live here where I won't bring her so much goddamned shame."

She turned from Josie and faced the wall, hands on her hips, her shoulders rigid. Josie ran her hands over her face. She was frustrated, tired, and in a drunk man's house in a foreign country. She wanted a bourbon and her own bed.

"You know how hard it's been for your mom to work her way up to the job she has now? A woman serving as a respected police officer in a town like Artemis? There's a group of men in town who still expect their wives to serve them dinner barefoot. Your mom's worked her ass off to get where she is, and it wasn't to prove something to herself. It was to make a better future for you. Then she has to sit back and watch you piss it all away on some drug dealer who's playing games with your mind. You're a pawn in his game, Teresa."

Josie forced herself to quit talking. Teenagers were way past her area of expertise. The last thing she wanted was to make her so angry she would refuse to leave her father. At the same time, she was tired of watching the girl run all over Marta.

Teresa walked over to the candles and stood staring down at

the flames. She ran a finger through the fire several times, each time spending longer in the heat. "Half the shit my parents say isn't even directed at me. They use me to get to each other."

Josie stared at the girl's back and could think of nothing to say.

"You know where Enrico went after he got bail? He left. He went to hang out with that jerk at the pawn shop. No 'thank you.' Nothing."

"This is what I don't get. Who is the one person who stands by you, day after day, and still only wants what's best for you?"

Teresa turned finally to face Josie. "So, why are you here? Did you come to take me home?"

TWELVE

After Josie and Marta had left for the river, Otto met Skip at the morgue, where he quickly confirmed the body was that of Juan Santiago. Afterwards, Otto stopped back by the office and picked up the absence record for Santiago on Josie's desk. He stared at the paper, the words a meaningless blur, and allowed his frustration to surface. The timing for Teresa's escapades couldn't have been worse. Josie and Marta were both needed at the department to work the murder investigation and to help monitor the growing threat of flooding in Artemis. He couldn't help imagining what he would have done had his own daughter pulled the same stunt at that age. And, truth be told, he thought Marta needed to yank a knot in the kid's rope before she ended up pregnant, or worse. But most of all, he was more worried about Josie than he cared to admit to anyone.

He rattled the paper in front of him, trying to get his thoughts focused on the job at hand. He had to get the apartment printed and searched. He called Delores on his cell phone and left a message on their answering machine at home that he would be late for dinner. He finally read the address again, then folded the paper and

tucked it into his shirt pocket. He walked downstairs, wincing at
the pain in his knees, lamenting a second-floor office. He gave Lou
the address of Santiago's house and said he was going to check it
out.

"You know who the landlord is?" he asked.

Lou leaned back in her seat and coughed. Otto saw the pack of
Marlboros sticking out of her purse and considered saying something, but fought the urge. *Mind your own business,* he thought.

"That's Junior Daggy," she said. "Realtor?"

"Yeah, I know him. Junior can take a ten-minute conversation
and stretch it to sixty."

Otto drove to Junior Daggy's Realty, located next door to Dillon
Reese's accounting office. Otto parked and waved at Dillon through
his office window. He was standing in the waiting area smiling as
an older lady talked. He waved back over her shoulder.

Daggy's realty office window was covered in black-and-white
printouts of houses, land, and business property for sale throughout West Texas. Otto figured it had to be a rough way to earn a
buck. The area wasn't exactly booming.

Otto entered the front door and found Junior leaned back in
an office chair, feet propped on his desk, phone held to an ear with
one hand, snapping a ball on a string back and forth against a
paddle with his other hand. He wore a seersucker shirt, beige dress
pants, and huarache sandals. Average height, with a slight paunch,
he was deeply tanned with shaggy gray hair growing over the top
of his shirt collar. When Otto entered, Daggy sat up and said a
quick good-bye to his phone companion, flung his paddleball on
the desk, and came around to shake Otto's hand.

"How you doing, Otto? Haven't seen you in ages. How's your
lovely wife?"

Otto shook Junior's hand, smoothing his hair down and adjust-
ing his gun belt out of habit. "Delores is doing just fine. You and
Karen okay?"

Daggy nodded. "Yes, sir, never better. Celebrating thirty years in September. Got married in South Carolina so we're headed east to renew the vows. That ought to get us through the next thirty years, don't you think?" He pointed to a chair in front of his desk and went on to describe Charleston and all the reasons he and his wife loved the area. After ten minutes of nodding and attempting to redirect the conversation, Otto finally cut him off.

"I have a pretty serious matter I came to talk with you about. I believe one of your renters may have been murdered. I'd like to take a look in his apartment."

Daggy's eyes widened. "Murdered?"

"Do you have a renter by the name of Juan Santiago?"

He nodded once, his jaw hanging open slightly. "Yes, sir. Rents a one-bedroom above the Family Value."

"I'd like to take the key, have a look around."

"You bet. Let me make a quick call, and I'll go with you."

Otto leaned forward and raised a finger to stop Daggy from reaching for the phone. "We're still early in the investigation. I'd like to take a look first. We don't want any extra bodies in there that don't need to be. I'll keep you informed."

Daggy looked crushed. He'd just lost a great story to tell the fellas at the Hot Tamale.

Otto finally got a copy of Santiago's key and escaped Daggy's chatter. A light rain had settled over the area but the clouds looked as if they were beginning to break up for now. An end to the rain would hopefully allow Josie passage via the International Bridge by nightfall. Otto was anxious to get a call from Marta on Josie's progress. The Medrano cartel had been humiliated and severely impacted as a direct result of Josie's police work. If they knew she was there, they would kill her without hesitation, or more likely, kidnap and use her as a bargaining chip.

Josie used her single status as an excuse to jump into situations she thought were too dangerous for someone with a family. Otto found her thinking foolish and annoying. Crossing the border illegally, regardless of the reason, was grounds for dismissal. Still, had he been thirty years younger and fifty pounds lighter, he would most likely have made the same choice. The problem was, Josie either didn't understand or chose to ignore the male-dominated political structure of Artemis. A female was not on equal footing with her male counterparts. It was a simple fact.

Otto could have walked the two blocks to Santiago's apartment, but he counted on the protection his police car provided. The biggest threat to a cop's safety was complacency: the moment you let your guard down was typically when all hell broke loose. There wasn't a day he clocked on to his shift that he didn't fully intend to drive back home to Delores at the end of it. It was a mentality that had kept him safe through forty years of police work. He had worked with other officers in years past whose mentality was just the opposite. They went to work every day prepared for disaster, ready for it to be their last. Otto had never understood why a man would look at the world that way.

He parallel parked and grabbed his notebook and pen off the passenger seat. An unmarked wooden door faced the street front and was located between the Family Value and the San Salbo Pawn Shop. The door opened to a dimly lit stairwell that led to two apartments at the top of the landing. Otto took the stairs slowly and decided to interview Daggy's other tenant, Colt Goff, who also lived above the Family Value store, before he checked out Santiago's place. He trudged up the stairs, so dimly lit he wasn't able to distinguish the color of the walls, and knocked on Colt's door. The hallway smelled musty and old, but the small landing was swept clean.

Colt opened the door about twelve inches, but said nothing. She had spiked hair and facial piercings, and she narrowed her eyes at him with suspicion.

"Ms. Goff, I'm Officer Otto Podowski. I'd like to talk with you a few minutes."

She opened her door farther, stepping away to allow him entrance, while glancing back into her apartment as if trying to assess the damage. Otto walked in and noted a simply furnished space with a navy blue couch and love seat arranged in the middle of the living room. Otto thought he recognized the furniture from Red Goff's place. Colt's father had been murdered the year before after a nasty mess that involved gun sales to Mexico. Goff's daughter had disowned her father long before that, but Otto was certain the appearance of the police was still not a pleasant sight.

Otto sat on the couch and Colt sat on the love seat to his right.

"I appreciate you talking with me. Don't want you to worry. You aren't in any kind of trouble. I just have a few questions about your neighbor."

She looked at him blankly.

"Juan Santiago?"

She nodded once to acknowledge the name. "I know who he is. That's about it."

"You ever talk to him? About anything?"

"Why do you want to know?" she asked.

"He's missing from work. We found a dead body that matches his description." Otto paused and leaned back into the couch.

She raised her eyebrows, but made no other signs of surprise or alarm.

"You guys ever stop by somewhere with good news?"

Otto grinned at her. "Not likely," he said. "Anything you can provide us on Santiago's personal life would help. All we've heard is that he's quiet, stays to himself, and sends his money back to Mexico."

Colt frowned. "I didn't even know that much. I don't know what he does with his money. We say hi on the street and that's it."

"He ever have visitors?"

She shrugged. "Not that I know of."

"You never heard anyone in the apartment?"

She shook her head no, but then seemed to consider something. "I do remember seeing him talk to some men once. I got out of my car and saw them standing in front of the Family Value, just talking. It was weird, like a month or two ago. The guys were in suits. I remember thinking they looked out of place. Like FBI, or mobsters, or something."

Otto smiled. "They all look alike?"

She shrugged, smiled back. "A suit's a suit. Still looks out of place here."

"Did it look like a friendly meeting?"

"I don't know. Just some guys in suits. I didn't pay much attention."

Otto stood. "You might think of something after I leave. Give me a call if anything comes up. Deal?" He pulled a business card out of his shirt pocket and laid it on the coffee table.

"Yep."

Before leaving he stopped and faced her again. "I'll be next door for a while. I'm going to check out his apartment. If anyone else approaches you about Santiago, you give me a call right away. Okay?"

She nodded and he saw the question in her eyes.

"I don't want to alarm you. Just be cautious."

She offered a wry smile. "Red Goff was my daddy. Caution was the one good lesson he taught me."

Otto walked across the hallway to Santiago's apartment. He knocked several times and announced himself but heard no noise from inside. A dirty overhead fixture barely gave off enough light for Otto to see the keyhole above the doorknob of Santiago's apartment. He pulled a pair of plastic gloves from his pocket and jiggled the key until he finally gained entrance.

He pushed the door open with a shove of his foot and was blasted with sweltering heat and the smell of rotting garbage, a sure sign Santiago had been gone several days. Stepping into the apartment, Otto's first impression was that it was a place used to eat, sleep, and not much else. Otherwise Colt Goff's apartment had been a mirror image of the space: murphy bed on one wall, kitchenette on another, small bathroom framed into a corner. Her space had been filled with furniture, pillows, pictures on the walls. It made Santiago's apartment look all the more depressing.

The murphy bed was down, the covers neatly pulled up and covering two pillows. At the end of the bed sat a small TV on top of a footstool. A card table littered with newspapers and other papers was centered in the kitchenette area. Two folding chairs sat on either side of the table. The only other furniture was a bookshelf that served as a night stand cobbled together out of pallet wood at the side of the bed. A wind-up alarm clock sat amid several coffee cups on the top shelf. The second shelf held photographs, a few in frames, most of them propped up against the wood, the photos curling around the edges. They were the only visible sign that a person called the place home.

Otto's shoulders slumped. Walking into a deceased person's home gave him an uneasy feeling, especially when the death was unexpected or suspicious. Poking around someone's personal space with no chance for them to clean up the messes or to hide the secrets left untended bothered him in ways he had difficulty explaining, even to himself. Otto had always made sure Delores knew where all of the insurance and important papers were located, and that she knew how much money was in the savings and checking account each month. The idea of strangers rooting through his things, trying to make sense of his life, kept him awake some nights. But this man's meager surroundings felt especially depressing; dead, almost a week, with not so much as a phone call to the police from a relative or friend wondering where he was or why he hadn't called.

Before walking any farther into the apartment he used his gloved hand to turn on a light switch to the left of the door, then opened his evidence kit to remove the fingerprinting materials. Once prints were taken throughout the apartment he began a methodical search.

On the kitchen table he found a pile of mail, all addressed to Juan Santiago. Otto opened an electric bill that was current, no late charges, as well as a water bill. Hoping for a phone bill that might show a list of recent calls, he came up empty. Glancing around the room, he found no landline, nor cell phone. There were no letters, nothing more personal than junk mail and bills. He flipped through four days' worth of newspapers, the most recent dated last Thursday, the day after Santiago went missing from work.

Otto pulled Santiago's absence record out of his shirt pocket to check his memory. His last day of work had been Tuesday. That meant he wore his boots home from work that evening. And was wearing them again when he was killed. Otto thought about his own uniform boots. He never wore them off duty. They were ugly, heavy, and he had more comfortable shoes to wear. He walked over to the small closet and opened it. He found one pair of running shoes, a pair of loafers, and a pair of casual cowboy boots. Why would Santiago have chosen to wear his heavy work boots with a pair of jeans and a nice shirt? It didn't add up.

After searching through Santiago's clothing in his closet and drawers, he searched the bathroom cabinet and vanity, finding nothing unusual there, nor in the kitchen. He opened the refrigerator, looking for anything amiss, and winced at the smell of sour milk and moldy food.

The most promising area was saved for last. Otto pulled a folding chair from the kitchen over to the bookshelf and sat down. The alarm clock was set to ring at 6:00 A.M., although it was not turned on. The coffee cups were used but empty, and there were no lipstick stains. The second shelf held several photographs, three in dollar-store frames. The first picture was a photo of Santiago amid seven other people who appeared to be family members. A heavy woman in the middle of the photograph smiled proudly, and had the distinct facial features that made it obvious to Otto that he was looking at the matriarch. The second photo was more interesting; Santiago and an attractive woman about his age stood together in front of a small home, arms around each other, heads leaned toward one another. It looked to be a picture of a man and wife. The third picture was the same woman but twenty years younger, leaning over a shallow kids' pool, splashing and laughing with three small children. The other unframed photographs were similar family photos. Otto checked each for writing on the back, and found several dated two years ago, but no names were included.

The next shelf held pay dirt: a shoebox filled with letters.

Otto set the letters aside to take back to the police department for Marta to translate. His uniform shirt was soaked through.

On his way out of the house he took the trash bag in the kitchen, as well as an empty one he found under the sink, and stood by the Dumpster in the alley behind the Family Value. He donned a fresh pair of plastic gloves and pulled the trash apart, throwing away food garbage, and keeping mail and paper to examine later at the office.

As Otto pulled into his parking space in front of the police department, he received a cell phone call from Marta.

"They found Teresa! Sergio just called. She was at her father's. Josie's with her now."

Otto breathed deeply and exhaled, relieved for everyone. "That's great news, Marta."

"Sergio called the bridge authority. The bridge will remain closed tonight, but they hope by morning it may open again. Teresa and Josie are staying at a church tonight. They'll be safe."

Otto said nothing. He knew, as well as Marta, that "safe" was a relative term in northern Mexico.

———————

Josie and Sergio waited outside Javier's apartment while Teresa packed her backpack and left a note for her father. Josie wondered if her father would even remember she had been there. Teresa walked out of the shabby apartment wearing a red tank top with ruffles around the hem, a denim skirt cut at mid-thigh, and sandals that wrapped leather laces around her ankles. It wasn't that the outfit was inappropriate for a teenaged girl, but it certainly drew attention to the young girl's physical features.

"Sergio," Josie said.

He shook his head slowly and glanced at Josie sitting in the passenger's seat. "You do not need this kind of attention."

"Sixteen-year-old girls don't understand blending in with the crowd."

Sergio tilted his head toward the front of the car window. "We're driving a half mile south. El Sagrado Corazon is in the city, but enclosed within a stone wall, ten feet high. It's run by the nuns, a sacred place."

Josie watched an armored truck, driven by federal police in camouflage fatigues and black masks, pass by their car. Their concealed identities were indicative of the power wielded by the cartels. She had no camouflage in this foreign country and felt as if she was wearing flashing lights announcing her presence.

"You are welcome to stay at my place," Sergio said, although his expression showed reluctance. He was already risking his own safety by driving the two around town.

Teresa opened the back door and climbed inside.

"We'll be fine. Just take us to the church." Josie turned to face Teresa. "Do you have any sweatpants, or old baggy clothing you could change into?"

Teresa grimaced.

"I'm in this country illegally. We could be in a great deal of trouble if we're pulled over. Even worse trouble if the Medrano clan finds out I'm here. I don't want any undue attention paid to us until we get back home."

Teresa nodded, her expression suddenly sober. "I could go grab something of my dad's."

Josie nodded. "Do that. Dress down, pull your hair up in a ball cap. I don't even want to know you're a girl when you come out of that door."

Ten minutes later, Teresa walked outside in a pair of baggy men's jeans, oil-stained at the knees, with a large black men's T-shirt that effectively concealed the girl's body underneath it. She laughed when she saw Josie and Sergio watching her.

Sergio turned to face her when she got in the car. "Good girl." His voice caught in his throat as he watched her close the door. "You have your mother's beauty. No clothes or hat can hide the beauty you have inside. You always remember that."

The bell tower was visible above the caramel-colored stone wall surrounding the church. Sergio pulled up in front of a massive wooden door that blocked the buildings within from sight. He stepped out of his car and pulled a piece of thick rope that hung down the left side of the gate, and then spoke into a small microphone mounted onto the wall. By the time he had gotten back into his car, the left gate was slowly opening inward. Once it was fully open, a nun, dressed in black robes and habit, walked quickly across the stone path and opened the other gate to allow Sergio entrance into the courtyard.

Inside the walls was a maze of stone paths and winding patches of garden filled with red and white flowers and a variety of vegetables. The recent rains had beaten down the plants, but they were lush and full of color. Wooden benches and adobe archways gave way to secret gardens and cubbyholes for meditation. As Sergio pulled his car inside the gates, the bell tower rang to announce it was seven o'clock. Sergio stopped his car and pointed out his window for Teresa to look up and watch the nun pull the rope with both arms, using the weight of her body to move the magnificent iron bell. The sound gave Josie chills. Another nun smiled and waved at Sergio and waited for him to pull the car forward so that she could shut the gates behind them. He followed a round driving path that circled past the church, then past a row of four rustic doors located under a steep overhang that shaded them from the blazing sun. Josie assumed these were the guest rooms.

As they got out of the car, Josie saw Teresa turn and watch the nun replace a thick piece of wrought iron across the gates, then padlock it on both ends. The enclosed churchyard was small and intimate and Josie felt a sense of peace settle over her that she had not felt in quite some time.

Sergio introduced the nun who closed the gates as Sister Agnes. She walked quickly up the stone path, smiling and talking to Sergio as if he were an old friend. She spoke in Spanish, her voice pleasant. After several minutes of friendly chatter the nun pulled a key out of her pocket and unlocked the wooden door closest to them. She stepped back and allowed Josie and Teresa to enter first. A window on the opposite wall let in filtered light through a gauze curtain. Shade trees on the opposite side of the room kept the breeze coming through the window warm but comfortable. A twin-size bed was pushed up lengthwise to the left side of the door and another to the right. On either side of the wall was an armoire and a small washbasin, mirror, and shelf for toiletries. The floor was ancient wood plank, and waxed to a high shine. The walls were stone, like the outside of the building, and helped keep the temperature comfortable without air-conditioning.

Josie smiled and nodded at the nun to show she was pleased with the room, then turned to face Sergio. "Can you ask how much I owe for the room?"

"The rooms are for friends of the church. No cost. If you would like to make a donation, that is up to you."

After Sergio and the nun left, Josie sat on one bed and Teresa sat on the other, facing each other.

"Now what?"

Josie smiled. "Beats me."

"I guess we can't take a walk?" Teresa asked.

"Not outside these walls. I'm not very well liked here by some pretty bad people."

"Mom told me." Teresa looked uncomfortable. "I'm sorry you had to come bail me out. I never meant to cause all this trouble for you."

"Just tell that to your mom tomorrow, and we'll call it even."

———————

Mitchell Cowan, Arroyo County coroner, stood at the autopsy table and stared at the black and green flesh in front of him, frustrated and angry at his inability to put all of the pieces together. He had originally declared the time of death at forty-eight hours, possibly longer, but over the past several hours he had changed his mind, placing the time of death closer to thirty hours. Otto had called as he was getting ready to go home that evening to inform Cowan that they had confirmed the man's identity, and the fact that he was part of the cleanup crew at the closed nuclear weapons plant. Cowan had originally estimated the man's age to be in his sixties. Otto had said the man's work records put him at forty-four. Something had caused the man's decomposition to increase at a faster rate than normal.

After four hours spent reexamining the body, and reformulating his theories, he summoned Otto to his office at almost eight o'clock that night. Otto knocked, entered the lab, and was then directed to wash and suit up before Cowan would talk with him.

Garbed in a blue gown, latex gloves, and a blue mask and cap, Otto approached the body. Cowan noted that his gaze rested on the dead man's feet, the only part covered by a cloth. Cowan retrieved the black plastic sheet that lay under the autopsy table and covered the rest of the body in deference to Otto.

"We have some issues," Cowan said. "Time of death has proven elusive."

Otto asked, "What about the blowflies? I thought they identified time of death."

Cowan nodded. "With the wet nature of the sores on the body, it wouldn't surprise me if the blowflies were on him within an hour of death. The blowfly eggs were hatching into larvae when Josie found the body. It usually takes time for the body to decompose, but he was decomposing before he was dead."

Otto winced at the thought.

"Judging by the decomposition of his body, the green and black marbling of his skin, and the insect larvae, I'm going to change my original estimate. At this point, I think he was killed Saturday night. Gauging the lividity, his body was transported several hours later and deposited in the desert late Saturday night, early Sunday morning."

Otto nodded in appreciation. "Nice work, Cowan."

Cowan frowned. "It's not so easy. This whole case is troubling me."

"How so?"

"After you called, first thing I did was go back to the internal organs. This wasn't the body of a forty-year-old man. I found the intestinal track highly putrefied. The intestinal tract is always first to disintegrate, especially in high heat circumstances, but his entire GI tract was further decomposed than it should have been. The rest of his organs were more in line with the twenty-four-to-thirty-six-hour theory."

"Can you translate that?"

"Something ate up his arms, and then ate up his digestive tract."

Otto blew air out in frustration. "We're all thinking radiation. The guy worked at the Feed Plant. Is that where you're headed with this?"

Cowan placed his hand on the black plastic sheet covering the body, and then paused. "I'm putting him away for the night. Turn your head if you want."

Otto walked over to the laundry tub and began taking his mask and gown off.

Cowan began preparing the body for the cooler as he talked. "That's the angle that makes the most sense. But why his GI tract?

If he'd had a massive dose of radiation and chemo he could have developed sores. Some cancer victims develop open wounds and they fester over a year before the body's immune system can heal them. Conceivably, radiation or chemo could have caused the sores on his arms and head. But I saw no evidence of cancer."

"That's not what I was getting at. Could he have picked up that kind of radiation exposure at the cleanup site?"

Cowan eyed Otto over his reading glasses, then rolled the metal gurney and body over to the freezer. "I know what you were getting at. I can't answer it, though. I don't have any idea what kind of radiation might be leaking out at that plant. I find it highly unlikely it caused the sores on this man's arms, though. My opinion is that it would take a prescribed, intensive, and malicious intent to cause the sores on this man's arms."

"Cause of death?" Otto asked.

"I'm just not ready to commit. There are three distinct traumas. The exterior sores, the GI tract, and the blow to the head. I'm not able to piece together how they are related."

"*If* they're related," Otto said.

"Obviously, I'm no expert in radiation poisoning. I'll be contacting the Centers for Disease Control in the morning." Cowan peeled his latex gloves off and dropped them in a hazardous waste container.

Otto left Cowan's office at the Arroyo County Jail and stood outside for a long while before entering his jeep to drive home. The case was a mix of barely related details. The victim worked at a nuclear weapons plant that was in the process of being dismantled. A handful of people in the entire nation took part in that kind of specialized cleanup, so who knew if the plant employees were providing good information. The man had been knocked unconscious by a blow to the back of the head, but more than likely he had been killed by some horrendous sores that the coroner couldn't identify on the man's arms. Were the sores caused by radiation from the plant, or by some unidentified virus infecting everyone who came in contact with the victim? To top it all off, the coroner just said that his digestive tract was disintegrated as well. And, how had the man's wallet, empty of ID but containing cash, been found in Cassidy Harper's beat-up car on the side of Scratchgravel Road?

THIRTEEN

By ten o'clock that night Josie and Teresa were both sitting in T-shirts and shorts on Teresa's bed playing gin rummy with a well-worn deck that Teresa had taken from her dad's apartment. They had relaxed into one another's company and were both enjoying what had started out seeming like an endless night.

Josie laid an ace of spades in the middle of their rows of cards. "What do you see yourself doing after you graduate high school?"

Teresa rested the cards in her lap and shrugged.

"You're young. You have plenty of time," Josie said. "Just find something other than law enforcement."

"I want out of here. I want to live in a city, away from the desert. Somewhere nobody knows me."

"Don't you have something in school you love to do?" Josie asked. "A hobby?"

Teresa looked at Josie for a moment too long and she could tell Teresa was struggling with something she wanted to say. Josie laid her cards on the bed, ready to listen.

Someone knocked on the door and a woman said something in Spanish, her voice urgent but unclear.

Josie and Teresa looked at each other, confused. It was after ten o'clock and the nuns locked up the church at nine.

Josie stood from the bed and automatically looked for her gun, then remembered she hadn't brought it.

The woman spoke again in a hoarse whisper, still banging on the door frantically. There was no peephole in the ancient door. Josie motioned Teresa to stand against the wall so she would be hidden behind the door when it opened. The girl looked terrified.

When Josie opened the door, Sister Agnes rushed inside. She wore a full-length white nightgown and her short gray hair was tousled. She stood in front of the door for a moment and took a long stilling breath. In a much calmer voice she gestured toward the door and said something in Spanish.

"No hablo Española," Josie said, and looked to Teresa, who was fluent. Her face had gone pale. "What is she saying?"

"She says the Federales are here. They've come to take us out of the city."

"Why?"

Teresa shook her head no and Josie feared she would go into shock.

"Teresa! Ask the nun why they want to take us! What have we done?"

The nun walked over to Teresa, who still stood with her back against the wall. The nun put her hands out and held both of Teresa's hands in her own. She spoke slower and Teresa nodded, calming down some.

"She doesn't know anything. There's a Federales van behind the church, waiting. She wants us to go now before there's trouble."

"Tell her I have to talk to Sergio."

The nun pointed to their bags on the floor and spoke rapidly.

Teresa said, "She says go now. We can't make them wait or they'll enter. She doesn't want attention drawn to the church."

Josie felt the blood rushing to her face and knew she needed to keep her calm. They had no choice. They threw their belongings into their backpacks and followed the nun across the courtyard and through the front doors of the church. They walked quickly down the center of the darkened sanctuary. The pews were barely visible from oil lamps lit on the altar. The nun slowed slightly and spoke, then stretched her hand out to Teresa. She motioned for Josie to hold Teresa's other hand and opened a door behind the altar.

"She says it's dark. To hang on to my hand and trust her."

Holding hands, they were plunged into complete darkness. The hallway smelled damp and musty and the floor turned to a ramp sloping downward. They walked slowly; the only sounds were their footsteps and the nun's reassuring whispers. Josie realized Sister Agnes had made this night trip before, and she wondered if the nun had imagined herself living a life of danger when she took her vows.

Josie ran into Teresa, who had stopped suddenly. They listened as the nun jiggled a metal key into a padlock, opened it, and then finally pushed a heavy wooden door open into the night. In front of them were three grim-faced men wearing black SWAT-style Federales uniforms. They spoke quickly to the nun, then grabbed Josie and Teresa roughly by the arms and pulled them to the back of the van where they were shoved inside and the doors were closed. In less than a minute they were moving down the road, and Josie and Teresa were sitting on the floor of a cargo van with no idea where they were going or why. Josie reached out and grabbed Teresa's hand and the two sat in silence.

After a fifteen-minute ride, with no explanation from the officers, the vehicle slowed and Josie felt Teresa's grip on her hand tighten. They listened as the men talked quietly in the front of the van, but Teresa couldn't hear their conversation enough to translate. Josie thought they were headed northwest but there were no windows in the back of the van and she wasn't able to hear other cars.

Once the van stopped the rear doors were yanked open and two officers pulled Josie and Teresa from the back. Once they were standing on the side of the road, the men slammed the back doors, said nothing more, turned, and got back in the van. Teresa began yelling as the van completed a U-turn and started back the way they had come. Josie grabbed her, wrapped her in a tight hug, and finally placed a hand over her mouth to get her to calm down.

"Stop. Teresa, you have to quit. There may be houses we can't see."

Teresa finally calmed somewhat and Josie tried to get her bearings. It was almost impossible. The sky was covered in clouds: the night was completely dark.

"Just stand here a minute. I need a sense for where we are."

Teresa began to cry, and Josie found her patience wearing thin. At that point, she had no desire to comfort the girl. She was exhausted and frightened herself, with no plan how to proceed.

Teresa grabbed her shoulder and Josie turned to see far-off headlights coming slowly down the road.

"What do we do?" The girl sounded terrified.

"Hold my hand." She pulled Teresa across the road. "We'll stay on this side so I can see the driver." They felt their way down a slight embankment off the side of the road, but could feel nothing to hide behind.

"Just lie flat and keep your head down. Don't do anything until I tell you to. If I tell you to run, you get up and run straight out into the desert. You run like hell for as far as you can. Then find something to hide behind until daybreak. Just don't run until I say so. Got it?"

Teresa murmured yes and lay flat, her hands under her face to keep the sand from her eyes.

Flat on her stomach, Josie watched as the car approached. All she could see were the headlights until the car rolled past them with the windows open. The interior light of the car was on and Josie recognized Sergio. She leaped up from her position and yelled his name. The car stopped and Josie and Teresa ran to it. Josie climbed in the front, Teresa in the rear, and Sergio sped off.

"Everyone all right? Teresa, you're okay?" Sergio asked. His voice was taut with stress and he reached an arm out to Josie's shoulder.

Teresa wasn't talking and Josie turned around. She shook her head yes, and fell into a slump against the backseat.

"We're okay. But I have no idea what just happened back there," Josie said.

"It was paranoia, nothing more. One of my fellow officers checked on the church this afternoon. A routine stop. One of the nuns told him who you were and he went straight to our commander. I am sorry to say, your name is connected with Medrano. He was afraid the Medrano cartel would find out you were staying in the church and take revenge." In the dim light from the dashboard, Josie saw Sergio turn toward her, his expression full of sorrow. "He ordered you out of the city."

His words stung. It was a terrible thing to hear as someone who had spent her life trying to uphold the law. When the Medrano cartel had invaded Artemis last year, and she had killed members of the clan in a battle for territory, she had lost her ability to move freely in Mexico.

"We live our lives preparing for disaster, trying to avoid it," he said.

Josie nodded. She understood but it didn't ease the sting.

"It isn't you. It's the idea there could be trouble. We've made some improvements in the city since the blowup in Artemis, but we can't afford to risk anything. Yes?"

"What do we do now?"

Sergio looked at her again and smiled. "We drive to Juarez. I've already arranged your crossing and there's a rental car waiting in El Paso. It will be two in the morning before we get there. It will be a long night."

FOURTEEN

The metal roof on Mitchell Cowan's one-story ranch home thrummed over his bed as he lay staring at the ceiling, imagining the black swirling clouds above him. The rain had started again sometime during the night, and he had awoken to booming thunder at 5 A.M. He rolled over and felt around in the general vicinity of his night table until he found the pull switch for the lamp. He sat up and arranged his pillows behind him, put his reading glasses on, and then opened the book he had started the night before.

Before leaving work that night Cowan had searched his professional library, and then drove home and pored through his extensive collection of books and scientific journals, gathering anything he could find concerning radiation poisoning. Having no wife or kids, he looked forward to a night spent deep in the pages of medical research—his favorite place to be.

At nine thirty he'd climbed into bed with a peanut butter and honey sandwich, milk, and a stack of books. At one in the morning, he finally forced himself to turn the light off. He thought he might have cracked the case. And it was a doozy.

In the book he was currently reading, he had found a fascinating story involving former Russian KGB leaders all related to some nasty business of poisoning a rogue agent who came too close to the truth. Cowan had no interest in the "truth" the young agent was attempting to expose, nor in the conspiracy theories being spun out in detail, but he was very interested in the man's grisly death.

Alexander Litvinenko was poisoned by a highly radioactive isotope called polonium-210. The drug can be touched with no danger done to the skin; however, once ingested, it destroys the tissues inside of the victim. Pictures of the former KGB agent, the only person known to have been intentionally killed by a lethal dose of polonium, were frighteningly similar to Juan Santiago. Both men showed augmented signs of aging, and had obliterated digestive tracts.

At six A.M., Cowan took a quick shower in order to be in his office by seven. Atlanta, Georgia, was just an hour ahead of Artemis, and he wanted to catch his contact before he got caught up in meetings.

Mark Preston was a research scientist at the CDC and Cowan had attended graduate school with him. Cowan remembered little of him, other than that he was friendly and studious, and his dream in life was to work on communicable diseases. Cowan knew Preston was working for the CDC because he had seen a paper co-published by him several months ago in *The Journal of the American Medical Association*.

Cowan cleared off a place at his desk in the coroner's office and put his notes in front of him. He didn't plan on bringing up the Litvinenko case for fear of being taken for a quack, but he needed some basic information on radiation poisoning. After speaking with an operator and receptionist he was finally connected to Preston.

"Of course I remember you. You went back to Texas, is that right?"

"That's right." Cowan smiled, pleased Preston had remembered him from so many years ago. "I'm the coroner for a small West

Texas town. Our resources are limited, but it doesn't keep us from getting the occasional odd duck case. That's why I'm calling."

Preston laughed. "Odd ducks are my favorite. Fill me in."

Cowan spent several minutes explaining the basics of the case, from the body's exposure to the elements, to the lesions and internal decay.

"Well, that's a unique one," Preston said. "Do you suspect radiation exposure, meaning body penetration? Or are you thinking internal or external contamination?"

"Possibly both. The intense desert heat will obviously speed up putrification, but I'm still concerned about contamination by ingestion. The deceased's digestive tract is destroyed, more so than his other body systems. But the lesions on his arms appear unrelated."

"Do you know what kind of dose the deceased may have received?"

"No."

"Here's the truth. Radiation exposure is typically not that deadly. The amount of radiation exposure, even from a dirty bomb, would typically not be enough to cause immediate danger. Years down the road, the people directly hit would probably be at greater risk of certain types of cancer, but that doesn't sound like what you've got."

"I'm not referring to terrorists. There is a nuclear weapons plant that is currently being dismantled and cleaned up. The deceased worked on the cleanup crew at the plant. I'm concerned the company's practices could have led to contamination."

There was silence on the other end for several moments. "The name of the company?"

"Beacon Pathways," Cowan said.

Another pause. "Do you suspect ARS? Acute radiation sickness?"

"That's my fear," Cowan said.

"A telltale sign is a day or two of intense vomiting and diarrhea.

Next, the patient makes a recovery for a few days and feels good. Then it hits again with a vengeance. Fever, no appetite, exhaustion. Does that fit the profile of the deceased?"

"I can't answer that. It's all speculation. We found the body and we're still trying to track down information. He lives by himself. He's a loner. We don't have any medical information for him."

"Do you have a dosimeter set up in the morgue yet?"

"No."

"So, you don't have any radiation readings on the body?"

"No, I'm just now starting to put together a picture of what might have happened. And even that is speculation," Cowan said.

"We need to establish low-dose and high-dose rates. You keep everyone out of the lab until you get some readings. That's your first task."

"Okay."

"It's critical you get a baseline reading to see what kind of radiation the body is emanating. If you've got someone who died within a week of contamination, then he was hit with a massive dose. You need to get your office checked immediately." Preston paused on the phone and mumbled something to himself as he wrote a note, then continued. "We'll need to get you several meters. It's critical to find out the type of radiation that was used. Without knowing that it's hard to know what kind of danger you might be in."

Cowan rubbed his forehead. He was feeling completely overwhelmed.

"You need dose rate readings for everyone who's been in contact with the body. You need a pancake probe to check your equipment and lab. Survey the remains tub, the body bag, everything. Are you wearing a Tyvek suit when you're in contact? Checking your feet when you leave the lab? Those kinds of precautions?"

"Somewhat." Cowan wrote down notes as Preston talked, but he knew he was missing details. Worse yet, he had no idea how to get the necessary equipment Preston was referring to. Cowan finally broke in. "I'll be completely honest. Radiation is not my area of specialty. I'm not sure where to even begin. I don't have any equipment, or any money to purchase the equipment. We're on a nonexistent budget."

"Ah. Understood. Let me put you on hold a minute." Preston was gone for almost five minutes before returning and apologizing for the delay. "I have good news though. I'm going to send you a certified hazardous materials technician. Her name is Diane Patel. She'll be able to help you put together a plan and get things moving quickly. This is exactly what she's trained for."

"That would be much appreciated." Cowan sighed, the relief immense. "I can work with Beacon to see what kind of equipment we have available."

"Diane will bring the necessary equipment. Without knowing Beacon professionally I'm hesitant to trust their monitors. Diane will get a flight out first thing in the morning."

"Here is my worry," Cowan said. "I don't think there is a public health menace. The body was discovered several days ago, and I haven't seen any indication that anyone else was involved. My bigger worry right now is for the officers who came into contact with the body."

"Absolutely. Those officers must be checked immediately. As well as yourself."

FIFTEEN

At six thirty Thursday morning Josie called Teresa's name, and woke her from a deep sleep in the backseat. Through the night Josie had finished two cups of cold McDonald's coffee that she had stocked up on in El Paso, and drunk on the long ride home. She had spent an hour on the phone with Dillon, who had forgiven her for taking the trip, and then told her stories from his childhood to keep her from falling asleep at the wheel. Now, her eyes felt as if someone had sprinkled sand in them, and although she was exhausted from driving and the stress of the night, she was also thoroughly satisfied.

Josie pulled into Marta's driveway, turned the rental car off, and stretched her back after the long ride. It was a bleak morning. They'd had a one-day reprieve from the rain. Now, it was back and forecast to stay for several days, dumping another several inches. Josie sat for a moment, watching the rain streak down the car window.

Marta opened the front door to her home. She was wearing jeans and a loose-fitting striped T-shirt, her face filled with worry. She looked confused when she saw Josie exit the rental car. From the front door of her home she couldn't see Teresa in the backseat, and Josie could see panic fill Marta's face.

"It's good news, Marta. I've brought her home. She's getting her stuff together in the backseat."

Marta's eyes widened and she ran through the rain to the car as if she wouldn't believe the news until she could see her daughter herself. She peered through the back passenger window and covered her face with her hands. After a moment she walked around to the other side of the car and approached Josie.

"You, my friend, I will never be able to repay."

Josie hugged Marta, who pulled away suddenly and said, "I just checked the Internet an hour ago. They don't expect to open the International Bridge today. The flooding is too bad. How did you?" She motioned to the car.

"It's a long story. Let's get out of the rain. Teresa can fill you in. I'm headed home for a shower and few hours' sleep."

After a tearful reunion and apologies and promises from Teresa, Josie pulled back out of the driveway. She drove the ten minutes to her home, glad to let her thoughts wander over not much of anything. She planned to collect Chester from Dell's house, go home and eat a fried egg, take a shower, and sleep until eleven when she would get up for second shift. It would be good to put the past twenty-four hours behind her.

Josie pulled down her lane, drove past her own home, and down the long drive to Dell's place. She found him inside the horse barn, with the sliding doors pulled all the way back, standing over a raised fire pit. Dell had mounted a tire rim from an old semi horizontally onto a metal tripod. He'd welded a grate in the bottom of the tire rim to hold the fire and coals. The tripod lifted the rim off the ground, and with a metal bottom inside the rim, it made a sturdy fire pit. Dell was sliding a swinging grate over the red coals when she ran inside the barn and out of the rain.

"How do?" he called, and set a metal coffeepot on the grate.

"You having smoke withdrawal?"

"I need some blue sky. Can't stand all this rain. We'll have us some cowboy coffee and that'll cheer us up."

Chester came loping around from the back of Dell's house. He knew the sound of Josie's car engine and made a beeline to greet her. He came into the barn and shook water all over both of them. Dell threw Josie an old towel and she dried the dog off and scratched his chest and ears until he wandered away to check one of the horses making a racket in the back of the barn.

Dell dragged two bales of straw over to the fire and they both sat watching the smoke drift out of the barn into the rain.

"Dig into that cooler, there against the stable. I kept Chester some scraps from breakfast."

Josie smiled when she found a half pound of fried bacon wrapped in tinfoil. "You have better dog scraps than what I keep in my refrigerator for people."

Chester smelled the bacon and came back to sit patiently in front of her, accepting each piece as if it were a delicate morsel, chewing carefully before swallowing. He always appeared to sincerely enjoy the taste of a good snack, and Dell couldn't resist spoiling him.

Dell stood, arms crossed over his chest, and watched the interaction. "That dog's got better manners than most kids."

Josie and Dell watched the coffee percolate as she caught him up on the dead body and the connection to the old Feed Plant.

"What do you know about that place?" she asked.

"Nothing. Don't want to either. Go talk to Sauly. He worked there for years before they fired him. Sons a bitches."

She grinned.

"Why on God's green earth would a man make something that can't be touched for ten thousand years just so he can heat his house? They call that clean energy?" Dell stood and jammed his poker stick into the coals and then placed a small chunk of wood into the fire. "We're so smart we're stupid. I can't even talk about it. Pisses me off too much."

Dell walked to a storage room in the back of the barn to retrieve two coffee cups. By the time he came back to the fire and poured the coffee he'd calmed down and moved on to a topic that didn't raise his ire.

"How about the pencil pusher?" Dell asked.

She sipped her coffee and took her time answering. "His name is Dillon."

"I know his name. Where's he been? Haven't seen his car much."

She shrugged and tried to figure Dell's angle. "He's been at a conference. I just saw him a couple days ago."

"Seems like I haven't seen him all that much," Dell said.

"What is this?"

"Conversation. I thought that's what you females liked."

"Well, I'm not your typical female." She fell quiet, assuming the conversation would turn.

"So, how is he?"

Josie sighed. "He's okay. He's good. Why do you care how he is?"

Dell held a hand up. "I'll restate the question. How are you and Dillon together? As a pair?"

"Dell! Why are you asking me this? It's too early in the morning." She blew air out in frustration. "I don't know. What does that mean, how are we as a pair? Am I one way on my own, and another with him?"

"Sure. Lots of people like that."

"We're fine." She patted her leg to get Chester to wander over and lie down at her feet. She stroked his head and hoped Dell would let it go.

He was quiet a minute as he stared at the fire. "Here's why I ask. You went through hell and back a few months ago. Had gunmen shoot up your bedroom with you laying there. That's enough to fry anybody's brain. But, it should also make you think. You're not getting any younger. If you like this fella then maybe it's time to do something about it. If you don't, or if you're happy the way you are, then leave it be. Nothing wrong with that. Just don't let fear hold you back."

"Who says I'm afraid?"

"You're a cop. What happens if you let fear influence your decisions as a cop? You get your ass blown to kingdom come. Same thing happens in your relationships. You let fear influence your relationships and you end up living alone on a beach."

"That what happened to you?" she asked.

"I don't have fear. I just don't want what other people seem to want. But I think you do."

After four hours of sleep that left her body feeling heavy and her mind sluggish, Josie dragged herself out of bed and into the shower. She drove to work on autopilot and walked into the Artemis Police Department at noon, ready for a second shift. She had a quick conversation with Lou and then found Otto upstairs glaring at his computer, and Marta brewing a fresh pot of coffee.

Otto heard Josie enter the office and turned toward her, his lips pursed in anger. "This blasted thing won't let me in. Something's timed out."

She approached his desk and leaned over him to examine his screen. "You need to learn a little patience."

"Weren't these things supposed to save us time? We were supposed to get rid of all our paperwork. We were sold a big fat lie." He picked up his mouse and pitched it across his desk. "How many heart attacks you think are caused each year because of these damned things?"

"Otto. Calm down. And don't throw your mouse." Josie sat down and discovered he was entering the wrong username and password for the new department e-mail system. While she logged him in he poured her a fresh cup of coffee.

Marta sat down at the conference table, her eyes bleary, looking slightly better than the day before.

"How's Teresa?" Otto asked, sitting down beside her with a handful of paperwork, notes, and his steno pad.

Marta wore a silver cross necklace that she pulled from underneath her uniform shirt. She rubbed absently at the back of the cross with her thumb. "'Repentant' is I think a good description. She's not one to apologize, but she is truly sorry this time. As she should be. She knows that she risked not only her life, but Josie's too. And she realizes the pain and anguish she caused me." Marta turned and watched Josie approach the table with her coffee and notes. "You must have said something that clicked with her. She's awful impressed with you."

"I think it was the midnight car ride that did it," Josie said. She turned to Otto. "So, fill us in on the Santiago investigation."

"I called Cowan yesterday to let him know we think we have the victim's ID. I told him Santiago's work records indicate he was forty-four years old. Remember, Cowan first estimated he was closer to sixty. He reexamined everything, including internal organs, and discovered some were decomposing at a faster rate than others."

Marta frowned. "How does that happen?"

"Cowan thinks he ingested something that ate up his insides," he said.

"How does that connect with the open sores on his arms?" Josie asked.

"That's what I wanted to know. Sounds like he got nuked," he said.

"Like he was over-radiated?" Josie said.

Otto shrugged, his expression skeptical. "Cowan says medical records need to be subpoenaed, but we don't even know where to start. Our best bet is tracking down his family to see if he was getting chemo or radiation. He claims cancer patients can get sores that won't heal sometimes."

Marta winced and shuddered.

"He's got a call in to Centers for Disease Control this morning," Otto said. "I have to give him credit. Cowan's working overtime on this one."

"Is Lou running down family?" Josie asked.

"Yep. The Feed Plant didn't have any records outside of his address here in Artemis. Lou's tracked back a Juan Santiago to four cities in northern Mexico. She's starting with those families first. See if she can get a match and notify the family. Then she'll go for medical records." Otto opened the shoebox in front of him. "I found these at Santiago's place. His wife's name is Abella. That'll help Lou make the connection."

"That's great," Josie said.

"He hasn't been at his apartment for days. No surprise there. The only thing I found of interest was this box full of letters." He looked at Marta. "They're all in Spanish. I can get the gist of the letters, but I'll need your help."

"Sure."

"I'll get them in order for you first."

Josie took notes as she talked. "You didn't find any money? No stash he was hiding to send home?"

"Nothing."

"Might give us a motive," Marta said.

Otto shook his head. "That doesn't work with the body in the desert and the wallet with twenty-four dollars left in Cassidy Harper's car," he said.

Josie switched tracks. "I also want to get Dillon to dig up what he can on Diego Paiva. See what kind of records he can find on Beacon."

"That Paiva seems like a shady character," Otto said.

"Why? Because he's smooth and polished?" Josie said.

He considered Josie for a moment, obviously annoyed by her question. "Disingenuous was more what I was thinking. I'm just not sure we can trust him as a reliable source at this point."

Josie stopped herself from commenting further. Otto was typically a good judge of character, but sometimes he jumped to conclusions about people, and Josie thought he was sometimes led astray by his initial judgment.

SIXTEEN

Otto picked up the shoebox full of letters he had obtained from Santiago's apartment and sat down at the conference table with a pencil and tablet of paper to take notes. The envelopes were not present, so he was hoping to find mention of cities that would help them find Santiago's home and family. Otto opened each letter and stacked them on top of each other in the same order they had been inside the box. About half the letters had dates noted in the upper right-hand corner of the paper. The sequence of dates made it obvious that Santiago kept the letters organized, the most recent on top. With Otto's rudimentary ability to read Spanish he was able to discern that the majority of the letters appeared to have been written by the man's wife, Abella. Otto pulled the photographs from the bottom of the box and found the black-and-white picture of Santiago and his wife, the sides of their heads touching, squinting and smiling toward the camera. The edges of the photograph were worn from being handled so often. Otto imagined Santiago lying on his back in bed, staring at those pretty smiling eyes, wishing for the day he could return home.

Otto understood the pain of leaving one's family. When he and Delores left Poland as young newlyweds, he'd been assigned a simple task: attend school in America, become a doctor, and return to the family village a trained physician. At nineteen years of age, with no preparation, no training, no travel experience outside of Poland, and no understanding of the process for acceptance into even the most mediocre of medical schools in America, Otto learned within six months the task his parents had given him was un-achievable. He and Delores discovered their limitations together, learned of the betrayal their families felt at their failure, felt the same intense guilt at the shameful waste of their parents' hard-earned savings, and realized that they had little more in life than their love for each other. They fast learned the lessons of poverty: that life isn't a journey with options, but rather a ladder to climb day after day, methodically taking one rung at a time.

Otto stared at the photo in his hands and pictured the couch in his comfortable living room, neat and tidy with Delores's personal-ity touching each pillow and needlepoint and rug, creating a co-coon of warmth he never took for granted. He realized that he'd climbed off the ladder, the one he'd visualized for so many of his younger years, and he'd found his place to rest. And it saddened him that this family would never find that same peace.

Once Otto had reviewed the letters, he asked Marta to read them for specific details that might help them narrow down where the family lived, or for information about Santiago's health. Marta sat beside Otto at the conference table and read through each of the letters, jotting down very few notes. She handed them back to Otto when she finished.

"Mostly, they're filled with family milestones. It's the stuff that means nothing to you and I, but breaks the heart of the one miss-ing it."

"No mention of towns or cities?"

"No. There were several letters from Santiago's daughters and one from his son, written just before the boy entered the Ejército Mexicano, or the Mexican Army, last year. But they didn't mention where he'd be stationed."

"Anything about Santiago's job?" Otto asked.

"It's obvious that his wife understood very little about his work at the Feed Plant. The job provided a paycheck and little else."

———— ·———

Josie left Marta and Otto at the police department and drove out to talk with Sauly Magson. His house was located just south of the mudflats on the Rio, surrounded by thick swaths of three-foot-high prairie grasses that rippled in the breeze like ocean waves. Mountain runoff and natural springs kept the area green year-round, and with the recent rains it looked almost tropical. Sauly's house was a three-story grain elevator he had painted purple and converted into an artsy space. He had become something of a local celebrity the past year after he was photographed by a writer from *Western Art and Architecture,* writing a story on free expression. Josie doubted he had even seen the article.

She heard a boom, like that of a cannon, explode behind his house. Anyone else and she would have been concerned—with Sauly it was the norm. Josie walked around the back of the grain elevator toward the sandy slope that led down to the river. She found him, bald-headed and bare-chested, with a blue bandana tied around his neck. He was wearing a pair of jean shorts with no shoes, holding an aerosol can and lighter. He turned and Josie saw he was shaking the can and laughing aloud.

"Did you hear that? Glory!" he yelled. Raindrops from the drizzle slipped down his chest, but he didn't seem to notice.

Sauly stood by a seven-foot-long plastic pipe that looked like a giant bazooka gun. Beside the pipe lay a bag of potatoes and several small cans of propane and aerosol propellant.

He seemed to realize he was talking to a police officer, and his smile faded.

"You here to ruin my day?" he asked. "It's just a potato gun."

She smiled. "Nope. What's with the pipe?"

He picked up a potato and rammed it down into the pipe. "The potato seals the end. Then I hook up the propane at the other end of the pipe. It mixes with air in the chamber, then I light it. Want to watch one? The sound shakes things up on your insides."

"I was actually hoping to get some information from you. Do you have a minute?"

He smiled a wide, toothless grin. "For you? Anything. Let's go inside and have a sip of cold tea."

Sauly asked her to carry the potato bag and he picked up the propellant along with the pipe. They walked through the wet grass to the back of his house and placed his toys underneath the green-and-white-striped awning that covered a deep back porch.

Josie followed him inside, through a small mudroom and into the kitchen. Sauly had picked a series of fifteen differently sized square windows and built them into the elevator's sides at differing angles. The effect was somewhere between sophisticated architecture and fun-house carnival, and Josie loved it. His kitchen was outfitted with two such windows. Josie sat at the kitchen table, in front of a four-foot-square window turned sideways to make a diamond shape. From the table, the Rio appeared to flow directly from one corner of the window to the other, splitting the outdoor scenery in half. Josie was certain the placement of the window was no accident and she was amazed at the precision.

As Sauly poured their tea and chatted about building his potato gun, Josie looked around the room. It was painted a deep maroon with buttery yellow cabinets and sage green trim. On the table was a collection of cactus plants arranged around the inside of a twelve-inch snapping turtle shell. Black-and-white photographs of the Rio were framed in old barn wood and hung around the dining room.

He placed two glasses of tea and a small glass dish with sugar cubes and spoons on the table.

"So, here's the deal," Josie said. She dropped several sugar cubes in her tea as Sauly sat down beside her. "We found a body out in the desert. It looks like murder. No identification on the body. We tracked him down through his work boots to the nuclear plant. We think his name is Juan Santiago. He worked on the cleanup crew."

Sauly leaned back in his chair, startled, and rubbed his bald head. "Yes, ma'am. I know who you mean. I worked with him about a year before I left."

"I need to know anything you can tell me about him."

Sauly made a low hum. "Can't give you much. It's been two years since I worked with him. And he never said nothing to anybody. Earned his dollar and left."

"That's what everybody said. Surely he connected with someone. You don't remember him hanging around anyone? Maybe sitting by someone at lunch?"

"Not a one. He wasn't unfriendly, but he just didn't make friends. You get my meaning?"

Frustrated, she stirred her tea and watched the sugar at the bottom of the glass. "What was your job at the plant?"

"Same as Santiago. Safe cleanup. That's what the bosses called it."

She nodded. "What made you leave?"

"They found me out. Fired me."

She laughed at his abrupt answer. "Fired?"

"Walked me to a room, took my clothes and boots. I tried to keep my Geiger counter for a souvenir but they caught me. They kicked my ass all the way to the parking lot. Gave me a personal escort."

"What did you do?"

A conspiratorial grin lit up his face. "Sabatoge."

Josie was shocked, but only mildly. She smiled at his grin. She could never keep a poker face with Sauly. "How so?"

"They were cooking soup."

"What's soup?"

"Nuclear soup. That's what we called it. The chemicals were in big silver vats and we always said they were cooking the soup."

"I thought you were working cleanup?"

"New soup. Blow-up-the-world stuff. I knew nobody would listen to me. So I pissed in the soup," he said.

"Literally?"

He gave her a look as if she should have known better. "Figuratively."

Josie decided not to pursue the sabotage line of questioning. Some things she preferred not know.

"What made you think they were making new stuff?" she asked.

"You need to mix chemicals to tear a building down?"

She shrugged. "I don't know. I never worked at a nuclear plant."

"The answer's no."

"Who was doing it?"

"Beacon! The cleanup company."

"How do you know it wasn't something legitimate? I talked with Diego Paiva this week."

Sauly rolled his eyes, obviously not impressed.

She continued. "He said they're combining waste product with glass, melting it down, and making new material where the nuclear waste can be stored while the radioactivity wears off."

Sauly ignored her explanation. "I'll tell you a secret. Guess who blew the whistle to the EPA?"

She looked at him skeptically. "You mean the Nuclear Regulatory Commission?"

"That's the one."

"I thought it was the group of women from Artemis. The ones who first suspected the higher cancer rates."

He grinned widely. "That's what they want you to think. Beacon blew the whistle. They go around the country scouting out old sites, getting their numbers in order. Then they feed a bunch of green-loving mamas some figures and coach them how to file a lawsuit." He threw his hands in the air. "Wha-la! The government knows they have to clean up the mess before they get hammered with another lawsuit. Pretty soon, Beacon has a new multimillion-dollar contract."

Josie shook her head. "Is this Sauly theory, or do you have something to back this up?"

"Dig around on the Internet. You'll find it all."

Josie turned her line of questions back to the reason for her visit. "So, you were in the room where they were cooking the new soup?"

"They caught me there twice. Second time they fired me."

"You didn't have clearance to be there?"

"Nope."

"Seems reasonable, then, that you got fired."

"I never said it wasn't. I didn't really need the money anyway," Sauly said.

"Did you ever see anyone hurt working there?"

He rubbed his head again and considered her question. "Not that I can remember."

"No one ever got radiation poisoning from working with the chemicals?"

Sauly turned his chair away from the table and stuck his legs and arms out in front of him and studied them. "I think I got a green glow at night, but that's about it."

Sauly sent Josie off with a loaf of zucchini bread he pulled out of his freezer. She sat in her jeep in his driveway and called Lou on her cell phone to check in.

"Cowan called," Lou said. "He wants to meet with you, Otto, and the county health nurse today. I already scheduled you all at the Trauma Center at three o'clock."

"That's perfect. Thanks, Lou."

"Otto and I got a lead on Santiago's family. Otto's running it down."

Josie could hear Otto talking in the background and Lou finally put him on the phone.

"I need sustenance. I haven't had a Coke all day. How about the Hot Tamale?"

"I need to run by Dillon's office first. I'll meet you in thirty minutes."

Josie drove back into town with the radio off, trying to sift through the details. It wasn't the information she expected to get from Sauly, but then again, it rarely was with him.

She pulled her jeep up to the curb in front of the office of Abacus and left her car running. She entered the office and found Miss Christina Handley sitting at her desk looking radiant in a silky white shirt and cream-colored skirt. She smiled broadly and said how nice it was to see Josie again. If Dillon's secretary was the least bit uppity Josie could have hated her, but she seemed genuinely kind. And, Dillon claimed she was an excellent secretary, which did nothing to help Josie's struggle with the lovely Miss Handley.

"I need to talk with Dillon for a few minutes if he's available."

Christina winked. "Certainly." After a momentary quiet conversation into her headset she motioned Josie back to his office.

Dillon stood from his desk as she entered. He raised his arms over his head and leaned back, groaning and stretching. He wore his standard attire: khaki pants, starched button-down blue shirt, and conservative yellow-and-blue-striped tie. His hair had been freshly trimmed and his face was clean shaven.

"I need a masseuse," he said, and flashed her a smile. He came around the desk and kissed her, then pulled back and asked, "Did you come to buy me lunch?"

"No, but Otto would. He's at the Hot Tamale waiting on me."

"Actually, I already ate. Christina brought me in homemade lasagna and fresh-baked bread for lunch today. She's serving the tiramisu later this afternoon."

Josie felt the hair on her arms stand on end. "You're lying to me, aren't you?"

He smiled. "I ate a peanut butter and jelly sandwich I brought from home."

She smiled. "I could make you some soup for supper tonight."

"How about you come to my place? I'll cook this time."

"Deal."

"Now, I assume you want something other than dinner," he said.

She sat down in the chair in front of his desk, he resumed his seat, and she filled him in on the Santiago murder.

"I'm hoping you can dig around and find out some information on Beacon. See what their reputation is, how solvent the company is, that kind of thing."

"Sure, I can do that." He narrowed his eyes and considered her for a moment. "Don't consultants usually get paid for working with police departments?"

She smirked. "What fantasy cop show have you been watching?"

He grinned and nodded his head. "Then we'll negotiate. I'm cooking dinner, and offering free consulting services. What will you be providing?"

Josie gave her best sleazy grin. "I've been staying up late sewing my lingerie apron. If you're lucky, maybe I'll model it tonight."

The Hot Tamale was raucous. The returning rain, coupled with the forecast for more, and a flood level that would not peak for several days, had the regulars on a manic high waiting for the next disaster.

West Texans had a complicated relationship with rain. Many a person spent time on their knees praying for rain for months on end, and after a few days of thanksgiving, flipped to prayers for the rain to cease. Josie couldn't think of anything else that was so desperately needed, worshiped, feared, and loathed as desert rain.

Otto had wangled their favorite table in the front of the diner. By the time Josie stopped to chat with a few patrons along the way and made it to the table, Sarah had left two Cokes and moved on to the next group.

"What's up?" Josie asked. She felt fairly good from a productive day, coupled with dinner plans that didn't involve cooking.

"Good news. Sort of. Lou tracked down Santiago's family. I spoke with his wife. I explained that we suspect her husband was killed. Her English was sketchy, but her daughter was there. I spoke to her as well."

"How did they take it?"

"They were shocked. They had already begun to think something was wrong because he hadn't called. His wife sobbed in the background as I talked to his daughter."

"You get anything new?" she asked.

"Santiago was married with four kids. Lived in Chiapas. Took his wife his paycheck each month to pay off a parcel of land in Central Mexico. A safe place where they could move their family. His wife said Santiago's dream was to raise the grandkids with no fear." Otto sipped his Coke and looked at Josie, his expression discouraged.

"Would she talk to you about his medical records?"

"She spoke Spanish and I could only understand about half of what she said," Otto said. "Her daughter said her father was in great health. She said she was certain he hadn't been receiving chemo, because he had no health insurance."

Otto frowned and leaned back as Sarah placed a bologna sandwich in front of him. She reached across the table to set a cold tamale and chips in front of Josie.

"How's it going, Sarah?" Josie asked.

"It's okay."

"You mind if I ask you a question about Juan Santiago?"

She looked surprised. "No, go ahead."

"I just wonder what your take on him is?"

Sarah shrugged, looking confused by the question.

"All we've been able to figure out is that he's quiet."

She smiled. "That's pretty much it."

"Quiet because he had no social skills? Maybe he was shy?" Josie asked.

Sarah narrowed her eyes and looked skeptical. "I don't think that was it. Brent drove him to work every day. And he still didn't talk! We even invited him over to dinner a couple times. He always said no." She tilted her head. "I hate to say this, but he just wasn't very friendly."

"Why did Brent drive him?"

"Juan didn't have a car. He used to have an old beater, but it basically died. Brent offered to help him out, and Juan never replaced his car! He said he was going to a few times, but he was saving his money. He took a bus home to visit his family each month."

"How's Brent taking all this?" Josie asked.

She shook her head. "He's not doing so good. He's taking it really hard. He stayed home from work today. I can't hardly get him to talk."

Josie glanced at Otto and leaned back in her seat. "I'd like to talk to one of Juan's coworkers about the plant. How about we stop by and talk to Brent today?"

Sarah lifted a shoulder, a helpless gesture. "Sure. Maybe talking it through will help."

Josie sipped at her drink as Sarah walked off. "I don't know where else we go with this. We can't go barging into the Feed Plant with nothing to tie the dead body to their operation."

"And what would we even look for?" he said.

"I don't know whether I hope there's a connection between the sores and his death, or whether I dread it."

"How about you? Sauly enlighten you?" he asked.

"As always. He claims Beacon is loaded. Their operation works like this—they find old nuclear plants. Then they convince a group of citizens—Sauly says women—that their town is contaminated and they need to file a lawsuit to make the government clean it up. Beacon lowballs a bid, gets hired, then a few years later requests more time and money from the government. Milks the contract for every drop it can get."

Otto smirked. "And the government is so happy to avoid a lawsuit they roll over belly-up. Beacon gets whatever it wants."

"Sauly's got life figured out," she said. "He should run for mayor."

Otto grinned. "You could be his campaign director."

Josie arrived back at the station at two thirty and finished up a case report from a drunk-driving incident and stood to stretch. She walked to the window at the back of the office and stared at the continuing rain. A small clock radio on Otto's desk played softly. They had both spent the afternoon listening to frequent updates about the flooding along the West Texas border. Mexico had received the most damage, but Presidio was evacuating all along the river. Sandbagging crews were working around the clock in Artemis. If the rain kept up as predicted, there was a chance Artemis would need to begin evacuations by week's end.

"You about ready?" Josie asked.

Otto looked up from his computer and glanced at his watch. "Day's flying. You driving?"

Josie borrowed Lou's umbrella to avoid the downpour, unlocked her jeep, and let Otto in the passenger door. She drove south two blocks to the Arroyo County Health Department—a brick ranch-style building that was located in the same structure as the Trauma Center.

The health department entrance led into a large fluorescent-lit room with rows of blue plastic chairs and low coffee tables covered with magazines, puzzles, and Legos. Several young mothers sat with small children in the plastic seats, most likely waiting for the free immunizations, the department's primary purpose in town.

They stared openly at Josie and Otto as they approached the receptionist who sat behind a glass window with a sign-in clipboard.

Otto spoke to the lady behind the counter like an old friend. She was in her fifties, a cheery woman with a short haircut that accentuated big brown eyes and a flashy smile. Josie didn't know her and remained behind Otto while they laughed about some event that had taken place at the Kiwanis meeting. The woman finally led them through a door and down a hallway and into a small office with a sign that read SHEILA MAGNUS—COUNTY HEALTH NURSE. The receptionist sat them both at a small round table and offered coffee and soft drinks before going back to her post. The door shut and a shriek rang out from an examination room down the hall. It sounded like a young child in serious distress.

Otto smirked. "They don't make kids like they used to."

Josie nodded. "They're not tough like we were."

A few minutes later, a harried middle-aged woman walked into the room, smiling and chattering, patting them both on the back before sitting across from them at the table.

"You have to quit beating the little ones," Otto said.

She laughed, her eyes still wide from the incident. "That little bugger tried to bite me! I gave him a shot in the butt and he went for my leg!"

Sheila wore a nurse's white top, pants, and shoes. Her wavy black hair and deep tan looked even darker against the stark white of her uniform. Josie had known her for years and had worked with her on several domestic and child abuse cases. She was a high-energy, conscientious worker whom Josie respected and liked.

Sheila sat down at the table. "Mitchell called and said he's hung up at the coroner's office. He'll be here in about fifteen minutes."

Josie nodded. "That will give me time to give you some background. I assume you've heard about the Santiago murder? The body found in the desert this past week?" Josie asked.

She nodded. "It's horrible. I heard the illegal crossing theory's already been shot down. Any leads?"

Josie tipped her head. "It's gotten complicated. We're coming to you with confidential information today." She paused.

"I understand."

"We have a male, name is Juan Santiago. He's in his forties, but we're still struggling with cause of death. He had multiple open wounds on both his arms. We're leaning toward some kind of radiation poisoning."

She pulled her head back and frowned in surprise. "You think he was over-radiated?"

"Not from a hospital. He worked at the Feed Plant. He was on the cleanup crew."

Sheila grimaced. "The old nuclear weapons plant?"

"We're concerned he may have been poisoned at the plant, but it's all conjecture," Josie said.

"Have you had any community members with strange wounds, or ailments that you can't explain?" Otto asked.

"Honey, people would be amazed at some of the strange things that can't be explained in here. But, outside of one patient, I haven't had any kind of sores like you're describing." She stood from the table and pulled a manila folder out of a filing cabinet behind her desk. She sat down and rifled through the folder and laid a photograph in between Josie and Otto. "Is this what you're referring to?"

They both nodded. Josie was certain they were looking at Juan Santiago's arms in the picture. She also knew HIPPA laws would prevent Sheila from confirming Santiago's identity.

Josie glanced at the photo and asked, "Can you tell me when this patient was seen?"

Sheila looked at the folder again. "The patient came in last Wednesday afternoon. I dressed his wounds and asked him to come back on Friday to let me reexamine him. I hoped to see him again, but you never know."

"Why not?" Otto asked.

She laid the folder down and crossed her arms on the table in front of her. "We see some people on a weekly, almost daily basis. Some of them are old and don't have any other contact with people. Some are lonely or social misfits. They just need to interact with people. Then there's the other side of the spectrum. There's a group of people who so mistrust us that they would choose death over receiving proper care. They associate us with the government, and they figure we're out to get them." She lifted both shoulders and turned her palms up. "What can you do?"

"Obviously the patient we're referring to was in the second group," Josie said.

"Hard to say. He was very nervous. I tried to reassure him. Tried to make him feel comfortable, but it didn't work. It was as if he thought the police would bust in the doors at any minute to cart him off to jail."

"Or back to Mexico," Otto said.

"I hate to admit it, but I think the pictures I took—only of his arms—freaked him out." She squinted at Josie as if feeling guilty. "But that's standard for anything we fear might be communicable."

"What was your diagnosis?" Josie asked.

Sheila grinned. "You know I can't tell you that. Nice try though."

Josie smiled in return. "Have you filed any reports to the CDC in the past month?"

She put a finger in the air. "That I can tell you." She stood again and rifled through her filing cabinet, and then laid a paper in front of Josie. "That's the CDC list of Nationally Notifiable Infectious Conditions for this year. We only report to them confirmed cases. Mystery diseases, like what we saw last week? There's nothing to report."

There was a quick knock, then the receptionist opened the door and stood back as Mitchell Cowan entered.

"Afternoon," Cowan said. "My apologies for being late."

Sheila stood and scooted a chair out for Cowan, who eased his considerable weight into the chair and sighed heavily as he hit the seat. Josie noticed Sheila smiling fondly at Cowan and wondered if there might be some interest outside of work.

"You look like you need a shot of caffeine. Can I get you coffee?" Sheila asked.

He looked up from the briefcase he was opening in front of him and smiled, although it was a sad, tired look. "That would be wonderful."

Sheila bustled out of the room and Cowan said, "I assume you've got her up to speed."

"We gave her the basics on Santiago. She showed us pictures of a man that was examined last Wednesday here at the clinic." Josie slid the picture over to Cowan, who glanced at it and scowled. "She couldn't provide much information, other than she didn't have any idea what the sores were caused by."

"And, she tried to convince him to come back for followup, but he didn't come back," Otto said. "She said that he seemed afraid, or at least mistrustful."

Sheila came back in and placed a steaming mug of coffee in front of Cowan. Josie was glad to see the cream in the coffee. She had known how to fix the drink without asking.

Cowan thanked her and opened a small laptop in front of him. His expression turned grim. "This morning I talked to a contact at the CDC who is quite knowledgeable about radiation diagnosis and treatment. He's sending us help tomorrow. We need to get a radiation assessment of the body, my lab, and each one of us. We'll need to include Cassidy and Danny as well."

Josie and Otto both looked at him in surprise. "What does that mean?" she asked.

Cowan pulled up notes on his computer and read from them. "Here's the crux of it. From what I was able to provide the CDC this morning, the scientist I spoke with confirmed a strong possibility of acute radiation syndrome. Considering the speed with which Santiago died, there is a chance he was hit with a massive dose."

Josie broke out in a cold sweat. "We stood right over the body and examined it. Are we in similar danger?"

"We won't know until we get the proper equipment and get each of us tested. Meanwhile, Sheila, it is imperative that you call immediately if you see any additional cases. At this point, we're approaching this as an isolated incident. If we find more people are affected, we could have a serious disaster looming."

"What about the Feed Plant? Couldn't they get us equipment?" Otto asked.

"The CDC is sending a certified hazardous materials technician. She'll help us with the equipment, help us assess the situation and come up with a plan. My contact at the CDC suggested as this point that we wait and use CDC equipment, as well as their staff. Beacon Pathways may be very well trained, but then again, they may not be. I'm not willing to take the gamble."

Josie was struggling not to look down at the picture of the sores lying in front of her on the table. "What do we do in the meantime?"

Cowan sighed heavily. "I know this goes against your grain. This is very unsettling. It is for me too. But I think we wait another half a day."

"You don't think a quarantine is in order?" she asked.

"Radiation is its own special kind of beast. Some radiation can be wiped on your skin and nothing will happen. You ingest the same thing and it will eat your insides up like battery acid. Some spreads through the air, others via surfaces. Some particles are radioactive for miles from the source and can be detected by a Geiger counter if a trace amount is on the shoe of a pedestrian that walks by. Other forms are only radioactive within centimeters of the source."

Josie listened to Cowan, trying to make sense of what he was saying. "I think we call Diego Paiva and get a list of anyone who had contact with the area of the plant Santiago worked in during his last three days there. We recommend they stay at home until we find some answers. I don't know what it could hurt."

Otto gave her a skeptical look. "Gossip travels at the speed of light in Artemis. The Hot Tamale would have it broadcast by nightfall. The trauma unit would be full. And what would we tell people?"

Josie looked at Sheila, who nodded in agreement with Otto. Josie finally shrugged. "Okay. We wait."

Josie left the meeting feeling numb. It had always been the unseen things in life that caused her the most fear: diseases, plague, nuclear radiation, bacteria, and parasites. She liked police work because the dangers were tangible. She could formulate a plan and attack it. A gun was a comfort. When she rested the palm of her hand on the butt of the gun in her holster she typically felt calm and in control. With this investigation she felt none of that.

She drove to Brent Thyme's at 4:15. After talking with Sarah that afternoon, Josie opted not to call Brent to tell him she was stopping by. Josie was curious why Santiago's death was troubling him so much, given that they weren't close friends. She realized the fact that Santiago had been murdered could be reason enough to upset Brent, but it was worth exploring.

The couple lived in a small beige stucco adobe behind the police station. Brent and his wife Sarah were sitting in lawn chairs just inside the open doors of a two-car garage, staying out of the downpour. Josie pulled her jeep up and noticed a small boy pedaling a tricycle in circles inside the garage. Josie got out of her jeep and ran for shelter. Brent stood and shook her hand.

"Sorry to barge in on you like this. I'm hoping I can ask you a few questions about the Santiago investigation."

Sarah offered drinks and when Josie declined Sarah took the little boy off the tricycle and said she needed to lay him down for a nap. She disappeared inside the house and Brent and Josie settled into the two lawn chairs facing the rain.

"Sarah said you're pretty upset about Santiago. Anything in particular?"

He looked surprised at her comment. "Well, no, other than my coworker is dead. That's pretty troubling."

"What can you tell me about him?"

Again, he looked surprised at the question. "What do you want to know?"

"No one knows anything about Santiago other than he loved his family and wanted to return to Mexico. There has to be something more."

Brent lifted his hands in a futile gesture. "I don't know what else I can add to that. I wish there was more we could help you with."

"Yet, this man with no connections to the community, no money, no friends, no family here in the U.S.—he ends up left for dead in the middle of the desert." Josie almost added, "wearing his work boots," but few people knew that information and she hoped to keep it that way.

Brent looked out into the rain. "I feel lousy about it now. I wish I'd made more of an effort with him. Tried to connect with him somehow."

"What about the work he did at the plant? Can you tell me what part of the plant Santiago was working in?"

"I can't provide you with that information."

She sighed. She should have anticipated his reaction, but opted to play the game out. "Why not?"

"When I was hired I signed a nondisclosure agreement. I'm prohibited from giving you any information about the inner workings of the plant."

Josie gave him a quizzical look. She was asking the questions to gauge his attitude toward the plant, more than his actual answers. If his answers were hesitant, unsure, she was fairly certain he would crack with enough pressure. "It's not as if you're giving out company secrets. The plant is closing down."

"They're still making new materials," he said.

She raised her eyebrows.

Brent groaned in frustration. Josie could tell he realized he'd already said too much.

"Look. I could get fired for talking to you. I was told it doesn't matter who comes asking for information, whether you're with the police or not. We're supposed to refer you to Paiva."

"I'll be talking with him later."

"I'm not allowed to discuss the plant."

Josie nodded. "I'm not here to cause you problems. I'm here because a man was murdered. Not only do I want to find the man's killer, but I want to make sure it doesn't happen again."

Brent turned in his chair and glanced back at the door leading into the house. "Are you able to keep my name out of this if I tell you something?" he asked.

"Absolutely."

"I mean, this remains completely anonymous."

"Yes, that's my intent," Josie said.

Brent sat for a moment and wiped the sweat off the back of his neck, then onto his shorts. His face was beet red and he looked miserable. "Santiago had been working in the pilot unit before he died. I know because I was working with him."

"I thought you worked in Unit Seven?"

"That's our assigned area. We spend most of our time there, but we have side projects in other areas. We'll occasionally do work out of the pilot unit. Santiago and I were assigned to the pilot for two days to sanitize equipment we'd been using in Unit Seven."

"What kind of work takes place there?" she asked.

"New projects. Pilots. Basic lab work. It's stuff Beacon tries out before the systems go live."

Josie narrowed her eyes in confusion. "Once again, I thought you were supposed to be closing the plant down. Why test new stuff?" She wondered if Brent's answer would match what others had told her.

He shrugged once. "Supposedly, it's new technology for radiation cleanup."

"You try new technology in the pilot unit, then try it out in the plant. If it works, I'm guessing Beacon sells it to others in the industry?"

He shrugged again. "Or the government."

"So, our government is paying them to clean up the plant, and they are using part of that money to develop new technology?" she asked.

He nodded.

"And then they turn around and sell it back to the government?"

"And the private sector," he said.

"So they're double-dipping."

"I guess you could call it that," he said.

"Can you give me an example of the kinds of projects that take place in the pilot unit?"

His face twisted in frustration, and he rolled his head as if stretching tight neck muscles. After a long moment he said, "After you left the other day? Paiva called all the plant supervisors in for an emergency meeting. Supervisors were told to personally meet with every one of their employees within twenty-four hours, even if it required home visits. Afterwards, Skip gave us copies of the nondisclosure agreement we signed. Someone had taken an orange highlighter and underlined the information on grounds for dismissal." He pointed his finger at Josie, then at his own chest. "This right here? I'll be fired if they find out. And I have a two-year-old, and a wife that makes little more than minimum wage."

Josie felt a stab of guilt for pushing him. If he chose not to share information she could call the company attorney and ask for assistance, but legally there wasn't much in her favor. A person could not be forced to talk.

She finally said, "Disregard the last question. I'll be talking with Mr. Paiva. I plan to ask him the same questions I've asked you. Your name will not be mentioned, nor will the information you shared with me. At least now I have a point of reference."

"I understand."

Josie opened the manila folder on her lap and pulled out several five-by-seven color photographs that Lou had developed for her earlier in the day. She handed the stack to Brent, who grimaced immediately.

"I'm sorry to have you look at these. They're pictures of Juan Santiago's arms the day we found his body. The sores are a big concern for us. They may be tied to his death. We have no medical records, so we're not sure if the situation was medical or possibly job-related. We're also concerned there may be a public health hazard that we don't know about." Josie paused and Brent nodded once. He flipped through the photographs, holding the edges as if he didn't want to touch the gruesome images.

"Did he have those sores on his arms when you last saw him?" she asked.

"Juan had some sores, but nothing like this." He stared at the last picture for several moments and appeared to consider Josie's question. He finally passed the photos back. "The last day he was at work I saw them. Just some red blisters on his arm. I saw him in the cafeteria, but he didn't talk to anyone. Most days he sat with us. That day he didn't. He went off by himself and ate. I saw the sores though when he went through the line. I wondered, you know? But it could have been a hundred different things. Then, we didn't see him again."

"You didn't mention the sores to anyone else you worked with?" He shook his head.

"Why didn't you bring this up at the meeting we had in the cafeteria?" she asked.

He gave a cynical laugh. "In front of Paiva?"

"This information could be critical to the investigation. It helps establish a timeframe. It could help the coroner determine a cause of death."

His expression had changed, but she couldn't read it.

"We have a radiation specialist from the CDC coming to talk

to us tomorrow. I would like for you to tell him what you know about the sores on Juan."

His face clouded over with anger.

"They're coming to help us, Brent. They want to make sure no one else ends up like Santiago." She stared hard at him, but he wouldn't meet her gaze. "You know more than you're telling me," she said.

After a moment, he held his right hand toward her, palm down, and pulled a bandage away from his skin. A blister, the size of a dime, was in the middle of his wrist.

Josie tried to hide the shock she felt. Her skin burned at the sight of it and she flashed back to the horrible images she'd just shown him of Santiago's arms.

"Sarah doesn't know. She thinks I burnt my hand on the iron."

"How did you get the sore?"

He shrugged, his eyes frightened. "I don't have any idea. When I saw the sores on Santiago, I didn't talk to him about them. I wondered. But, like I said, it could have been anything." He looked down at his hand and replaced the bandage. "Then I woke up this morning with this sore. It scared the shit out of me. Then you come here with these pictures and they're way worse than what I saw."

"Does anyone else at the plant have these same lesions?"

"I don't think so. No one has said anything."

"You need to tell all of this to the CDC tech. Show her the sores and tell her everything you can remember about the work you were doing."

He nodded, his expression sober and frightened. "If Paiva thinks we had an accident, and I didn't follow reporting procedures, I'll lose my job."

"Did you have an accident?"

"No! But he'll assume we did if he finds out I've been affected too!"

"If you didn't have an accident, then other people could be involved. You need to get checked immediately."

"You don't have kids. You don't have a family and a house payment."

Josie ignored his comment. "You say you don't know where the sores came from. Give me your best guess. Do you think it was exposure to radiation?"

His gaze was steady, but Josie was certain the internal struggle was seismic. He said nothing.

"I know you're worried about your job and your family. I'm not judging that. I respect it," she said. "But sometimes you have to be willing to look beyond your own self for the greater good. If this was a radiation accident, there could be other people affected. I touched Santiago's body. The coroner has worked on his exposed flesh for hours on end. There may be others at the plant who were affected that you don't even know about. And we don't know what kind of internal damage this could be causing to any of us." Josie could feel her face getting red, and anger creeping into her voice.

His expression never changed. "I'm telling you, I don't know how it happened."

"It's no longer a suggestion."

Brent bent over in his lawn chair and held his head in his hands for a long while, staring at the ground. He finally sat up, his expression resolute. "I'll meet with your CDC expert tomorrow. I'll give them everything I know."

SEVENTEEN

When Josie left Brent Thyme's house it was 5 P.M. She called Dillon and explained the radiation scare. She tried to cancel their plans for the evening, but he told her she was being paranoid and she agreed to a late dinner. Next, she called Cowan. He answered his cell phone on the first ring.

"It's Josie. I have some disturbing news."

"That's the only kind I get. Go ahead."

"I talked with another worker from the Feed Plant this evening. I just left his house. He found a sore on his wrist this morning when he woke up."

Cowan exhaled loudly. "Anyone else know yet?"

"No."

"Has he been to the doctor?"

"No. I'm the only person that knows about it. He's afraid if he talks about the plant he'll lose his job."

"I'd say the fellow has bigger issues than his job to worry about right now."

"I forced the issue. He's agreed to meet with the CDC in the morning to explain everything. I'm sure there will be an internal investigation at the plant, but I want him to talk with the CDC first."

"Good."

Josie drove toward home not seeing the road or the landscape. Her skin felt cold and damp. "You're still comfortable waiting until tomorrow before we make this public?"

"We can't let this information out without facts, Josie. The last thing we want is for people to panic. I should be back in my office by noon tomorrow with the tech. Just give me a little more time."

She hung up with Cowan feeling no better about their situation. The media thrived on stories like this, and they never ended well for the authorities. If the police spoke up too soon there was a mass panic. If the police waited too long they were hiding potentially deadly information.

Josie drove home, then fed Chester and gave him fresh water. He wandered into the living room and curled up on his rug. She took a hot shower, and in the bright light of the bathroom, looked over her body carefully for any bumps or blisters or sores. She knew she was being paranoid. She had read enough about radiation on the Internet to know that second- or thirdhand exposure was most likely not dangerous, but the worry nagged at her. After all, it was enough of a concern that the CDC was flying a technician to Texas the next morning.

She changed into a pair of ancient Levis and a soft pink T-shirt. When she was ready, she loaded Chester in the back of her jeep. He lay down on the backseat with his head on his paws. His eyes were closed before she made it back around to the driver's side, like a baby conditioned to sleep as soon as the buckle clicks on the car seat.

Dillon lived north of town in a small, trendy subdivision. His neighbors were primarily young to middle-aged career couples with at least one of the partners making a weekly commute to a larger city. Two of the houses were second homes for couples who spent winters in West Texas and summers up north. Dillon enjoyed the neighborhood and the eclectic mix of people and participated in the occasional block pitch-in. He could small talk and charm at a dinner party with ease, and Josie enjoyed people-watching while he carried the conversation. The *opposites attract* rule had worked well for her through the years, and was especially true with Dillon.

She pulled up his paved driveway and stopped in front of the garage. The house was a limestone-and-glass structure with long sloping sides and expansive windows. Even his sleek, stylish home, with its neutral colors, contrasted sharply with the warm colors of her little adobe in the foothills.

She knocked once and opened the front door. The air was cool and smelled like clean linen. Eggshell white walls and minimal gray trim were used throughout the house. The focus was the floor-to-ceiling windows in the living room and dining room that faced a landscaped garden Dillon had designed and planted. Smiling and breathing deeply, she felt the serenity of the space settle around her. She gave Chester his bone and he lay down in front of the couch, not even making it all the way to the kitchen to visit Dillon. She marveled at the dog's laziness.

Josie walked through the living room and found Dillon whistling along to classical music that filled the kitchen. His head was bent over a cutting board where he appeared to be slicing cabbage into thin strips. He looked up and smiled when she entered, then laid his hands on the cutting board and gave his full attention to her. She had encountered very few people in life who ever gave their full attention to anyone.

She crossed the kitchen and stretched up to kiss him lightly on the lips.

"You taste like Merlot," she said.

"You taste delicious."

She patted him on the back end. Dillon turned the music down and told her to dip the cabbage into the sauce in a bowl behind the cutting board. She dipped, and moaned at the taste.

"That's amazing. Sweet and tangy and creamy. Just a little heat. Where did you come up with this?"

He winked. "You set the table. We're almost ready."

"Hmm. What else?" she asked, scanning the kitchen.

"Apple sage pork chops. Wine in the fridge. French bread in the oven."

"You are the best," she said.

Dillon washed and dried his hands on a dish towel, then came over and wrapped one arm behind her back, and slowly ran the tip of his finger under each of her eyes. He leaned his face next to her ear and whispered, "You need sleep."

She shivered and smiled as he turned his head into her neck, running goose bumps up her spine.

"Maybe you can feed me and then tuck me into bed for the night."

Dillon trailed kisses from her neck, along her jawline, and finally to her lips. Her knees were weak before he finally pulled away and whispered, "My chops are burning."

She followed him outside where he opened the grill and poked a meat thermometer into the thick chops.

"How's Teresa? Think she learned a lesson?" he asked.

Josie looked doubtful. "I don't know. For a while, maybe. She's a tough kid with a lot of anger."

Dillon took the pork chops off the grill and they walked back inside. Josie pulled plates and glasses out of the cabinets, set the table, and poured wine as Dillon cleaned off the countertops and talked about his work and his ongoing frustration with government bureaucracy.

"It used to be red tape. Now it's policy written in such overwrought language you have to hire an attorney to interpret," he said.

Once they were seated, the dinner conversation eventually turned to Josie's work and Dillon's investigation into Beacon Pathways.

"You didn't need me. Sauly was right on it. Everything is out in the open. Much of what they do with small towns like Artemis is an image game. They portray themselves one way publicly to disguise the bigger picture. It's all completely legal and companies do it all the time."

"Give me an example," she said.

Dillon spooned sautéed apples over his pork chops and cut more French bread as he talked. "It's like the large companies with plants overseas. They pay their workers paltry sums so we get cheap clothing. They portray themselves as companies taking care of the little guy, but the *true* little guy gets screwed in the sweatshop. Or the companies who climb into bed with quasi-terrorist groups because it's the only way they can get to the bananas, or the coffee beans, or the spices they want."

Josie frowned, not sure she understood the connection. "Beacon is a little different, though. They aren't misrepresenting themselves as much as they are drumming up business."

Dillon sipped at his glass of wine and cocked his head. "On one level. But they don't make it clear their real profit doesn't come from the cleanup. It comes from developing new technology. They just submitted a patent this past year aimed at cleaning up spent fuel rods—some of the most radioactive of all waste materials. If the technology does what they claim, they stand to make billions."

"Which means they don't want to clean up the plant too fast if they can test new products in the meantime, and get paid to do it," she said.

"Exactly."

She sat back in her seat. "And what happens if a little radiation slop-over takes place and an employee gets burned? Would they risk a billion-dollar profit on a possible lawsuit?"

"Or the end of the company's impeccable safety record?" he asked.

"Maybe we know why they have such an impeccable safety record."

"Because they dump their mistakes in the desert?"

Josie hesitated. "You haven't heard the rest of it yet. I didn't give you all the details when I called this afternoon."

"Let's hear it."

"This goes no further."

He gave her a quizzical look. "That's a given."

"I talked with one of the other workers today from the Feed Plant. He woke with a sore on his wrist this morning. The same type of sore found on Santiago's arm."

Dillon looked up in surprise. "Did he get it from the plant?"

"He doesn't know."

"Have you told anyone?"

"Mitchell Cowan. He talked with the CDC today. They're flying someone in tomorrow morning to help us figure out what's going on."

He frowned. "Should this guy be quarantined?"

"I talked with Cowan. He thinks it's radiation. Santiago and the other man both worked in the same building together before Santiago came up missing. Now, it's a matter of calling in the right help to narrow down the cause. Cowan doesn't want to panic people before we have some answers. We at least need to get some direction." Josie drank her wine, glad for its bitter dryness. "There's another problem for the guy with the sore on his wrist. He's got a wife, son, and a mortgage, and he signed a clause on his contract that strictly forbids him from sharing any information about the plant."

Dillon was quiet. He was cutting his meat, studying it as if deep in thought.

"Hey. Do you want me to go home? Are you worried this could be contagious? Because it's crossed my mind too."

He looked up at her, surprised. "No, of course not! I'm just thinking. Nagasaki is about the extent of my knowledge of radiation sickness. But it sounds horrible. It just makes me wonder how many other employees might have been exposed."

* * *

After dinner was finished and supper cleaned up, Dillon went through a stack of information he had printed for Josie on Beacon Pathways. The information included their current holdings, profit margins, even a mission statement and ten-year business plan.

"Honestly? It's the kind of information that makes me want to buy stock in their company," Dillon said. "Beacon is opening another plant in California. They have a crew there now, taking stock and running environmental tests."

Josie frowned and scooted her chair away from the dining room table. She stared out the glass at the cactus and agave plants in Dillon's backyard. The sun had slipped below the horizon and left a purple haze across the desert floor. The whole situation bothered her on some level that she couldn't express. She felt jilted. It was the angry taxpayer syndrome. As a kid she used to listen to her grandpa rant and rave about people abusing the system. She'd just thought of him as an angry old man, but she'd been paying taxes long enough now that his words seemed less angry and more rational.

Dillon smirked. "Okay. What's your issue?"

"Where are the boundary lines? Beacon seems to be benefiting on all sides by dragging their contracts out as long as they can."

He shrugged. "Not against the law."

"Here's my issue. We're dealing with material that is so dangerous Paiva talked about burying it for thousands of years. I don't want him dragging his feet on this. I want this mess out of my backyard!"

"You'd have to prove negligence on their part," he said.

"That's just it. Who would do that? They're so specialized, and insulated out here. Who's keeping tabs on them?" she asked.

"I don't really know. I guess the Nuclear Regulatory Commission."

"The whole operation makes me feel helpless. And I hate that."

"So what are you going to do about it?"

"You in the mood for a late-night drive?"

He looked surprised. "I figured after your foray into Mexico last night that you'd get to bed early."

She raised an eyebrow. "How about a late-night trip around the Feed Plant?"

Dillon laughed. "You're serious. Right now?"

Josie nodded. She was wearing down from the previous night with little sleep. She knew she ought to go home, but curiosity had her. She wanted to see the Feed Plant on her own terms, away from Diego's careful watch.

He finally shrugged. "Let's do it."

Just five minutes outside of town, all other civilization disappeared. The night had cooled down to a comfortable eighty degrees, and the wind from the jeep's open windows felt like silk on Josie's skin. A smattering of stars shimmered around clouds that stretched down south into Mexico. By the time she reached the gravel on Plant Road, they hadn't seen another car for several miles. She stopped the jeep and turned off the engine. The chain-link fence that stretched around the perimeter of the plant appeared like a solid wall in the dark. Josie unclipped her Maglite from underneath her seat and shone it on a large rectangular sign that loomed in front of the gate. The sign read PRIVATE PROPERTY: BEACON PATHWAYS: TRESPASSERS WILL BE PROSECUTED.

Dillon pointed to a darkened gate shack. "They still use that?"

"No, there's a microphone and gate." Josie was looking through her night-vision binoculars and spotted a security camera at the top of the gate. She hadn't noticed the camera when she and Otto checked in. Diego had said the cameras were mounted at the gates but that they weren't monitored, only checked if a problem arose. She hoped that was true.

Dillon placed a hand on her thigh and whispered, "Listen."

They could hear the yips and barks of a distant pack of coyotes.

"Sounds like a bunch of drunken kids at a party," he said.

"The Christo Ranch connects to this side of the plant. I read an article in the *Sentinel* last week. He's got coyotes tearing up his calves," Josie said.

She got out of the jeep and shone her Maglite on the eight-foot-tall gate in front of them and was surprised to see it was unlocked and slightly ajar.

"There's a lawsuit waiting to happen." Josie looked at Dillon, who had followed her to the fence. "Either the security guard is really lazy or there's a reason they leave it unlocked."

Dillon pushed open one of the sides far enough to allow Josie to drive through. Leaving it open, he got back in on the passenger side. She eased the jeep forward, leaving the headlights off.

"I feel like I have a free pass to break the law when I'm with you," he said.

"Explain that one?"

"I'm forty-two years old, and I've never trespassed. At least not intentionally. And, as far as I can remember, I don't think I've ever driven at night with my headlights off."

"You're such a city boy."

"I grew up living in a house off a busy interstate in Los Angeles. I played at the Boy's Club, not outside."

"Why not outside?"

"My mother's biggest fears were baby-snatchers and smog." He lifted his hands straight up to the night sky. "It's why I love it out here. You get a sense of what eternity is."

Josie grinned. "It's a rush, isn't it?"

Leaving her headlights off, she drove slowly down the narrow gravel lane until they reached the second set of gates into the factory. Josie pulled her jeep off the gravel path and drove through rocky sand, around to the right of the fence.

"I noticed when Otto and I were out here, there was a gate the maintenance guys used."

Three hundred feet down the fence line they came across the

gate and found the padlock hanging unfastened on the fence. Josie made a mental note to tell Diego about his lax perimeter security and drove through the opening and down a rutted, muddy path that led to the main area of the plant. She pulled to a stop and killed the engine. They sat and listened to the silence, then slowly picked up the humming of various machinery and engines running throughout the plant.

She pointed to a building to the right of where they were parked. "See the sign in front of the building? That's the pilot unit. That's where the experiments are taking place. That's the last building where Juan Santiago worked before his arms became full of sores, and he ended up dead."

"You sure you want to go over there?"

"We'll just poke around."

"Maybe that's what got Santiago dumped in the sand," Dillon said.

Josie ignored the comment and opted to walk instead of starting the engine again. She had counted five cars in the front parking lot when they drove around the fence. She didn't know if they were security or night-shift workers.

A security light was posted in front of each building, but the muddy courtyard area between the buildings was dark in shadows. There was no rain forecast for the night, but the ground was still a mess. She stopped and pointed at the ground.

"It looks like a stream running through here," she said. "The rainwater is funneling in and washing out a path through the center of the plant."

As they approached the crane and dump truck that she and Otto had seen on their visit, she said, "Those haven't moved. Look at these buildings. Beacon has been here for over ten years. Even if they are working on new technology, you'd think they would have dismantled some of the buildings."

He pointed upward, toward the skyline, where the exposed beams of one of the larger buildings looked like a giant metal erector set. "They've obviously done some work. The outside walls are down."

"There were ten units when it was in full production. Count them now. Still ten. Actually eleven with the new building. They've expanded the plant!" Josie said.

They approached the pilot unit from the right side in order to stay out of the security light. Dillon caught her hand before they reached the side door. "You're sure this is safe? We don't have any protective gear."

"We wore hard hats the other day. That was it. Same as Paiva. With his experience, I can't imagine he'd walk around outside if things weren't safe."

As they approached the side door, Josie realized the door's window was blacked out with a tinted film, but light was visible around the edges. She placed her head against the glass and saw lights on inside the building and the vague outline of several men in white suits working around machinery.

The door opened suddenly and Josie faced a man wearing a full hazmat suit and helmet.

"Who the hell are you?" he yelled. The sound was muffled from the headgear, but his voice was loud and angry.

After the initial shock of getting caught, Josie pulled her badge from her back jeans pocket. Dillon stepped back into the shadow of the door. "My name is Josie Gray. I'm chief of police in Artemis. I'm investigating the possible murder of an employee of the Feed Plant."

"It isn't safe for you to be walking around without someone who works here. That's why we have No Trespassing signs posted. If you want to see someone, call ahead."

"I understand. I called too late tonight to meet with Mr. Paiva. I'll call in the morning. Sorry for the problem. We'll head back out." Josie waved and turned and walked away. The door closed immediately behind her, but she was certain they were being watched.

"Did you smell that place when he opened the door?" Dillon

said. "I felt like the smell alone would be enough to burn my insides."

"Like sniffing battery acid," she said.

"Don't you think it was odd he didn't ask what you were talking about? You mentioned a murder investigation and he didn't even acknowledge it."

"I'm sure the news of cops showing up spread like wildfire."

When they climbed back in the jeep Josie said, "Let's make one more detour before we leave."

"We're already busted. Why not?"

"I'm pretty sure you have latent criminal tendencies," she said.

He squeezed her thigh as she turned the engine on and drove the jeep toward the back of the plant with the headlights still off.

"Wait till you see this," she said. Josie pulled in front of a lot the size of a football field, filled with black barrels, some of them double-stacked. She turned her headlights back on so Dillon could get the full effect. "This used to be the back parking lot when the factory was in full production. As the waste started to pile up, the back parking lot filled. The number of workers decreased as the waste increased, until the barrels eventually took up the entire lot."

They both sat in the car for some time, staring at hundreds of barrels, most of them rusted and corroded. "It's one thing to read about this in the newspaper. It's entirely different to see it in your town's backyard," she said.

"They didn't actually make the bombs here," Dillon said. "This plant was just a part of the bigger process?"

"The Feed Plant took raw uranium ore and turned it into uranium metal. They shipped it east to factories where they fed the uranium into reactors for nuclear weapons. See the numbers painted on the outside of the barrels? They tell the plant operators what kind of waste is inside each one. Enriched. Remelt materials. Whatever."

"How the hell do you know all this?" he asked.

"After lunch today I spent some time on the Internet. While you were checking Beacon's financials, I looked into their so-called safe-cleanup operations. I have to admit, they have a pretty good record. They seem to have a good reputation in the field." Josie looked to her right and saw the miniature headlights from a golf cart approaching fast. "Damn."

"I hope you have bail-out powers. I don't want to spend the night in jail," he said.

The golf cart stopped and a very angry Diego Paiva exited and approached the jeep. He was wearing blue jeans and a white T-shirt, leather sandals, and a Cincinnati Reds ball cap.

"I believe you just informed one of my employees that you were leaving, not continuing to trespass." His voice was controlled but angry.

Josie nodded slowly. "You're right. I apologize. We're on our way out now."

"Who is this man?"

"This is Dillon Reese, a local accountant. He's doing some pro bono work for the police department."

"What exactly does an accountant have to do with Beacon Pathways?"

"This is a murder investigation, Mr. Paiva. The police ask intrusive questions from every possible angle. I understand what you're feeling."

"I doubt you do."

"Investigations often make innocent people angry at what feels like an invasion into their privacy."

He pursed his lips and looked as if he were trying to calm his temper before speaking. "I assume that as an investigator, you are not given carte blanche to wander private property aimlessly? I believe that's what warrants are issued for. I also believe you are way out of line."

Josie looked away from Diego and out across the barrels, and tried to phrase her response without cynicism, but he beat her to the punch.

"Let's not cloud your murder investigation with what appears to be your bigger issue." He nodded his head toward the barrels. "I'm not sure what you expect here. Over two billion pounds of waste were my inheritance when I took over cleanup. Two *billion* pounds. That's not waste you can take to a landfill. You can't burn it. You can't dump it in the ocean or bury it. So what do you do? People expect companies like Beacon to come in and clean things up with a broom and dustpan, but this is what I was left with." He nodded again toward the barrels. "It doesn't help when the police and media snoop around trying to find conspiracy when there is none. I'm not trying to hide anything here, Chief Gray. I'm trying to safely and effectively process this waste so you and I can raise our grandkids on this land without worry."

"I didn't go looking for a conspiracy theory. Juan Santiago showed up in the desert with open wounds on his body." She paused to gauge his response. His face remained impassive. "Preliminary findings are consistent with some form of radiation poisoning. He didn't have cancer. That leaves one rational explanation."

Diego crossed his arms over his chest and smiled slightly, as if her explanation was amusing. "If this happened anywhere but here you wouldn't even consider radiation. It would seem like a ridiculous idea."

"But it did happen here." Josie could feel Dillon tense beside her and hoped he would remain out of the conversation.

"There are a million different reasons a person might have open sores on his arms."

Josie caught his response. She had said Santiago's sores were on his body. Diego obviously knew about the sores.

"I have a few follow-up questions. Mind if I ask them now?"

He said nothing but didn't turn to leave, so Josie continued.

"I'm wondering about worker safety. When workers go home at night, do they leave their work clothes here at the plant?"

"Of course. We have strict safety guidelines. You'll find Beacon's safety record to be the best in the business. We have lockers where workers change into coveralls when they arrive. They wear something similar to a Geiger counter while here, and it is monitored by staff at the plant. They don't leave before changing back into their civvies."

"But when we found Santiago's body, he was wearing your company boots." She paused for a moment. Diego said nothing. "It means his dead body was either carried out of the plant, or the safety rules aren't followed as carefully as you imagine."

EIGHTEEN

Friday morning Josie woke early. She lay on her side, staring at her open closet door in the moon's predawn light, trying to find the detail that would connect the Santiago case. Finally, at a little before six she took a quick shower, dressed in her uniform, sent Chester out the kitchen door to lope back to Dell's house, and left for work by 6:45. Sprawling gray clouds covered the sky and blocked out all traces of the morning sunrise. It was a dismal day, and Josie intended to make good use of it.

When she arrived at the station, Brian Moore, the part-time night dispatcher, was hunched over a thick college-level textbook at the dispatcher station. He looked up with bleary red eyes and gave her a feeble smile. Brian had finished his law degree last year and was studying to take the bar exam for the second time. He had huge college debt and was working two part-time jobs to clear it. He was a nice guy who deserved a break.

She smiled and pointed at the page. "There's more yellow than white. Aren't you supposed to narrow that down some?"

His smile disappeared. "This will be the death of me yet. How do you highlight when every detail is important to the case?"

Josie nodded. "Wish I could answer that myself. Any action last night?"

"Nope. All's quiet."

"Good news. Can you hand me the evidence key?"

Brian fished the key out of the drawer in front of him and passed it across the desk to Josie. She wished him luck and headed for the evidence locker, where she signed her name on the clipboard hanging to the right of the door and flipped on the fluorescent lights. She found the Juan Santiago/Cassidy Harper document box on the shelves labeled *2012–2014*. She left the larger box with the bowling ball and college textbooks on the shelf, and carried the shoebox-sized container over to the examination table.

She looked at the paltry evidence through the plastic bags, fingering the wallet, the loose change, and the Case knife. She finally sat down at the table and aimed the desk lamp on the official inventory sheet that she had typed up. It listed all the items that were associated with the crime scene and that were either stored in the evidence room or were currently quarantined. She noted the clothing, the boots, the items in Santiago's pocket, and tried to find anything amiss. She considered the wallet found in Cassidy's car with no identification, but twenty-four dollars left behind. Had anything else been taken from him before he was left for dead?

And then it hit her like a bump to the head. He had no keys. Otto had told her he picked up the keys to Santiago's apartment from Junior Daggy. Otto had said the door was locked and the partial fingerprints he collected from the apartment all matched the set Josie had taken from the dead body. So, where were Santiago's keys? Did Cassidy Harper have the keys, same as she had his wallet?

Josie quickly packed the box back up, replaced it on the evidence shelf, and signed out on the log-in clipboard. Otto was just walking inside the front door of the department as Josie was giving the keys back to Brian.

"Morning all," he called.

"Same to you," she said.

"Son. You need a bed and a pillow," Otto said to Brian.

He nodded. "Lou will be here any minute."

Josie walked beside Otto toward the back stairs. "I studied the evidence list this morning for the Santiago case. We missed something. What about the keys to his apartment?"

"I know. I had to get them from Daggy," Otto said.

"If the keys are gone, what else might be gone?"

"I didn't find anything out of place. No stray fingerprints."

They reached the top of the stairs and Josie unlocked the office door and turned on the lights. She walked to the back of the office to make coffee and continued talking while Otto started his computer. "What was Santiago's sole motivation for being here?"

"He wanted to get enough money to buy a parcel of land," Otto said.

"And you didn't find a dime in his apartment?"

He shook his head. "Not a dime. No checks. No credit cards. Which I considered, but dismissed. He drove his money back home."

"We need to confirm what we heard from the workers at the Feed Plant. They claimed he made a trip to Mexico once a month to visit and take money home. We need to talk to his wife. How much did he bring home at a time? When was the last time he sent it?" Josie measured two heaping scoops and slid the basket into the coffeepot. "Maybe we've been so hung up on the radiation poisoning that we missed the real motivation for his killing. Maybe someone killed him for a shoebox full of money."

"Doesn't explain the sores. Or the wallet with twenty-four dollars left in Cassidy's car," Otto said.

Josie sat down at her desk and turned her chair toward Otto. "It's driving me crazy. I feel like we're missing something. A detail that's right there."

"That means we're close," he said.

"I had an interesting night last night."

"Maybe I don't want to hear this," he said.

"Dillon and I drove over to the Feed Plant and snooped around."

He raised his eyebrows. "You get caught?"

"Yep. We found the pilot unit up and running. Men in white suits hard at work behind black-tinted windows. They caught us peeking in the door. They ran us off and we took a side trip to check out the barrels in the back lot. That's when Paiva showed up on his golf cart to run us off."

His eyebrows went up again. "That guy must live there." A smile spread across his face. "Got run off by the big dog. He give you grief?"

She nodded. "He gave me a lecture on their safety record. The precautions they take, like changing into the company uniform when they arrive. Back into civvies before they leave. He acted surprised when I told him about Santiago wearing the company boots. I haven't told him yet about the plant gates that were both unlocked to anyone wanting entrance."

Otto looked puzzled. "Hang on. Let's think about the timeline."

Josie rolled her chair back over to her desk and found her notebook. She opened it to a blank page, propped it on her lap, and turned back to Otto.

"Let's work backwards from the time his body was found," he said.

"The body was found on Monday, the fifteenth. Cowan believes Santiago was killed late Saturday night or early Sunday morning," she said.

"We have nothing Friday or Saturday. Thursday was the last postmark on the mail I found on his table."

"Wednesday was the first day he didn't show up to work." Josie looked up from her notebook. "And it was the day he visited the nurse."

They both stared at their notes in silence, formulating their own questions.

"First thing I want to know is Santiago's work duties on Monday and Tuesday last week. I'll call Skip and ask him to e-mail a detailed list," Josie said.

Otto was leaned back in his chair with one arm resting on his stomach, the other elbow resting on his forearm as he rubbed his chin. Josie had seen the pose countless times through her years of watching him puzzle through various cases.

He said, "I want to know what he did on Thursday, Friday, and Saturday. When I call his wife about receiving the money, I'll ask if she knows what he did in his spare time. She said she hadn't spoken with him for over a week on the phone, but that wasn't unusual. They each had a disposable cell phone with limited minutes."

Josie squinted at Otto, trying to remember the details. "What was the situation with his cell phone?"

"We haven't found his phone, although his wife says he had a throwaway model. She told Lou the minutes were gone on her phone and her grandson took it. He's now lost it. She claims the whole family is trying to track her phone down. Hoping he left them one last message."

"I want to visit Cassidy again too. See if she found a spare set of keys." She stared at her notebook for a moment. She finally said, "I'll check out Santiago's place again. Maybe I'll find a shoebox full of money we can send to his wife. I'll stop by and see Diego Paiva on my way back. I'm sure he has an earful for me." Josie stood and picked her jeep keys up off her desk. "Call me if you learn anything."

Santiago's apartment was barely illuminated from the gray morning seeping inside one curtainless window in the kitchen. Josie pulled a pair of latex gloves from her back pocket, pulled them on, and flipped the living room light switch.

She broke the one-room apartment into quadrants to make sure that she didn't overlook anything. She started with the bathroom, which was a quick search. She found a shower stall that allowed no storage of anything except shampoo and a bar of soap, and a medicine cabinet over the sink that held a few over-the-counter medications and shaving supplies.

The kitchen area took more time. Josie checked each cabinet, top and bottom, the refrigerator, the oven and the drawer below it. Everything was neatly organized; the cans lined up with the labels facing out and three pasta boxes in a row. She checked under the bed and mattress, behind the headboard, and then tried the closet. She rifled through his clothing, arranged with shirts on the left, pants on the right. She checked the pockets for any stray papers.

When she bent down on her knees to check the bottom of the closet, the shoes caught her eye immediately. A pair of tennis shoes and a pair of inexpensive loafers were lined up under the pants. A pair of cowboy boots were lying on their side, half on top of each other. A beige hand towel, the same color as the carpet that covered the entire apartment, lay partially over the boots and the loafers. She pulled her flashlight off the clip on her gun belt and shined the light on the floor. In the corner of the closet, behind a slight imprint made by the heels of the cowboy boots, was another flattened area. A space, roughly twelve inches by eight inches, was pressed into the carpet. Josie was certain a box had once been kept in the closet, covered by the towel: someone had knocked the boots out of the way and made off with Santiago's money.

After Josie left, Otto sat at his desk and rifled through his notes until he found Abella Santiago's phone number. It would have been better to have Marta call and talk with her, but she wouldn't be on duty for several hours. Abella answered on the third ring.

"Hello?"

"Mrs. Santiago?"

"Yes?"

"This is Officer Podowski. Could I speak with your daughter?"

After several minutes the same daughter Otto had spoken with during his last phone call came on the line.

"Yes. You have news?" Her voice was soft but anxious, her speech heavily accented.

"I'm sorry. Just more questions. I'm hoping you can help me track down some information that may help us better understand what happened to your father."

"Yes," she said. "I'll try and help you."

"From information we've gathered from people your father worked with, it sounds as if he was in the U.S. to save money to send home to his family. Would you agree with that?"

"That was why he went to Texas." Her voice broke as she continued. "He worked so hard for us."

"Can you tell me when he last sent you money?" Otto asked, his voice gentle.

"Oh, he never mail money. He never—" She paused, obviously trying to come up with the correct words. "No banks in America. No mail. He was afraid of jail, then the bank would take the money."

Otto paused. "But he was here legally."

"I tell him that! But he was always afraid."

"How did you receive the money?"

"Once each month he came home. He most of the time came home on the middle of the month."

"So, you saw him the weekend after the first of July?"

"No." Her voice was distant and he could hear her speaking Spanish with her mother in the background. She finally came back on the line. "He last came home June sixteen."

"Was he paid every two weeks?" Otto asked.

"No. On the first and the fifteenth of each month. He brings two checks with him."

"He hadn't been back since June to see you?"

"No."

"Why didn't he visit you over the July fifteenth weekend? He had two checks for you, right?"

She began crying softly. "He never said why. He just could not come yet. My brother is angry, asking when we can get his money to pay bills. I told him it's disrespectful to talk about money just now. We have to be patient."

"Do you know where your father kept the money in the apartment?"

"In a box. In a closet."

Otto thanked her for the information and hung the phone up. His body felt heavy with the knowledge. He knew there would be no box. He'd checked the closet and found nothing but shoes.

He called Josie on her cell and she answered immediately.

"Are you still at Santiago's?" he asked.

"I'm on my way back."

"You check the closet?"

She paused. "The missing box?"

"Damn it. His daughter said he kept the box in his closet."

"I found the spot. The carpet was pressed down. Someone has Santiago's keys and his money," she said.

NINETEEN

Josie parked her jeep outside the department, intent on going back to the evidence room. Something had occurred to her at Santiago's house and she was anxious to check the information. She retrieved the key from Lou and logged in on the clipboard.

Inside, once the fluorescent lights had flickered on and warmed enough to light up the dark room, Josie found the smaller of the two evidence boxes for the Santiago case and carried it to the examination table. She turned on the table lamp and lifted the box lid. Inside, she found the plastic bag labeled LIBRARY RECEIPT. She opened it and lifted out the receipt that Leo Monaco had provided her for his visit to the library during the time that Cassidy Harper was finding the dead body.

It had occurred to her that she couldn't remember Leo's purpose for driving all the way to Presidio to check out library books. Granted, the Arroyo County Library was nothing to brag about, but most people didn't drive out of county, especially with an interlibrary loan program.

She unfolded the small white slip of paper and read the light purple ink. He had checked out four items: *Radioanalytical and*

Nuclear Chemistry; *Physics and Chemistry of Fission*; *Concepts and Trends in Radiation Dosimetry*; and the one Josie could have kicked herself for not seeing before: *Dirty Bombs*.

She carried the library slip to the photocopier in the main office and made a copy, then tucked the receipt back into the plastic bag and replaced it in the box. She put the evidence box back on the shelf, signed out on the clipboard, and handed the key back to Lou, who was talking on the phone.

Josie took the stairs to the second floor two at a time and found Otto sitting in front of his computer looking glum.

She pulled her rolling chair over to his desk and sat down, facing him.

"Not only do we know someone stole Santiago's keys and stole his money either before or after his death, we also finally have a lucrative connection to Cassidy Harper."

Otto raised his eyebrows.

"I just went back to the library receipt that Leo gave me. He used it to prove he had nothing to do with Cassidy being in the desert."

Otto nodded. "Yeah?"

"Guess what books he checked out?" she asked. Grinning, she handed him the copy of the receipt.

Otto read the list. "Son of a buck." He looked up at Josie, his expression incredulous. "You suppose he's plotting something?"

"Dirty bombs?"

"What if he was working with Santiago? Maybe they were selling uranium on the black market." Otto slapped his knee. "When I interviewed Colt, she mentioned seeing Santiago talking to men in suits. She even thought it was odd."

Josie shrugged. "I say we pay Mr. Paiva a visit."

"What about Leo? Any chance we can get a warrant? Check for the missing box, the missing keys? We've already found Santaigo's wallet in his car."

Josie shook her head. "Not his car. Cassidy's. I don't think a judge would see a close enough connection to Leo at this point. So he has some library books on radiation. He was a science instructor."

"Cassidy's dad told me he doesn't have a job. Didn't you say he's got something part time?"

"He said he's doing research part time. He made it sound like the books he checked out were used for his research. Let's find out if he's telling the truth," she said.

Otto stood and walked to the back of the office where his gunbelt hung on a hook. As he buckled it around his waist, he glanced out the back window in the office and stopped. "We may have bigger issues to deal with. I talked to Smokey. He said if this rain keeps up today, we'll probably have to start evacuations by tomorrow."

Josie rubbed at the muscles in her neck and felt her energy drain. "Have you thought about how this flooding may affect the Feed Plant?"

Otto gave her a look that said he had not.

"I keep thinking about those metal barrels at the back of the plant. If the foothills north of the plant start washing we could have a mess," she said.

Josie pulled her cell phone out of her shirt pocket and dialed the sheriff.

"Martínez."

"It's Josie. You doing okay?"

"Been better. Figure out how to keep people from driving down flooded roads I'd be a hell of a lot better," he said.

"What's the flooding status?"

"We've shut down four county roads. Pulled out three cars from flooded roadways. All three drivers were people who should've known better."

"Anybody hurt?" she asked.

"No injuries. South Branch Road is the worst. We've got two houses we'll need to evacuate by tomorrow."

"What do you know about the Feed Plant?" she asked.

"What about it?"

"I need to catch you up on the body that was found off Scratchgravel. The deceased worked at the Feed Plant so we've spent some time out there. I'm just wondering if they have any kind of evacuation or emergency plan."

"They have an emergency plan. I've got a copy in the office. I don't imagine there's a big contingency for flooding. That area has a decent slope to it."

"As long as it doesn't wash out."

"Why do you ask?"

"Have you seen the number of old rusty barrels they have stacked behind the plant?"

He made a noise but didn't respond.

"I'm wondering about runoff from the mountains surrounding the plant."

"I can't take any more men off the road right now."

"I'll check it out and keep you posted," she said.

Josie hung up and faced Otto, who stood ready to walk out the door.

Josie pulled her chair back over to her desk. "Let me call Paiva's office and make sure he's in." She checked her phone list on her computer and found his number. She reached Sylvia Moore first.

"Mr. Paiva has a full schedule today. The first I can squeeze you in is Monday morning at nine thirty."

"Please tell him this is urgent. We need to speak with him this morning."

"One moment."

Josie covered the receiver with the palm of her hand. "I don't imagine he'll be very happy to have to see me today."

After several minutes she came back on the line. "He'll see you in thirty minutes."

"We'll be there."

* * *

Otto drove and Josie sat in the passenger seat making a list of questions they wanted to address. The sky was overcast, but the rain had stopped for the moment. The streets in downtown Artemis were passable, but once Otto and Josie hit the county, mud and streams of water crossed the roads making it almost impossible in some places to determine where the road began and ended. Some of the arroyos were overflowing, and the sheriff's department had already prohibited travel to certain areas of the county. The maintenance crews had been putting in mandatory twelve-hour days and were still barely keeping up with the workload.

Otto pulled onto Plant Road and they saw a large dump truck blocking the road a half mile ahead. As they drove forward, the truck advanced slowly, dumping a layer of gravel behind it. They could see that sections of the road had washed out completely and were now being built up again. It looked like a losing battle, but at least they were fighting.

As was the case with their first visit, by the time they stepped out of Otto's jeep, Sylvia was walking briskly across the lot toward them. After a sour "good morning," they walked into the building and were taken to Diego Paiva's office where he met them at the door and showed them to the conference table.

"We appreciate you changing your schedule for us today," Josie said.

"Absolutely. I hope you've come with news about Juan."

Josie noticed his demeanor was a bit cooler than their first meeting, but it appeared he did not intend to bring up the previous night.

"We've come for two different reasons. We have follow-up questions regarding the Santiago case."

He nodded once.

"I also talked with Sheriff Martínez this morning. He asked that I check to see if you need support in regard to the flooding situation."

"I appreciate that."

"If the rain continues we're concerned how the flooding may affect the plant."

"I have an engineering team handling the preparedness plan."

"I'm most worried about the wash from the foothills to the north of the plant," Josie said.

"As are we. This is not being taken lightly. The team is to have recommendations to me by this afternoon. You are welcome to attend the meeting."

Josie nodded. "Good. What about someone from county maintenance? I think we need to keep them in the loop."

"Absolutely. I'll have Sylvia make the call."

"Okay. Switching topics. We're making progress on the Santiago murder," Josie said.

Diego's expression was focused and attentive but unemotional. She figured he played a great hand of poker.

"What can I do to help?" he asked.

"Is the name Leo Monaco familiar to you?"

His eyebrows rose in surprise. "Yes. He's working as a consultant for us. He's actually conducting scholarly research."

"Which means?" Otto asked.

"Beacon performs laboratory research, but there is a lot of information that must be culled through in order for us to stay current. You can imagine, any company conducting scientific research has to stay up to date in the field. Just as important, we need to stay abreast of past research that may inform current projects. We often don't have the time or manpower to conduct the scholarly research, so we'll hire out to grad students."

"How did you connect with Leo?" Josie asked.

"He applied for a job here last year for a lab position, but he had no direct experience. He was, however, bright and well versed in physics and chemistry. I called him and offered him a job collecting research on a current project we're working on."

"What kind of project?" she asked.

He considered her for a moment before responding. "We're conducting a dose reconstruction process for the area."

Josie frowned. "Which means?"

"We're looking at the amount of various chemicals in the environment versus the amount of various diseases typically associated with those chemicals."

Surprised, Josie let her reaction show.

Paiva smiled. "Contrary to popular sentiment, we're the watchdogs. We're here to keep you safe. Leo has access to several thousand documents and historical records that were collected during the lawsuit. He's compiling data. Our internal researchers will then assess the data."

"Is he a good employee?" Josie asked.

"He's done an excellent job analyzing and synthesizing data for us."

"What kind of pay does he make?"

"Just above minimum wage."

"And he's working part time?" Otto asked.

Diego nodded. "I'm sure he deserves more for the work he's doing, but that's the pay structure. That type of research is considered data entry on the pay scale."

"Can you imagine any reason he would want Juan Santiago dead?" Josie asked.

He gave her a look as if she'd said something ridiculous. "Why would you ask that?"

"Would he stand to gain anything by killing Santiago? Or disposing of his body for someone else?" she asked.

He smiled slightly, obviously put off by her questions. "I cannot imagine any reason why Mr. Monaco would gain something by killing a coworker."

Josie frowned. She didn't like to share details of the case without good cause, but sometimes one detail was sufficient to bring out additional information. She had reservations about Paiva, but she was also willing to bargain.

She said, "Leo Monaco's girlfriend discovered Santiago's body.

She's been evasive, hasn't been able to provide any reason why she was walking in the desert on a hundred-and-four-degree day. Or how she happened to find a body a quarter mile off the roadside." She paused. "Then we discover today that her boyfriend is a consultant for the same company that Santiago worked for."

Diego's eyes narrowed. He crossed his legs and laced his hands over his knee. "I don't know if it's typical police procedure, or whether the vibe is genuine, but I have gotten the feeling from the beginning that you find either me, or my company, culpable in my employee's death. I'm not sure what you expect from me. Perhaps it's time our company lawyers became involved."

Otto stepped in, ready to take the focus off Josie. "It isn't that we think any one person or company is innocent or guilty. The murder investigation is open. Someone murdered your employee. So far, every credible lead we've had has been linked to the Feed Plant. That doesn't make anyone guilty or innocent."

"But we'd be incompetent if we didn't pursue those leads," Josie said.

"Fair enough." Paiva stood from his chair. "Please understand, I've been with this company from its early years. Beacon Pathways is highly respected in the industry. And regardless of your own personal beliefs about the plant, our safety record is unbeatable. I find it highly unlikely that an employee was irradiated and left for dead."

Josie nodded, but she was fully aware that every guilty man she'd ever interviewed made similar pleas of innocence. "One more question on Leo. One of the books he was reading was about making dirty bombs. Does that concern you given his connection with the plant?"

He sighed. "This plant used to aid in the production of nuclear weapons. It does not surprise me that people who work here, or even people who live in this community, would have a curiosity about such things. I would hope the police wouldn't judge a man based on his reading list."

Josie smiled slightly. "One more question. Would you ask Mr. Bradford to provide me a detailed list of job duties that Juan performed his last two days at work?"

"Certainly."

Josie glanced at Otto to see if he had further questions, and he stood from the table.

"We appreciate your time this morning. I know you have a busy schedule." She and Paiva stood and he extended his hand toward her.

"I want justice for the Santiago family. Whatever it takes."

TWENTY

Josie followed Otto outside the building and into the rain.

"I thought we were supposed to get a reprieve today. Didn't you tell me that?" Josie asked as they jogged to the car.

"I was thinking positive. Isn't that what you're always harping on me to do?"

Once inside the jeep Otto turned on the local weather station. He drove down Plant Road grousing about Paiva's arrogance. Josie had found his demeanor more down to earth at this meeting, but she let it go. She could tell Otto's mood had turned dark. She had worked with him long enough to know the missing money box in Santiago's apartment would be eating at him. He would feel responsible for not making the connection earlier.

"So where are we with Leo? What would give us enough for a search warrant?" he asked.

Josie rubbed her temples and sighed. "I think he stole the money. The judge may allow it since we've got the wallet and Santiago's fingerprints on it. But I doubt it."

"Hell, he's not going to have that box. Making minimum at a

part-time job? He'll have that money long gone or squirreled away somewhere," he said, dismissing his own idea. "Out of Cassidy's reach."

Josie considered Otto's comment. "Or, we catch a break, and Cassidy knows Leo took the money. I'll pay her a visit. Ask her if she's found an extra set of keys."

"I know you don't want to hear this," Otto said, "but maybe we discounted Cassidy too soon. Maybe she factors in."

Josie frowned. "It's crossed my mind. I hope I didn't misjudge her."

"She and Leo could both be tied to the murder. The evidence supports it," he said.

The cell phone in her pocket vibrated, and she slipped it out.

"Chief Gray."

"This is Diego. We have a problem. Can you come back? Now?"

"We're on our way." Josie twirled her finger in the air to signal Otto to turn around. He gestured to either side of the road to show her it was too washed out.

"What's going on?" she asked.

"Sandy Davis, the lead engineer studying the flood problem, is here in my office. She and another engineer took a helicopter up to check the mountains. They spotted a breach this morning. The chance of a mudslide just increased tenfold."

"How much time do we have?"

"She said it was hard to speculate. They spent all morning checking measurements. There's so many variables. Including the current rain."

"What kind of problems are you talking about?"

He sighed. "It's best if we talk in person."

"Okay. Worst-case scenario. How long?" Josie listened to Diego's muffled voice as he conferred with his engineer. He finally came back on the line. "If the mountain runoff breaks loose, a mudslide is imminent. She thinks worst case is three hours."

Josie felt the panic well up in her throat. "Have you started making calls for resources—people and agencies who can help with an evacuation?"

"Sylvia is on the phone. Another engineer is helping her place the calls. She's already called your county maintenance."

"We'll be there in five."

On the drive back to the plant Josie reached Lou and filled her in on the situation. She requested that Lou call Marta in for assistance but was told that the mayor had just sent her over to Presidio to aid in an evacuation. Two families were stranded in their homes due to flooding and the water was rising.

"I was picking up the phone to call you and Otto out when you called. I've lived in Artemis twenty years and never seen flooding like this," Lou said.

"Keep me updated. I'll check in after my meeting at the Feed Plant."

Ten minutes later Josie and Otto were sitting in a large meeting room at a conference table. Sylvia Moore had ushered them in and placed coffee on the table for them, then sat down at the far end where she turned on a laptop. Diego entered shortly after and one woman and three men followed behind him. Lines radiated from his eyes as he talked quietly to the woman, who Josie assumed was the lead engineer at the company. He pulled her chair out for her and she sat, the conversation never missing a beat. She had short gray hair cut close to her head and wore a tasteful starched blue shirt and dress pants. Josie figured she was in her late fifties and thought she appeared to have an easy disposition.

Diego remained standing and called them together with few formalities.

"I realize we don't have the full group. As more people become involved, we'll update as needed. Sylvia will be typing up our plan so we'll all be clear on the details." He glanced at the wall where her notes were being projected.

He sat down and cleared his throat. "First, introductions. To my left is Chief of Police Josie Gray. She and Officer Otto Podowski actually met with me earlier this morning about our disaster preparedness plan. I appreciate the department's fore-thought." He gestured to Otto, who nodded to the engineers across the table. "They will be our liaisons with the law enforcement agencies and will be key to moving this plan forward. If we need additional manpower I will count on Josie's help to work with area residents."

Diego looked at Josie and she nodded in agreement. Rarely were the local police afforded the respect that they deserved for their experience and expertise in dealing with local disasters.

"To my right is Sandy Davis. She is our lead engineer. She knows the layout of the plant, including the danger areas, better than anyone." Sandy introduced the three men sitting to her left, all of whom were engineers. They obviously would be taking their orders from her. And, finally, she introduced Scott Franklin, a chemical expert.

Diego took over the meeting again. "Sandy, I'd like for you to first explain the concern you shared with me before the meeting. It's important we put this into perspective for everyone."

She straightened her back and folded her hands on top of her legal pad. Her face was lightly freckled and it reddened as she began speaking. Her voice was quiet but controlled and confident.

"I have been following radiation disasters throughout the world for thirty years. There have been surprisingly few. Given the potential for disaster, the industry has put strenuous safeguards in place. With that comes a cost. When a catastrophe does strike, there is very little to fall back on in terms of response and baseline data. To my knowledge, I don't know of another former weapons plant that has faced flooding, or more specifically mudslides." She turned to Josie and Otto. "This is new territory, and we don't have a sufficient response. The tsunami that hit Japan was a completely different situation. We're not dealing with reactors or meltdowns. We're dealing with enriched uranium byproduct. Waste that is highly radioactive."

"Are you referring to the barrels?" Josie asked.

She nodded. "In part. They are the most immediate concern because the mudflow would hit that area first. But there are other areas of the plant that could be in more serious jeopardy. The pilot unit has a significant amount of high-level radioactive matter. It would be disastrous if that building was compromised. We also have two concrete silos that are not in good shape."

"What's inside them?" Otto asked.

"Sludge. Radioactive byproducts. The waste is safe inside the concrete, but you know the immense damage that can be wrought by a mudslide. If the slide gains momentum as it comes down the mountain, and picks up debris along the way, it will act like a bull-dozer by the time it hits the plant. My greatest fear is that it will pick up those metal barrels and they'll have the force needed to tear down the silos and certain buildings in their path."

She stopped, and no one spoke for a time.

Finally Diego broke the silence. "Our current disaster plan does not sufficiently prepare us for a mudslide of the magnitude that we're facing. Mudslides have never been a serious risk until now. In the past, heavy rains have funneled to the east of the plant due to the natural contours of the land."

Sandy broke in. "It's the mountain range behind the plant. Specifically, Norton's Peak. Our pilot's been flying over it the past two days. It's crumbling. And there's a great deal of mud and debris coming with it. We have concrete barriers in place, but the response won't be enough if we have an actual slide."

Diego said, "I'd like to list the major issues we're facing, and then we'll prioritize." He turned to Josie. "Finally, we'll come up with a command group and dole out responsibilities." He glanced around the table and received nods.

Over the next twenty minutes the engineers made a list of key areas that had to be protected. They also agreed they needed the helicopter back in the air to monitor the flow. Once the list was generated, they prioritized and starred the situations that had to be dealt with immediately. Finally, Sylvia took the list and put it into a table format and they began listing agencies and key personnel that needed to be called for information or manpower.

One of the engineers walked to the back of the room to call the helicopter pilot, who was fueled up, ready to fly, but on hold waiting orders. He was told to take two other engineers to fly the area and collect information to share with Mike Ramey, one of the engineers at the table. In his early twenties and fresh out of graduate school, Mike wasn't quite smiling with excitement, but he was obviously glad to be a part of the response group.

"Let's get a camera up there too," Mike said. "We can get a live feed in here to monitor what they see from the air."

Sandy gave him a thumbs-up and he left the table to get it set up.

Diego was saying, "Our number-one goal is to shift that slide so it moves around the plant, not through the middle of it. This was part of our emergency plan, but we hadn't seen it as an immediate threat. The flows have always taken place east of here, but something broke loose in the mountains with the foot of rain we received this week. Everything has shifted course."

"Wouldn't it be faster and more reliable to organize a quick-response team to move the material? Why not get as many flatbed trucks and semis—every truck we can find—to move those barrels to higher ground?" Josie asked.

Diego stared at Josie for a moment and she assumed he was choosing his words carefully.

He pursed his lips and ran a finger between his neck and shirt collar as if trying to stretch the fabric. "The barrels are not in moveable condition. We've held off on the waste in the barrels because we're close to a better solution for storage. They were better off stationary than moving them twice," he said.

"So what you're saying is that the barrels are corroded to the point that we can't move them?"

"That's correct."

"What happens if they're moved in the mudslide?" she asked.

"The barrels in the back third of the parking lot were placed there first. They've received the most weathering. They are what we're most concerned with. The metal on some of the barrels has weakened. They are not leaking. There's no groundwater contamination. However, I would not feel comfortable moving them without precautions."

"We don't have the time to move them safely," Sandy agreed.

"How do you divert a wall that could weigh hundreds of tons by the time you figure in the momentum of the moving debris?" Otto asked. "I've seen news footage of people trying to divert mudslides, and they usually end in disaster."

Sylvia raised a finger and held a phone receiver against her chest. "Mr. Paiva?"

He nodded for her to continue.

"Department of Transportation is sending a team. They should be here in thirty minutes. Environmental Protection Agency is flying in a team as well, but they're about an hour out." Paiva thanked her and she put the phone back to her ear.

He continued. "We're in agreement. We've all seen the slides in Japan where entire interstate systems were wiped out in a matter of seconds. Those massive structures didn't even slow the mudflow." He glanced at Sandy, who took over the conversation.

"Fortunately, we're not facing a mudslide of that magnitude. It is the location of this slide that is our concern. We're thinking our best bet is to go down, not up."

Josie said, "In other words, dig a trench instead of building a wall."

Diego nodded. "Have you had any experience using explosives to divert mudslides?"

Josie and Otto both shook their heads no.

"We have the explosives. But we need an explosives expert to develop a plan."

Otto said, "You want to blow holes in the ground. Make a trench to divert the flow?"

"That's exactly it," Sandy said.

"Why not just use a trencher?" Josie asked. "Wouldn't that be safer?"

"We can use it to lay the explosives, but not for the whole diversion," Sandy said. "We have a Ditch Witch Quad trencher on site, and it'll dig down eight feet, but only twenty-four inches wide. That won't help with the mudslide. We need a five- to ten-foot width to do any good."

Diego's face was grave. "Here's another concern. We can make estimated guesses, but in the end, we don't know what the explosions are going to do to the equipment and the volatile nature of some of our experimental solutions."

"When you say volatile nature? Are you referring to a nuclear explosion? What do you mean?" Josie asked.

The chemical engineer sitting to Sandy's left raised a finger and looked at Diego. "Mind if I take this?"

Diego nodded. "Please do."

The man had been introduced as Scott Franklin. He was a chemical expert who said he specialized in designing and implementing cleanup solutions.

"Part of my job is to supervise volatile chemical experiments in the pilot plant. We deal with chemicals that quite honestly are just as dangerous as the radiation everyone fears. The explosive nature of some of the chemicals is enough to kill us all several times over." He pursed his lips and glanced around the room, letting the weight of his words sink in. "I guess my point is that we're working in unpredictable conditions. I have chemical compounds that haven't been exposed to tremors. There are a lot of variables with explosives that I don't personally feel comfortable with. What kind of tremors will be felt in the lab?" He frowned and looked around the table, his expression full of worry.

Sandy's face reddened and her eyes widened. "We've been through this. None of us are comfortable with any of this! We're operating in crisis mode here, Scott. This isn't the time for covering your ass. We need your expertise to help us figure out solutions based on the facts we have. Not what we would like to have."

Scott looked hurt by her response but he said nothing in return.

"Do you have an explosives team?" Josie asked.

Diego smiled grimly. "I was going to ask you the same. Sandy and I have talked. We've got the explosives, but no one on site with the experience to work with them."

Josie glanced at Otto, who nodded agreement.

"Otto and I know someone who might do it. He works at the County Maintenance Department in Artemis as a mechanic. He was in the army. Served as an explosives ordnance disposal tech."

Diego looked skeptical. "How long ago was he in the service?"

"He's been out of the service a little over a year," Josie said. "He served two tours of duty in Iraq. I don't think you'll find a better option than Mitch."

Otto said, "The local paper had a writeup when he came home. He was a master EOD specialist when he left the army. Received some kind of commendation for valor."

"Let's get him out here then," Diego said.

TWENTY-ONE

Cassidy stood in front of her living room window and peeked through the curtains. She watched Leo back out of the driveway and drive toward town, where he was headed to pick up groceries. Cassidy had convinced him she had a headache and felt too sick to run errands. Begrudgingly, he had left.

Cassidy figured she had twenty minutes. She sat at the kitchen table where Leo kept his laptop set up, where he conducted his research for the Feed Plant. She had stood behind him while she was making dinner on two different occasions and was able to figure out his login and password to unlock the computer, and to connect to the Internet. Cassidy had shown no interest in computers or the Internet, and she was hoping she could use this to her advantage. She was hoping once she logged in to his computer, the information wouldn't be protected or hidden.

First, she logged in to his e-mail account and read everything for the past two weeks, both sent and received. She found nothing that connected to the body or Scratchgravel Road. In order to cover her tracks, she marked the new e-mail she had just opened as unread, and then closed the program. She had no idea if he would be able to tell that she had opened his e-mail, but she couldn't worry about it at this point.

Next, she opened Internet Explorer and checked his book-marked sites. She clicked through several Web sites and found hor-rific pictures of radiation poisoning and chemical burns. She could barely force herself to look at the pictures, worrying that Leo might have killed the man in the desert in the same way the people in the pictures had been killed.

Since the evening she had come home from the hospital and threatened to move out, Leo had changed. He had been talking to her more, helped her cook dinner the night before, actually acted interested in what she had to say. But his attempts were too little, too late. She thought it was all an act. He was spending countless hours on the computer each day, and she suspected it was related to the dead man.

Cassidy was scrolling through his list of "Favorites" and saw a link to First Bank and Trust—not their bank. She clicked on the link and a login appeared with Leo's name preloaded. As far as she knew, they only had one account, with Bank of America, where both their checks were automatically deposited. She typed in the same password that she had used to log in to his computer and was taken to an account page. A few clicks later and she dis-covered Leo had made a deposit the day before in the amount of $1,200. She leaned back in the chair, staring at the computer screen, with no idea how to move forward.

Mitch Wilson entered the conference room thirty minutes after his conversation on the phone with Josie. He was wearing a grease-stained navy blue mechanic's shirt and pants. With his shaggy black hair, tattooed arms, and deep southern drawl, he seemed more Hell's Angel than ordnance specialist, but Josie felt confident in his abilities. She hoped the group from Beacon wouldn't judge his skills by his appearance.

She introduced him to the group, and he apologized for his uniform.

"Had my head under the hood of a plow. Trying to keep those old machines on the road in this kind of mess is a never-ending problem," he said.

"Please don't apologize. We appreciate you coming on such short notice," Paiva said. "I understand you worked as an EOD for the army?"

He nodded slowly. "Trained at Fort Lee. Served six years."

"I served as an engineer in the army for twenty years. My experience led me here."

Mitch nodded.

"I believe Chief Gray gave you a rundown on our situation. If the rain keeps up, we're facing the potential of a mudslide in a matter of hours. And that's just a guess. We don't have time for options. Diverting the flow is the best idea we've got right now."

"Makes good sense to me."

"Are you experienced in laying and detonating explosives?"

"Take 'em apart, put 'em together, blow 'em up." He grinned. "You name it, I can do it."

Diego laughed. "It's good to see your confidence. I'm afraid we're well out of our comfort zone here."

"C-4 explosives?" Mitch asked.

Diego nodded.

"You have enough det cord, blasting caps, and so on?"

"We've got everything you need. One of our engineers will get you set up," Diego said.

"Excellent. Let's do this."

Paiva nodded, and Josie could see the relief in his expression.

"We're ready to pull officers in from several different agencies. They're waiting in the lobby. I'll just ask that you listen to the briefing so you're brought up to speed. Then we'll start making plans." He stood and placed two keys on the conference table in front of Josie. "For you and Otto to get in and out. Please return them at the end of the day. I've got to make a phone call to headquarters in Boston, and return a call to the NRC. Can you get the group organized in my absence?"

Josie nodded. "I'll be glad to."

Sylvia left the room and came back moments later, escorting a large group of officers. Smokey Blessings, three Texas Highway Patrol officers, and four agents from the Department of Transportation took chairs around the table. It was a quiet, grim-faced group of men.

"On behalf of Mr. Paiva, I want to thank you all for coming. Mr. Paiva is on a call with the NRC, so I'll get introductions started." Josie went on to introduce herself and Otto as well as Sylvia and the engineers. She then asked each officer to introduce himself and describe his position. She knew one of them, Aaron Crowe, a well-respected officer who lived halfway between Marfa and Artemis. The DOT officers were all associated with West Texas, and they were all familiar with the weather conditions and mudslides that were an occasional threat. Aside from one DOT officer who described himself as a "take-charge man," Josie thought they all appeared levelheaded and ready to jump in where needed.

Josie went on to summarize the notes Sylvia had posted on the projection screen. She had taken several questions when Diego entered the room and returned to his seat. He nodded to Josie and thanked her for stepping in.

Diego spent the next ten minutes efficiently describing the situation and explaining the various risks to the plant. When he'd finished his summary he directed their attention to the projector screen, which was showing a still image of the plant and the surrounding mountain range. "I want to give you a clear visual of what we're dealing with." He pointed to a rectangular area dotted with buildings and said, "This is obviously the plant. The range runs along the sides of the plant. The largest amount of runoff comes down this eastern slope." He ran a finger along the eastern ridge where a V appeared to have been cut into the mountain. "This is a natural valley where rain has eroded the rock and formed an arroyo that captures runoff, and, in the past, has funneled excess rain and floodwaters a half mile to the east of the plant. To date, the plant has never faced a serious flooding issue due to the natural contours of the land." He pointed to the highest point on the ridge, to the west of the valley. It was a jagged outcropping of rocks that stood precariously at the top of the ridge. "This peak is what's causing us concern. We've been watching this area for years, but the erosion has been minimal. Until now."

Sandy said, "This has always been a stable range, but the rain this season has eroded it to the point we fear it will collapse. If that happens, the runoff will be significant, and we fear it will change course. Instead of following the arroyo, the water and the potential mudslide could funnel directly through the plant, hitting the barrels in the back parking lot first."

The sober-looking group of law enforcement officers said nothing as they processed the information and Diego continued. "One of our engineers is filming for us." He paused and took a sip out of the water glass in front of him. Josie noticed beads of sweat along his hairline, the only visible sign of nerves.

"We'll be able to listen in and get a good look at the current flooding," Diego said. "From where he's flying, it's almost two miles to the back lot where the metal barrels are stored. The two concrete silos are located in the back of the plant as well."

One of the highway patrol officers asked, "What's inside the silos?"

"They store radioactive waste materials."

"And what if one of the silos is compromised?"

"Then the ground around the plant would be contaminated," Diego said.

He turned to face Sylvia. "Do we have a live feed from the helicopter set up yet?"

Sylvia nodded and the still image was replaced with a live image of the mountain range being filmed during a downpour. As the helicopter flew in closer to the mountain, large fractures among the jagged boulders at the top of the peak became visible. Diego ran his finger down the length of the mountain. "This area below the peak is highly erodible, and the water has begun to funnel into this location from several areas on the mountain, dragging debris with it."

Sandy walked back into the room and sat down by the phone at the end of the table. She said, "The pilot is on the line. I'll place him on speaker so we can all hear his report."

She looked at Diego, who nodded that he was ready.

"Michael?"

"I'm here."

"Can you zoom in to the area that's washing? Get up by the peak if you can. That's where we're most concerned." She addressed the group again. "If we can make it through this rain without that area of the mountain giving way we'll be fine. If it breaks loose we've got a real mess."

Suddenly the view of the mountain tilted right and Josie felt as if the bottom fell out of the room. The pilot banked a hard right and circled around the mountain.

"I'm going to take you to the front of the peak so you can see the water coming down. It's really flowing right now. More rock has broken loose since I was up here this morning."

The picture on the screen enlarged, the mountain coming at them quickly as the pilot continued to describe the scene. Suddenly the rocks on the mountain came into focus, and Josie could see water rushing down at an alarming rate. The water was devouring the side of the mountain, washing away large chunks like sand. As the pilot flew down the slope it became obvious that other streams were being funneled toward the same path that converged on the valley floor.

Diego asked the pilot to pull the shot back and get a picture of the stream that was draining in the direction of the plant. "We've successfully diverted this water to the left of the plant. However, if we get a significant mudslide, the diversion won't hold. We've been using concrete barriers in key places, but it's just not enough."

"It wouldn't be enough to reinforce with additional barricades? Stretch it from the mountain down past the plant?" one of the officers asked.

"Mudslides have the ability to wipe out entire neighborhoods in a matter of minutes. There's enough of a grade from the mountain to the plant that it could produce significant speed." Diego pointed back to the screen. "You can see the lay of the land. See how the water funnels straight down that mountain, through the sandy stretch in the desert, and toward the plant? Those barriers are okay with the water, but if we lose a significant piece of that mountain, and pick up sand and mud from the foothills, the mud could flow heavily."

Sandy nodded toward Mitch, who had been listening intently. "This is where Mitch comes into play. We'd like to lay a line of explosives that will blow a trench to divert the water flow from reaching the plant."

One of the DOT officers asked, "Why hasn't something been done before now to prevent this?"

"That wash wasn't there before the peak started to crumble. This is all new erosion," Diego said. He paused for a moment and steepled his fingers in front of his chest, gathering all eyes on him. "I'll make one request of the group. After this incident is finished, you have my word, I will review the entire operation: what worked, what didn't, what should have been done and wasn't. For today though, I would request we focus on the events at hand. We don't have the time to point fingers. Today, we work as a team to figure out answers." He looked around the room and received head nods from everyone.

Diego cleared his throat. "We have a team setting up a decontamination area. They are consulting with FEMA as we speak. We're approaching this proactively. God forbid, if part of the plant is taken out by the mudslide, if radiation is released into the environment, we're prepared to handle the aftermath."

Josie felt as if the wind had been knocked out of her lungs. A table filled with first responders, people trained to handle crisis, and they were all speechless, imagining their own nuclear nightmares.

"We're at the unfortunate point of weighing our odds." Diego looked at Sandy, who was not able to meet his eyes before he stood to break the room into working groups. Prepared or not, it was time to move.

TWENTY-TWO

Diego and Sandy assigned groups of officers to specific tasks. Diego had called in plant workers earlier that morning to remain on standby and they were now being put to work. A team of ten was surveying the metal barrels to determine their ability to withstand movement, and it was quickly determined that about a hundred of them on the front end of the lot were stable enough to handle a move. Scott led the DOT team and county maintenance around the site to establish transportation routes for evacuation and removal of the barrels. Next, they began the nerve-racking task of moving the barrels to a fleet of semi trucks that were also being equipped for radiation monitoring. Meanwhile, a team of five scientists from the EPA landed in a helicopter and was quickly briefed on the situation by Diego. Sandy took the Department of Energy team and the three highway patrol officers with her in a four-wheel-drive Excursion to check out the runoff in person. Josie was amazed at how well orchestrated the effort appeared. She gave credit to Diego's leadership and started to believe the company's outstanding reputation might be deserved.

Diego had asked Josie and Otto to follow Mitch Wilson into

the area behind the plant where the water was currently flowing. They followed Diego down a hallway to the back area of the staging facility, where he grabbed them each rain ponchos and wader boots from a storage closet.

"You can still set the charges in the rain?" Josie asked Mitch.

He grinned. "I can detonate explosives in a tornado."

Instead of driving, Mitch asked to walk to check the ground and the effects of the rain. After they were dressed, Diego led them through the back of the building to see the path the water was taking through the plant.

"There's about a thirty-five percent grade behind the mountain that levels off to fifteen percent," Diego said. "The problem is the rain that's pouring down Norton's Peak is pushing all the water and debris right through the center of the plant."

Diego led them through the gate and into the production area of the plant. Josie pulled her rain poncho hood up around her face and looked at the dismal, gray sky. The rain continued steadily. She could not remember ever standing in a more depressing place. The partially disassembled buildings and empty machinery, the muddy holes and washed-out pathways were surface issues, but underneath lay a ticking time bomb. She was very aware that Diego and Sandy had avoided explaining the aftermath of what would happen if the mudslide hit the buildings with the massive force it was capable of. Sandy had made it clear they weren't facing a nuclear explosion, but she hadn't filled in the blanks.

The walk up the hill to the base of the mountain took just fifteen minutes. As they walked, Mitch stuck spikes into the ground to represent placement of the charges. Norton's Peak, at the top of the mountain ridge, was directly above them, ending approximately fifty feet up. It was in bad shape. It was obvious to Josie the base was crumbling and would most likely fall that day if the rain didn't halt immediately.

Mitch had kept up a running commentary to Otto and Diego, who both seemed interested in the logistics of the explosives.

Josie wasn't much interested in the mechanics, as long as it worked and didn't blow the plant sky high. For that, she had little choice but to have faith.

With Mitch shouting orders, they began digging a shallow trench to hold the C-4. He was laying a sample line of explosives to see how the saturated ground would react.

After Josie had already become covered in mud, the cell phone in her shirt pocket rang. She had no choice but to wipe her hands on her streaked uniform pants, before popping open the snaps on the poncho and flipping open her cell phone to an unfamiliar number.

"Chief Gray."

"I'm so glad you answered. This is Cassidy." She sighed deeply and continued. "I need to see you."

"I'm in a mess right now. Are you in danger?"

"I don't know."

"Do you need police help?" Josie asked.

"I found stuff on Leo's computer. Weird shit. I think it's connected to the nuclear plant. Maybe to the dead guy."

"Like what?"

Cassidy moaned. "There's all this weird stuff about radiation and death."

"What made you search his computer?"

She hesitated. "Leo knew where the body was in the desert."

"How do you know?" she asked.

"I overheard him one night on the phone. I wrote down the directions that he was telling someone. That's why I took a walk in the desert that day it was so hot. I thought maybe Leo was having an affair or something."

Josie clenched her jaws and tried to keep her calm. "Why didn't you just tell us this? You withheld serious information from the investigation."

"I was afraid! I was afraid he'd kill me if he found out I told you! I'd already seen one dead person!"

"Is Leo there with you?"

"No, but there's something more."

Josie waited.

"Leo deposited over a thousand dollars into a bank account I didn't even know we had."

"When?"

"Yesterday. He works part time at the plant. And his paycheck gets deposited in our bank. I don't know where that money came from."

Josie knew exactly where the money came from but didn't have time to enlighten Cassidy. "Have you found a set of house keys?"

She hesitated. "Yeah, there were some in Leo's desk drawer." She sounded hesitant, already expecting the worst.

"Leave the computer. Take the keys. Get to your parents' house. Now."

"I don't want to drag them into this," Cassidy said. "This is my mess, not theirs."

"Trust me on this. Your dad wants you out of there. Go tell him everything. Then sit tight until we can get to you. Don't talk to Leo. Don't talk to anyone but your dad. Got it?"

Josie hung her phone up and walked back to Otto and Diego. Otto stabbed his shovel into the mud and looked up at Josie in surprise, as if thoroughly absorbed in his task. Water dripped from the edge of his plastic hood and down into his face, red from the exertion of digging the trench.

"What's the problem?" Otto asked.

"I just received a phone call from Cassidy Harper. She was snooping on Leo's computer and discovered he deposited over a thousand dollars into a bank account yesterday. An account she didn't know they had."

Otto made a fist. "We got him!"

Diego looked at them in confusion. "What's the significance?"

"Juan saved his paychecks, took a bus, and delivered the money to his family once a month. He kept the cash in a shoebox in the back of his closet. The box is missing."

Diego took a step back. "And you think Leo stole Juan's money?"

"It gets better. Cassidy also said Leo knew where the body was located in the desert." Josie recounted the conversation for Otto.

"I don't understand people. How could she sit on information like that and not tell us?" Otto said.

"She claims she was afraid he would kill her if she told anyone." Otto shook his head. "What about Leo?"

"I won't bring him in until I know the charges will stick. We'll have to wait until we're finished here."

They returned to the mud and spent another thirty minutes digging a ten-foot-long shallow trench, each of them lost in their own thoughts, spinning their own theories as to how Juan Santiago lost his money and ended up left for dead. After the trench was finished, they stepped back and watched as Mitch assembled the pieces for the trial run. He laid the C-4, then attached blasting caps to the explosives. Next he crimped the detonation cord into the caps and attached the primer to the end of the det cord. Josie was impressed at his efficiency. He took charge of the situation with ease and had no trouble shouting orders when necessary. She tried to imagine the danger he had been in, setting up similar explosions in a war zone, and figured his life had often depended on his ability to react with confidence.

Mitch was wearing a headset with a direct line to Sandy, who was checking out the peak farther up the mountain. He talked intermittently with Otto and Sandy, explaining his moves as he went. Otto was fascinated by the setup, and Josie was certain he would light the fuse himself if given the opportunity.

"That's it," Mitch yelled. "Let's get these charges set!"

He took off at a fast walk on legs long enough to leave the rest of them jogging to keep up. As he walked, he unraveled the det cord from a large spool hanging on his right hip. At twenty feet he stopped, cut the cord, and told Josie, Otto, and Diego to keep heading toward the plant. They did so, maintaining the jog. They didn't turn around until they heard Mitch yell, "We have smoke!"

About four minutes later, the ground exploded, spewing mud into the air like a fountain. The mess fell to the ground in patties, splattering their clothes and boots, falling onto the hoods of their rain ponchos like a hailstorm. In its aftermath, a ten-foot-wide swath of ground was carved out of the desert to the depth of about four feet. Mitch and Otto cheered as Diego looked on smiling. It was exactly what they had hoped for. Josie could imagine the sight when a half mile of dirt flew into the sky and landed back down onto the wet ground.

After the explosion Sandy had a four-wheel-drive SUV pick them up for a quick trip back to the parking lot so that Mitch could assemble his equipment and the explosives crew he had called in. A ragtag group of twenty-something-year-old guys climbed out of an extended-cab pickup and high-fived Mitch before he proceeded to explain his plan. Josie was impressed how quickly they turned to business.

The weather remained dismal: the sky full of dark clouds, and the rain continuing to fall in a steady downpour. The clothes under Josie's rain poncho and the socks inside her boots were soaked. Water dripped down the sides of her face even with the large hood pulled over her head.

Josie noticed Diego and Skip in a serious discussion on the other side of the truck that was carrying the explosives. She realized the timing was lousy, but she couldn't shake the investigation from her thoughts, especially given the information Cassidy had just provided. She decided to ask Skip about the information on Santiago that she had requested.

When Josie reached them, Diego put a finger in the air to halt her. "Sylvia called and said the NRC is on the line and refusing to hang up before I talk to them. I need to take care of business. Anything urgent?"

"No, I just need to talk with Skip," Josie said.

"Excellent. I'll be back shortly." Diego walked quickly toward the main office building and Josie turned to Skip. "Did Diego tell you I need Santiago's work duties for the days before he disappeared? I sent you an e-mail too."

Skip sighed and rubbed his eyes. "I'm sorry. I actually pulled that together for you yesterday. I just haven't had time to call."

Josie gave a noncommittal shrug. "Discover anything?"

Skip squinted his eyes and looked guilty. "I knew Juan was working on the vitrification project in Unit Seven. Our team has been in the building for almost a year now."

"Okay."

"What I forgot, in all the commotion the day you arrived, was that he was working in the pilot unit the week before. Just a short assignment to clean equipment."

"Why is that important?" she asked.

"The vitrification project is still experimental. We're working through issues constantly. Our goal is to perfect the science and share it with other scientists."

Or, sell the science and make a fortune, Josie thought. "What kind of work was he doing?"

Skip squinted at her again. "He was working cleanup with caustic chemicals. If he was careless, if safety precautions weren't followed and the chemicals reached his skin, he could have ended up with some nasty sores on his arms."

"I thought they wore the white hazmat suits?" she asked.

"That's the company rule. In fact, it's grounds for dismissal if a worker's caught performing certain tasks without the suits. I'm just saying, maybe he didn't follow protocol."

Josie knew the answer but asked to see if Skip would be honest. "Was anyone working with Santiago those days?"

He nodded. "Brent Thyme."

At least the stories match, she thought. "Have you talked to Brent about his own safety yet?"

"No, he called in sick yesterday and today. I was planning on visiting him tonight after work." His expression was vacant, as if his brain had reached its capacity to process. "And now this. One week it's business as usual. The next, the whole world crumbles."

Josie glanced at her watch and wondered if Brent had arrived at Cowan's office yet to talk with the CDC. She made a mental note to call Cowan when she was done talking with Skip.

Josie took a leap of faith. "There's something that's bothering me about this case that I want to share with you," she said.

Skip met her eyes, his expression earnest. "Sure."

"When Juan's body was found, he was wearing his work boots. From the Feed Plant."

Skip took a second to respond. "That's against company procedures. It doesn't sound like Juan. He was one to follow rules."

"It's more than that though. Have you ever had any desire to wear your boots outside of the plant?"

"No."

"Even if it weren't against regulations. Would you wear your boots because they're comfortable? Sturdy? Maybe they're good for walking outside?"

He curled a lip up. "The boots are made for industrial work. I would not wear them if given the choice."

"Then why would Santiago wear them two days after he left work? He had a pair of boots in his closet at his apartment that looked much more comfortable. He was wearing a nice pair of jeans and a Western shirt. His cowboy boots would have been the natural choice."

Skip looked at her and shrugged. "I don't know. It doesn't make sense to me either."

They both turned and watched a DPS car pull into the parking area, splashing water onto one of Mitch's crew. To the man's credit, he looked at his pants, already soaked from the rain, but didn't react.

Josie looked back at Skip, her mind still focused on the details. "What if Santiago came back? What if he realized he'd gotten into something, and he came back that night for help?"

Skip raised his eyebrows.

"Are there antidotes? Or first-aid procedures you follow for chemical burns?" she asked.

"Sure, to an extent. If he truly got into the chemicals I'm afraid he touched, he'd need much more than a first-aid kit."

"But he might not know that."

Skip looked skeptical. "He certainly knows basic first aid and safety procedures. He would have washed the chemicals off immediately and treated the skin. He's been through a number of mandatory safety trainings. If his skin came into contact with those chemicals, he knew to approach a supervisor immediately for treatment."

"What if he came back the night before he died and stopped at his locker to put on his boots? Would he have access to them?" she asked.

"Yeah. He'd been working here for several years. Had a clean personnel record. Some of the guys have keys so they can have access to the buildings they work in. We keep the buildings locked at all times, so we give them keys so they can get in and out during the day. He's worked here long enough to have his own set. It's kind of a badge of honor to have a set of keys. A trust issue."

Josie nodded, putting together the pieces in her mind.

Skip's cell phone rang and Josie listened as he spoke to someone about a request that the NRC had for paperwork. He glanced at Josie. "Diego needs help for a minute. Do you mind?"

Josie motioned toward the building. "Of course not. I'll catch up with you later."

She watched Skip jog across the parking lot and considered Santiago and the timeline of events. She felt certain his death was connected with the plant, and her hunch was it took place at night. When she and Dillon had come to the plant the security was lax. She assumed the plant had operated for so many years in the isolation of the desert with no security issues that the gaurds had become complacent. And it wouldn't take long for the wrong person to pick up on the complacency.

Josie walked over to where Otto stood listening to Mitch brief his crew.

"I got a hunch," she said.

"Do you now?" His surprise turned to a grin as he turned away from the group. "Fill me in."

"Skip just confirmed that both Santiago and Brent Thyme were working with hazardous chemicals in the pilot unit the week before they both developed lesions on their arms or hands."

Otto rubbed at the stubble on his chin. "Well, that could change things."

"We could be looking at chemical burns—not radiation."

"Maybe the CDC can sort that one out."

"I'm still stuck on Santiago's boots. I'd lay money on the fact that he and Thyme got into something they weren't supposed to, and he came back to make it right. He came back into the plant and put his boots on as a security measure. My hunch is, he left a dead man."

Otto nodded slowly, thinking it through.

"Remember the first day we came and met Diego, and he took us for a quick tour around Unit Seven?"

He nodded.

"There was a small room on the right side of the building that houses their security tapes. Diego said they don't monitor them, but they're digitally archived. I worked with a similar setup last year when the Family Value installed their system."

"I remember." He frowned. "You planning on viewing the tapes after we're done here?"

"I'm going now. Skip just said employees with good personnel records are allowed keys to the various buildings. I want to get to those tapes before someone else does."

"Diego know you're planning on viewing the tapes?" Otto asked.

"He's busy."

"Skip know?" he asked.

"He's busy too."

"And what if one of those two killed Santiago?"

"All the more reason for me to check this out now. Cover for me?"

Otto sighed and pulled his cell phone out of his shirt pocket. He flipped it open. "It's on with the volume turned up. You call if anything looks out of place. Let me know when you get the video pulled up."

Josie walked quickly across the parking lot and through the gate into the production area. She walked around the track until she reached the building labeled as Unit Seven, keeping an eye open for Diego and Skip, but she saw no one. The action was currently taking place outside the plant, not inside the buildings, and she felt fairly secure. While the chance was remote, she wanted to at least scan the tapes in case evacuation became inevitable. If Skip or Diego questioned her, which she had no doubt they eventually would, that would be her excuse for operating without their knowledge.

Josie used the master key that Diego had provided her earlier that day, and she let herself into Unit Seven. She quickly scanned the building and determined it was empty, and then proceeded to the security office.

The room was cool, but not like the arctic temperature in Skip's office. It was a small space filled with electronic equipment and one computer with a flat, wide-screen monitor. The desk and shelves were organized and clean, but she noticed the faint corroded battery smell that Dillon had commented on when they were digging around the plant.

Josie flipped the overhead light switch on and closed the door behind her. She booted up the computer and the system loaded, but a login screen appeared. She looked around the desktop for a login-password combination, hoping to find something taped to the desk, a card left out in the open. She rifled through three desk drawers and was surprised there wasn't a paper somewhere that contained the logins. She had found most people, even businesses, were often careless with security issues. She scanned the shelves above her and found a dozen software manuals and computer books. The computer login screen said STATEN SECURITY SYSTEMS, V.4.3. She found the manual with that title, opened the front cover, and hand-printed in pencil on the first page was *login: BeaconP1* and *password: password1A*. She entered the two terms into the system and was in within twenty seconds.

Once inside the program it was a fairly simple search. She entered dates into the appropriate fields, entered the time range she wanted to view, and then had to choose from thirty-five different locations that were notated with a number from one to thirty-five. Going back to the manual she found a pocket in the back of the book stuffed with someone's notes. A sheet of paper with the words *Cheat Sheet* written across the top listed the specific location next to the numbers. She found *Pilot Lab* next to number twenty-nine and within a minute she was watching a clear black-and-white video of the empty lab in the pilot unit. Over the next several minutes she practiced using the various controls to scan at differing speeds, and to pause and stop.

In real time the tape showed a static shot of the laboratory that Santiago and Brent had been working in. Skip had indicated it was the only lab in the plant. The room was approximately six hundred square feet and was brightly lit and filled with metal lab furniture.

Lab equipment and paraphernalia were stacked all around the room, which appeared to be less orderly than other areas she had seen in the plant. From the rotating security camera, Josie could see everything but the far corner of the room, opposite the entrance door.

After scanning both Thursday and Friday nights, she was able to determine a set schedule that the security guard used to walk the building. He arrived within ten minutes of his three-hour rotation both nights. Josie was pinning her hopes on Saturday. If Santiago knew the schedule as well, he could have slipped in unnoticed. And so could his murderer.

TWENTY-THREE

Otto looked over the shoulder of one of the workers who was checking the satellite picture on his cell phone and whistled at the band of green that signaled rain across West Texas and northern Mexico; it looked as if the rain would continue for at least another hour or two, and from the looks of the radar there would be increased flooding all across West Texas.

While the rest of the men were piling into the pickup truck, Otto and Mitch each climbed on an ATV that Diego had provided. Otto felt as if twenty years had fallen off his back. Maybe even thirty. He wished Delores could see him riding through the desert on a four-wheeler, flinging mud like a kid again.

Mitch took a wide path around the plant and the pickup followed with Otto in the rear. Otto noticed places on the hillside where the ground was cracking in ten- and twenty-foot horizontal stretches, as if big slabs of earth were ready to separate. It was a frightening sight and sobered him quickly. He wondered what the trencher would do to the already unstable ground. They might cause their own mudslide trying to avert another one.

Beacon's Quad trencher was already at the location Mitch had designated as the starting point for the explosives. Otto had never seen a trencher in action, and this one was obviously top of the line. Otto figured his tax dollars were paying for it, so it ought to be good.

The machine was red, built similar to a bulldozer, but with a large arm on the back of it that looked like a three-foot-wide, five-foot-long chainsaw blade. It sat atop tracks similar to those used on army tanks, however these were triangular in shape, and there were two separate tracks on either side of the machine. It looked as if it could move through about any terrain. The operator left the machine running and hopped out of the cab to meet up with the group.

Mitch got off his four-wheeler and approached the operator with his hand outstretched and introduced himself as the explosives tech.

"Name's Bob Smitty." He was a short, heavyset man with a two-day beard and leathery skin.

Mitch pointed to the tracks. "How's she do in this kind of mud?"

The operator smiled and laughed as if he'd heard a good dirty joke. "You have to try to get her stuck." He looked up into the sky, where the rain still came down. "She can run in this for sure."

<hr />

Josie called and gave Otto an update on her progress and said she needed another thirty minutes to scan the video through Saturday night and Sunday. She was convinced she knew who the murderer was, and the tape would prove it. She pressed Play again and set it to fast-forward. On Saturday at 10:40 P.M., just thirty minutes past when the security guard last made his rounds of the pilot unit, she saw unexpected movement and clicked Stop. She took a deep breath, certain she was about ready to break open the case, and clicked the Play button to watch the video at standard speed. A person in a white hazmat suit, wearing black work boots, walked into the room.

"Here we go," she whispered. She could feel her heart race in her chest as she watched another person dressed in a similar white suit enter the room. The two figures walked across the room to a lab table that held various equipment and glass beakers. One of the figures held a hand up to a glass overhead cabinet and unlocked it, pulling out a white box, what appeared to be a first-aid kit. The container was placed on the counter and the two figures faced one another, apparently discussing something. One of them took a tube of something from the kit and tried to give it to the other person. The two appeared to be arguing. After several minutes, the individual who refused the tube turned and started to walk away. The other person picked up a metal stool, lifted it over his head, and came down with incredible force on top of the other man's head. Josie knew that she'd just seen the blow that caused the injury to Juan Santiago's head.

"Josie?"

Josie gasped and turned to the door. She had no idea there was anyone else in the building. "Brent! What are you doing here? I thought you were home sick."

He looked just as surprised to see her. "I was. Someone called and told me about the mudslide. Said I needed to get here and help."

Josie breathed out, trying to calm her nerves. She noticed him staring at the video. She turned back to the computer and clicked the monitor off to lose the picture.

"What are you watching?" he asked. He narrowed his eyes at her.

"Have you talked to Skip or Diego yet?"

He shook his head no.

"Go find your supervisors to see how you can help."

Pointing at the monitor he asked, "Does this have to do with Santiago?"

"It doesn't concern you. We've got a mess out here."

Brent held out his wrist, covered with a large bandage. Josie could see the discoloration underneath. It was obvious the blister on his wrist had worsened and was seeping blood.

"I think I deserve to be a part of this conversation. Look at what's happening to me!"

Otto stood on the side of the hill with two of Mitch's crew. His skin felt sticky under the plastic poncho where the rain had trickled in between the gaps and openings to soak his uniform. The smell of wet, sweaty skin was giving him a headache and he was beginning to long for a cool shower. He imagined sitting in his kitchen with a glass of iced tea and a bowl of vanilla ice cream.

They watched as the trencher slowly worked its way down the hill. Two men were laying the blocks of explosive down into the ditch, and Mitch was coming behind them attaching the blasting caps. Another man was attaching the detonation cord. The entire operation was moving smoothly, and Otto had just begun to have hope, when the man standing beside him cursed and pointed to the top of the peak.

"Son of a bitch," whispered Otto.

They watched in horror as a large chunk on the face of the peak broke free, slamming against the side of the mountain as it tumbled down. The cracking rocks reverberated down the hill. Everyone stopped what they were doing, holding their breath, waiting for the rest of the peak to fall. Amazingly, it did not.

Otto dialed Josie's number, anxious to get her out of the building before Mitch lit the explosives. She didn't answer.

Josie felt the cell phone vibrate against her chest and ignored it, not wanting to spook Brent before she understood his motivation.

She stood and gestured with her hand for him to walk out of the small room, but he didn't budge. The room was too confined and she felt extremely uncomfortable. His attitude had changed considerably. She realized he was holding one of his arms awkwardly behind his body, just behind the door frame.

He spoke again, his voice low, with a forced calm that made him sound even more unstable.

"I came here to tell you that you're wanted outside. Things are going bad out there. Someone stopped me and said to get you. They want you out there now."

His words were carefully enunciated, and his eyes had grown wide and unfocused. Josie wondered if he was on something, prescription or otherwise.

"Let them know I'm on my way. I need to lock things up." Josie rested her hand on the butt of her gun at her waist.

His face turned red, his eyes wide now. "You do not understand. Things are completely screwed. I will take care of things here. They need you outside!"

His voice had become rigid. It was clear he had no intention of leaving the building.

Josie tried to remain calm and took a step forward to move them into the larger area outside the room where she stood a better chance of defending herself. She brought her hand down toward her gun, but he stopped her with a yell.

"Don't do that!" He brought his hidden hand around to the front of him. He held a pint-sized glass beaker half filled with liquid.

Her skin grew cold.

"I did not want to do this," he said.

When the rock tumbled down Norton's Peak, the trencher operator stopped and left his machine for further direction. Mitch stopped laying the explosives and ran to catch up with him.

"The trench is about halfway done. I got several hundred pounds of explosives laid. For now, let's keep going, digging the trench and laying the C-4. If the rest of the peak crumbles, we stop and detonate what we have. Start back up where you left off. Keep running where I have the flags laid."

The man nodded and took off toward his machine.

"Hey!" Mitch yelled, and the man turned back. "When this blows it's gonna rain shit on all of us for half a mile. You'll get hit with some heavy mud. Just be prepared. I'll call first."

The man said nothing, just gave a thumbs-up and climbed back up in the trencher.

Mitch turned to Otto. "Get Sandy on the phone. Tell her we're going to light the fuse soon. This is her last chance to call it off if she's still worried about the tremors."

Otto got Sandy on the cell phone and explained.

"It's not good," she said. "We're just east of the peak. Everything is crumbling, breaking loose. Tell Mitch to blow us a hole in the ground before this mess plows through the middle of those barrels and causes a real disaster."

Sandy hung up before Otto could respond.

While Mitch briefed his crew on safety precautions and each man's location, Otto called Josie again and got no answer. He started to worry.

Otto interrupted Mitch's talk. "I'm taking the four-wheeler to check on Josie. She's not answering her phone. I want her out of there."

Otto got on his four-wheeler. Spinning mud behind him, he quickly got it up to third gear, and made it back to the front of Unit Seven. He pulled his gun and used the key to the side door, which opened behind and to the left of Skip's office. He hoped he was being paranoid and overly cautious, and that Josie would give him hell for playing mother hen.

He opened the door slowly, and stepped inside, then shut it behind him with a slight click of the latch. The humming of the filtration system drowned out most of the background noise, but Otto could hear voices coming from the other side of the office. He made his way down the side of Skip's office, against the wall, his gun at the ready.

He paused and listened. An angry male voice sounded as if it was facing away from Otto. When he heard Josie respond, her tone forced, reasonable, he knew she was in trouble. He slowly looked around the corner of the office and saw Brent Thyme facing her, standing just outside the door of a small room. He could see part of Josie standing behind Brent, but he was certain she had a clear view of him.

Brent held a glass jar in one hand, his other hand pointing at her. Otto watched Josie nod her head calmly, acknowledging Brent's words, trying to get him to continue. Otto hoped she had seen him. He walked into the open expanse in the middle of the building, his arms extended, his gun pointing directly at Brent. Otto hoped he could make it to Brent before he sensed movement and turned.

Josie saw Otto enter the room from the corner of her eye, but kept her focus on Brent.

"Destroy the tape or I throw it. Your skin will melt just like Santiago's." He held his hand out. "You don't want this."

Brent's face was filled with a rage that Josie would not have believed he had inside of him.

"We'll look at the tape together. You explain it to me," she said.

"That tape means nothing," he said. "It distorts everything. What Beacon did to us. They killed Santiago! That tape proves nothing, and they'll make it look like I'm the guilty one!"

"I can help you work through this. You have to trust me, Brent."

"It's bullshit! I have a family to take care of. They don't care about any of us! It's smoke and mirrors."

Josie let him rant, and kept her eyes focused on him, encouraging him as Otto made his way toward them.

Otto approached and she watched the expression on Brent's face change from rage to shock the instant that she knew the barrel of Otto's gun had reached the center of Brent's back.

"If you drop that glass, or you raise your arm, you'll get a bullet through your back," Otto said. "You'll die here on the floor, in a pool of your own blood."

The hysteria from moments before hung on Brent's face as if frozen in time. He appeared paralyzed.

"You're going to bend slowly down, and you're going to set that glass on the floor. Very gently," Otto said.

His face grew slack, as if Otto's words were sinking in, and he slowly bent forward.

About a foot from the floor, Brent rose up with all his power, knocking Otto's gun arm out of the way. He flung the liquid at Josie. She ducked, but received a splash across the right side of her face, and down her right arm. She screamed in shock, then anger propelled her forward and she leaped onto him as he was turning to escape. Otto brought his gun arm up at the same time and hit Brent in the temple. The beaker fell, sending glass shards scattering across the floor. Blood appeared immediately and Brent fell backwards as Josie landed on his side.

She flipped him on his stomach where he lay limp. Her face began to burn.

"Jesus, Josie, get that washed off you," Otto called. "Go!"

As Josie squatted with one knee on Brent's back, her arms and legs felt numb, as if weighed down with lead. She couldn't believe what was happening to her.

Otto pulled a set of handcuffs off his gun belt, and clicked them around Brent's wrists.

"Damn it, Josie! Get up and find a bathroom. Get that washed off. Who knows what the hell that might be!" he yelled.

He grabbed Josie's arm and pulled her up and out of her own thoughts. "Go. I'll call Diego and get him over here."

She walked, then ran toward the back of the building in search of a bathroom.

She heard Brent groan as if the wind had been knocked out of him. She imagined Otto beating the life out of him, but she couldn't think straight. She just knew she needed to get water on her face. The visions of Santiago's arms, the fresh image of Brent Thyme's wrist, were terrifying.

She stumbled through a door with a sign that said RESTROOM. She turned the water on full force and pressed the lever for the hand soap, rubbing the foam into her face, splashing water, then doing the same on her arm. She wondered suddenly if water would do more harm than good, but continued splashing water and washing with soap until the skin on her face turned bright red. After ten minutes of continual soap and water Josie decided to stop because she didn't know what else to do. Her face burned, but no blisters were forming yet. After several minutes the burn worsened and she went back to the water and soap routine. She was certain Otto had called the medics. She figured the most effective treatment at that point was continued washing until she heard otherwise.

She looked in the mirror at the red patch on her face. She'd seen pictures of women in Pakistan, disfigured by acid thrown on their faces and bodies as a punishment for accused infidelity. She imagined her face scarred and withered.

The door opened and Diego entered the restroom. "Where did you get hit? Do you know what he threw on you?"

She looked up from the running water and saw his reflection in the mirror behind her. She shook her head. "It was a clear liquid. It hit the side of my face and my arm. It's burning."

He looked panicked. "Otto and Skip are taking Brent to the storage room where he found the chemicals."

She looked at him blankly.

"Keep applying a cool water bath to the area until we find out what the chemical was."

Diego stayed with her, touching wet cloths to her face, talking to calm her nerves. After what seemed an eternity, Skip entered the small bathroom carrying a glass jug half filled with a clear liquid.

"This is it, Josie. Brent led us to it. The lid was off. It's hydrochloric acid. In its most concentrated form it would do terrible damage to your skin. The pain would be unbearable. These acids have been prepared for disposal, though. It's been combined with a base in order to neutralize the acid."

"So what are you saying?" she asked, wanting irrefutable proof that she would not be scarred for life.

Diego laid a hand on her back. "He's saying you'll be fine. You need to see a doctor, but the acid has been mixed with something to make it less harmful. I'm so sorry for this."

Josie looked at Skip, who stood looking helpless. "Brent poured the acid from that container into another jar? And that's what he threw on me?"

"Yes."

She noticed he was wearing latex gloves. "Keep the gloves on so we don't lose his fingerprints. I need you to get that container to Otto. Ask him to get it labeled for evidence. It's crucial that doesn't get misplaced in the middle of all the commotion here."

Skip left the room with the acid and Diego continued to stare at her face.

"My face still burns." She looked toward the mirror and saw a red patch the size of her palm along the side of her face.

"The skin on your face is sensitive. I would expect it to turn red. It will fade. You need to get to a hospital to have a doctor treat you, though," Diego said. "The chemicals are neutralized to make them safe to dispose of, but it's not an exact science."

Josie nodded. "Where's Otto?"

"Skip said he took Brent outside in handcuffs."

Diego placed his hand on her shoulder and turned her slowly toward him. He touched the red area gently with the back of his fingers. "It doesn't feel hot to the touch. You need some cream applied to it to stop the burn."

Josie held her arm out and saw the red that stretched down her forearm and across her wrist.

He removed his hand from her shoulder and looked at her in confusion. "Why would Brent attack you?"

"I watched the security tapes from Saturday and Sunday. I'm sorry. I couldn't afford to wait for permission."

Anger flickered across his face, but he nodded.

"Brent killed Juan Santiago."

"What?" Diego looked incredulous, as if he wasn't capable of hearing one more horrendous piece of news.

"That's why he attacked you? You saw him kill Santiago on the security tapes?"

"I was watching the tapes. Brent came into the security room carrying the beaker. When I refused to leave the room, he threatened me with the chemicals. That's when Otto approached with his gun drawn. Brent threw the acid in an attempt to break free."

Looking at Diego's stunned expression she was hit by a sudden realization. *This is the difference between cops and other people. He still feels shock and disbelief at the atrocities people do to one another.*

"I haven't watched the rest of the security tape," Josie said. "But I have no doubt what we'll find."

They heard a boom like thunder ripping through the inside of a metal drum. The sound lasted for what seemed like an eternity. Mitch had just detonated the explosives in the trench. They left the bathroom and ran outside to find Otto with one of the DPS officers who had been helping with the mudslide, locking Brent Thyme in the backseat of his patrol car.

Otto turned to Josie. He looked bad, Josie thought.

"You okay?" he asked, his voice cracking.

She could see he was searching her face for signs of damage, and she realized how shaken he had been over her safety.

"I'm fine. Skip says it was a neutralized chemical. The burning is already easing up. I'm going to be fine."

Otto's shoulders slumped in relief.

She noticed Brent in the back of the police car. The anger and betrayal she felt over his attack toward her, and toward Santiago, were too much to put into words at that point. She turned away from the car to keep from looking at him. She needed time to mentally cool off before she had to confront him at the jail.

Diego and Skip left for the parking lot to meet with Sandy to check the results of the explosives. After Brent was driven away in the DPS car, Josie and Otto stood in the courtyard, surveying each other without word.

Josie finally said, "Hell of a day."

"When I left to get you, the peak was just crumbling," Otto said.

Josie looked toward the mountain range but one of the buildings blocked the view. "You need to get to the hospital. You need to be examined," Otto said.

"Let's go check the hillside. If it's under control I'll take off."

Otto climbed on the four-wheeler, and Josie slid on behind him.

TWENTY-FOUR

As Otto drove around the side of the Feed Plant, the mountain range came into full view. Josie couldn't believe the sight. Losing the peak, the highest point on the mountain range, completely changed the landscape, creating a void in the sky.

Two streams of water were flowing down the mountain: one down the original arroyo a half mile to the left of the plant, the other a newly formed stream that was flowing through the trench Mitch had blown into the earth. Mitch was on the ATV. His crew was located between the two flows, and they were beginning to drive the truck back toward the plant. Josie noticed the trench operator was to the left of the newly blown ditch.

"He needs to get that trencher out of there before he gets stuck!" she said, pointing at the machine. It appeared to be caught on the edge of the path of water and mud moving down the hill.

Otto yelled back to her. "Looks like he lost traction in the moving water."

The trencher was pointed east, away from the runoff, but the machine wasn't built for speed. It probably only moved about two miles per hour.

Using the four-wheeler, Otto drove to where Mitch and his crew had stopped their pickup truck to watch the trencher. The Excursion, several four-wheelers, and the pickup truck were all congregated, watching the operator try to beat the slide.

Josie was amazed at the fast-moving stream of mud and debris. She'd seen the aftermath, but she'd never seen an actual mudslide in person. It looked to be alive, engulfing everything in its way, completely unstoppable. She realized now how ineffective the concrete barriers would have been in the wake of its widening path.

Otto killed the engine and the group turned briefly to ask if everything was okay, but the focus was now on the mudslide. Massive slabs of earth were dislodging and collecting with the debris and water sliding down from the base of the mountain. The mess was fortunately following the path Mitch had predicted, headed straight for the ten-foot-wide ditch that would bypass the Feed Plant. The problem now was the mudslide was spreading wider than the ditch and was about to catch the trencher and pull it along.

"We've got to get him out of there!" Otto yelled. Josie could tell he was ready to start up their four-wheeler and take off toward the machine, but she was afraid it would just put another vehicle in the way of the slide.

Mitch turned. "You gonna throw him a rope? What the hell can we do?"

Josie yelled over the engine, "Let's at least get up there closer." She looked at Sandy and Diego, who stood together watching off to the side. "Do you have any chains?"

Mitch yelled, "It's too late! Somebody call and tell him to leave the machine. Just get out and let it roll."

"He can't jump into a mudslide! He could kill himself getting out. That trencher could roll on top of him," Josie said.

In a matter of seconds the slabs of mud had gained momentum, floating on the loose desert sand, mixing with the slew now pouring down the mountain. It had turned into a river of thick mud. The edge of the slide reached the trencher and began to turn the machine, finally taking it down the hill with it. The operator had no control. The tracks would be useless with nothing solid to grab on to. Josie prayed the massive machine wouldn't tip.

Otto and Josie followed Mitch and Diego on the ATVs, up the hillside toward the trencher, staying on the solid ground to the right of the flow. Josie looked behind her and saw Sandy driving the Excursion back toward the plant before it got stuck in the mud.

As they came toward the machine, it tipped on its side, the cab moving in slow motion, the massive trencher slipping down into the middle of the mudslide. The windows were covered in thick sludge and the driver was no longer visible. They watched in awe as it was swept away, on its side, like a paper boat floating in a pond.

The mudslide stretched for about two miles to the left of the plant before the slight slope it was following flattened out and the mud dissipated into flat, barren desert. The trencher lay on its side completely engulfed in brown sludge. Otto and Mitch each drove the ATVs within thirty feet of the machine and had to stop. A layer of mud stretched around them, slowly flowing outward in all directions. Josie and Mitch both waded through almost a foot of thick mud to reach the trencher. After several torturous steps, Josie pulled her feet out of her wader boots, which were forever lost to the mud, and then pulled her muddy socks off. She pulled her poncho over her head and left it in a heap on the ground.

Josie yelled out to the driver, but heard nothing. In her bare feet, she approached the tracks and tried to find something to grab hold of to pull herself up, but every surface was slick. With the trencher lying on its side, it was almost impossible to find a foothold. Mitch stood beside her and laced his hands together.

"Step up here. I'll boost you up," he said.

She placed a foot in his hands and he easily pushed her up and onto the side of the machine, almost on top of the door.

She took careful steps on the slippery surface, then, bending over, she reached down for the handle and twisted it. She pulled hard on the door to break the mud seal that was caked around the edge, yanking at the door until finally it broke free. She pried the door open and found the operator looking dazed and confused, still sitting in the cab chair, still strapped in by his seat belt.

"Any place on you that hurts?" she asked.

"I don't think so." He struggled to speak, sounding disoriented.

Mitch managed to climb on to the machine and was suddenly standing at her side. He held one of her hands as she climbed inside the cab. The driver was lying on his side, one of his hands still clenching the steering wheel. Josie bent over the top of him and unbuckled the safety belt from around his waist.

"You think you're okay enough we can move you? No broken bones?" she asked.

"Hard to tell. I think I'm okay."

"I got you unbuckled. Mitch is going to put his hand down here, and we're going to both pull you up out of the cab. You yell if anything hurts and we'll wait for the medics. Okay?"

He finally turned his head to the side and made eye contact with Josie. "Scared the shit out of me."

She laughed, relieved to hear him coming around. "Scared me too. And I wasn't inside this thing! Let's get you out of here."

Josie and Mitch each took a hand and helped pull him to a standing position. His head appeared out of the cab and he seemed fine, just shaken up. The rest of the group had assembled and watched as he was slowly pulled from the cab. Cheers and applause broke out as he made his way down from the machine, hanging on to Josie and Mitch for support.

Back at the staging facility, Josie and Mitch rinsed the mud off their feet and pants using a water hose outside the main office. Sylvia Moore brought them each another pair of waders and they got back to work. The mudslide lost intensity but continued for another three hours, then finally stopped after the rain ended. Additional workers were called in and spent the day monitoring the mountainside and cleaning up the aftermath. The crew moving the barrels had managed to move only twenty-five of them into the semis before the peak crumbled. Debris and water had flowed through the center of the Feed Plant, but not enough to topple any of the decaying barrels or to invade the buildings. The explosives had worked as hoped.

When it was clear that the crisis had been averted and moved into cleanup mode, Diego called the cafeteria workers and asked them to prepare meals for the crew. A large group of women and men showed up and began preparing meals for a team that had grown to almost seventy-five. As the day drew to a close, Diego called the officers and company employees who had been a part of the initial planning effort into the cafeteria to debrief. As the bedraggled group entered the room, the cafeteria workers stood in a line and clapped. When Mitch entered he smiled and waved to a room full of cheers and applause. Josie looked around the cafeteria at the mud-covered, exhausted group of people and was proud of what they had accomplished. They had worked together as a team and achieved their goal. It didn't always work that way.

After Diego thanked the group, the cafeteria ladies began serving a sit-down meal of meatloaf and mashed potatoes. Josie and Otto stepped away from the group to plan their next steps.

"Can you go meet with Cowan and the CDC technician? I want to make sure that what we suspect matches with what the CDC has found on the body."

Otto nodded.

"I'm not leaving until I get back into that security room to watch the rest of the tape. I'll call you as soon as I can."

Diego and Skip approached them. Diego looked exhausted. Josie knew there were many plant managers who would have sat in a dry office all day barking orders. She was impressed with his willingness to work alongside of, instead of in front of, his employees.

"Quite a day," Diego said.

Otto grunted. "You could say that."

Diego turned to Josie. "I'm assuming the security tape will be taken as evidence. Is it possible for me to watch the tape before you take it?"

"That's where I'm headed."

Diego considered her thoughtfully for a moment. "Can I ask you a question regarding the case?"

"Sure."

"Why did you suspect Brent Thyme? I thought Leo was your primary suspect. You just discovered he stole Santiago's money."

"Leo was used. He was broke. I had no trouble believing he stole the money, but there was never a good connection between Leo and Juan."

"But Brent and Juan were coworkers. Friends even," Skip said.

Josie gave him a skeptical look. "Maybe on the surface. This whole case came back to the boots for me. I felt certain the murder took place at the plant. And then I remembered, Juan didn't have a car. Who took Juan to work every day?"

"Brent did," Skip said.

"Then we discovered Brent had a sore on his arm, similar to the sores that were on Santiago's arms."

Skip and Diego both looked at each other in surprise. "I had no idea," Skip said.

"Brent didn't want you to know. He was afraid he would lose his job."

Diego stared intently at Josie, processing the information. "I'm sorry, I still don't see the connection," he said.

"From what I've seen in reports, things I've read on the Internet, and even what we've heard from employees, there's one thing you stress to your workers. Above all else."

Diego nodded. "Safety above all else."

"There are Safety First signs everywhere. Crews are called Safe Shut-Down Crews. Then when I interviewed Brent and he told me about the sores, he practically begged me not to tell you. He was terrified you would suspect protocol hadn't been followed. That he'd lose his job. He said he had a wife, kid, mortgage. The job meant everything to him."

"Brent was a great worker," Skip said. "We were grooming him for a promotion."

"When I talked to him at his home, I was disappointed in him for not doing the right thing. For not going to you with the truth about what had happened. But the more I thought about it, I realized, he had probably sat on information that could have saved Santiago's life." She turned to Diego. "Let's pull up the tape from the pilot unit. From the last day Juan and Brent worked together. My guess is, safety was compromised and led to their injuries. Juan was going to blow the whistle, and Brent could only find one way to stop him. He lured him to the plant and killed him."

Otto said his good-byes and left for the health department, and Skip joined a group of police officers for dinner in the cafeteria. Josie thought he still looked shell-shocked by the day's revelations. Diego and Josie walked to the pilot unit under a gray sky that looked as if at any moment the thin membrane holding back the rain might break, allowing yet another drenching. The forecast called for rain through the evening, but promised an end to the deluge by morning. Josie glanced down at her soaked uniform, her pants covered in mud from mid-thigh down. She had pulled her wet hair back into a ponytail again, but it had done little to help her appearance. Diego somehow managed to still look businesslike even with mud splattered across his suit pants and shirt. He'd lost his suit jacket and tie sometime earlier in the day.

Apparently sensing her train of thought, Diego said, "You look quite good in brown. It might be your color."

She laughed as they walked. She could feel him studying her face.

"I can still see the burn, although it's faded. There's a fair chance the top layer of skin will turn brown and peel. You should still have your face checked, but don't panic."

"Don't panic. Phrase of the day."

They reached Unit Seven and Diego unlocked the door, then led them to the security office. The building appeared empty.

They sat next to each other on chairs facing the computer screen. Diego had closed the door behind them and Josie could smell the damp from their clothes in the small space.

"I never dreamt one of my employees could be capable of such an act," he said.

Josie cued up the tape, then reversed it so that Diego could watch from the moment the two men wearing hazmat suits entered the laboratory. They watched as the box was taken from the cabinet, the tube declined by the man Josie identified as Santiago, then finally as he was hit over the head by the stool.

They watched as he fell to the floor, and the minutes of indecision as the other man paced the floor, then stood for a long while just staring at the body.

"What a horrific thing," Diego said. "He is rationalizing the death of his friend."

After a full five minutes of indecision, the figure bent down and unfastened the hood of the man on the floor, then pulled it off. Josie and Diego both leaned forward, straining to see his face. When the other person stood, they got a clear shot of Juan Santiago. Diego made a noise, then cleared his throat. "I recognize him from his photo on his ID. And I've seen him around the plant. There's no doubt."

The other person kept his hood on and Josie assumed he was doing it to hide his identity. He opened several cabinets, and rifled through their contents, obviously searching for something. He finally pulled out a glass jug, similar to the one Brent had used earlier in the day against Josie. He uncapped the liquid and bent down beside Santiago. They watched in horror as he pried Santiago's mouth open with his hand and poured the liquid down the man's throat.

Diego made a sound of disgust.

Josie said nothing. She imagined Sarah, Brent's wife, and their small child at home right now, probably still oblivious to the horror he had unleashed upon their family.

"What in god's name was he thinking?" Diego said.

Shortly after, the man replaced the chemicals and bent down to pick up the lifeless Santiago. He struggled, but finally managed to maneuver him over his shoulder and walk out of the lab. Diego fast-forwarded through the rest of Sunday to when the tape ended at 6 A.M. Monday. Other than one security guard walk-through, the lab remained empty.

Diego faced Josie. "How can you be certain that was Brent Thyme?"

"Let's pull up the tape from last Monday, the last day that Brent and Juan worked together in the pilot plant."

Over the next fifteen minutes they fast-forwarded through tape, watching scientists and technicians come in and out of the lab. Then, at 11:10 A.M., two men in hazmat suits took off their helmets and peeled down the top portion of their suits, allowing their upper body and arms to be exposed.

"Brent and Juan. There's the safety breach," Diego said.

Several minutes later they watched Juan drop a glass jug of something and both men jump away from it. They appeared to argue, Brent obviously furious with Juan for the accident, Juan apologizing. Then both men pulled their suits back up and put their hoods on and began cleaning the floor.

Diego looked at Josie in astonishment. "They didn't even wash the solution off their arms! There's a sink in the lab. Why wouldn't they have cleaned up first?"

Josie shook her head. "I assume they were afraid if someone came in and saw the spill, and their suits off, that they would be fired."

Diego sat back in his chair, a look of defeat spreading across his face. He said, "It makes me question everyone I know. I would never have guessed him capable of this kind of evil." He considered Josie for a moment. "It would be hard to not become jaded in your position. Do you reach a point where everyone in your life is suspect?"

"Aren't we all capable of evil at some point?"

He looked surprised.

Josie leaned back in her seat and crossed her arms over her chest, chilled from her damp clothing. "Given the right set of circumstances I think we're all capable of doing bad."

He gave her a cynical smile. "You're twisting my words. I asked if you suspect everyone, even those you love, of doing evil. I agree we're all capable, but most of us have internal triggers that stop us."

Josie nodded, acknowledging the distinction. "You're probably right. I suppose I suspect most everyone. I assume guilt until the facts prove otherwise. Hazard of the profession." She paused for a moment. "Or a severe personality flaw."

Diego smiled and shut down the viewing equipment. "I'll ask Skip to make you a copy of the last two weeks of tape. I don't think you want me to try it. I'm afraid I may erase something in error."

"That's fine. I'd love to be able to pick it up tomorrow."

Diego nodded and they stood to leave. With his hand on the doorknob, he turned to Josie.

"Have dinner with me tonight."

Her eyebrows arched in surprise. "Dinner?"

He smiled. "I think we deserve a nice dinner, a glass of wine, calm conversation. No stress, just dinner."

She felt the flush to her face and chest and knew that Diego saw it. She felt guilty at the hesitation. "I can't. I'm sorry. I would agree that we certainly deserve a stress-free dinner, but I'm already committed."

He tilted his head back but his smile remained. "Committed. That can mean any number of things. I will assume that means you have a previous engagement, although after the events of the day, it would be difficult to maintain comparable conversation with someone who had not experienced this."

He opened the door and stepped back for Josie to exit first. He walked beside her as they left the plant. "When you aren't so committed, I would like to take you out to express my gratitude. You are one of the most unique women I've had the good fortune to meet, and I would like to get to know you."

Josie smiled. "I appreciate the invitation. I'm sure we'll talk again soon."

She left Diego and walked through the plant toward the parking lot when she heard a female voice calling her name. She turned and saw Sylvia Moore walking quickly down the sidewalk in her high heels and dress, carrying a brown paper bag.

"You left these!" she called.

Josie turned and walked toward her, and accepted the bag.

"It's your uniform boots. You left them when you changed into the waders."

Josie looked down at the pair of waders someone had given her after she lost the first pair in the mudslide with the trencher.

"Thank you. I forgot all about these. If you'd like I'll come back inside and change," Josie said, expecting her to be a stickler for the rules.

"No, no. You can return them later." She hesitated, her face conflicted. "We appreciate everything the police did for us today." She paused, obviously struggling. "People view Beacon as the bad guys. We're the scoundrels, when all we want to do is help. The company is here to clean up our community, not destroy it. It just gets frustrating."

Josie put her hand out and the two women shook. "I understand the feeling well."

Josie sat in her jeep for a few minutes, her body sore and tired. She called Otto and he stepped out of the meeting with Cowan and the lab tech from the CDC.

"She's got her equipment checking out all the stuff in the morgue. She checked Santiago, his clothing, the evidence we collected. Santiago has elevated radiation."

Josie sighed, feeling the last bit of energy drain from her body. "Did she check you and Cowan?"

"Yep, and there was nothing. Looks like chemicals were the culprit. We'll know more shortly, but I think we're out of the woods. Radiation, or negligence from the plant, weren't what killed Santiago. It was human intervention."

Josie explained what she and Diego had discovered on the security tapes.

"If Brent had gotten to those security tapes before you did, we'd have trouble."

"I want to interview him, get his statement. Marta finished with the evacuations about an hour ago. She brought Cassidy Harper and Leo Monaco in for questioning. I'll see you back at the jail when you're finished."

Josie called her family doctor, one of two in Artemis, and met him at his office before she went home to clean up and change. She gave him the name of the chemical that burnt her skin and explained the neutralization. He checked her thoroughly, gave her an ointment to apply twice a day, and sent her home with a clean bill of health. Before she left the parking lot at the doctor's office she called Dillon and said she wouldn't be coming over. She was too exhausted for company. When the day finally ended she wanted a hot bath, a warm tumbler of bourbon, and clean sheets all to herself.

TWENTY-FIVE

Josie made a quick trip home to shower and change into a clean uniform, and then drove to the Arroyo County Jail. She was led down the hall by the intake officer. Maria was one of Josie's favorite employees at the jail; she took pride in her work and was a cheerful woman who rarely let the stress of the job bring her down. That evening, however, she was clearly agitated by the arrest of Brent Thyme.

They reached the interrogation room and Maria stood in front of the door with her arms crossed over her chest, the keys firmly grasped in her hand.

"I'd like to get him in the back parking lot and beat the tar out of him myself. That precious little boy at home? A wife who depends on him?"

"Hard to figure people out," Josie said. She'd already suffered through the thoughts now plaguing Maria and was anxious to get to the questioning.

"Sarah will lose that house. She can't afford it on a waitress salary."

"We'll see what he has to say for himself."

Maria shook her head and seemed to realize she was detaining Josie. "His attorney is with him. It's Oliver Greene. Public defender from Presidio. Brent's been read his rights." She turned to unlock the door. "Have at him."

Brent looked wired. He wore the same jeans and navy blue long-sleeved T-shirt that he was arrested in earlier that afternoon. His pupils were dilated and he appeared to have difficulty focusing and paying attention to the directions his attorney was attempting to provide. Josie wondered again if he was on something.

Oliver Greene was an expatriate in his sixties with a soft, dignified British accent and bearing. He was a private man who had never explained to anyone in the law enforcement community how he'd ended up in West Texas. Greene was not a showman; he was an excellent public defender with no patience for theatrics. Josie liked him a great deal.

Once the preliminaries were out of the way, and the tape-recording equipment set up, Greene provided an additional verbal warning to Brent.

"I expect you to consult with me about anything that could possibly be construed as incriminating. I realize that isn't always clear. If in doubt, stop and ask me. Understood?"

The warning seemed to have no effect on Brent. He remained hunched over the table, staring at his folded hands. Greene finally sighed heavily and told Josie to proceed with questioning.

"I watched the surveillance video. Have you explained to your attorney what's on it?" she asked.

Brent stared at his fingers as he shredded the trash from a sugar wrapper used to sweeten his coffee. He said nothing and Greene finally shook his head once. Josie could tell he was in the dark and frustrated.

"The tape clearly shows you and Juan Santiago entering the pilot unit at the Feed Plant, Saturday night, July twenty-first at 10:43 P.M. Both you and Santiago are wearing full protective hazardous materials suits, as well as company work boots. After several minutes of discussion, you open a cabinet and remove a first-aid kit. You place it on the laboratory counter. You try and convince Mr. Santiago to use some of the ointment for the sores on his arms."

Greene cut Josie off. "Is there audio on this tape?"

"No, but it's obvious that—"

"No, ma'am, watching a security tape with no audio does not give you the ability to determine my client's intent. Doesn't work that way."

Josie nodded and rephrased. "There was a discussion between the two men after the kit was placed on the counter. Mr. Santiago finally turned from the conversation and walked toward the door, as if leaving. At that time, Brent picked up a stool and slammed it into Santiago's head, causing him to fall unconscious to the floor."

Brent stared at his hands as Greene took notes on his laptop. Brent's identity on the tape had not been confirmed, but his lack of protest just sealed it for Josie. She had no doubts now.

There was a knock on the door. Josie looked up and saw Officer Marta Cruz's face in the window, beckoning Josie outside with a crooked finger.

Josie didn't mind the interruption. She hoped his attorney would counsel Brent to make things easier on everyone and confess.

Josie excused herself, closed the door behind her, and found Marta in the hallway, her face animated.

"Sorry to interrupt, but I think you'll want to hear this."

"What's up?"

"You might want to have a word with Leo Monaco. He just admitted driving the body and dumping it in the desert late Saturday night. He claims he'll provide details only if you can assure him leniency," Marta said.

"Nasty little bastard. Where is he?"

"Jail's full up," Marta said. "We've got him secured in the conference room." She pointed to the room directly across the hallway. "A jailer's sitting with him."

Josie looked into the small square window and saw Leo sitting at a table by himself, the jailer sitting in a chair in the corner of the room reading a magazine.

"Where's his attorney?" she asked.

Marta stood behind her and said, "Refused one. Said he could speak for himself. I got the refusal in writing. Score one for us."

Josie walked into the conference room fuming. She could feel the pressure in her chest. "Are you serious?" she asked, skipping introductions.

Leo looked surprised to see her.

"You admit to dumping a dead body in the desert? And you want leniency?" Josie laughed, leaned a hip against the wall, and crossed her arms. "You are a piece of scum. Your life here in Artemis just ended. You have no girlfriend. Your job with Beacon? Gone. Your dream of a university position? Gone."

She walked toward him, leaned in within six inches of his face. "You have no bargaining chips, Leo. You got this all backwards. You tell us everything you know. Beg for mercy. Then you hope like hell the judge decides not to give you the maximum."

The jailer smirked, and Leo turned his head away from her. He tried to lean farther back in his chair, away from Josie, who was intentionally invading his space. He raised both hands in the air in a show of innocence.

"I had nothing to do with that guy's death. I got a call from Brent Thyme. He just asked if I'd meet him at the plant. He said I could make some quick money if I came immediately. That's what he said. Get here now."

"To do what?"

"He wanted to know where he could hide something in the desert. Where no one would find it. I said I knew a place on Scratchgravel Road. I didn't know I was picking up a body until it was too late."

"You couldn't walk away?" she asked. "Call the police and report a crime like any other person with a conscience would do?"

He looked confused for a moment. "No! He told me he'd kill me if I didn't follow through. He'd already killed once. I figured he'd do it again."

Josie didn't believe that but let it go. "Did he tell you he killed the man?"

Leo averted his eyes. "No. He didn't say anything, other than he wanted it dumped that night. I didn't ask questions. He paid me to do a job. That's it."

"How much?" she asked.

He looked confused. "How much what?"

"How much did he pay you?"

He stared at her, thinking.

"He didn't pay you," she said. "He gave you a key to Santiago's apartment. Told you to go inside, collect the money box with the dead man's cash in it."

"I don't know what you're talking about."

Josie smiled. "Yes, you do. So does your girlfriend. She found the house keys in your desk drawer." His expression changed from shock to anger in a matter of seconds. Josie preferred the anger. An angry suspect mouthed off information instead of trying to hide it.

"Brent just told me the money was in this apartment, in the bottom of a closet. He gave me the keys and said I needed to dump the body and get the money the same night. That's the honest to god's truth. That's all there was to it."

"What about the dead man's wallet in Cassidy's car?" she asked.

Leo tipped his head back and groaned as if the questions would never end. Josie wanted to reach over the table and grab him by the throat but she remained still.

"I ran errands in town before I left for the library. I had breakfast, got gas, that kind of stuff. As I was leaving town that afternoon I saw Cassidy's car headed out of town on Scratchgravel. She wasn't supposed to go anywhere that day, so I followed her. She parked on the side of the road where I had parked." He put his hands in the air. "I have no idea how she knew the body was there. She never would tell me. She played dumb."

"You haven't answered my question."

"I just wanted to scare her. Get her to keep her mouth shut. I had the guy's wallet in my car, so I stopped, unlocked her car, threw the wallet in the backseat."

"Where's Santiago's license?"

"I took the license out so she wouldn't know who he was. I figured that would freak her out. Let her know that somebody saw her snooping around. Then she gets picked up by the police." He shook his head like he couldn't believe her stupidity.

"So, you left Cassidy to die in the desert too? Just like the body you dumped?"

"No! I had no idea Cassidy was sick. I couldn't see her from the road. That's why I left the body there. It looked like a place no one would ever find."

Josie collected the rest of the details and left Leo. His information tied up the last major hurdle in the investigation. She thanked Marta for excellent work, and asked Maria to let her back into the interrogation room.

When she entered, Greene was turned in his seat, his forearms resting on his thighs, leaning toward Brent. Greene had the frustrated look of a father trying to talk sense to an obstinate teenager and having no luck.

Josie sat down at the table and said nothing for a moment, waiting to see if Brent wanted to talk.

Greene continued staring at Brent, his lips compressed into a thin line, obviously waiting on a response from his client. The defense attorney had been through enough interviews to know that his bad day was about to get worse.

"When I left the room, I had just explained that I've seen the tape that shows you slamming a stool into Juan Santiago's head when he tried to leave the laboratory."

Greene objected but Josie waved it off. "After knocking him unconscious, Brent found chemicals in the laboratory cabinet. He poured them down Santiago's throat." Josie watched him closely, but he refused to make eye contact. "The chemicals that disintegrated his friend's insides."

"Friend? He took advantage of me for three years! I drove him to work every day. Not once did he offer to pay me gas money. I offered to help when his car died. Then he never got another car. Never even said thanks."

"I would encourage you to—"

Brent cut Greene off. "He was so damned self-righteous. He was doing something noble for his family, so it gave him the right to treat everyone else like dirt."

"And then he spilled the chemicals that were going to get you fired."

Brent stared at her with a burning hatred that surprised her. "He didn't care! It was always about him."

Josie realized he'd said nothing to implicate himself to this point. Greene was staring at him intently.

"But you did more than poison Santiago. You had his body dumped in the desert by your friend, Leo Monaco."

He clenched his jaws, his face turning a deep red, and Josie wondered why this news would cause such an angry reaction. Maybe he thought Leo was a faithful friend.

Josie turned to Greene. "Brent called and told Leo he had a way he could make some extra money. Leo drove to meet him at the plant and discovered a dead body in the backseat of Brent's car."

She turned to face Brent. "A place where Juan Santiago's DNA will show up like neon paint."

He looked silently back at her, seeming to evaluate her words.

Facing Greene again she said, "When Leo arrived and found the body, he tried to back out, but was afraid Brent would kill him, as he had killed Juan Santiago."

Brent made a face as if she'd told a ridiculous story. "He didn't care what he was dumping! He found out there was a box of money in the apartment and he couldn't have cared less what he moved."

Josie felt the thrill of closing in. She lowered her voice and pulled a chair directly across from him, leaning toward him across the table. "Why, Brent? Was the job really worth his life?"

He looked across the table, his face feverish. "It was his fault we got splashed. He was trying to hurry the job and he didn't take precautions. I followed the book. I was working toward a promotion. I was next in line."

Brent stopped talking and Josie kept quiet, waiting for the admission.

After staring at the table for some time he seemed to resolve something internally. He leaned back in his chair, his face slack, his expression resigned.

"Juan and I were working on a project in the lab for a couple of days."

"In the pilot unit?" she asked.

He nodded. "It's company policy to wear the hazmat suits whenever we work with certain chemicals. Grounds for termination if you don't. The day we were working it was hot. We were both sweating so we just pulled the top half down to get some air. We were the only ones scheduled in the lab so we figured a few minutes of fresh air wouldn't hurt." Brent finally glanced at his attorney. Greene scowled and motioned for him to continue.

"We were using sodium hydroxide. Juan wasn't watching what he was doing. He knocked the container onto the floor. It spilled everywhere. Our legs were protected, but we got it on our arms. We had gloves on our hands, but I still got some inside my glove as we were cleaning." His hand was lying on the table and he looked down at the bandaged sore. "I have sores on my forearms too. Juan panicked. We both pulled our suits back on to clean the floor up before a supervisor walked in and saw us cleaning a spill with no protection."

"You didn't wash the chemicals off your arms first?" Josie asked.

Brent propped his head on his hand. "I panicked. We probably could have talked our way out of trouble if a supervisor had seen our hoods and tops off. But with a chemical spill? We'd have been fired. Then Skip walked into the unit as we were sweeping up the cleaner. He asked some pointless question about lunch or something. But he kept talking."

Josie remembered seeing someone in the security tape come into the lab and talk with them.

"I could feel my hand burning. I knew I had gotten it on me by that point but we had to wait for him to leave. Juan had it all over his arms. He was already on fire by the time Skip left."

"When did the open sores show up?" Josie asked.

"His were a day later. Mine showed up after his. I didn't get burnt as bad. He freaked out though when they kept getting worse. We have fact sheets at the plant about all the chemicals. He started reading about cancer and side effects. That's when he went to the county health nurse."

"Did you advise him not to visit?" she asked.

He shrugged. "He never asked. He just went. When he told me he was going back for a follow-up visit I said he was crazy. He was going to get us both fired. He kept talking about the side effects and treatment and not having insurance. Then he decided to go to Skip Bradford and tell him everything."

"And you told him not to?"

"It would have been my job!"

"Why not kill Juan in the desert? Why go to the trouble of taking him to the plant?" she asked.

"He *asked* me to take him! Practically demanded it. He couldn't go to work with the sores like they were. He wanted me to take him to the plant that night so he could find some salve or ointment. I finally agreed." He looked at Josie, his face imploring now. "I never set out to hurt him. He just backed me into a corner!"

"And when he tried to walk out?" she asked.

"We both realized the sores had gotten too bad for anything in the first-aid kit. He wanted me to take him to Skip's house. To tell him everything. I wouldn't do it so he said he'd walk. I panicked."

"And you killed him."

He looked at her, his face a conflicted mix of anger and sadness.

Josie looked at him for some time, taking in the facts, realizing that a few bad decisions had reduced his life to nothing. "Why did you tell me about the sores on your hand?"

He shook his head, offered a regretful smile. "By the time I talked to you I'd had them for a couple of days and they weren't healing." He raised his shirt sleeve to reveal bandages on his forearms. "I don't have insurance. I couldn't afford to see a doctor. I thought if I could get help from your CDC doctor then Paiva wouldn't have to know."

Josie changed directions. "So why get Leo involved? Why not dump the body yourself?"

"I just freaked out. I didn't know where to take it." He struggled for words, obviously still confused by his own decisions. "It was all too horrible. I called Leo because I knew he was in debt. The guy has no conscience. I knew I could talk him into helping."

Josie let his reference to a lack of conscience slide. "What happened to Santiago's money?"

"That was the deal Leo made. I gave him Santiago's keys. After he left the body in the desert he got the keys and whatever money was in the apartment."

"Did you tell Leo where the money was located?" she asked.

Brent looked up from the place on the table he'd been staring at and nodded.

"How did you know where the money was?"

For the first time the anger in his expression was replaced with pain and guilt. "Juan told me the money was in his closet. He made me promise if anything ever happened to him, that I would make sure his wife got the money."

Otto arrived at the Arroyo County Jail as Leo Monaco was being booked. Brent Thyme had already been processed and led back to his cell. Josie left Maria to attend to Leo's fingerprints and went into the hallway to talk with Otto.

"What's the word from the CDC?" Josie asked.

"Santiago had slightly elevated levels of radiation, but it was caused from the chemical Brent Thyme gave him. Skip Bradford found a large amount of uranyl nitrate missing from the cabinet at the pilot unit."

"The cabinet that's visible on the security tape? The one Brent got into?"

"Yep. It's a crystal that had been dissolved in water. It has no odor, but it's toxic by ingestion. It's what ate up Santiago's insides."

Josie grimaced at the thought. "So, the Feed Plant is in the clear," she said.

Otto nodded. "Marta has Cassidy Harper in the conference room Leo was in. Marta's already entered Leo's laptop and the keys into evidence."

Josie patted Otto on the arm. "We're close."

"By the time you finish with Cassidy I'll have paperwork finished for tonight." He smiled and sighed. "Home is on the horizon."

The interrogation room smelled of sweat and day-old coffee, and the air-conditioning was on the blink. Josie figured it had to have been close to eighty degrees. Cassidy's face was bright red from the heat and her lingering sunburn, and the curls around her face had turned to frizz. She looked surprised when Josie entered the room, and Josie figured she was waiting for the hammer to drop. Josie, however, was exhausted and too tired for anything but the truth. She pulled the chair out across the table from Cassidy and sat down.

"I suppose you heard," Josie said.

"Leo's in jail."

"What do you think about that?"

Cassidy lifted a shoulder. "When I went to my parents' house, after I called you? My dad asked me why I keep hooking up with rejects."

Josie smiled at her dad's description, but Cassidy's expression remained serious.

"I keep thinking about that. It wasn't that Leo was a bad guy."

Josie groaned and allowed her head to fall forward in frustration.

Cassidy grinned. "Okay, I didn't mean it that way. In the beginning he wasn't bad. He was just miserable. And I thought, I can help him feel better. If he just had someone to believe in him, maybe he could get better. Feel good again. You know?"

Josie stared at her, struggling to remain quiet.

"But it didn't really matter what I did, he was still miserable. I could make a nice dinner, dress up, or lay on the couch and eat potato chips. It didn't matter. He could fake it, but I could tell, on the inside he still hated himself. And he probably hated me too."

"What now?"

"I'll move back in with my parents. Dad said he'd help me find an apartment as soon as we know Leo's gone for good."

"There's little doubt. Leo is gone. At least for now."

Cassidy nodded. "My dad's all worried that he'll come back for me after he gets out of jail. Like some stalker. I tried to explain to him though, Leo doesn't care about anyone enough to stalk them. He'd probably be happier being the one stalked."

Josie smiled and thought it was one of the most perceptive things she'd ever heard Cassidy say. There was hope for her after all.

* * *

Josie finished with Cassidy and found Otto talking with Maria in the command center.

"You get her straightened out?" he asked.

A tolerant smile spread across Josie's face. "I'll keep my fingers crossed."

"What about her withholding information?" Otto asked.

"The prosecutor would never press charges against her. I just hope she learns something out of this mess."

They fell into silence for a moment.

"Are we done here?" he asked.

Josie gave him a weary smile. "I sure hope so. Let's go home."

———————

It was ten o'clock before Josie finally clocked off and drove toward home. The air outside was damp with the retreating rain, almost balmy. She rolled the windows down and allowed the night air to blow through the jeep. The forecast claimed the rain would subside for the next forty-eight hours, and she hoped it would be enough to allow the flood level in the Rio to drop. For now, it just felt good to be dry.

She left the radio off, preferring silence, and considered her options for the night. She'd already canceled with Dillon. She could eat popcorn and zone out in front of the TV for an hour. Or, she had a new Harlan Coben book on her bedside table she could start. She briefly considered calling her mother, whom she hadn't talked to in months, but discounted that idea.

Josie craved time alone, but once she got it, the emptiness closed in around her, and the desire to be alone would be replaced by a deep sense of loneliness. She wondered what a shrink might make of her behavior but decided she really didn't care to know.

She turned onto Scratchgravel, heading toward Schenck Road, and saw the dark shadow of the watchtower in the distance. As she drove closer she spotted a car parked on the side of the road, in roughly the same place she had found Cassidy Harper's car a week before. She felt a heaviness overtake her. She was too exhausted to deal with more drama. She pulled her jeep behind the car, her headlights revealing Teresa Cruz's little white Honda Civic. Josie sighed heavily and turned her jeep's engine off. She grabbed her flashlight, checked her sidearm, got out of the vehicle, and locked up. She shone her flashlight in and around the car and saw no signs of disturbance, and then picked up a single set of footprints in the wet sand leading out toward the direction the body had been found. A nauseating sense of déjà vu came over her.

Josie called in her location to Brian, the night dispatcher, and took off walking toward the grove of bushes. It occurred to her that Teresa might be visiting the Hollow, the doper hangout, but the kids parked their cars in an off-road arroyo to keep from being seen. If she was partying, Josie assumed Teresa wouldn't be naïve enough to park her car on the side of the road.

As she walked toward the bushes she was thinking through the information that had been made public. Very few people knew the location of the body. She couldn't imagine why Marta would have told her daughter, or what connection Teresa could possibly have had with the dead man.

As Josie approached the bushes she stopped and shone her flashlight around the area, then walked back around to where the body was found.

"Teresa?" Josie called.

After several seconds she heard, "Chief Gray?"

Josie directed her light over the large boulder and saw Teresa crouching beside it.

"What's going on?" Josie asked.

Teresa was wearing dark jeans, a T-shirt, and her hair was

pulled behind her head. She squinted into the beam of the flashlight and looked younger than her sixteen years, like a kid caught misbehaving.

"Is there something you want to tell me?" Josie asked.

"I don't know." Her voice was timid, not a typical response.

"You know it's not safe out here by yourself," Josie said. "What are you doing out here?"

She began to cry and slumped back onto the rock behind her. "I don't know. I don't even know who I am anymore."

Josie paused for a moment. She was mentally and physically exhausted and her patience with people was at a low. She refused to play word games with the girl.

"You know what? I always thought that was a bullshit statement. I think that's a way for cowards to get out of moving forward in their life. I think you know exactly who you are."

Teresa sniffed and wiped her eyes with her T-shirt.

Josie pointed to the ground where the body had lain when Cassidy found it. "As far as you know, do we have the right person in jail for killing the man we found out here?"

Teresa looked up suddenly. "I don't know who killed him." It was too dark for Josie to read her expression, but her words sounded sincere.

Josie nodded, relieved. "Is there anyone else we need to question? Someone who was involved in killing that man that we don't know about?"

"I don't know." She hesitated again, obviously still confused by the questions. "I don't think so."

"Do you have any additional information that would change the guilt or innocence of anyone related to this case?"

Teresa shook her head, as if finally understanding the line of questioning. "No." Her response was resolute this time.

Josie nodded then and looked out toward the Chinati Peak, in the direction of her home. She took a long while to gather her thoughts. "I don't know any human being who doesn't grow up making mistakes. Sometimes big mistakes. Someday, when you're looking back on your life, you'll probably decide those mistakes are what changed you. Made you a better person." She glanced at Teresa. "Now's your chance."

She nodded and stared at Josie as if preparing to tell her something.

"The people who fail in life are the ones who keep making the same mistakes. They never learn anything. Don't be that person."

The anxiety came back into Teresa's expression and she started to speak, but Josie cut her off.

"Look. Take your confession to your priest. Beyond that, it's time to move on. I don't want to see you out here again. You leave Enrico and this mess behind you." Josie pointed in the direction of the Hollow and saw the surprise in Teresa's expression. "Is that who you are? Are those the people you want to hang out with?"

She shook her head no.

Josie pointed to the place on the ground where the body was found. "Is that who you are?"

"I know who I am. I know right from wrong," Teresa said. Her tone was humble and sincere. "But when you start making bad decisions you start wondering when it'll stop. Who says I won't do it again?"

"An old friend told me that scars are nature's way of making sure we remember all the stupid stuff we do."

Teresa nodded and rubbed her thumb along her jawline. "When I was eleven, Mom told me I wasn't allowed to play in the drainage ditch across the road from the house because it was dirty. It had rained though, and the ditch was full of water. Me and a bunch of kids went swimming in the ditch. I fell on a metal pipe and cut my jaw open. I ran home with blood dripping down my face. She had to drive me to the doctor. I had to get stitches."

"Did you play in the ditch after that happened?"

"Never went back."

Teresa turned her head to the side and Josie could see the small line of raised white flesh along her jawbone. Josie watched the girl run her finger along the hard edge and they sat quiet for a time. Josie thought about her own scars, and whether she ever learned from them. Maybe Dell was right. Maybe it was fear that kept her from moving forward in life, and fear that made her keep repeating the same mistakes. Maybe it was time to have a little faith.